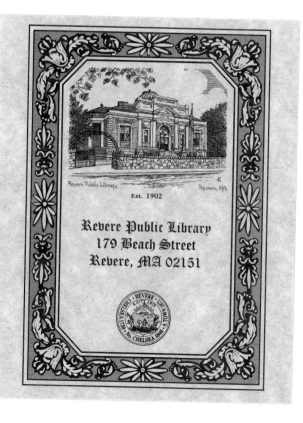

MEAN WOMAN BLUES

MEAN
WOMAN
BLUES

Julie Smith

A TOM DOHERTY ASSOCIATES BOOK
NEW YORK

MEAN WOMAN BLUES

Copyright © 2003 by Julie Smith

All rights reserved, including the right to reproduce this book, or portions thereof, in any form.

Book design by Mary A. Wirth

A Forge Book
Published by Tom Doherty Associates, LLC
175 Fifth Avenue
New York, NY 10010

Forge® is a registered trademark of Tom Doherty Associates, LLC.

Smith, Julie.
    Mean woman blues / Julie Smith.—1st ed.

    "A Tom Doherty Associates book."
    ISBN 0-765-30552-6

Printed in the United States of America

To the best and truest of friends,

Mary Ann and Larry Walker

Acknowledgments

Many thanks to the regulars: retired NOPD Captain Linda Buczek, Kathy Perry, Greg Herren, Betsy Petersen, Dr. Ken White, Charlotte Sheedy, Vicky Bijur, Win Blevins, and, of course, my incomparable husband, Lee Pryor. Can't do a book without 'em.

Also, thanks to Dr. Mark Cousins, Kit Wohl, retired District Fire Chief Dave Tibbetts, Kathy Fontenot at the Louisiana State Penitentiary, Kathy White, Kiley McGuire (my Dallas expert), Lynn Kuriger Stanton (on Texas divorce law), and Ace Atkins (for title consultation). Any mistakes are my own and not theirs, bless their hearts—they did their best to make it simple.

The ugly affair of the bank is based on a real incident. A thousand thanks (and all my sympathy) to the person who shared details of the ordeal.

MEAN WOMAN BLUES

Chapter ONE

*M*ay is the cruelest month.

September has its moments, being hurricane season, but its meanness is unreliable. May is a sure thing.

On Mother's Day, give or take a week or so, the Formosans swarm, only slightly less consistent than the swallows at Capistrano. They continue their inexorable flight, sometimes in terrifying indoor clouds, well into summer.

Formosan termites, accidentally imported some years ago, are eating the city of New Orleans. They are doing it not in bug-sized nibbles, but in greedy gulps that some people say they can actually hear. They swear that in the dark of night, as they lie awake kissing their investments good-bye, they can hear the buzz of so many tiny saws, mandibles chomping their floorboards.

Perhaps they are merely blessed with good imaginations, but a visitor who arrives in the merry month, strolls a few blocks, and finds himself wearing a vest of termites may be inclined to credit them.

The unsuspecting stay-at-home finds himself in a fifties sci-fi film. It begins with a single bug. It may fall on his clothing or perhaps the desk upon which he's writing. He brushes it off, and another falls, like an earwig from the eaves of a porch. He looks up and sees a few winged creatures bouncing off the chandelier. Odd, he thinks, and goes back to his reverie. And soon there are more bugs. And more. And more. The room may fill with them, thick shrouds of them, circling, diving, turning the air into a seething dark mass.

It may seem the sensible thing to run screaming for cover, but in fact there is an easier way: Our hero can simply turn off the light, and they will leave or die. Or he can just wait, if he can stand it. The winged ones, the alates, or breeders, have about a two-hour life span, between seven and nine P.M., usually. Unless, of course, they manage to mate, in which case they will start a nest. The largest nest found to date had a diameter of three hundred feet.

Unlike other termites, these can build aerial nests, right in your walls. Brick or stucco houses are fine with them; they'll eat the door frames, windowsills, picture frames, furniture, and telephone bills, plus your favorite hundred-year-old shade tree. Except for exterminators, who shake their heads and look grim, like oncologists delivering the bad news, they have no natural enemies. The alates, so shocking in their thick, swirling clouds, are only a small percentage of the population, according to entomologists. A mature nest may contain five to ten million termites, though seventy million isn't unheard of.

Formosan termites now infest eleven Southern states, plus California, New Mexico, and Hawaii. Louisiana has the most severe infestation in the world (despite headway being made by state and federal baiting programs), and it is only natural that the bug has become, like the *loup-garou* (or Cajun werewolf), part of the local mythology.

The stories are legion: An alfresco wedding attacked by something resembling a Biblical plague. A window shut just in time, as hundreds of tiny bodies, drawn by the light inside, smash as if on a windshield. An ordinary backyard, covered in minutes by a carpet of termites. Fat garbage bags of wings, as many as ten or twelve, shoveled from the floor of a house.

Indeed, the month of May affords a brush with nature rarely seen by urban dwellers. Those of a metaphorical bent try not to think about the Mother's Day aspect.

*D*etective Skip Langdon, a veteran of many Mays in New Orleans, was trying to help her beloved through his first, mostly with diversionary tactics. She had seen Steve Steinman's face when he discovered the termite launching pads on his newly purchased, newly painted, hundred-and-twenty-year-old ceiling. He looked as if someone had died.

"Am I insured for this?" he said, and she desperately wished there were something she could do. The insurance companies weren't that dumb.

"Why didn't they find them when they inspected?" he asked, outraged.

"You can't know they're there unless you rip out the walls."

"Uh-oh. I've got a bad feeling that means I've got to do that now."

"Maybe you won't. They can probably drill holes for the poison." But she was lying. They might well have to rip out the walls.

No exterminator would be available for weeks, of course, and it's said the Formosans can go through a floor board in a month. The thing to do was keep his mind off it.

JazzFest was over, and the heaviness of summer was nearly upon them; Mother's Day brunch at a fine old restaurant sounded like a prison sentence. Yet Skip was a mother of sorts, or at least an aunt to the adopted children of her landlord, Jimmy Dee Scoggin. Dee-Dee was gay, and his partner, Layne Bilderback, had recently joined the household shared by Jimmy Dee and young Kenny and Sheila Ritter, the offspring of his late sister.

Dee-Dee wheedled. "We have to do something to remember their mother, keep the feminine spirit alive. Isn't it the decent thing?"

Steve said, "How about a hike?" and Dee-Dee countered, "Don't you get enough wildlife at home?"

But Skip pounced on it. If Steve wanted it, she wanted it. She wanted him in a good mood about Louisiana. He had moved there recently and restored a house (the one being gnawed), after months and years of thinking about it. A documentary filmmaker and film editor, he'd lived in California the entire time he and Skip had been dating. Their long-distance relationship had deepened on proximity. Skip was getting comfortable and liking it a lot. Steve had come to New Orleans for her, and his being there had enriched her life so much more than she'd anticipated that she felt responsible now— And motivated—eager to make him happy. A walk in Jean Lafitte Park, over in Jefferson Parish, ought to be wonderfully therapeutic.

There was almost a no-go when Jimmy Dee said they'd have to leave the dogs behind—Steve's shepherd, Napoleon, and the kids' mutt, Angel—because they couldn't go in the park itself and it was too hot to leave them in the car.

But in the end the three kids—Dee-Dee's two and Steve—rose above it.

They went in two cars, the uncles and Sheila in one, Kenny with Skip and Steve. There was a reason for this; Kenny, being in his early teens, hero-worshipped Steve. The two uncles could have gotten their feelings hurt but had the sense not to bother. The average fourteen-year-old preferred baseball to opera; metaphorically speaking, it was that simple. And Kenny was such a gentle soul, even as a teenager, that no one could imagine he'd ignore anyone on purpose. Sheila was another matter. She'd probably chosen to ride with the uncles just to snub her younger brother.

Spilling from the cars, they stepped onto the natural levee that ran along Bayou Coquille and instantly heard the silence of the swamp. It was louder than the bullfrog croaks and insect ditties and birdsongs and animal slitherings that, in fact, were a concert in themselves. The two conditions were like stereo—you could listen to either or both, and the effect was like being on another planet. As the trail descended to the flooded forest of the swamp, the noises grew louder, and so did the silence. The air, though it was nearly ninety in the French Quarter, here seemed fresh and soft with breezes. It was too late for the wild irises, which bloom in great fields of purplish blue, but a few of the pale lavender water hyacinths, to some more beautiful than orchids, still floated on the water, gorgeous to look at, but in fact choking out the life of the bayou. In its way, the water hyacinth—imported from South America rather than Asia—is as deadly as the termites. A single plant can produce fifty thousand others in one growing season, killing the native plants, thus reducing available food for animals.

Yet to Skip, the day was so beautiful, the views so tranquil, the natural mix so seemingly harmonious that it was possible to forget unharmonious nature: weed against weed, man against bug, cop against thug. People were oddly quiet as they walked the trail; even Sheila, given to complaining about the personalities and intellectual capacities of her companions, was as sunny as the day, which would have been perfect even if they hadn't happened upon a Cajun band on the way home, playing at an outdoor restaurant where people danced under a shed. They stopped and had iced tea, enjoying the dancers, some of whom wore shirts from a Cajun heritage organization and one of whom wore a masterpiece of taxidermy on his hat: an entire duck, feet and all, intact except for its innards.

Afterward, they went home and barbecued. While Layne cooked, the other grown-ups sat in the courtyard Skip shared with the Ritter-Scoggin family, drinking gin and tonics while the kids watched television, Napoleon snoozed, and Angel tried to wake him up. The air was velvety, with a little breeze, and the mosquitoes weren't yet biting. It was absurdly familial. Skip was completely, deliciously happy, a feeling she sometimes distrusted.

But that night she dreamed, and the dream was like life. In the dream, she had a beautiful house, and then a tiny hole appeared in the wall; out of the hole came swirling hordes of termites, traveling in vortexes like tornadoes. More and more swarmed until the air turned black, and then there was no air, only chaotic, moving, living walls, trapping her and invading her nose, her ears, smothering, strangling . . .

Steve shook her awake, and she told him the dream, still moaning, shivering though it was late spring, unnerved out of all proportion.

"They aren't that bad," he said. "It'll be okay. But thank you for your empathy."

*T*he dream wasn't about his termites. Someone could have said it was about him, about her fear of their relationship, her dread of becoming engulfed. But she knew it wasn't that. She knew what it *was* about, and she knew why she couldn't stop shaking.

It was about fear of dropping her guard, of looking away for even a second, of forgetting the danger that always lurked.

She had been happy too long, and something was happening to wake her up, to alert her to be wary. Yet the task was impossible. She couldn't be wary every second of the day. She couldn't protect even herself, let alone those she loved. No wonder she had dreamed of a pulsating monster, a force of nature that overwhelmed and smothered.

Fear was like that, a shrink might have said. But that wasn't it, not quite. Her enemy was like that.

Nearly two years ago, Errol Jacomine had disappeared, but he would not stay gone. She knew this; she had destroyed two of his careers, twice thwarted his attempts to win control over his fellow human beings, to gain a following, and to dominate. He would be back, and he would try to kill her sooner rather than later. To forget it for a day in the woods, for an evening in her courtyard, for a moment, for a millisecond, was dangerous and possibly deadly.

Jacomine's son, Daniel, had been arrested, charged with half a dozen crimes, and eventually convicted of murder as the result of one of Jacomine's schemes. He was due to be sentenced in a couple of days.

How that would affect his father, Skip couldn't know, but it had probably precipitated the dream. Jacomine might not even notice, perhaps having written Daniel off. He could do this; he seemed sometimes to have no feelings.

On the other hand, he perceived himself to be at the center of the universe. He might feel proprietary toward Daniel, no matter how unlikely he was to have true paternal feelings. And if he did, he might . . . what?

Surface. Treat it as an occasion to make himself known. Trade an eye for an eye: kidnap Kenny and demand Daniel.

Anything.

That was what the dream was about.

She left for work feeling hunted and resentful of her psyche for rubbing her nose in it. She knew all that, and what could she do about it? Exactly *what*? she asked herself angrily. Later, the dream seemed more a premonition than a warning.

That morning as always, she walked the few blocks to the garage where she kept her car, pointed the remote at the automatic door (a process that never failed to give her childlike pleasure), and waited for the door to raise itself high enough to allow her ingress. Instead of the familiar rumble, an explosion ripped through the quiet morning, followed by a loud *ping*, like a beer can hitting a metal drum.

She felt an arm around her waist, another at her back and then she felt herself falling, a great weight upon her. She tried to fight it, but it was too heavy. She was helpless. Her head hit the pavement.

It took a second to put it together. The explosion had been a shot, the *ping* a ricochet.

Another shot blasted the momentary peace, a second bullet thunked into the sidewalk. Closer. She felt her muscles contract, involuntarily seeking shelter.

She heard a woman scream, and she held her breath, but a shocked hush had enveloped the corner.

After a moment, a man said, "Owww." The man on top of her, she realized. Someone was shooting at her, and he had pushed her down, remained on top of her so that she couldn't move.

When she had waited long enough to be sure the shooting had stopped, she said to the lump atop her, "Police. Are you hit?"

The man rolled off, and she saw that he was a light-skinned black, well-muscled, wearing jeans and a white T-shirt—laborer's garb. He said, "You're police?" Her detective status meant she wore no uniform.

She didn't see any blood. "Are you all right?" She was frantic.

He was examining himself. "Yeah. Yeah, I'm all right. That was real close, though."

A crowd was gathering around them. Unless the sniper was in it, he no longer had a clear shot. Skip scanned the rooftops, wondering where the shots had come from.

The idea of asking what happened made her feel shamed somehow. She closed her eyes for a moment, trying to get it together, and the man said, "Somebody just tried to kill you."

"You saw him?"

"No. I was right behind you when I heard the shot. Didn't stop to look around, you understand?"

"Thanks. I appreciate what you did. But how did you know he wasn't shooting at you?"

The man shrugged. "I didn't ax no questions. Just hit the pavement."

When they paced it off, she could see that the man wasn't really right behind her; he'd had to run a step or two to tackle her. She'd been facing the garage door, and the bullet had hit it immediately to her right. She was between it and her rescuer.

There was no doubt in her mind that it was meant for her. She grabbed for her radio.

After that, it was chaos. A sniper in the French Quarter was a big deal, shots fired on a police officer an even bigger deal. But when it was Skip Langdon, it was nearly enough to declare a state of emergency. Everyone in the department knew Jacomine was as likely to come for her as get up in the morning and put on his clothes.

He might even come in person, and catching him would be as big a coup as discovering the whereabouts of D. B. Cooper.

Certainly her sergeant—her good friend and sometime partner Adam Abasolo—knew all this. Skip knew he was going to call for the works investigating this one, and the works was what Skip got. In minutes, District cars blocked the whole place off, the streets crawled with cops, and the downside—TV cameras.

The poor man who saved Skip's life was treated like a threat to society, taken over to the Eighth District, questioned and bullied until he well and truly understood that no good deed goes unpunished. Skip made a mental note to thank him somehow but wondered how. What did you do for a perfect stranger who risked his life to save yours, and then found himself in a living nightmare? He'd obviously been on his way to work. Maybe he'd even get fired.

She was having an extremely pessimistic day.

It seemed she'd barely picked herself up when Turner Shellmire turned up, a rumpled, pear-shaped figure in the midst of all the glamour of sirens and flashing lights. Shellmire was an FBI agent she'd worked with on the Jacomine case—or cases, actually. Though he came from the agency the New Orleans police liked to call Famous But Incompetent, he wasn't either. Certainly not incompetent. He was one of the best cops she'd ever worked with, and he was a straight shooter. They were as close to being friends as a police officer and an FBI agent possibly could be.

She played it light. "Hey, Turner. Slow day today?"

He didn't return her grin, instead examined the dented door and sidewalk. "He almost got you."

"What about the kids?"

"I've sent people to get them. Also Jimmy Dee, Layne, and Steve."

"Layne? Even Layne?" He'd only married into the family; it didn't seem fair to him.

Shellmire nodded. "Jacomine would go for him."

Skip knew it was true. Jacomine played mind games. If he couldn't get at her through somebody really close, he'd try for someone once removed, knowing that would pile guilt on top of her other emotions—guilt and the outrage of the person closest to the one targeted.

"What are you going to do with them?"

He opened his arms in exasperation. "That's the problem. We can keep them safe for a day, maybe, but they've got to have a life."

At the end of the day, when all the questions that could possibly be asked had been asked, the lifesaver—a man named Rooster Blanchard—had finally been released, and still the sniper hadn't been found and not a single fact more was known than the kind of gun he'd used and the angle the bullets had come from, Skip went to see her sergeant. "A.A., my nerves are shot. I've got to get the son of a bitch."

"You sound like you're asking for a leave of absence."

"Just a transfer. I want to go to Cold Case for a while. Please. Just let me try it."

"Skip, he's a needle in a haystack. And furthermore, you can't just work on one case."

"At least I could work on it some. That's all I ask."

The sergeant's eyes went shifty on her. "Langdon, you're not the person to work on this. You know that. Anyway, I can't spare you."

She ignored his last sentence. "Oh, come on. I wouldn't be working the shooting, just the cold case."

"Did you hear me? I can't do it. I've got to have you for the cemetery thefts. I want you to head the task force."

Here in the Third District, where Skip had been sent when the department was "decentralized" and the Homicide Division disbanded, things were usually pretty quiet. But the cemetery thefts were big, about as high profile as a case that wasn't a triple murder could get in New Orleans.

Somebody—probably a ring of professional thieves—was removing cemetery statues and selling them through the lucrative antiques market. In a city that took its saints and angels as seriously as it did its pre-Lent festivities, this was big, bad crime. A department that stopped it was going to be a popular department. Heading the task force was a handsome plum.

Still, to Skip's mind, it was trivial compared to getting Jacomine. She said, "A.A., I'm flattered, but . . ."

"The superintendent asked for you. Says it's the mayor's idea. Two city councilmen have also called—at the mayor's request, probably."

"Oh, shit."

He could have made a crack about the price of fame, but Abasolo looked as downcast as she probably did. "Yeah. I'm sorry, Skip. Wrap it up fast, and we'll see about the transfer."

Chapter TWO

*T*erri Whittaker stared at herself in the bathroom mirror, wondering how she was going to get through the day without Isaac. And with blue hair.

She had gone ahead with the hair, anticipating that her boyfriend would act as a buffer between herself and her parents, particularly her mother. Now, with no Isaac for the evening, it was a beacon inviting her mother's attack. She would just have to hope the barbed-wire-looking thing around her neck and the thorn bracelet tattooed on her upper arm would look so scary no one would comment.

Now, *there* was a pipe dream.

Mother's Day would be Judgment Day, as usual. Her parents were Christians of a sort: the sort who seemed to think they were channeling God with a bug up his butt. She toyed with the idea of saying she was sick.

But she knew she would go. She always went; to this and all family gatherings, no matter that she felt less kinship with her kin than she did with gibbons and lemurs. She didn't exactly hate her parents; she merely disliked their company. In fact, she was perfectly aware that they were decent people who'd done the best they could for her and her sisters, both of whom had had the gall to move out of state. That left her to cope, and it would have been a lot easier with her new boyfriend.

Her parents wouldn't be rude in front of a stranger; in fact they'd go out of their way to be friendly. And Isaac, truth to tell, would be quite a prize to show off. The man was handsome, and he was talented, and he was polite and well spoken. Best of all, he was just eccentric enough to intimidate them—and she got along with them best when they were intimidated.

Yet she didn't know how to pull it off by herself. In fact, she'd cover up the tattoo with sleeves, and she'd leave the barbed-wire thing at home. She was aware that, for all her blue hair and bravado, there was still some piece of her that was deeply timid and submissive. And frightened.

She sighed, hoping this time would be better. She had baked a lemon chess pie, her mother's favorite. It was something, anyway.

Her parents lived in a small, depressing house in one of the few neighborhoods she could name that actually had no charm. This was a hard thing to pull off in New Orleans, but the house was in Kenner, out in the burbs. It might have been the sort of thing you'd hide from a new boyfriend—and so might her parents be—but Isaac was so perfectly sweet and tolerant, he probably wouldn't even be offended when they questioned him about whether he was Jewish or not, on account of his first name.

It was still light when she arrived for dinner, and when her mother saw the pie, she said, "Oh. I thought you liked chocolate. I got a cake."

"Mom, the pie's for you. Happy Mother's Day." Her mother looked as if she didn't know how to respond. Neither of them made a move to kiss the other. Her dad was in the den, watching television.

"What'd you do to your hair?"

"Dyed it. What's for dinner?"

Terri stayed in the kitchen while her mother finished cooking: ham, sweet potatoes whipped with orange juice, frozen green beans, and Waldorf salad—her mother's idea of festive food. She hadn't started the salad yet. This way she could keep Terri in the kitchen by herself while she complained about her husband.

He never talked to her, she said. Their marriage wasn't close; it never had been. Sometimes she was so depressed she didn't know what to do.

"Pray?" Terri suggested.

And her mother snapped, "A lot you know about it," as if Terri were being deliberately insolent.

When they were at the table, in the small dining room papered with a stiff brown and yellow floral pattern, her mother said, "You're welcome to bring your boyfriend. We hope you know that."

"Thank you," she said.

"You got a boyfriend?" Her dad seemed suddenly interested. "Who'd want a blue-haired gal?"

"A very nice man. An artist."

"You meet him in some bar?"

"At school. He went back for his degree."

Her dad pointed a fork at her, speared with a great hunk of pink meat. His face was perennially red, and his neck was thick and always had been, even before his middle matched. Though he'd never hit her—it was her mother who had—she'd always found him frightening. "He older than you?"

"A little bit. He's very mature." She wasn't sure that he was, but at least he made money, which was more than she could say for herself.

Her dad made his voice low and somehow seductive. "You gonna marry him?"

She felt the hot rush of blood to her face. "I don't know. We've just been dating a couple of months."

She didn't even know if she wanted to marry him, but she sure wished he'd ask her to move in with him. Sharing rent and groceries would take a huge financial burden off her.

"Just so you don't go living in sin."

Terri lost it then; sometimes it didn't take much. "I wouldn't consider it a sin to live with somebody you love."

It was like throwing a mouse to a cat. Her mother sat up straight as a pole and narrowed her eyes. She was in territory she loved. "It is in the sight of God," she said.

"Who decided that? The male chauvinists of the Roman Catholic church?"

"Thou shalt not commit adultery."

"If you aren't married, it isn't adultery."

"Why, it certainly is."

"You know, if you're not a Christian, it just doesn't matter. You don't have to listen to what anyone says. You get to make your own rules."

"You don't believe there's such a thing as God's truth?"

"Will y'all *stop*?" Her father was furious. "My stomach's churnin' and churnin'." That was his unvarying reaction to conflict, which was inevitable in all Whittaker family visits. When there was silence, he said, "Now tell us about school, Terri."

The rest of the evening continued that way: a pocket of peace, followed by an eruption of aimless, unfocused anger. And when it was over, her parents thanked her for coming and said how much they'd enjoyed the evening and how they didn't see her enough and wished they could see her more and when could they do it again. This happened every time and never failed to make her feel sad. They clearly didn't have a clue how to communicate with her, didn't approve of her, and didn't enjoy her company, yet they wanted to. Actually, she wasn't sure of that; in some dim corner of her soul, she knew that *she* wanted to. She thought that perhaps they just wanted to think they did.

Her mother had given her half the bought chocolate cake, which Terri took because she thought Isaac might enjoy it. (She herself avoided sweets and fats lest she turn into a balloon.) Why not take it to him now, she thought?

She was desperate for someone to talk to. Being with her parents always made her feel desperate, as if she were alone in the world and there was no hope.

She could simply go over to Isaac's house and surprise him—have a second evening after the first fiasco. Actually, they hadn't seen each other all weekend. Isaac had gone to visit *his* mother—in Atlanta, she thought—but he was coming back tonight. He'd said he'd call her; that meant he'd be home.

He might be too tired to see her. Well, in that case, she could just drop off the cake and kiss him good night. What could be wrong with that? Who wouldn't be glad to see half a chocolate cake?

If she'd really thought about it, she'd have known she had expectations beyond cake delivery. Isaac lived in the Bywater, and Terri lived in Carrollton, two neighborhoods about as far from each other as you can get.

She felt a little rush of happiness as she got out of her beat-up Toyota and saw that the lights were on in his living room. She was nearly up the front porch steps when she noticed the curtains weren't completely closed. What was he doing? she wondered, and peeked.

He was sitting in a chair, and someone was with him. A woman about Terri's age, maybe even younger, was packing a suitcase lying open on his sofa. Terri got it instantly: The woman was about to go home after spending the weekend with him!

He had lied to her. He hadn't gone away to see his mother at all. The serious little talk she'd had with him about whether he could possibly join her at her parents' house now seemed a sham. He'd said he really cared about her, but he didn't think they were at the stage yet of meeting each other's parents.

She stopped dead in her tracks and watched a moment. But only a moment. Before she knew she was doing it, she threw the cake at the door. The plate her mother had left it on banged satisfactorily and maybe broke. She couldn't be sure, she didn't look back.

She only heard the door open suddenly and then voices, laughing, she thought.

Yes. She was almost sure she heard them laughing at her.

He had to know who it was, even from the back; who else had blue hair and a beat-up, dented, rusty old Toyota? He didn't even call to her. That was how much she meant to him.

She drove back to her shabby little place in Carrollton, tears nearly blinding her, the tension of the evening giving way to despair. She flopped on her bed and stared up at the ceiling, wishing like hell for a cigarette, though she no longer smoked, not, for one thing, being able to afford it.

That—and everything—was so damned expensive. She did tutoring, errands, and intermittent clerical work for a few off-campus clients, but she never had two nickels, as her father would say, to rub together.

Almost not realizing she was doing it, she got up, slipped into her shoes, picked up her keys, stuffed five dollars in her pocket, and went back out to get cigarettes.

She was nearly home, a fat unopened pack on the seat beside her, when she saw the blue lights of a police car. Its driver was signaling her. Her? Terri? *Thank God,* she thought, *she hadn't been drinking.*

Wondering what on earth was up, she pulled over and got out of the car, as she'd once read you were supposed to do—it made the cops feel more comfortable or something. Too late, she recalled she had blue hair; that may not have been so reassuring.

Oh, well, she thought. *Good thing I resisted a nose ring.*

The cop looked okay: mid-thirties, maybe, slightly heavy; but not a redneck. That was good.

"What's going on?" she said.

"What's your name?"

"Terri Whittaker. Have I done something wrong?"

"I noticed you don't have a brake tag." He pointed to her windshield. Louisiana law required a brake check every year; if you passed, you got a tag that said so. If you didn't, you got a ticket.

"I'm really embarrassed. I just . . . uh . . . well, I work two jobs and go to school . . ."

He smiled, showing he understood. "See your driver's license?"

"My . . . uh . . . omigod. I came out without it. I just went to . . ." She turned around and reached through the windshield, meaning to show him the cigarettes. His hand closed around her arm, hard, and she screamed, it was so unexpected.

"Stay where you are, please."

"I just . . . I mean I was going to . . ."

"Just stay where you are." She saw him glance in at the seat and, apparently having reassured himself there was no gun there, he said to her, "Insurance?"

"I, uh, keep everything together. Someone broke into my car once and took everything, registration and all, so I . . ."

"You keep everything together." He smiled at her.

She decided to flirt a little. "Now, how'd you know that?"

"Oh, just a lucky guess." Thank God. He was being nice. "So you don't have your registration, either."

"I'm sorry. I can't believe I was so dumb. I was upset and I just came tearing out without even thinking about it."

"Where are you going?"

"To get cigarettes. I've already gotten them. I'm on my way home now, just a couple of blocks away."

"Terri, have you been drinking?"

She shouldn't have been shocked by the question, but she was. "No. Why would you think that?"

"Say the alphabet for me."

Impatiently, she raced through it.

"You messed up, Terri."

"I did? How?"

"You know what I want to know? How come every time I ask you a question you answer me with another one?"

"Am I doing that?"

"There you go again, Terri."

This was getting out of hand. She tried to head it off. "Listen, Officer, I meant no disrespect. I really didn't know I was doing it."

"Let's try it again. Say the alphabet."

This time she went through it more slowly.

"Okay," he said. "Close your eyes and touch your nose with your index finger."

She did it easily.

"All right. I'm going to write you up. Get back in the car, please."

He asked her her date of birth and a few other questions, and then he got back in his car and scribbled for a long time, so long she was pretty sure he was playing some passive-aggressive game with her, making her wait for no reason, and then he picked up his radio mike.

He talked awhile and returned.

"Everything okay?" she said.

"You need to step out of the car again."

She opened the door and got out, quickly stubbing out the cigarette she'd finally gotten to have.

"Now step away."

"Why?"

"You're *answering* me with a question."

She obeyed him, feeling nervous.

"Now put your hands behind your back."

Once again she obeyed, and before she had a chance to think about it, he'd handcuffed her. She stared at him, utterly bewildered. She wanted to ask him why he did it, but it seemed questions were suddenly against the law.

He said, "Terri, you got any warrants out against you?"

"No, I don't."

"Have you done anything?"

"Well, no. I haven't."

"Yes, you have."

She remembered her parking tickets. There were so many they'd threatened to boot her car, so she had a little stash at home meant to take care of them at the end of the month. "It must be my parking tickets."

"I'm going to have to take you down to the police station. Maybe you can call somebody to come pay your tickets."

He wouldn't let her move her car, but it hardly mattered; she'd be out in an hour or two.

But he didn't take her to the station. He took her somewhere with doors like an elevator that opened automatically and then you were standing in a space with more of those doors. Once you got in, there was a large room with lots of hard plastic chairs, like a bus station. The room was like a hub: opening off it were other rooms— cells. One, way at the back, was a holding tank for women.

"Where are we?" she asked.

"Central Lockup." He took her handcuffs off and left her. When he came back, he said, "You know what you did, Terri? You committed a felony. This isn't about parking tickets. This is forgery. Why didn't you tell me about it?"

"Forgery? That's ridiculous! Whose name would I sign?"

"There you go again. With that question thing."

*B*efore he opened his door to find it smeared with chocolate, Isaac James had been enjoying the last moments of a near perfect weekend, a weekend spent with his niece, Lovelace, who, because Isaac had a much older brother, was only a few years younger than he.

On seeing blue hair and a trim behind flying down the walk, he had taken in the hopelessness of the situation as quickly as a breath and laughed outright, there being little else to do. Lovelace, apparently horrified at the chocolate, the hair, the retreat, and the laugh simultaneously, looked as shocked as if someone had just opened fire. "What's happening?" she said, and, knowing she had plenty to fear, he wanted to reassure her immediately. But he couldn't. He thought later that it must have been the phenomenon called hysterical laughter.

"That's Terri. It's Terri," he sputtered finally, knowing Lovelace would know who he meant. He'd talked about his girlfriend all weekend.

"Why is that funny?"

"I can't say you're my niece—who'd believe *that*?"

She looked so completely unbelieving that it sobered him up. He cared deeply what Lovelace thought about him; except for his mother, who was some kind of missionary and was never in the country, his niece was all he had—by no means his only relative but all he had nonetheless. And since she was almost a contemporary, she was more like a cousin or a sister than a niece.

She was born when he was seven and just entering second grade. At the time, the thought of having a niece—or, more accurately, of being an uncle—was far and away the most important thing that ever happened to him. His short life up till that point hadn't been a bowl of cherries. He was the sort of child adults describe as sickly, and there was a reason for that. He hadn't yet decided whether to live. He had bronchitis when Jacqueline gave birth, and it happened they were in the same hospital, so his mother, Irene, took him down to the nursery to look at the baby. There was a window in the wall like a television screen and through it, he could see a nurse wearing a mask and holding a human being smaller than a cat. He'd seen plenty of babies, of course, but he had no idea they could come this small. He started to cry.

His mother said, "What's wrong, honey?" and he could tell by her voice his response was what was wrong.

"Will the baby be all right?" he asked.

His mother looked confused for a second, and then comprehending. "Oh, yes. The baby isn't sick. She just came here to be born."

But that wasn't what he meant at all. He knew perfectly well babies were born in the hospital. He couldn't have said what he meant, but seeing the baby terrified him. He was hugely, horribly afraid that she wouldn't be all right, that something bad would happen to her. He couldn't have said what; he didn't even think he knew. He just knew she wouldn't be safe.

At the time, he hadn't eaten in three days, but he went back to his room and asked for a milkshake. He thought that he might as well put off dying for a while and go on ahead and grow up. He made that decision without really knowing why, but he remembered it all his life, realizing much later that it was somehow connected to the baby.

Exactly how, he didn't know to this day. But he had always taken an extraordinary interest in Lovelace. Always. People had remarked on it, said how sweet it was for a boy to be so interested, how unusual. Some people had thought it too sweet and called him a faggot, though mostly behind his back (his father being the exception to that).

Maybe she was lucky for him, maybe they were connected karmically. Whatever it was, he had a soft spot for Lovelace, and it had continued through the macho years of adolescence and the awkward, searching ones of his twenties. He always sent her birthday and Christmas cards, no matter if he had no connection at the time to another human being and no desire for one, and that was what, in the end, had brought them close.

When you're the son and the granddaughter, respectively, of the most famous, maybe the most dangerous, killer on the planet, you'd better be close. Especially since Lovelace's mother was hopeless, and Isaac's was not only never around, but also pretty much a broken woman from all the years she'd spent with his father.

Neither of them called themselves "Jacomine" any more. They had chosen "James" together, so they could still have a family name in common yet avoid embarrassing questions.

Lovelace's father, who was Isaac's brother, Daniel, was about to be sentenced for crimes he'd committed with his infamous father, and that was why Lovelace was here. Exams prevented her coming for the actual sentencing, but she had wanted to come down and see him this weekend instead, as some kind of gesture Isaac didn't understand. Motivated by guilt, maybe. From everything he read, most people felt guilty for not loving their parents enough, not doing enough for them, just not being the cookie-cutter kids their parents had ordered and, truth to tell, Isaac felt somewhat that way toward his mother. He certainly didn't toward his father.

The way he did feel toward his father didn't bear thinking about, though maybe one day he'd have to sit down and go over it with a shrink, the way most people seemed to. But maybe not, because he painted. That took a lot of the edge off.

Lovelace was going to be fine, he thought. It was the first time they'd seen each other since Thanksgiving, and she was much stronger, much happier. She was like Isaac: Her work kept her going.

On Saturday, they'd gone to see Daniel and then to a movie, slowly getting reacquainted, and today they'd talked. He made her brunch first, one of his justly famous vegetarian omelettes with a side of home fries, and then they went for a walk along the lakefront.

Some things they'd already caught up on at Thanksgiving. Things like life among the talking classes. (Isaac had once lived under a vow of silence.) Things like her new environment—she'd transferred from Northwestern to Cornell to attend the hotel school. Today, they'd kind of filled in the details.

Lovelace wasn't having her nightmares anymore, but she was still on Prozac. Isaac was on it too, and it was working (though his complaint was much different). He was living close to a normal life these days, having gotten tired of being an outsider artist and gone back to UNO for a fine arts degree. That way, he figured, he'd get respect, and he could teach. And he had this girlfriend, Terri.

"What's your favorite thing about her?" Lovelace had asked, which made him think about it. What *was* his favorite thing about her?

At first it was just that she was nice to him. She had been the one to make the advances: to strike up a conversation, to ask him to coffee, finally to ask to see him again. "I figure she must like me," he said.

Lovelace laughed. "I'd say that's a fair assumption. But why not, Uncle dear? You're a pretty handsome dude."

"I'm not exactly the type you'd pick out of a crowd."

She pretended to assess him. "Little short, maybe." And that was good for another laugh, as she was about five-ten.

He never thought of himself as handsome, and anyway the whole subject of sexual attraction embarrassed him, especially talking to his niece. Hastily, he soldiered on. "Well, we got to know each other, and, really, what I like about her is, I admire her."

"Well, of course, silly." Lovelace was wriggling around on the sofa like some twelve-year-old sex kitten. She was visibly enjoying his discomfort.

"I mean I like her values." When you've been raised in hell, values get important.

"How so?"

"She's a hard, hard worker. Nothing's easy for her, and she works her butt off to keep her life together."

"A cute butt, I bet. What does she do that's so hard?"

"She's also an art student—an undergraduate."

"Aha. A younger woman."

He was about to say, "I like younger women," meaning it as a compliment to Lovelace, but he was afraid it would come off as flirtatious. He let the comment go. "She goes to school and does clerical work for somebody two days a week, and in addition to that, she has her own business, Aunt Terri's Rent-a-Wife."

Lovelace laughed out loud. "She's not full service, I suppose?"

"Hell, no. She comes from a good Christian family—and believe me, they never let her forget it."

"So what does a rent-a-wife do?"

"Errands, mostly. She picks up your dry cleaning, does your weekly shopping, takes your elderly mom to the doctor. Her clients are mostly married women who work."

"Wow. What a great idea. I'll bet I could do that. I could combine it with cooking."

"The only trouble is, the work's a little sporadic, so she never really knows where her next nickel's coming from."

"Poor baby, I know that one. Well, I can see what you mean about her values. She sounds like a very plucky person."

"She's a *good* person. She really is."

"An admirable quality in a girlfriend."

They'd had the talk right after dinner. Then, while Lovelace packed, they talked about their own crazy family, and then Terri arrived and came to the obvious but erroneous conclusion. He'd had a great time with Lovelace, but Isaac missed Terri. He'd thought about her last night in bed, realizing they hadn't been apart on a Saturday night for a while, and for the first time he began to wonder if this was what people called a "serious" relationship. Whatever that meant. Maybe it just meant missing someone when you weren't with her.

Lovelace said, "I'd better clean this mess up," and left to get paper towels and sponges.

Isaac just watched her, not offering to help and not even thinking about it, just feeling a little dazed. What had happened here? He couldn't let Terri run out of his life, just like that, on a misunderstanding.

"Maybe," said Lovelace, "we should go find her."

"What?" He wasn't moving ahead; instead of trying to think what to do next, he was still trying to comprehend what had gone on.

"Look. If we both turn up, it'll be abundantly obvious I'm no threat to her. *Nobody* would go over to their boyfriend's girlfriend's house and claim to be his niece. Think about it."

Isaac smiled, as he saw the truth of it. "Let's do it."

"Let me put on some lipstick and change my T-shirt."

Isaac waited impatiently, wondering why it took any woman on Earth at least ten minutes to perform any act of grooming, no matter how small.

He drove so fast and was so obviously preoccupied that Lovelace remarked upon it, in that all too straightforward way she'd developed lately. "Hey, Uncle. You seem like a man in love."

He ignored her, which was probably the worst thing he could have done.

"Methinks," she said, "thou doth protest too much."

"I didn't protest at all. I didn't say anything."

"It's like the curious incident of the dog in the night—in the Sherlock Holmes story. 'The dog did nothing in the night; that was the curious incident.'"

"Maybe," he said. "You should give up this cooking thing. You could be a great lawyer."

"Well, I notice you're not saying you're not in love with her."

He couldn't have said if he was or he wasn't; he hadn't even thought about it. But the sight of Terri's house ablaze with light cheered him immensely.

Each got out of the car, and they fell into formation, one beside the other, Lovelace a little taller, dressed in jeans and white T-shirt, still a little awkward from adolescence. Lovelace was a beautiful girl, but surely Terri would see that she was a child, young enough to be someone's niece, though technically only a year or two behind Terri herself.

He pushed the bell and they waited. Terri usually came springing down the hall, but this time he didn't hear her. Anxiously, he looked around for her car and didn't see it, either. "Her car's not here."

Lovelace peered up and down the street. "You sure?"

"Pretty sure."

"Maybe she went out for a minute. For cigarettes or something."

"She doesn't smoke."

"Why don't we wait around a few minutes, just in case?"

They sat down on the steps, but Isaac couldn't handle it. He was getting more and more depressed with each passing minute. Finally, he said, "I don't think she's coming," and Lovelace nodded. He hated looking at her, knowing her sad face reflected his.

Chapter THREE

$\mathcal{I}$t was freezing cold in the lockup. Terri couldn't help thinking what an incredible waste it was of the taxpayers' money—and then thinking, *What a weird thing to think in jail.*

Jail. How could this be? But she'd be out soon, at least there was that, and at least they'd taken off the handcuffs. There were two banks of phones, but you could only call collect, because of course they'd taken your money. The phones were in use right now (and most of the time), and from time to time, it appeared, the guards turned them off just to be ornery. Anyway, sometimes they just wouldn't work, and then all of a sudden they did.

For the moment, that was okay. She was thinking, weighing consequences. Her parents would certainly bail her out, but there'd be a big fat price. Two prices: the problems she'd have dealing with their judgment about it and the problems they'd have with worry and shame. And there was an additionally complicating factor: It was a precarious feeling, not knowing why she was here. She felt unaccountably guilty. Could she have forged checks in her sleep or something?

There was only one person she wanted to see, one person who could make her feel as if she weren't scum after all, one person who wasn't going to judge her, and that was Isaac. She was pretty sure she loved him, or could love him if he'd be kind enough to return the sentiment, but the simple fact was, she'd just caught him with another woman.

Everyone else in the place was a career criminal and didn't care who knew it. Some of the women dozed, but they perked up when someone new came in. When it was Terri, a prisoner hollered at her, a skinny woman who looked drugged-out and tired and used up. "Hey. What you in for? You look like a *good* girl."

"Thanks for the vote of confidence."

"What'd you do?"

She couldn't say she'd done nothing. Everybody knew there were no innocent people in jail. She didn't want to listen to a dozen hags laughing at her. She fudged her answer a little bit: "I'm in for *forgery*." The word felt so odd on her tongue. Forgery was something that happened in movies; she wasn't even sure how you did it. With great care, surely. You must have to practice the other person's signature and maybe steal their driver's license. Even in her sleep she couldn't have done that. Maybe she was a multiple personality. Maybe today's multiples went in for money instead of sex.

"Oh, forgery. That's nothin'. My sister-in-law did that once."

"What happened to her?" Terri was avid.

"I don't remember." The light went out of the woman's face, replaced by what looked like a twinge of pain. She was probably coming down from whatever she was on.

Terri had a semicomforting thought. Once when her bank statement had come, she saw that some other Terri Whittaker's check was in the package, a check that had been paid from her account.

She took it in and was shocked to be asked to sign an addidavit of forgery. "But I don't think there's forgery," she had said. "I think this check is from someone else's account—another Terri Whittaker." She didn't say, "This is some dim-witted bank error," but she certainly thought it.

In the end she signed the affidavit because they told her it was the only alternative to paying the check herself, but she'd always felt guilty about it. Had the chickens now come home to roost? Had someone signed an affidavit against her, as the result of a clerical error? At least it was an explanation.

She felt frozen in more ways than one. She thought later that she must have been in shock. She sat immobile and shivering, trying to take in her surroundings, comprehend her situation. She really didn't want to put her mind to what to do next.

They called her for prebooking, and she felt a shock of betrayal. How could they hold her without booking her? Forgetting the question prohibition, she blurted it out. The deputy laughed. "We can hold you seventy-two hours without booking you."

Seventy-two hours!

"You've got to be kidding! You can't do that."

The woman smiled, not a worry in the world. "Sure can."

She was so damn smug and superior, like she enjoyed making Terri miserable.

Every cell in Terri's body protested. *But I'm a good citizen. I pay taxes. I vote. I'm a good girl.* She knew better than to say it.

When she came back to the lockup, one of the phones was free, so she grabbed it. But she didn't do anything, just stood there and dithered some more. Finally, someone said, "You gonna use it or not?"

Timidly, Terri moved away.

There was a toilet of sorts in the holding tank, a toilet partly shielded by a waist-high concrete wall, but from certain angles everyone could see you sitting there doing your business. Someone was sitting there now and hollering for toilet paper.

"Goddammit!" one of the deputies hollered. "You bitches are out of control. Get off the phones. Up against the wall."

And then he locked them all in the holding tank, where they stayed for the next twenty or thirty minutes.

Terri was terrified. "What's going on?" she asked no one in particular. Most of the women ignored her, but one of them shrugged. "Never did figure it out. Think they go on break."

A woman deputy was standing outside the holding tank, in plain view of everyone, eating a small pack of chips. Eating it slowly. Very slowly. One chip at a time.

She was either talking to herself or to someone just out of Terri's sight. "Ain't had a minute to myself all day. I'm going to *enjoy* my snack." She spoke almost as slowly as she ate.

Terri was becoming increasingly panicked. All bets were off in jail. She might be furious with Isaac, might never be his girlfriend again, but she could worry about that later. Right now, she needed him to bail her out.

Eventually, another guard came along and unlocked the cell. With access to the phones once again (and with the fear of God in her), Terri dialed Isaac's number, fingers flying, before she talked herself out of it. He came on the line.

A recorded voice said, "This is Orleans Parish Prison . . ."

Isaac hung up.

That was the last thing Terri expected. He wouldn't even talk to her. She sat back down, humbled, and shivered some more. Gradually, she realized the hang-up wasn't personal, Isaac just wasn't used to getting calls from prisoners, which, when you thought about it, spoke well for him. Finally, she got up the nerve to try again, and this time he heard the recording out. "This is Orleans Parish Prison. Will you accept a collect call from . . ."

"Terri," she said, almost shouting. "Terri!" She'd nearly missed her cue.

"Terri?" He spoke as if he'd never heard of her, and the phone disconnected itself.

A guard came in again. "Okay, everybody off the phones. Up against the wall."

It was a long time before Terri got a chance at a phone again, and in the interim she debated once again the wisdom of calling this man who'd betrayed her. But every time, in spite of what she'd seen, Isaac won the argument simply because the thought of him was so comforting. She knew she'd be putting him out in a way that wasn't right. With great embarrassment, she even remembered that her last message to him was a cake thrown against his door. And in a way, that was the thing that tipped the scales. Because deep in her heart, she knew that Isaac would leave the other woman—if she hadn't already caught her plane—to come bail Terri out, no matter if he was planning to run away and get married first thing in the morning.

He just wouldn't be able to stand the thought of Terri in jail. He'd probably do it for any of her current six or eight cellmates without even knowing their names. This was the kind of guy you wanted to see on the other side of the cell door. She might never see him again, she might wear out her welcome sometime in the next two hours, but she couldn't help it, Isaac was the person she needed.

Once out of the cell and back in the holding tank, she tried him again. A woman answered, accepted the charges.

"Terri? Terri, this is Lovelace, Isaac's niece."

Niece? *Niece?* Terri was too astonished to answer. He hadn't cheated on her. But why the hell had he lied about going home to see his mother?

"I guess you saw me through the window tonight. Listen, Isaac said to tell you he's on his way."

"On his way where?"

"To bail you out. You poor thing. Did you get stopped for traffic tickets?"

"Brake tag," she said, nearly swooning with relief.

"Oh, you poor, poor thing. I'm so sorry."

Terri barely heard her. She was getting out within the hour.

*A*fter their wild goose chase, Isaac and Lovelace had gone home and had a glass of wine. She was flying first thing in the morning and felt the need of a soporific; he was upset.

He called Terri every fifteen minutes, growing increasingly anxious. He talked his niece into another glass of wine.

But, finally, as the living room was Lovelace's bedroom, he had no choice but to leave her to get some sleep before her flight. He read for a while and finally fell asleep. He had no idea when the first call came, but he went back to sleep afterward. The idea that it might be Terri just didn't penetrate. He'd gotten that kind of wrong number before; he thought nothing of it.

When the second call came, and he actually heard her name, he snapped to as if someone had yelled "Fire!" It was instantly clear what had happened. Furious with him (maybe broken-hearted, he flattered himself), Terri had gone out and gotten drunk. She'd either gotten into some kind of altercation and been busted for disturbing the peace, or she'd gotten a DUI. Thank God she hadn't been hurt.

He got up, pulled on some jeans, and headed for the nearest ATM for bail money, stopping only long enough to tell Lovelace what was going on.

He took about five hundred dollars, not knowing how much he'd need but figuring that would do it.

He had never been to Central Lockup, and certainly not at night. Thus, he was unprepared for the knots of shady characters hanging out in front, as if it were a crummy bar. What a weird place to hang, he thought. Why *not* a bar? As he went in, one or two accosted him: "Sir? Need a bail bondsman?"

So that was it. They were bail bondsmen.

There was a deputy at the desk. "Have you got a Terri Whittaker?"

He looked at something, maybe a computer screen. "She's not showing up."

"Theresa. Theresa Whittaker."

After about ten minutes, maybe twenty, he finally nodded. "Yeah, we've got her."

"I'd like to bail her out, please."

"You can't bail her out."

"What do you mean I can't bail her out?"

"Bond hasn't been set." He seemed to take pride in this.

"Well, can I see her?"

"Are you kidding?"

"No. Why?"

"She hasn't even been booked." As if that was supposed to mean something.

"Well, when will she be booked?"

The deputy shrugged.

"Look, when is bond going to be set? Can I get it set tonight?"

"Not unless you know somebody who has the nerve to wake up a judge. She'll be in court at ten o'clock tomorrow morning. At the very latest, four."

Isaac flat out couldn't believe it. Not only was she going to have to spend the night in jail, she might end up there all day. He couldn't even imagine that. There was no way he could let it happen.

"What court?"

"Criminal."

"Well, whose?"

"What?" The man was a cretin.

"What judge?"

"You're going to have to check the docket in the morning." The guy was clearly dying to get back to his solitaire game.

"Could you possibly tell me what the charge is?"

The deputy looked utterly exasperated, as if the idea of spending this much time with a member of the public was out of the question for a man in his position. Obviously irritated, he fussed again with the computer.

"Forgery and bad checks."

"What?" Impossible. It just couldn't be.

"She wrote some bad checks."

"She *wrote* some bad checks? You mean you've already convicted her?"

The deputy didn't even bother to answer, just turned around and walked away, leaving Isaac alone except for the herd of bail bondsmen.

He couldn't believe this. He never heard of a law-abiding citizen spending a night in jail unless they mouthed off at a cop.

Something nasty was nagging at him. How well did he really know Terri? Maybe he'd attracted some female version of his father and brother. He was no psychology scholar but he was perfectly aware that people with big-time criminals in their families might have to be careful about something nasty surfacing in their relationships. It was the same deal as children of alcoholics finding their nice, teetotaling spouses turning into alcoholics. Nobody knew how it happened, just that you attracted what you were used to.

Anyway, that was the theory, but Isaac figured his father was so mean and so dangerous, a mere bad-check passer wasn't half bad enough to fit it. Still, he had to wonder.

Well, he could wonder later. The thing was, to get Terri out of jail—he couldn't think of anybody he *wouldn't* bail out except his father. The problem was, he couldn't bail her out. He was way out of his depth. He needed to have a lawyer in court with her the next day at ten. How to get one?

He went home and called the lockup, but getting to speak to a prisoner was the same as talking to one if you were there—an "are-you-kidding?" situation. Isaac had never felt so helpless in his life. In the end, there was nothing he could do but set the clock for seven, thinking to get up and get on it early. Lawyers ought to be up by then—he could call them at home, while they were picking out the power tie of the day.

At four, the phone rang. "Isaac? Isaac, I'm freezing."

"Terri, I'm really sorry; they wouldn't let me talk to you, or anything. I can't bail you out until a judge sets bond, which they said will be at ten A.M." He didn't mention the "four at the latest" part.

"I'm so cold. It's about forty degrees in here. Isaac, why did you lie to me about going home for Mother's Day?"

He couldn't speak; he felt so helpless. No way could he tell her. He said, "Let's talk about it later. I've got to focus on getting you out."

She sighed. She was in no position to argue. "They just booked me a few minutes ago. I have the place where I'll be: JPSO. Wait a minute, that's not it. CDC Section J."

"I'll be there, Terri. They said you're in for forgery." He blurted the last before he could stop himself.

"That's what they told me at first too. Now I've got an official blue slip that says the charge. Are you ready for this? It's bank fraud."

"Bank fraud. What does that mean?"

"I wish I knew. Bank fraud! Me! I can't even balance my checkbook; how would I figure out a bank fraud?"

That was reassuring, anyhow. "I'll get you out," he said. "Don't worry. I'll get you out. Whatever happens I'll be there at ten A.M."

"Thanks." There was so much gratitude in her voice he felt his chest get tight. Dammit, if there were just something he could do! There wasn't, not till tomorrow at seven, but the anticipation of it was so strong he couldn't go back to sleep.

He got up at six, and, to Lovelace's surprise, made her breakfast. She had been asleep when he came back from the lockup. "Get her out?" she asked.

"I couldn't; bond hadn't been set."

"I thought she got stopped on a brake tag . . . she called right after you left."

"That might be why they stopped her, but she's in for bank fraud."

Lovelace brushed red-blonde hair from her eyes. "My God. What did she do?"

"She says she doesn't know. Want me to make you some grits?

"Sure."

They ate in near silence. Isaac's stomach was in knots, with worry about Terri and regret that Lovelace was leaving. As always when she left, Lovelace seemed sad too. In a way, it would have been better if he'd let her sneak away in her taxi, but in another way, he wanted to prolong their time together. He understood why people hated good-byes, though he found them indispensable.

Eventually, they got through theirs, with promises to see each other soon, and Isaac got out the phone book. First he called every lawyer specializing in criminal defense who also had a listed home number. Not one of them answered the phone, and he didn't blame them; with that kind of clientele, he wasn't sure why they were even listed. Next, he started calling their offices. Finally, he found one open, that of a Mr. Alvin Puglia. He poured it all out to the receptionist. "Listen, I have an emergency. A friend's been arrested, and she's going to be in court at ten o'clock. Could I please speak to Mr. Puglia?"

The lady couldn't have been nicer. "Oh, my goodness. I'm afraid he's not in yet." She paused, and Isaac could see her looking at a clock. "He's usually in by now. Shall I have him call you?"

"Could you, please? My name's Isaac James."

Isaac hung up, feeling anxious. He needed to move around. He went to take his shower and, to his surprise, found that a normal shower wasn't enough.

"Oh, no," he thought. "There isn't time for this." But there was no way around it. He had to stand in the shower until the hot water ran out.

He called the lawyer's office again, and still Puglia wasn't in. So, very carefully, he dressed for court. He had no tie and, in fact, no summer sport coat. He had a tweed one, for winter, but it was boiling outside. What to do? Had to wear it. No choice. He couldn't go to court in shirtsleeves. Terri deserved better than that.

It was after nine. Once again, he called Puglia. He still wasn't in. Isaac wondered if he should try to get another lawyer but decided it was too late. He'd have to go to court alone. Somebody had to be there.

"Listen," he said to the receptionist, "I'll call from the court-house. Can you tell me where it is?"

She hollered the question to someone else in the office, neglecting to put her hand over the receiver. That nearly blew out Isaac's ears, but then she came back all soft and pleasant, "Four-twenty-one Loyola."

He hustled on over on his scooter, and when he got to Section J, out of breath, only minutes to spare, the judge wasn't in and wasn't scheduled to go on the bench.

"There must be some mistake," he said, and at almost the same moment saw the sign that said CIVIL DISTRICT COURT. A criminal lawyer's office had sent him to the wrong court, wrong courthouse, wrong part of town.

"You want magistrate's court," the clerk told him. "Over on South Broad. Near the police station."

Once there, he asked and was directed a second time to the wrong court and finally arrived at ten fifteen to find that there was no Section J. He was winded by now, carrying the sport coat over his shoulder, his shirt nearly soaked through. *A tie,* he thought, *would have killed me. And the stress might still.*

He was astounded at how hard this was, this thing that ought to be simple. *And I'm white and educated,* he thought. *They say it's really hard if you're black and poor.*

Finally, someone directed him to the office of the clerk of court, where he was told that Theresa Whittaker wasn't on the docket. "She's got to be." Futilely, the words came out. Nothing so far had worked out as it was supposed to. But, still, she'd spent a night in jail. They had to bring her before a magistrate (or so he thought).

The clerk looked at his records again. "Sorry, I just can't find her." He seemed a nice and sympathetic man, which might be quite a trick in the job he had.

Not knowing what else to do, Isaac prowled the halls till he found an office labeled INDIGENT LAWYERS. It wasn't a phrase he'd heard before, but surely it meant public defenders. He marched in and stood before a woman whose desk nearly spanned the doorway. "Can I help you?"

"Yes. I need a lawyer."

"All of our lawyers are court-appointed." Naturally. Another roadblock.

Isaac considered. "Well, maybe I just need help. A friend of mine's supposed to be in court at ten A.M., and the clerk says she's not on the docket."

"Did you ask him if she's scheduled for four o'clock?"

"Well, no, she was arrested last night. Surely she's scheduled for morning."

"Not necessarily. If a lot of people came in, they might not get to her till then."

So it was back to the drawing board, and once again the clerk was patient, but no Theresa Whittaker was scheduled for four, either.

Feeling wrung out, Isaac called Puglia yet another time, and still he wasn't in. He was out of ideas and out of starch, as limp as if he'd done a whole day's work, and he'd hardly started and hadn't accomplished a thing. Plus, he'd already missed his first class.

The hell with classes. He wasn't going to make it today.

He went and called his next-door neighbor, who was more or less like a guardian angel to him. "Pamela, it's Isaac."

"Oh, hi, Monkie." This was her nickname for him, a holdover from the days when he called himself The White Monk. "Want some coffee? I'm just making some."

He did. He wanted some desperately, and, more, he needed it. He was fresh out of adrenaline. "Thanks, but I can't stop, I'm trying to get someone out of jail."

"Not Terri, I hope."

"Terri? I didn't even think you knew her."

"Of course I know her. She and I visit all the time."

"Pamela, listen. Do you know any criminal lawyers?"

"Sure. My brother's wife, Tiffany."

"Tiffany? That's a lawyer?"

"Tough little cookie. Just ask Leo."

"Well, I mean, would anybody take her seriously?"

"Only everybody. She used to be an assistant D.A. Give her a call, why don't you? And listen, let me know if there's anything I can do. Terri's a good kid." Good old Pamela. She not only had what he needed, she offered more, and no questions asked. Everyone should have a friend like her.

"Someday, you know, I'm going to buy you that castle in Spain."

"What castle?"

"The one I owe you."

"Oh, by the way, about your lawyer—her friends call her Tiffie."

If he hadn't been so desperate, Isaac might have disqualified Tiffie on grounds of cognitive dissonance, but he *was* desperate. And Tiffie was in. Quickly, he explained the problem.

Tiffie wasted no words. "She must be in Jefferson Parish."

"No, she can't be. I was at Central Lockup myself. She was there."

"Maybe they transferred her this morning. What did she tell you when she called?"

"She said CDC Section J—oh, wait. JPSO, she said first. Could that mean Jefferson Parish?"

"It might."

"But she was stopped in Orleans. Why would they take her to Jefferson?"

"Simple. That's where she wrote the bad checks."

There it was again. Instant conviction. It was one thing coming from a jailer and quite another from Terri's lawyer. "I guess," he said, "there's really no such thing as the presumption of innocence."

"What?"

"You just convicted her."

There was an edge to Tiffie's voice. "You're going to find, Isaac, that most people who get arrested are guilty."

Well. He really needed *that*. "Look, do you think you can find out where she is?"

"Let me try."

She called back in ten minutes. "She's not in Jefferson Parish, but she's not in Orleans either. I just talked to the clerk of court. He remembers you."

"Well, where does that get us?"

"I don't know. I just don't know. Let me try calling a few people I know."

Isaac fidgeted while she did, unable to do anything worthwhile, way too keyed up for a catnap, not hungry and not thirsty. He supposed that normal people watched television at times like this, but he absolutely couldn't abide the medium. He went in the bathroom and washed his hands a few times.

After forty-five minutes, the phone rang. Tiffie said, "I've found her, or at least I know where she's supposed to be. They did transfer her to Jefferson. But over there they're still saying they have no record of her. They must not have processed her yet."

"What do we do now?"

"I'm going to lunch. I'll call you as soon as I know something."

Isaac was nearly mad with anxiety. He wondered if he should call her parents and decided definitely not. He sat down and meditated, something he should have thought of a long time ago. He used to do it several times a day, but he was kind of out of practice.

Afterward, he felt calm enough to go to the kitchen and make a tuna fish sandwich, though he was usually a strict vegetarian. Today, he needed something solid. He was slicing green onions when Terri called.

"Hi. I'm in Gretna. On the west bank of the river. Jefferson Parish."

"So I hear. Well, I was in court this morning even if you weren't. You should have seen me in my power jacket."

"Isaac, what's happening?" Her voice was full of fear.

"Well, the good news is, you've got a tough cookie of a lawyer."

"Great."

"The bad is, she's named Tiffie."

She didn't laugh. "Oh, very funny."

"I swear. She's Pamela's sister-in-law. She's very good." He felt a twinge, realizing he didn't yet know how good she was. "Anyway, she's very conscientious."

"Well, then, why am I still in here?" She sounded as if she were losing it.

"To tell you the truth, you were lost in the system for a few hours. We'll get you out soon. I promise."

By one o'clock, Tiffie had caught up with him. She called to say that Terri was indeed in Jefferson Parish Lockup and a judge would set bond at five o'clock.

Isaac had a question, but he didn't really know how to ask it. "I'm wondering, ah—"

Tiffie closed in on his indecision. "Look. Isaac. That's it. That's the whole story. There's no way to get her out till then."

"I wasn't . . . I was just . . ."

Her voice was supremely tired. "Isaac, there's nothing more I can do."

He had no idea why she'd so suddenly gone off on him, but he really needed an answer to his question. His urgency gave him sudden clarity of speech. "Look," he said, "would you just hear me out?"

Tiffie backed off. "All right."

"Can you go to court with her?"

"What are you talking about?"

Of all things he expected to hear, that was the last. Maybe this woman wasn't a good lawyer. Evidently, she had a poor comprehension of English. He tried again, "When she goes to court at five, can you be there?"

"She's not going to court."

"I beg your pardon?"

"They'll just do it on the phone."

"I never heard of that."

"I guess that's the way they do it over there."

Okay then. Nothing more to be done. He could grab a much-needed nap and then go get her. Ah, but how was he going to do that on his scooter? He really needed Terri's car. He hoped she'd call back and tell him where it was and where to find the key.

He lay down on his bed but found himself absolutely unable to relax. *Dammit, okay,* he thought, and turned on the TV that Pamela had insisted he take when she bought a better one. He'd had it on about twice. Some sort of midday news show was on, a sniper somewhere . . . Jesus, in the French Quarter. The shot had "narrowly missed a police officer," the reporter said, and all of a sudden he was looking at an inset photo of someone he knew well—Skip Langdon.

His stomach turned over, and his heart started pounding. Jesus. Did it have to do with Daniel? His father had good reason to kill Langdon—a string of them, actually—and would. Oh, yes, his father certainly would. If the thought entered his head, he wouldn't rest till it was done. And the timing. Somehow, with Daniel about to be sentenced . . . he couldn't explain it, it was just the kind of thing his father would do.

Isaac was working up to a pulse rate of about a thousand when the phone rang. He snatched it up, unable to believe he'd been distracted for a moment. He felt like Chicken Little: The sky was definitely falling. "Terri?"

"No, but Terri asked me to call." It was a man's voice. "This is Mike with Lincoln Bail Bonds over in Gretna. Terri said you might be willing to help her."

"I'm trying, but bond hasn't been set yet."

"It'll be about five thousand dollars."

"Mike, what are you telling me? It hasn't been set and won't be until five this evening." How dumb did they think he was?

"I can get a bond set right away."

"I beg your pardon? Her lawyer can't even get a bond set. Why should I believe you can?" Isaac was outraged. He saw the scam immediately. You went all the way across the river, and they said it would just be a few minutes and then three hours later, when the judge was scheduled to set bond, he did, and you were already committed to Lincoln Bail Bonds. Furthermore, you'd wasted your afternoon.

But just to be sure, he gave Tiffie a call, pretty much expecting to be brushed off again, yet determined to do whatever it took to get that poor scared girl out of jail. To his surprise, the lawyer said, "I'd go for it. Bail bondsmen are in business; if they say they can do it, they must have a way."

It sounded crazy to him, but he was still too keyed up to sleep and too tired to do anything else. Why not just take a ride over there?

In the end, he borrowed Pamela's car, and to his enormous surprise, all the papers were filled out, awaiting his signature and a non-refundable cash accompaniment.

Nothing was what he expected. The bail bond office wasn't any cheaper or uglier than any other office—indeed it had been rather nicely furnished with fake oriental rugs and fake Queen Anne desks—and the people seemed perfectly nice. Not at all the sort hanging in front of Central Lockup the night before. There was a young black man with a huge cross around his neck, a yuppie-looking dude in a blue polo shirt, and a middle-aged lady with as polite a manner as you'd expect in a person whose customers weren't a captive audience.

"I'm Kay," she said. "Come on. I'll take you over."

"Just like that?" Isaac couldn't believe the hours of anxiety were really over.

Inside the lockup, there was a wall of glass, behind which sheriff's deputies were displayed at work—or, rather, horsing around and talking on the phone. They assiduously avoided Kay's eye. She didn't even shrug, just leaned an open hand containing the papers against the glass so they could see what she was there for, in the event they wanted a break from flirting and arranging their kids' soccer schedules.

Kay was telling Isaac about her job. "Every hour," she said, "we come in and get the docket. Then we can start calling people's relatives."

Actually, Isaac found it pretty riveting, but he couldn't help thinking about poor Terri chewing her nails in there. He tried, unsuccessfully at first, to catch a deputy's eye, but he kept at it until he succeeded, a task that took about ten minutes, while Kay just leaned and chatted as obliviously as if this were a way of life she was used to.

When someone finally took the papers, she left with a nice friendly good-bye. "How long," Isaac asked, "before Terri comes out?" He dreaded the answer.

"Well, I'm sorry to tell you it could take as long as forty-five minutes if they haven't processed her yet."

"That doesn't sound so bad."

An hour and forty minutes later, the doors finally opened, and out walked a bedraggled Terri, who started crying the second she saw him. "The asshole ate french fries!" she managed to blubber.

Isaac wasn't sure he'd heard right. "What asshole?"

"The deputy. They processed me an hour ago, but he knew I hadn't eaten all day, so he made me sit on a bench and watch him while he ate his fries. One at a time. Slowly. Chewing twenty times each."

Chapter FOUR

*D*avid Wright ("Mr. Right" to an increasing number of Americans) sat in his paneled wood den in University Park and nervously fingered his remote as he tried to digest what he was seeing on television. It was a news story about his own son's sentencing for what the newscaster called "heinous crimes." He flicked the remote again and again, trying a bunch of other stations, and it was the same damn thing.

He should have been watching a story about the shooting death of New Orleans's hot-dog cop Skip Langdon. He tried not to think about that part because if he did, it was going to make him mad, and he was going to throw the remote, wrecking the expensive oversized screen and scaring Karen half to death. This kind of fuckup just didn't happen when Errol Jacomine was there to run the show. The ironic part was that it was Devil-Woman's fault Jacomine didn't exist anymore. So she got to live a little bit longer while Daniel spent the rest of his life in the joint. David Wright simply could not countenance it. Absolutely had to make it Right. Was driven to.

Actually, Daniel had defied the Lord and deserved what he got. David Wright had no real problems with that part and in truth had nothing but ill will toward his son. It was Langdon's arrogance that galled him, that she could think she could do this to him, David Wright, and get away with it. That was what he found insupportable.

He was afraid of her too. She was probably the only person in the world who could bring him down at this point and not because she was so almighty smart and talented.

Because she had special knowledge, goddamn her.

"Honey, what's wrong? You look like you're 'bout to cry." Karen spoke in that Texas twang so many of them had around here, that soft feminine musical way that let you know the speaker was a blonde before you even saw her.

He said, "I'm listenin' to the news. That's all." (Sometimes, at home, he dropped his *g*'s; he never did in public any more.)

They had two big, deep, plaid-covered sofas arranged in an L for watching television, which was now part of his job; when you're in television, you watch it.

Karen came and cuddled up with him. Idly, he grabbed a breast. Ever since he could remember, he'd gotten all the pussy he wanted, but he'd had very few women in the same class as Karen.

Rosemarie Owens now, that was another matter. She was one of a kind.

He always pretty much expected the best around to come his way; he just hadn't been around the ones like Karen much. Karen came to him because she had a problem—the reason a lot of people had come to him over the years and especially came now—and she had stayed and become his wife.

There were things about it that tickled him. She didn't know either of his true ages; in fact, she thought he was in his mid-fifties, though his body was older. That part would probably fly, she was so crazy in love with him. But he was also less than two years old. That would probably give her a start.

The last time he saw that bitch Langdon he knew Errol Jacomine had to disappear, and fortunately he had the wherewithal to make it happen. Or Rosemarie Owens did. He'd laid low for a while, staying in cheap motels and wearing a pulled-down baseball cap in the daytime, and found it was pretty easy to get along if you looked like nobody in particular. He wore jeans and T-shirts like everybody else, and for a while he shaved his head, but nobody paid him any mind anyway. He was just another itinerant nobody, going no place and no place to go.

For the first few nights, he had a hidey-hole, an abandoned house scoped out far in advance. He also had enough money to last awhile and a car registered to someone else, but not stolen—a car someone had bought for him under their own name; thus, a perfectly legitimate registration. The house was in a neighborhood where there were both blacks and whites, neither with much money, none with any love of the police. He'd stocked it with canned goods, so he didn't have to go out much, but the place was disgusting. After a few days he got on the road, figuring as long as he didn't get stopped, he was safe.

He needed to stay in the South, because that way he'd blend better, and he needed to stay in fairly big towns so he wouldn't stick out. The Redneck Riviera ought to be about perfect; everyone looked the same and talked the same, and no one cared what anyone else was up to; they were too busy falling all over each other trying to make their money disappear.

So he headed for the Mississippi Gulf Coast, where he found any number of losers hanging out in casinos and bars, two of his least favorite kinds of places, yet better cover for it. These were people who needed help, people to whom the Reverend Errol Jacomine could have given direction and purpose. People whose money he could have saved—his followers didn't gamble because it was forbidden, and it was forbidden because it wasn't smart. Jacomine was known as Daddy, and it wasn't for nothing. Daddy didn't let people throw away their lives and their money. That was for suckers, and that was what most people were. They needed to be taken care of, and Daddy was a natural-born caretaker. You just treated them like children, that was all: set boundaries and didn't let them cross. They toed the line, or they got punished. If they did right, they got rewarded.

But he needed a bigger canvas to get his message across. It wasn't any big unusual thing, just that God was love and people who did right and followed His laws would be saved. Everybody knew that anyway.

The thing about Daddy was, he had a unique talent for saving them. It was like—he didn't say it much, only to his very closest associates—but it was like he was the one who'd been sent by God to get everybody saved. He felt the power; he knew that was his mission. Not just everybody for a few miles around. Everybody in the world.

Things at the start of the millenium were not going so well, and all of a sudden nuclear weapons were in the news again. Somebody had to do something. In his heart of hearts, Daddy knew the somebody was he; he just wasn't sure yet what the something was. But he did know that, in this period before he could call Rosemarie, while he was lying low and pretending to be a loser, he would be given a sign and he would know what to do. And then he would find Rosemarie, and she would help him do it.

For the moment, he just wished he could get these dumb fucks to quit gambling their lives away. It made him sick to see corporate gangsters taking these poor people's money this way. He read up on gambling, so he knew just how much the odds were stacked in favor of the house, and now and then he'd tell somebody but never in a casino and never if it wasn't a pretty loose situation.

Nobody cared. Nobody was interested. But he knew it was all a matter of the way you put it. When the Lord was in him, Daddy could convince a cat it was a dog. He couldn't wait to get back to his calling.

During those grim and gray days, Daddy watched a lot of television. It was a good alternative to throwing his money away, and, the more he sat in his room out of sight, the less chance he had of being recognized.

The Lord spoke to him while he was watching television, though not in one single blinding-white moment. The message came gradually and surely, the way an idea starts from a germ and refines itself. But since Daddy had prayed for a message and since God often spoke to him, he was able to recognize the divinity of this one almost as soon as it was given to him. What he had prayed for was divine guidance regarding God's future plans for him.

Daddy had never thought highly of televangelists, finding them rather slick and transparent, but he tuned in from time to time because he felt it was part of his job to keep up with the competition. One Sunday morning, as he was watching one of his least favorites, the kind of thought came to him that for various reasons made him uncomfortable: *This guy is an amateur. I'm a million times better than this guy.*

Having had the thought, he almost immediately forgot about the preacher and went into a reverie about envy and the Biblical prohibition against it. It occurred to him that when you had a thought like that, even if it happened to be true, other people, at the very least, would *take* it for envy. Even if you knew it to be God's truth.

God's truth. How had that phrase come into his mind? God had put it there. He knew that, because he was good at recognizing that very thing—God's truth.

So he was better than the other preacher. That was a given. Why was God being so insistent with him? He turned it over in his mind a couple of times, knowing that the rest would unfold in its own good time, exactly as God intended and no other way.

He knew that God did not intend him to become a televangelist. He couldn't have said how he knew, but he knew it quite well, perhaps because it was an anticlimactic idea. Daddy had been a preacher and he had been a politician and he had been a soldier for justice. Deep in his heart, he was still a preacher, but he knew that that was only the core of God's plan for him. His mission was a much bigger one.

He forgot about the revelation of the televangelist—to the extent that it was one—until a week or so later when he was watching a talk show. *This guy is terrible,* he thought. *I could do that.*

And in a split second he had it: He understood how a talk-show host could spread the word of God (though of course he never need mention the three-letter word). And, perhaps not coincidentally, he saw how such a host could also be a politician and a soldier for justice.

He turned off the television, went out to get some yellow pads, brought them back to his nondescript motel room, and began to fill them up with the ideas that now flowed out of him like a sacred river.

He filled up two of the pads and then made himself a checklist of the things he had to do and the order he had to do them in. First on the list was call Rosemarie Owens. He couldn't do another thing until he did because she held the purse strings.

Rosemarie had all the money in the world, thanks to him. Thanks to Errol Jacomine and no one else. Not only that, she was family.

And fortunately the connection between them had never been publicly made, probably because Rosemarie had the money and clout to dissociate herself from him. Still, the FBI knew, and the Devil-Bitch knew. No matter how much Rosemarie wanted to help him—which was probably not at all—her hands might very well be tied. Her phones were probably tapped, and they very likely watched her house as well. Or did he give himself too much credit?

The media had made him into a monster (with the help of Detective Devil-Bitch Langdon), but maybe he was small potatoes to people with real crooks to catch. He'd have to proceed carefully.

When he judged enough time had passed, he fired up his car, checked it for any burnt-out lights or other excuses for cops to stop it, and drove to Dallas. Once there, he registered at a crummy motel, paid cash, and began to scope out the very fancy Ms. Owens.

She lived in the kind of neighborhood where any stranger was suspect, so it looked as if he'd have to watch from a distance. He didn't like that. If the FBI were also watching from another building, he'd be visible.

Maybe they were checking her mailbox. He had no idea what lengths they were willing to go to.

Should he send flowers with a rendezvous note? But what was to stop the feds from showing up at the meeting place?

The problem was, he didn't know enough about her habits to go wait for her at a place she might turn up. He racked his brain until it finally occurred to him that every rich Texas woman would have at least one habit.

Accordingly, he phoned Nieman-Marcus, said he needed to talk about his bill, and was referred to a Donald McCullough. He then went to the store itself (to get around the Caller I.D. problem) and, by means of a simple ruse or two, actually managed to make a call from the credit department. He was rewarded with the ubiquitous voice mail. Good. The real Rosemarie would probably have just blundered in and interrupted.

"This is Donald McCullough at Nieman-Marcus," he told the robot. "I'm returning your call about your bill. Four P.M. at my office will be quite convenient. See you tomorrow."

She would know his voice, but how she'd respond, he couldn't say. What he would do in her shoes would be to go to McCullough's office, look around for the caller, wait around a bit, and leave if they didn't show up.

If she did that, he could catch her at the bottom of the escalator on the next floor down. Of course, she might decide to turn him in, but he was willing to take the chance. He knew enough about her to make her extremely cautious when dealing with him. Besides, the two of them loved each other. Always had.

Feeling cocky the next day, he waited a few blocks from her apartment, on the route he knew she'd have to take, and the sight of her driving by in her big, sleek, white Lexus made him happier than anything had in months. In fact, it made him feel like a million dollars. Bulletproof. Absolutely on top of the world.

He decided to abandon the charade of waiting by the down escalator and in fact caught her as she was coming in the door and planted a big one on her just as she opened her mouth to say his birth name: "Earl Jackson! What the *devil* do you think you're doing?" He could just hear her saying his first name, the one he'd had when he married her, in that phony British accent of hers, but anything to keep his name quiet.

"Rosemarie. You're looking pretty."

"Well, you look like hell."

*R*osemarie Owens let him take her arm and stroll her around the store, pretending now and then to admire an expensive bauble. Running wasn't going to help anything. She figured he probably wanted money; she could just give him some and send him on his way. "The whole world's chasin' me," he said. "—or haven't you heard?"

Mmm hmm. Definitely money. She said, "Earl, that wasn't nice what you did to me—having me kidnapped that time."

"Well, the guy let you go, didn't he? I wouldn't let anything happen to you."

She was silent, for once at a loss for words. What kind of man had you kidnapped and didn't even say he was sorry?

"Now, Rosemarie, we may have both done a few things—regarding each other—that we regret . . ."

"Like getting married, you mean?" They had gotten married when she was fifteen, he sixteen. She was Daniel's mother.

"You hurt me, baby. You really hurt me."

She turned to him, smiling, and hugged his neck. "Oh, Earl, you know I'm kidding. I've still got a soft spot for you, damn your eyes." The sad thing about it was, she did.

" 'Damn your eyes.' Americans don't talk like that, Rosemarie."

She shrugged. "What can I do for you, Earl Jackson, former husband and the FBI's second–most-wanted man?"

"I thought you'd never ask, rich lady. First off, I need to talk different. More like you do."

What in hell? she thought. She gave him a look meant to convey that she'd just realized she was dealing with a being from a different solar system. And then she saw what he was getting at. "Ah. You need a disguise."

"*You've* got one. I figure you know where to get 'em."

Rosemarie was perfectly aware that people said she reminded them of Ivana Trump. She knew she had a certain brassy attractiveness they couldn't quite place. Her former husband was one of few who remembered she'd once been little Mary Rose Markey of Savannah, Georgia.

She weighed her words carefully, not wanting to give him ideas. "You want me to help you get away."

"Well, not exactly, honey bunch. I've kind of got plans to stick around."

Bad news. No good could come of this. But she couldn't let him know she was afraid of him, had to make the monster eat out of her hand. She did her best to look concerned for him and hoped it didn't come off as frightened for herself. She said, "Earl, it's too dangerous."

He nuzzled her neck to test the waters, and it took all her will power, but she didn't flinch. "I think you need some champagne to steady your nerves."

Really good idea, she thought, and made up her mind to seduce him. Hell, she still thought he was attractive. Not good-looking—not for a second. Earl Jackson always had been a warty little toad, and time hadn't improved him. But he had something. An energy or something. She needed time to think, and sex would put him in a good mood.

They went and drank some champagne, and then they checked into a hotel. And then, for the first time in forty years, she made love to her ex-husband. What he said in the afterglow was kind of interesting: "Know what, Baby? You're the only woman I ever loved. I mean that."

She doubted it, but there was a kind of respect between them; there was definitely something there. "Come on, Earl," she said. "You just slept with me to see if I was wearing a wire. Like some people I know."

It was a reference to a little insurance policy he'd bought for himself, a recording he'd made of a certain conversation they'd had and sent to her shortly after she'd come into her money. That is, he'd sent a *copy* to her and made that fact very clear. If he went down, she went down. She was still smarting about that.

She knew that she still had the soft, white, unspeakably delicate skin she'd had when she was a teenager, and he stroked her shoulders and her arms and her breasts and belly as he told her his crazy plan. So crazy it just might work.

And considering the alternative, it had to.

He started out slow. "I'm going to need some speech lessons."

She nodded, thinking it over. She could help him with that. The idea had appeal: Rosemarie Owens as Pygmalion. She wondered if she could pull it off, decided it might be a hell of a lot of fun to try.

"I know a guy," she said, "but he's in England. How would you get a passport?"

"Maybe you could bring him over. Say you've met a diamond in the rough."

She nodded, and Earl said, "Do you know an English plastic surgeon?"

That one was easy. "Mexican. Lots of them."

He sighed. "Looks like I'm going to need papers."

She made a little face, wondering how to find a reliable forger. The Internet, maybe. "We're just going to see what we can do, aren't we? May I ask what you're going to do once you've reinvented yourself?"

"Well, now. You own a cable television station, don't you?"

"I do."

"I'm gonna be a TV star. What do you think of that?"

Now he was getting way too close to home. She gave him the alien look again. "Frankly, Scarlett, I think you've got a screw loose."

"Just hear me out, now. Just hear me out. This is something The Lord showed me. And it's what I was meant for." His voice dropped on that one, as if he actually awed himself. "All these years and now I know."

Rosemarie rolled her eyes. "You and God, Earl! You and God."

"What's that supposed to mean?"

His eyes flamed fury. She'd forgotten that about him: how fast he could turn mean. Clearly this was no time to make fun of his new life's work, however crazy it might be.

"Nothing. Go on; I'm interested."

"Well, it was a sort of vision. I was holed up in some cheap motel in Panama City, and the Lord showed me what I had to do. I looked at those televangelists, and I looked at those talk shows, and I looked at those reality shows, and I thought, *You know what? There needs to be a whole different kind of talk show, a talk show that could help God help real people. A talk show with a mission.* And you know what that mission would be?"

She shook her head, wondering where on Earth he was going with this.

"The mission is to right wrongs, lady. Real people's wrongs. If somebody gets cheated, badly treated, or roughed up by the assholes in power, why, Mr. Right will have them tell the story on his show, and then we'll follow up with some solid reporting on the underlying phenomenon of whatever it was, and then the show'll sponsor a let-ter-writing campaign or whatever seems appropriate. To right the wrong. See?"

Her heart rate was starting to pick up by a good little bit. This was a bloody great idea, the kind of thing that could really catch on, breathe life back into her floundering cable station. He was right; it combined three incredibly popular genres, and it would give people a chance to act out their angst. Not just the contestants but also the viewers. With the right host, it could become a national sensation.

She sat up in bed and laughed, breasts flapping like tetherballs. She loved it, actually loved it. "Earl, Earl, Earl," she said. "Talk about thinking outside the box! You're a sketch, you know that? I'll have to keep you around just to amuse myself." It was daring and dangerous and so insane she just had to do it (leaving escape hatches for herself, of course). "I even like the name."

"Mr. Right. That's me."

"You?"

"Wake up, Rosemary. What the hell do you think the makeover's for?"

"You crazy bastard. You can't get away with that."

He rolled over on her. "It's worth trying, isn't it? Besides, consider the alternative."

She didn't care to.

"If you're going to jail, might as well be later rather than sooner, right, lady?"

"Oh, well. Maybe I'll meet an assassin before you get busted." Or think of some other way out.

In a matter of months, she made Earl Jackson into David Wright, host of a new show called *Mr. Right*. He now had a new way of speaking, one with no dropped *g*'s and a vaguely British cast to it; a new—and younger and handsomer—face, with a far, far better jaw-line; new, iron-gray hair, and lots of it; heel lifts; blue contact lenses; even, due to workouts and shoulder pads, a different body.

And *Mr. Right* was a now minor hit on its way to becoming a major one. It was a show that believed in action, and people loved it. Its popularity was growing at such a rapid rate that Rosemarie was dizzy with greedy delight, and so were her sponsors.

Earl was a natural for it; he'd been in show biz all his life, if you counted preaching. And he'd had plenty of practice sounding like Mr. Sincere. Of course, he was a killer and a snake in the grass and could get her thrown in jail for the rest of her life, but for now they were pulling it off.

After she'd made him over, he turned her on so much she had to put a stop to having sex with him before it got out of hand. And it wasn't because he was so all-fired hunky, she suspected; it was because she'd made him. Whooo! Way too big a turn-on. She got herself a nice, young, seriously buffed ex-football player first chance she got, and after that she kept her distance and her fingers crossed. She had to think of a way out of this.

Especially knowing what she did now. One night, in the throes of passion, he told her what was really going on: "Oh, Baby, I can go all the way on this! I know it! You know what I have done? I have finally, at long last, come to an understanding of God's plan for me. Everything else in my life has just been flailing around. God has finally put me where I belong, and God will take me to the highest office in the land, where I will do the work of the Lord on the grand scale I was meant to."

Someone else might have asked them to run that by her again. But she knew Earl Jackson. There was no question in her mind just how crazy he was, what he intended to do. A piece of her actually thought he could pull it off and was just dying to see him try.

Chapter FIVE

$\mathcal{T}$urner Shellmire was waiting for Skip in the parking lot of the Third District. It gave her a turn, seeing a male form looming so publicly. If Jacomine had found a kamikaze shooter to kill her, all he had to do was wait for her just like this. He'd have time to turn her into a sieve before anyone could return the favor.

In the old days—four or five years ago—New Orleans had had a homicide department, and Skip had been a hard-working member of it. But "decentralization" had come to the city on the river, along with community policing, "accountability," "comstat," and certain other fin-de-siècle crime-fighting ideas first tried in New York and increasingly considered the hip and groovy nineties way. New Orleans had hired the same consultants who'd successfully worked the plan in New York City and had adopted all their ideas except one:

The city that invented boob-baring for beads had zero tolerance for zero tolerance. (Or so the experts were told. Plenty of natives thought this was a sop to the tourists.)

The effect, however, was that decentralization became the most dramatic manifestation of the new order. Basically, it meant the detective bureau was dissolved and its members dispersed to the district stations, where they became what some of them called "gen dicks": general detectives rather than specialists. The only ones who were still exclusively homicide investigators were those on the Cold Case Squad, which handled murder cases for the Eighth District as well as the cold ones its name implied. They still worked out of headquarters, where you parked your car in an underground garage and no one could wait for you in an open parking lot. Seeing Shellmire, Skip was once again a bit resentful about being sent to the boonies.

"Hey, Turner," she called. "You my police escort?"

"For today," he said. "For today." He shook his head unhappily, the corners of his mouth turning toward the floor. "I don't know about tomorrow."

"Well, I do. Tomorrow, Jimmy Dee'll go to work, and the kids'll go to school, and the FBI won't be able to do a damn thing, and the sniper'll have a clear shot." She spoke with such hopelessness she hated the sound of it.

Shellmire looked at her in surprise. "You don't sound like yourself."

"I'm just worried, that's all."

"Have a drink with me?"

Skip liked the sound of that. Shellmire wasn't the sort who'd waste his time trying to cheer her up: if he wanted to buy her a drink, he must have something to say.

She suggested a place near the lake, since they were in the neighborhood anyway and Shellmire lived on its north shore. But the agent said he wasn't going home, had miles to go before he slept, had to work out a plan to keep her alive. She wished, as she let him follow her back to the French Quarter, that she had any confidence he'd be able to.

Being cops, they could park where they wanted, and Skip suggested the Napoleon House. "You might as well absorb a little color while you're down here."

Once again, Shellmire turned thumbs-down. "It's a CC's kind of night."

"Why?"

"Lightning never strikes twice." CC's was a coffeehouse in the same block where she'd been shot at.

"I didn't think you were a superstitious kind of guy."

"I'm not; we've got agents covering the block."

She laughed. "Fat lot of good that'll do."

He shrugged and ordered coffee for both of them. "Look, I've been working all day to get you some protection . . ."

"Just me?"

"Hell, no. Everybody down to Angel and Napoleon."

"Napoleon's safe: they've got to know how much we hate each other. They know everything else."

"Skip, I'm afraid you were right back at the station. We can't really do anything. I'm just as sorry as I can be."

She leaned back and looked at him, waiting for more.

Now that the bad news was over, he was all business. "Can you get them to pack up and go away?"

"For how long?"

"Long as it takes."

"Dammit, Turner, I hate it when you say dumb stuff."

"Intelligence isn't my strong point."

"Wrong. We're both here because you've got some ideas about how to get him."

"I don't. I thought you might."

"I'm out of ideas. I thought Daniel's sentencing might flush him out."

Shellmire took a long pull on his coffee and patted his mouth with a handkerchief, eschewing the paper napkin the coffee shop had provided. "Well, he did in a way. What's happened to the other son?"

"You mean The Artist Formerly Known as The White Monk? He's moved on to great things; he even asked to paint me."

"And did you pose?" Shellmire was a bit of a slob, but he could be attractive. At the moment, his face was lit up with amusement.

"Twice," she said. "Nude."

"Right."

In fact, the first part was true: She had posed twice. She liked The Monk.

Shellmire said, "Who else was Jacomine close to, besides that Owens woman?"

"Ah, yes, the first wife. The one he had kidnapped."

"That was her story. We never were sure she wasn't working with him, but we watched her for six months after he disappeared. Phone taps and everything."

"Nothing?"

"Nada." He chewed his lip. "How about the pregnant woman?"

"Ah. The lovely Bettina. Still scot-free, damn her."

"Sore point?"

"You got it." Bettina was a follower of Jacomine's who'd claimed she'd been held against her will and forced to have sex with all the men of The Jury, Jacomine's vigilante organization. Her baby—evidently a product of her time with the group—had turned out to have a congenital disorder that required hours of attention each day. And Bettina herself, not very bright but extremely good at people-pleasing, had managed to convince the D.A.'s office they couldn't find twelve people who'd convict her of anything at all, much less conspiracy to commit murder. She'd pleaded out and ended up with probation.

For all Skip knew, Bettina wasn't guilty of anything more than being young and dumb, but it still pissed her off that the woman had so easily walked away from a human train wreck.

Shelllmire said, "Any other followers?"

"Doing time." That, at least, was gratifying, but unless Jacomine wanted to mastermind a jailbreak, they were never going to be any use to him again, thus no use to Skip and Shellmire. "Look, I should be going."

"Don't go yet. We're just getting started."

But she wanted to go; the conversation was making her anxious.

"Would you like me to sweep your house?"

"Sure." This was something she hadn't thought of. "Could you do Steve's too?"

"Consider it done."

He sent someone out the next day and reported later that both her phone and Steve's were tapped.

So the feds checked Jimmy Dee's and found it clean, but that provided little solace. Skip felt as if she'd been kicked. How the hell was she supposed to think about cemetery angels when the devil himself was eavesdropping on her?

I've got to do something, she thought. *I can't just let it lie.*

An idea came to her: *Why don't I just work the case as if I'm assigned to it? In my off-hours, say?*

It was time, and she knew it. She'd let herself feel safe for too long. Why, she couldn't have said, except that she so desperately wanted to live a normal life. And because she didn't know what else to do. In reality, her safety was as fragile as a thread and had been for two years.

Maybe, she thought, *there's nothing you really can do. Maybe it's like owning a house in the French Quarter. You whack away at it for a while, rebuilding and painting and fluffing and buffing, and then you lie down exhausted; next thing you know you have termites.*

I have termites of the lifestyle.

She doodled on a yellow pad, stars and spirals that came out of nowhere. And she wrote: What would I do if I *were* working the case?

The answer was obvious: Go see Bettina.

Bettina Starnes, her name was, but she wasn't in the phone book.

Okay, fine. Maybe she was still on probation.

She was, and her probation officer had her address, in New Orleans East. After work, Skip drove out there, just to get a gander, maybe check out the neighborhood, see if it looked like Bettina had a sugar daddy.

But if Bettina was still in contact with Jacomine, it sure wasn't for material reasons. She lived in a rundown brick fourplex, poorly maintained and badly built to begin with, one of six or eight in a small, underfinanced development. One of the four apartments was boarded up.

Bettina was a smallish, youngish, plumpish woman, African-American with a round face that wasn't really pretty but managed somehow to be so downright pleasant you just couldn't imagine her involved with a bunch of thugs and murderers, no matter how sheep-like their clothing. She had frustrated Skip and the feds—and certainly the D.A.'s office—when she was arrested shortly after giving birth.

Surely, Skip thought at the time, *she didn't know what she was doing.* How *could* she have believed the vicious claptrap that came out of Jacomine's mouth? She couldn't possibly have a violent bone in her body.

But everyone did, according to Cindy Lou Wootten, the police psychologist. She'd evaluated Bettina and pronounced her a woman who practiced the fine art of manipulation the way a doctor practices medicine.

Damn, she was good—as her freedom attested.

She met Skip at the door in surgical scrubs, fuschia in color, an ear-to-ear smile showing slightly buck teeth, her baby on her right hip.

With her left hand, nails painted a pearl-white, she reached out and grabbed Skip's elbow, the best handshake she could manage with the baby in her arms. Skip was grateful for the encumbrance, reasonably sure the woman would have tried for a hug if she'd had her hands free.

"Detective Langdon! How've you *been?*"

"Just fine, Bettina. Mind if I come in?"

"You're always welcome. You know that, baby." Baby! To the

detective who'd tried to pop her for murder. She spoke in the soft maternal voice of a favorite aunt, a voice that wrapped around you like a comforter. It had to be half the reason she was free today.

Bettina stepped aside to let Skip in, revealing a living room so Spartan Bettina might have been a Shaker instead of an evangelical fanatic. There was a greenish square of carpet on the floor, probably a remnant. A wooden settee and a hard wooden chair that matched it were the only furniture except for a couple of ancient end tables, undoubtedly found at a thrift store. The chair sported a yellow pillow large enough to fit on the seat.

Two or three toys were scattered on the green rug, certainly not the exuberant litter one might expect in the home of a working mother with a child under two. Not a single picture hung on the walls.

The place was stifling. Bettina said, "Sorry it's so hot in here. AC broke; they never did fix it."

Bettina put the child down and pointed to a narrow hall, evidently opening out to a bedroom. At any rate, Skip could hear electronic murmurs coming from that direction. "Go watch television, darlin'. Go on, now."

The boy bounced on rubbery knees, raising his arms to be picked up. When his mother failed to respond, he began to make little whiny noises, his sweet face twisting and turning in panic. Bettina put a hand at the back of his head, "Go on, baby. We'll play with your toys in a little bit."

The kid stuck out his lip but seemed to decide TV was his best course of action. And once he'd made up his mind, he tore off down the hall like a chubby missile.

Skip grinned after him, as silly as any adult around a two-year-old. "Sweet baby."

"Ohhh, you don't know. You don't know what a devil that child can be."

Considering his suspected paternity, Skip was startled by the aptness of the phrase. The baby was light tan, a color that could easily mean a white father. "What's his name?" she asked.

"Jacob. You know Daddy. He liked names out of the Bible." She meant Jacomine, of course; his whole following called him Daddy.

Skip deliberately misunderstood. "So his father was the Reverend Jacomine?" It nearly killed her to give him the title.

Bettina sat down, motioned Skip to do the same, and gave her visitor the full benefit of her too-large teeth. "All children are the son of God. You know that, Sister."

She'd never called Skip "Sister" before, and never again would be soon enough. But it might mean they had a rapport going; Skip sure wasn't going to ruffle it. She said, "You're looking good, Bettina. How's everything going?"

The other woman, sitting on the wooden settee, rocked back and forth, turning what looked more or less like an instrument of torture into an imaginary rocking chair. She smiled again, this time barely parting her lips. Her red-orange lipstick, walnut-colored skin, and fuchsia scrubs formed a fascinating play of color. "Doing good. Doing real good. Got me a nice, good-paying office job, working for Ochsner Home Health." She pulled at her sleeve. "They give you a choice. You wear these or pantyhose, nothing in between. What would you pick?"

Skip smiled back at her, as if they were neighbors passing the time of day. "I'd wear those if they looked that good on me."

The comment apparently made Bettina uncomfortable; evidently she was so used to using compliments to her advantage she felt attacked when one came back at her. Her smile flicked on again (though she kept the wattage down), and she said, "What brings you around, darlin'?"

"I was wondering if you've heard from Daddy." Calling him that was worse than calling him Reverend.

Bettina surprised her by saying, "Ohhhh, Ms. Langdon, I just wish I *would*." She seemed to have forgotten the story that had kept her out of jail.

Skip was about to comment when suddenly the television blasted at them like an explosion. Jacob, bored and curious, must have unwittingly cranked up the volume. Great, broken-hearted wails began to layer themselves on top of a booming aspirin commercial.

Bettina was on her feet in an instant. "Goddamn motherfuckin' *shit!*" Without so much as a glance at Skip, she disappeared down the hall, screaming at her kid the whole time. "Jacob! What the *fuck* you think you're doin'? Can't you use the sense God gave you?" And then there were pounding sounds, a kid being systematically hit, louder and louder wails, and the television went off.

Slowly, Bettina walked back in, for all the world as if Jacob weren't sobbing his heart out in the background. For a second, Skip wondered if she should make sure he was all right but decided the sounds she'd heard were probably no more than a palm slapping against a disposable diaper. If Bettina didn't treat him any worse than that, she probably wasn't going to do him any physical harm, though she might end up raising another criminal.

Bettina's temper tantrum had passed like a squall in a harbor. Once again she gave Skip that too-broad smile and spoke in that saccharine voice. "Every day I pray for my Daddy's safety, and I pray to hear his voice, and I pray to be reunited with him. In my heart of hearts, I know the good Lord's keeping him safe, and I'm grateful for it every minute of the day."

"You haven't heard from him at all?"

"Oh, my Lord, my Lord. I only wish my savior, Jesus Christ in heaven, would send my Daddy home to me." She sounded almost as if she were in a trance.

Skip absolutely couldn't believe, given her official story, that Bettina could speak this way to a police officer.

"So you've forgiven him for holding you prisoner?"

"Lawd, he didn't mean nothin' by that. Daddy just thought it was the best thing for me."

"What would you do if called you?" she asked.

Anguish replaced the longing on the woman's face. "Well, I

couldn't do anything, Detective Langdon. You know that. Not and stay out of jail." She bit off the last sentence, for a moment sounding furious.

But almost immediately the rapt look came back, along with the spun-sugar tones. "I'd just give anything in the world to know he's alive and all right. Anything in the world."

"If you hear from him, are you going to call me?"

"You know I've got to."

And we both know you won't, Skip thought. She felt unsettled, as if her business with the woman were unfinished. Bettina's longing to hear from Jacomine, so freely and ingenuously expressed, was frightening, but then so was everything about the man.

She stood and said her good-byes. On her way out, she saw a familiar pear-shaped figure dodge into a doorway across the street. She wondered if Shellmire were following her—acting as unofficial bodyguard—or if he'd decided on his own to come see Bettina. She ignored him, knowing an acknowledgment could be a Judas kiss, and he, in turn, ignored her. He phoned a couple of hours later, catching her at Steve's. "Bettina went to a pay phone about half an hour after you left. Did you notice a phone in her apartment?"

"No, but who doesn't have one?"

"Yeah. Could be she's in touch with him."

Skip felt her neck prickle and her cheeks get hot.

Shellmire said, "We can do a few days' surveillance. Maybe we'll get something."

"Thanks, Turner. I appreciate it." She got off the phone, heart still pounding. The agent's diligence should have been reassuring, but she found her mind drifting in a thousand paranoid directions. She drank two glasses of wine, inducing an uneasy slumber, and sometime in the night Steve woke her. "You were having a nightmare."

She was clammy with sweat. The damn termites again.

Chapter SIX

You haven't eaten all day?" Isaac sounded as if he didn't believe it. "They *have* to feed you."

Terri felt sulky. No one believed her about anything any more. Probably if she mentioned her name was Terri, he'd challenge her on that. "They didn't, okay?" she snapped.

Isaac pulled into a McDonald's.

"What are you doing?"

"We're getting you some food. Now."

"No."

"Terri, you've got to eat."

"I can't eat. I've got to go home. Just take me home, all right?" She heard herself snapping and whining, but she couldn't help it.

Isaac drove her home without another word, the lie between

them hovering ominously in the background. She got out of the car alone, ran inside, ripped off her clothes, and got in the shower. When she emerged, some twenty minutes later, she staggered, weak and disoriented, to the kitchen, but there was nothing in the refrigerator. Literally nothing that wasn't in a jar or bottle or didn't have green stuff on it.

She lay down on her bed and cried, thinking of the chocolate cake she'd thrown at Isaac's door the night before. Had it really been less than twenty-four hours?

She didn't know how long she lay there before someone knocked. Frightened, she looked through the peephole, half expecting the police. It was Isaac, holding a fast-food bag. She flung open the door, feeling calmer and very much ashamed of herself.

"I'm sorry I was such a butthead."

"No, I'm sorry. I brought you some food. I'll leave. I know you want to be alone. I just—"

"No, come in. I feel better. I'm really sorry."

He came in shyly, holding the bag at arm's length, as if offering it to a slavering beast.

Nestled in the paper bag was a shrimp po' boy—her favorite. She fell on it while Isaac made her some iced tea.

She drank a little: The sandwich had made her thirsty. And she said again, "I'm so sorry."

"Would you rather have some wine?"

She managed a smile. "I guess I would. I think there's some in the fridge. From about a week ago. You?"

"I'll get it."

He got her a glass, handed it to her, and eyed her warily. "Terri, what happened?"

She sank back into a chair. "I was thinking about it while I was in jail. They gave us foam pads to sleep on, but I couldn't sleep. I think I know. I think it's something to do with that mix-up I had at the bank—you remember that?"

"Yeah, those fines. I thought you had it all straightened out."

"You know, I remembered something they said the last time we talked. They said they turned it over to security."

"What the hell does that mean?"

"I don't know. By then, I was so over it, I just . . ."

"Terri!"

"Isaac, don't yell at me!" He fell back against the sofa he was sitting on. She realized he hadn't yelled at all.

"I'm sorry," she said again.

"If you don't want to talk about it, I can understand."

"No, I do. I want to see if I can get it straight in my head." She looked down at the floor and up again, flinging her still-wet hair out of her eyes, surprised by the color of it. She couldn't believe she'd done a stupid thing like dye it blue to annoy her mother. "Remember when I talked to my friend Ronnie?"

"Uh-huh," he said, his voice nervous, as if he expected her to do the yelling.

"Well, I was doing such a bad job of keeping track, I had all these fines, and Ronnie said I needed a second account to keep everything straight. See, here's what I didn't know. Sometimes, when checks come in to banks, like other people's banks, you follow—?" He shook his head. "Like, say, my account's at First Carnivore, and my client's account is at T. Rex. Well, then, I deposit her check, but my bank holds it for seven days to make sure it's cleared."

"Why would they do that?"

"I don't know." She shrugged. "They just say it's a policy, but I don't think it always is. I guess it's because I never have enough money to cover the check if it bounces."

"I don't see what that has to do with what happened."

"Well, I didn't know they were doing it, and I'd think the checks had cleared, so I'd just write checks of my own, thinking I had money in the bank. But I didn't. And then the bank would charge me a fine every time I didn't."

"For the overdraft."

"Yeah, I guess." She felt her shoulders go up in a big, defensive shrug. "I don't know how banks operate. I mean, how could I know? See, they'd take out twenty-two dollars a check, and I wouldn't know it, then they'd put through the new checks I'd written, and they wouldn't clear, plus the old ones, and they wouldn't clear *again*. And I'd get charged again. Only I wouldn't know."

"Terri." His voice was accusing. "Surely you've had checking accounts before."

She shrugged again. "I have, but if I bounced a check, I'd pay the fee. It was no big deal. I've never seen anything like this."

"But what about your records?"

"Well, I never wrote anything down. I just couldn't be bothered. And I never saved bank statements either. I'd never had a problem. I'd think, *Oh, damn*, and I'd pay the fee. I just . . . never banked with a bank like this. But, anyway, I got all messed up, and my mom bailed me out—" She stopped, noticing her unfortunate choice of words. "I mean, she said she'd lend me five hundred dollars to get me out of trouble, and my friend Ronnie, who works at a bank, said he'd straighten everything out for me. So I went to see him—"

"You mean at a different bank?"

"Yeah, and he opened a business account for me. Then I'd just deposit money at whichever bank was convenient and write checks at both accounts. But when my mom gave me the $500 check and I took it to the first bank to straighten the whole mess out, no one would talk to me."

"What do you mean no one would talk to you?"

"They said, 'You need to talk to someone in security,' so I asked for security, and the same thing happened. No one would talk to me there either. I deposited the five-hundred-dollar check, and after that, they never sent me any more bills. I thought it was fixed."

"Oh, Terri!"

"I know, I know. Basically, I just ignored it, which I know was bad on my part."

Isaac was silent, probably thinking what a dummy she was. Finally, he said, "You're telling me they never told you they'd filed charges?"

She shook her head.

"Terri, that's not right. You went there in good faith. It's just wrong. You've got to call the D.A. and explain."

"Yeah. *Somebody's* got to understand."

He stayed with her that night and held her, making her think everything was going to be all right.

But she found out the next day that she couldn't call the D.A. and explain. Tiffie told her so, strongly: *"Whatever you do, don't call the D.A.! I'll see if I can get the charges reduced . . ."*

"To what?" Issac asked.

"I don't know. She said I did do something illegal, even though I didn't know it was. It's called check kiting."

"I've heard of it, but I never really knew what it was."

Tiffie had explained, but the truth was, Terri didn't have a clue what she was talking about. "Tiffie just said it's when you write a check and there's no money in the bank."

"It can't be that. It's some kind of scam."

"Well, how could I have been running a scam? Look, I'm an artist; this stuff makes no sense to me. *They* were the ones charging me twenty-two dollars a check and never telling me, or not until it was too late. Think about it. That's more than two hundred dollars for ten checks: my rent, the phone, a couple credit cards, . . . I write that many checks every month, and there's no money left over. None. You know how much two hundred dollars is to somebody like me?"

Isaac only nodded. She knew he knew.

*T*iffie, whose lips were as thin as her tiny little waist, wanted to plead Terri out and get her six months probation. Which meant Terri would officially be a felon.

She ate all the time now, when she wasn't smoking, and bit her nails, worrying that her parents would find out. She stopped going to class, and one day, instead, had her cards read in Jackson Square. "Look for a sign," said the reader. "Look for a sign and follow it."

She felt so damn miserable she just went home and put on her pajamas and turned the TV on. One thing: Her parents had given her cable for her birthday. *Really great for depression,* she thought. *All the TV you can eat.*

She was an hour into a session of channel-surfing when she heard the words "We right wrongs on this show."

Riveted, she turned up the volume. The host was a man named David Wright. (*Mr. Right* was the name of the show.) He was a handsome man, a little slick, maybe, a little Texas-looking, but well-spoken in a Southern kind of way. Truth to tell, Terri found him slightly smarmy, but she sure liked what he had to say. "Let's welcome Corinne Kay Walker for the second time in a month. Corinne, you look a lot better than the last time you were on."

Corinne was a big-breasted blonde who'd evidently just had an expert makeup job done by someone at the station. She looked bright and sassy. The host played a clip of the previous show. Corinne was crying, describing her unfair eviction by a landlord who wanted to sell his building before her lease was up. She was the unmarried, unemployed mother of two small children. In the clip, she had scraggly hair and wore no makeup. She broke down twice as she told her story.

"My ex-husband declared bankrupcy, and I was on one of his credit cards, so that wrecked my credit. It was as if I'd done it too, you understand? I couldn't get credit for seven years, and that was only five years ago. I lost my job when the company went out of business, and I got evicted a week later. Mrs. Browning said I broke the terms of the lease—well, I did, Mr. Wright . . ."

"David."

"Technically, I did, David, but I *asked* her first. I told her my story, and she said, sure I could have a few more days to pay the rent. But then she denied ever saying it. And then I found out about the firm that wanted to tear down the building and build a hotel. Do you see what she did? She used my own circumstances against me."

Mr. Right said, "You know what that reminds me of? It's like the kind of person who picks up a hitchhiker who's been robbed and then rapes her."

This was the first of the two occasions on which Corinne broke down. She just had time to cry out the words "You understand!" before she lost it. When she recovered, she said, "I mean, it wouldn't be so bad if, you know, I could just go out and get another apartment, but who's going to take somebody with my credit record? And I didn't have enough money for first and last months' rent, you know, and some people even charge a damage fee."

Mr. Right stopped her here and turned to the studio audience. "What do you think, folks? Can we make it right?"

A roar went up from the crowd. The show's theme music came up, and suddenly ushers appeared, as if in church, passing collection baskets into which people fell all over themselves to drop money and coins. The camera lingered over a child dropping nickels in, then an old woman unwrapping a hanky.

Terri wrinkled her nose. *Pretty hokey stuff,* she thought.

And then the video stopped. The camera went back to the present-day, well-groomed, confident Corinne beaming and once again tearing up.

"Tell me, Corinne, did we make it right?"

She seemed a bit overwhelmed. "I won my case," she said. "People wrote letters. And I had lawyers . . ."

Wright stopped her again. "Our staff lawyers, yes. You won your case, you say?"

Corinne added, "People picketed too. She just . . . dropped the eviction. She said I could stay there until I got on my feet."

In addition, someone had offered her a job. She was working now as a secretary but taking computer courses at night toward the moment when she could make enough money to get out of the hole she was in. Subsidized child care had been found for her. The show's viewers had contributed food and clothing. The show had gotten her a makeover at a salon.

After Corinne's story was told, the second guest was called, an elderly woman who'd run a red light on the way to visit her daughter in the hospital, the victim of a traffic accident. The cop who stopped her found she was driving without her glasses, because she grabbed the wrong pair in her rush, and he'd taken away her license, which meant that she now had no way to get to the daughter's house to take care of her grandchildren while their mother was recovering.

This time, in the present, Terri got to see the offertory baskets being passed and hear an optometrist offering to fit her with new glasses. She was betting the police department of the woman's town was about to be shamed into returning her license.

A piece of her recoiled at the cheesy show-biz tone of Mr. Right's particular brand of justice, but it wasn't a big enough piece to stop her from copying down the phone number and e-mail address that flashed on the screen when the show was over. "Do you have a wrong that needs righting?" Mr. Right intoned. "Call or e-mail us before your life spins out of control. It's what we're here for."

Deep in her heart, Terri knew that she'd been the victim of a scam. Maybe not a deliberate scam—she doubted the bank actually meant to get her thrown in jail—but there wasn't a single aspect of what had happened to her that was right. She wanted justice, and darling Tiffie wasn't about to get it for her. She felt as if someone had thrown her a rope.

She obeyed the impulse and dialed. She got a recording saying to tell her story briefly and someone would get back to her.

And then it was like her brain returned from a short vacation. "Oh, sure, you will," she told the phone. "I'm a student without enough money to stretch from one week to another. The bank never told me it was going to hold my checks for a whole week and then fine me twenty-two dollars for each check I couldn't cover. Do you realize how impossible that made it to cover the next one? I had to borrow money from my mom to pay them off, and they took it and didn't even have the decency to tell me they'd already put out a warrant for my arrest. They just waited till I got stopped for some traffic violation and had to go to jail! I've never knowingly broken a law in my life. And now I'm about to have a felony on my record. Sure you care. Sure you're gonna call me back. I'm really holding my breath on that one." But she left her name and number anyhow.

She had no idea why she'd sounded off on the phone, except that she couldn't help it. In disgust, she changed the channel to a daytime soap.

*A*t the same time, in Dallas, the former Karen Bennett turned off her television, reaching, as she always did, for yet another tissue. Mr. Right was her favorite show. It always got to her. She had been one of Mr. Right's first guests and was perhaps its primary beneficiary.

She'd fought the biggest Goliath of all—the IRS. She still had the tape of the show, and watched it frequently, reliving the Cinderella saga that had become her life. She was barely twenty-six, and she'd gone from riches to rags to semiriches again. When her life had gone wrong, it went wrong really fast. And it went all the way wrong.

It was the kind of thing that could only happen in a prominent Southern family, a Southern *religious* family in which the men think just because their God is male and they've made some money, they must be God too. In the end, she humiliated her father in front of the whole town, but she'd had to end up in the gutter first. Her father's mistake was he thought he could outbluff her. It might have worked if she'd had a lick of sense.

But she was a girl in love, with no idea in hell somebody like her could end up as Cinderella. She thought of herself as Juliet. It was simple (and in her mind, hugely romantic): The McLeans hated the Bennetts—really *hated* them—and she was a McLean. Charles Bennett, Sr., was her father's biggest rival in business, in politics, even at the stupid country club. For her to consort with his son Charlie was tantamount to bringing home a serial killer. Her mistake was she hadn't understood the depth of the rivalry—that it was more important to her father than she was.

Her father threatened to disown her if she married him, and the arrogance of it made her even more determined, made her want to do it sooner rather than later. What did *disown* mean, anyway? If he was going to be like that, her mother, too, and all her siblings—no one in the family opposed him—if they all were going to be like that, she didn't care if she never spoke to them again. It didn't occur to her she might need them sometime.

She could hear her father now: "You made your bed; you lie in it."

That was what he said when she told him, two years into their marriage, that Charlie was cheating on her. Blithely, she filed for divorce, which was exactly what Charlie wanted, having hidden all his assets from her. So there was really no community property except their reasonably modest house, and Texas law—notoriously unfair to women—is extremely stingy with spousal suport, not even granting it in a "young" marriage. Because Karen had been married less than ten years, she got none. But there was still the money from the sale of the house, and she could always get a job.

However, she failed to get one in her field, elementary school education, and ended up teaching aerobics. She invested wisely in a tiny condo—having just enough for the down payment—and could just scrape by. She was making it on her own, even going back to school, and proud of herself—until income tax time. She'd had no idea she was going to end up owing ten thousand dollars.

"No problem; they'll make a deal," her accountant said. "Just explain your situation, and they'll set up a payment plan."

But she could never get them on the phone, and they didn't answer her letters. Then one day they sent *her* a letter, saying they were going to put a lien on her house if she didn't pay them by a certain date.

Well, she couldn't have that. She needed a new car, but with a lien on her condo, no bank would give her a loan.

Panicked, she called the accountant, who asked her if she could come up with any part of the money. "Sure," she said confidently. "I still have my engagement ring. It ought to bring about five thousand dollars."

"Sell it," he said, eyes cold and unfriendly. "I'll make the deal myself."

And he did make the deal: five thousand up front and the rest in monthly payments.

She sold the ring, paid the five thousand, and within a week, the IRS slapped the lien on her. As if there'd never been a deal at all.

She was so depressed, she started watching daytime TV, which was how she found the show that changed her life. They *loved* her story.

Who wouldn't? Who doesn't hate the IRS? Hundreds of calls came in from taxpayers who'd been similarly burned, so many that the next week the station abandoned the normal Mr. Right format (one wrong righted, another stated) and devoted a special hour-long show to what it called "The Treachery of the Tax Collectors."

The IRS took such a beating they did something no one had ever heard of them doing before: They said there'd been a "mistake" and removed Karen's lien. Car dealers all over town called *her*, offering extraordinary deals. But as it turned out, she didn't need their charity. Her father, in a grand, public gesture of conciliation, gave her a car himself. She'd "suffered enough," he said.

But, really, social pressure had shamed him into reconciling, and she knew it. Not that she cared; she'd gotten used to her family's ostracism a long time ago.

But the best part was that David Wright, Mr. Right himself, a lovely man, seemed to take a personal interest in her, even got her a job at the station. Like Superman, he seemed to have swooped down from the sky to rescue her.

One day she asked him to have coffee with her, to thank him personally. He went, and he couldn't have been nicer or more gracious. But she had known that was how it would be. He didn't try to grab her leg, didn't tell off-color jokes, didn't flirt, didn't behave in any way at all that a perfect gentleman wouldn't.

A week or so went by, and he asked *her* for coffee. It got to be a regular thing before she realized she was falling for him. She'd never really met such a concerned, loving person. She was definitely interested in him, and she knew he wasn't married, but there was a problem: He treated her like a daughter.

She had to get up all her courage to ask him to dinner, and then he refused! She was flabbergasted. "But why?" she demanded, the words falling out before she thought.

"Because," he said, "the gentleman always asks the lady."

Stung by the reprimand, she kept her head down for the next three days, thinking maybe he wasn't nearly as nice as he seemed. Maybe he was just an old rattlesnake waiting for a chance to strike. Now he had, and who needed him?

On the third day, a Thursday, she picked up her ringing phone to hear his voice. "Ms. Bennett, would you do me the honor of accompanying me to dinner Saturday night?" It was the night she'd asked *him* for.

She couldn't help but laugh. "Why didn't you just say yes in the first place? In fact, why didn't you ask me first if you're so picky about who asks who?"

"First of all, I'm quite a bit older than you. I didn't want to presume on you. But once I learned you were interested, I thought we should do it by the book."

If she hadn't already been in love with him, that would have turned the trick.

That night he regaled her with stories of his life. The son of missionaries, he'd lived all over the world.

"Aha," she said. "That explains the accent."

"Excuse me?" He seemed slightly nonplussed.

"You sound slightly English."

"Ah. Boarding schools," he said. "But that was for convenience. Actually, my family were very simple, God-fearing people."

She found that she liked that—both his claim to simplicity and his announced spirituality. She had felt all along that there was something noble and fine about him. At the end of the date, lying in bed, assessing it, what she felt was safe. She felt that David Wright would never hurt her, would take care of her, would *cherish* her . . . *Now there was a word*, she thought, *that you never heard outside a marriage ceremony. Funny she should make that connection.*

On the other hand not so funny. She already knew she wanted to marry him.

Two months ago, she had. She was Karen Wright now, suddenly a young woman about town, all her family ties reinstated, in demand for committees and charity parties, and the fledgling founder of her own charitable foundation.

She was so proud of her husband she could burst. So much in love she floated through life, hardly remembering the difficult days behind her.

Chapter SEVEN

*B*eset by a strange combination of lethargy and restlessness, Skip Langdon sat at her desk, sighing, drinking coffee, looking at pictures. They were photographs of stone angels, urns, antique wire furniture—cemetery art—currently very hot (in more ways than one) on the antiques market. Aunt Mabel's angels, Grandpa's St. Francis statue.

Some of the pictures were from Atlanta, some from Charleston, some from as far away as Los Angeles. But so far, none from New Orleans, except the ones taken in the cemeteries themselves. The pictures from other cities portrayed art currently for sale in antique shops, the ones from New Orleans were blowups of family snapshots—the statues and urns in place at Aunt Mabel's and Grandpa's plots before they disappeared. These things weighed tons, quite liter-

ally. How were they getting from here to there? That was one of
many questions she had to answer, and fast, before somebody got
lynched, meaning the mayor or the superintendent. From the fury
around this one, you'd have thought Mardi Gras itself was threatened.

The problem was, she couldn't work up the same sense of outrage
as the rest of the citizenry; in fact, she could barely keep her mind on
the job. She was a lot more interested in finding the man who'd tried
to have her killed. And that wasn't all he'd done to her. At different
times, he'd kidnapped two children she cared about, with nearly fatal
results. That is, he'd *ordered* them kidnapped. Ordering was something
he did well.

He'd ordered more than a dozen murders that she personally
knew about, and he'd done it with the high-handedness of a dictator.
When people were convinced they had God on their side, they'd do
anything. Indeed, some of his followers seemed to think he *was* God
or had a direct line thereto.

It wasn't lost on Skip that Jim Jones, the person responsible for
the most deaths in the twentieth century who wasn't a head of state,
was also a preacher—also a white one—who preyed on people of
color by embracing liberal causes, matters of human rights and equal-
ity, claiming to be their friend. She sometimes wondered what
Jacomine thought of Jones, whether the dead preacher was a hero of
his or if he was unable to recognize their similarities.

She gave it up for the moment and gave Shellmire a ring.

"Skip. Glad you called. I've got something for you."

"Oh, Lord."

"Oh, Lord is right. The news is not good. I've been watching
Bettina. She's got a cell phone and a regular phone, but she makes a
lot of calls from pay phones. A lot of different pay phones."

"Near her house?" Skip asked desperately. If Bettina was calling
Jacomine, they had to get a tap.

"All over town. Never the same one twice."

"Damn." No chance of a tap. "Where do you go from here?"

"I just have to keep working the case." She could hear the exasperation in his voice.

"Keep in touch," she said, and hoped that he would.

She went back to studying the photos, trying to think what to do. Well, why try to figure it out alone? She'd been appointed to head a task force; she might as well get one together. After some thought, she decided on a seasoned detective she'd known since her days at headquarters, Danny LeDoux, and a relative rookie, Mercia Hagerty. They were both good officers—that was a given. In addition, they offered diversity. LeDoux was black; so was more than half the city. Hagerty was white, and she cleaned up nicely; she wouldn't look out of place shopping for antiques. Skip phoned them with the news, setting a meeting for later that day. And let her thoughts go back to Jacomine.

LeDoux and Hagerty arrived for the meeting rarin' to go. They couldn't thank her enough for giving them a piece of the case.

She thought, *God, I wish I had their enthusiasm.*

What she had to do was pretend. They couldn't know her mind was elsewhere. "Okay, here's what we know so far. Last week, the L.A. *Times* broke a story about stolen cemetery art. The *Times-Picayune* picked it up, with pictures. And next thing you know, their switchboard lit up, if they even had switchboards any more. People recognized stuff from their own relatives' plots. And that started a stampede: Everybody went to check on their family plots, and just about everybody has something missing." She sighed, knowing she was exaggerating, but wanting to convey the enormity of the task, its importance as a potential public relations coup for the department.

LeDoux said, "If it's all gone, that makes it kind of tough to catch anybody red-handed."

"Danny, for Christ's sake," Hagerty said. "It's not like you go out there and see bare ground."

Skip made conciliatory air pats. "Okay, so I exaggerated. There's probably enough ornate stuff around here that you could loot graves from here to doomsday and not run out. And there are way too many cemeteries to watch. That's the part that makes it tough."

Both faces brightened. "Hey, how about . . ."

". . . a sting."

The two officers high-fived, delighted at having thought of the same thing. *Good,* Skip thought. *They work and play well with others.* She'd chosen well: Some of their enthusiasm was starting to rub off.

Hagerty said, "Why don't I go up and down Magazine Street? I could say I'm a decorator from Texas or something; maybe I've got a client who needs some six-foot statues of saints."

"Oh, get obvious about it," LeDoux said.

She frowned. "Well, something like that."

"I like it," Skip said. "But you take the French Quarter; I'll take Magazine." These were the two main antiques districts in the city. "I live in the Quarter; everybody knows me there."

"Langdon," LeDoux said. "Everybody knows you everywhere. You're too high-profile for this."

It was true. She could go undercover on some things, but not this; her picture had been in the *Times-Picayune* too many times. And now that she thought of it, Abasolo had said he was appointing her for her publicity value. That meant her name was going to be in the paper again. That was going to play hell with the sting idea.

"I've got it," LeDoux said. "Let Hagerty do Magazine *and* the French Quarter. But we'll double-dip. I'll go in offering what she's looking for. Then, if anybody bites on that, we can haul them in for questioning."

Skip sighed. "Done deal. I'll do the phones and computer stuff. What else?"

Hagerty bit her lip. "I suppose we could pick certain cemeteries and do some kind of surveillance."

She was shouted down by Skip and LeDoux. "What if we pick the wrong ones?"

"Well, how about if we just took a day and visited the main cemeteries where the looting's going on—Lafayette 1 and Lake Lawn

Metairie, for instance; St. Louis 1 and 2; maybe St. Roch—and see what it looks like there, what hours the thieves can work, if they can get in at night, what sections offer the best pickings? We might even be able to figure out where they're going to hit next. I mean, if two rows are completely looted, and the next hasn't been touched, stands to reason . . ."

"Great idea!" Skip said. "And we can talk to the groundskeepers, anybody we see, and give them our numbers in case they see anything. Want to do it tomorrow?"

"You got it."

Skip went back to her office, thinking to call every antique store in L.A., Atlanta, and Charleston. But first she called Abasolo. "You haven't told the press about this task force thing, have you?"

"I'm going to tomorrow. Why?"

"Has it occurred to you it's like saying, 'Hey, hens, the fox is on the way'?"

"Work around it, Langdon. The chief wants it."

"Let's just hope the bad guys are real dumb."

"Or can't read."

But success didn't hinge on either of those things, and she knew it. It was all about how convincing Hagerty and LeDoux could be—and how greedy the thieves were.

She worked on her Atlanta calls for the rest of the afternoon, to no avail; nobody had seen anyone offering merchandise of the sort she described, or at least no one was admitting it.

She left feeling discouraged and frustrated, not an uncommon state of mind for her lately. She was looking forward to a soothing evening with Steve. He'd invited her over for dinner, and she figured he'd make something special. She was his first official dinner guest in his new house.

But first she stopped off at hers, to metamorphose from cop to guest. As she approached, she could hear voices in the courtyard. Angel, the kids' adorable black-and-white mutt, stormed the gate, barking as if Skip were a horde of barbarians. "Hey, Ange, it's only me," she said and watched the little dog change from a furious harpy into a wriggling love worm. For the first time that day, she started to relax. "Yeah, you love me, don't you? Why can't Napoleon be like you?" She'd never understood what Steve and the shepherd saw in each other.

But they had history: Back when Kenny first came to live with his uncle, he had a period of wetting the bed. Figuring he needed a friend, Steve found the dog and brought him to Kenny without consulting Jimmy Dee, whereupon Napoleon tried to attack not only Skip but also Dee-Dee and Sheila's boyfriend, Emery. Dee-Dee took him back to the pound, and Steve adopted him once again, for himself, earning a place in Kenny's heart forever. The shepherd had since settled down a bit, but he still loved only two humans: Steve and Kenny.

As she approached the courtyard, Jimmy Dee held up a martini glass. "Cocktail for the lady?" He and Layne were having a jolly old time. Even Kenny was there, trying to teach Angel some kind of trick.

"No, thanks. I'm going over to Steve's."

"There's a law against a predrink drink?"

Skip laughed. "There probably ought to be," she said and climbed the stairs to her refurbished slave quarters.

She stepped in the shower and washed off the office dust. Redressed in shorts, T-shirt, and sandals, she felt a hundred percent better. Here, in her own world behind the walls, megalomaniac killers seemed a million miles away. Jimmy Dee produced some white wine. "Come on. Sit a minute."

"Oh, what the hell. Steve's cooking; he won't care."

Kenny lit up as she plopped into a chair. "Hey, Aunt Skip, watch this. "Up, Angel. Up."

The dog jumped up to his chest, turned around in midair, and bounced off.

"Pretty good, huh?" He slipped Angel a treat. "The next step's jumping up to my shoulder."

Layne said, "She's too little. She'll never do that."

"She can. She has to use my chest like a stepping stone. It's in this book I got."

Sheila came outside, in jeans that rode on her hips and a T-shirt that barely grazed her bottom rib. She was a big girl, like Skip, but somehow, she got away with the bare midriff—on aesthetic grounds, at any rate. Uncle Jimmy was another matter. He didn't bother to hide his frown; Sheila didn't bother to acknowledge it. "Anybody know how to fold stuff in?"

For a moment, everyone tried silently to make sense of the question. Finally, Layne said, "You mean, like egg whites?"

"Yeah. Egg whites. How'd you know?"

"Come on. I'll show you." He got up to save the soufflé, and Skip took it as a cue.

"Gotta motor—I have to stop at Matassa's for some of my fabulous homemade hors d'oeuvres. Angel, you're a good dog. I want to see the whole trick by tomorrow."

Steve's house looked fresh and inviting in its new blue paint. Skip had been able to talk him into a little fuschia trim, which had turned it downright spiffy, never mind the feasting insects that infested it.

She stepped lightly to the door, carrying a bottle of decent wine bought a week earlier and the bag of cheese and crackers that was all she'd managed to score at Matassa's. The few sips of wine she'd had in the courtyard had lightened her mood even more than the shower.

She rang the doorbell, bracing herself for Napoleon's onslaught, not even particularly dreading it. She was greeted with silence. In fact, with even more silence than a nonbarking dog. The house was spookily quiet.

Fear flamed up her spine. Carefully, she set the groceries down and felt for the gun in her shoulder bag. She edged her way down the steps and around to the side of the house.

As she neared the gate, she heard faint noises, but what they were she couldn't figure out. She stopped to listen: It was a person's voice, twisted in an odd anguished sound, as if the owner were hurt. And the owner had to be Steve.

She wondered if she should call for backup and dismissed the idea. She had a key to the house; she could go in and assess the situation. She was about to move back to the door when she suddenly realized what the sound was. Someone was crying.

It occurred to her that a person had a right to cry in his own backyard without a cop with a drawn gun traipsing through his house. He wasn't pleading with anyone and wasn't the sort to cry if he were being held prisoner.

She decided to behave like a normal person instead of a paranoid fool. "Steve? Steve, it's Skip. Are you all right?"

"Skip? Oh, God. I'm coming."

She heard him walking toward her, which was reassuring, and when he opened the gate, she saw that he was alone, which was even more so. He was a big man, with a big chest and a lot of hair on his head. (Not for nothing did Jimmy Dee refer to him as her "bear.") The sight of him coming apart was nearly as upsetting as finding him in a hostage situation. In some ways, she was frightened, but she was also sad, soaked in *his* sadness, whatever its cause. She felt as if a relative had died and thought that must be what had happened.

She was frantic, danced up and down while he fumbled with the gate. "What is it? Steve, what is it?"

He didn't speak until he had his arms around her, giving her the bear hug they both needed, nearly crushing her ribs, a not-so-easy task given that she was nearly as tall as he was and had plenty of heft to take the pressure. "Someone killed Napoleon."

"Oh, Steve!" She'd never liked the dog, but she loved Steve, and the person who subjected him to this kind of misery would have her to answer to. "He got run over?"

"Come here." He drew her down the passageway and into the courtyard, where Napoleon lay on the flagstones, a miserable pile of rumpled fur. He looked helpless in death, nothing like the formidable animal he had been, a dog that never could make up its mind just to settle down and live a peaceful life.

Now, looking at all that was left of him, she felt herself tearing up.

Steve said, "They threw something over the back fence; that's all I can figure. See, the Harrisons aren't home."

"Harrisons." Skip couldn't follow.

"My next-door neighbors. Anybody could have come in and just . . . nailed him."

"He was shot?"

"Oh, I wish. He would have been if you'd been here. I'd have gotten your gun and done it myself. He was poisoned. He died in horrible agony."

"Oh, Steve! You saw it."

"Yeah . . . Yeah . . . I heard him out here, kind of making little whimpering noises. So I came out, and he just didn't look right, you know what I mean? I can't explain it, you could just tell he felt bad. And he was salivating a lot, so I knew he'd eaten something. Then I noticed his rear end was quivering and then his shoulders. Skip, he was shaking all over, like a Chihuahua. I touched him, and he yipped, like it hurt, and he was hot, like he had a fever. And then he fell down. Can you imagine how sad that was?" He was tearing up again, and his voice was getting loud and outraged.

Skip put herself in his shoes. "And you didn't want to leave him to call the vet because you were afraid he might die without you." She wondered which decision she'd have made.

"It wasn't even like that; I knew it was too late. I just had to watch him die. I couldn't even hold him or stroke him, because it hurt him. I just hope my being there was . . . I don't know—*something* for him."

Skip wondered if she could hug Steve, or if, right now, he couldn't be touched either. She opened her arms, and Steve folded himself around her. "I'm so sorry."

He spoke against her shoulder, so that she could feel his breath. "Who would do something like that to an innocent animal?"

For once, Napoleon did look innocent. "Jacomine," she said and wished she hadn't almost immediately.

Instantly Steve turned his outrage on her. "What did you say? Did you say 'Jacomine'? Skip, this isn't about you. This is about that poor dog lying over there."

"Napoleon . . . uh . . . had enemies?" She was trying to strike a semilight note without seeming completely heartless; she was also fishing for information.

"You ought to know," he said resentfully.

She knew what he was doing: that anger and sadness were closely related, that he was using one to cover the other. It was the sort of thing she might do herself. But it felt terrible when you were the object of the anger.

As if to restore the peace, Steve said, "The neighbors hate him. I get all kinds of complaints because he barks too much."

"It takes a really crazy person to kill a dog." Skip spoke neutrally, hoping he'd think about it.

"Naaah, it just takes a heartless redneck drunk."

"Anybody around here like that?"

"Everybody."

"I'm serious. This would take planning. You'd have to figure out . . ."

"You wouldn't have to figure out shit. You'd just go out to your garage, find something that said CAUTION! in great big letters, put it in a hot dog, and lob it over the fence." He shrugged to make his point. "Simple as that."

Could be, she thought. But her heart was about to pound out of her chest. She pulled out her cell phone. "Excuse me for a moment."

"Who're you calling?"

She twitched her lip a bit, as if mouthing a name, and turned her back slightly, hoping he'd think it was so she could hear better. She was calling Shellmire of the FBI.

Consulting his caller I.D., he answered, "How's it going, big girl?"

"Watch that 'big' stuff, Turner."

"Whatcha got, kid?"

"Someone poisoned Steve's dog."

"Jacomine?" he fired back, making it a question, but Skip was gratified that his mind had leapt to the same place hers had.

"Steve says not. He says the dog had enemies."

"You know how crazy someone has to be to kill a dog?"

She almost laughed, hearing her own words come back to her. "I wish we were on a speaker phone. He thinks I'm paranoid."

"Let me talk to him."

"Turner, he's not really in any condition to talk."

"Skip, I know he's your boyfriend. But this is a big-deal federal case, in case you've forgotten. Also, somebody just shot at you, and with that dog out of the way, you'll be a much easier target."

"Yeah, I thought of that." Sighing, she held out the phone. "Shellmire wants to talk to you."

"Shellmire? You called Shellmire?"

"Just listen to what he has to say."

Actually, judging from what she could overhear, Shellmire had more questions to ask than admonitions to deliver. But he must have gotten a few of those in too. Steve was even sulkier when he got off the phone. "I don't need this shit."

Unsure what the agent had told him, Skip waited.

Steve said, "My fuckin' dog's dead." It wasn't a way he talked at all; neither the profanity nor the pure childishness of the statement sounded anything like him.

Hoping for a laugh, she said, "Such a lovely animal too."

Steve got up and stomped into the house.

Shocked, she phoned Shellmire back. "What on Earth did you tell him?"

"First, I said not to call animal control or anything, that we'd send over our own guys to get the dog an autopsy and investigate the scene. After that I did my standard bit about taking the threat seriously, blah-blah-blah and etc."

"Oh. Guess that was the part that got him."

"I've noticed your average macho guy gets a little sideways over that kind of stuff."

Skip was silent.

"See, they hate things they can't control. So they just pretend it isn't happening. If you bring it up, they shoot the messenger. That's how my wife tells it, anyhow. That what's happening?"

"Pretty much."

"Not good, Skip; that makes him vulnerable. But the good news is, sometimes they sleep on it and get over it."

The bad news, in her opinion, was that unless Steve got over it soon, he wasn't going to be sleeping on it with her. She went inside to wait for the FBI and see what she could do to save the situation.

Chapter EIGHT

r. Right was pleased as punch with the success of his television show. He was helping people. He was getting to know people, influential people, some of whom he was related to by marriage. Every week he made more of an impact. The show got more and more letters, more and more volunteers to go on camera, more media attention every day.

Truth to tell, he was a lot more than pleased. He was so excited he could bust, as he might have said in the old days, the pre–Henry Higgins days, as Rosemarie called his former life. He wasn't entirely sure what she meant, but he didn't argue with Rosemarie, for any reason, because some day he might have a reason, and he was damn sure going to pick his battle carefully.

This thing he was doing, this Mr. Right thing, was snowballing so fast he could see it going all the way. Absolutely all the way to the top. There was really no reason why it couldn't. Even his fingerprints were different now; aside from dental X-rays, there was no way in hell to connect David Wright with Errol Jacomine.

He was changing his persona too. In all his previous careers—preacher, politician, and guerrilla fighter for justice—the last thing in the world he'd cared for was material things. Now he relished a well-cut suit, a good cigar. The joy of fine cognac was something he wished he'd discovered years ago, and yet it wouldn't have been appropriate. Wouldn't have fit into his lifestyle. It fit into this one just fine. Though he was just thinking that perhaps his littered, cheaply panelled office no longer did. Maybe he could get Karen to come down and work some magic on it. He had a moment to assess it because Bettina was late with her call.

They had to make dates with each other because it was so difficult for her to get to a phone. Messages didn't work at all. If he missed her call, he might miss something crucial.

Mentally, he improved his surroundings while waiting for the ring of his cell phone—an instrument in the name of Cecil Houseman, a man who existed only on paper. By the time it finally pealed, he'd worked up a backlog of resentment.

"Can't you do anything right?" he asked by way of greeting.

"Daddy, I'm sorry. Had to be careful. Fat man follow me the other day."

"What the hell you talkin' about?" He still dropped his *g*'s when talking to his flock.

"Pretty sure of it. I seen him twice. After Devil Woman come see me." Langdon, she meant.

"He follow you today?"

"Nooooo, sir. I be sure he ain' follow me today. Tha's why I be a little late."

"Not a little late, Bettina. Six minutes late." He switched gears quickly. "Langdon dead yet?" He knew she wasn't, or Bettina would have already told him.

"Well, Lobo, he——"

"Goddammit, don't use his name. What the hell ya usin' his name for?"

"Oh, it's okay. See, that's not his real name. Lobo, he say there was obfus—obcas—"

"Obstacles. What kind of fool is he? I never want to hear that word. Ya hear me?"

"He say he can't get near the bitch 'cause her boyfriend's got this big ol' dog. So first he has to poison the dog. He say that went real good, so . . ."

"What am I hearing here? What am I hearing, Bettina? Are you saying that ham-handed amateur poisoned a dog?"

"Well, yessuh, he poison a dog. See, he had to, 'cause . . ."

"I *did not* authorize any dog poisoning!"

"Well, Daddy, we . . ."

"What did that poor dog ever do to anybody?"

"Oh, he was a real mean dog. Like to took Wolf's, I mean Lobo's, hand off."

"Bettina, you fucked up. You fucked up big time this time."

"But, Daddy, I didn't . . ."

"Ya gotta do penance, Bettina. I'm gon' make you suffer a way you never suffered before."

There was a long pause on the telephone. Finally, she said softly, "Daddy, if I got to, I got to. Ain' nothin' I wouldn't do for you." He could tell she was getting off on the idea.

"I want you to take that ugly baby of yours . . ."

"Daddy, you ain't never even seen yo' baby."

"What did you say? What'd you say, Bettina? That's *your* baby. That's the curse the good Lord sent you for your weakness. Now I want you to take that ugly baby . . ."

"His name's Jacob."

"Every night for a week, now, I want you to take little Jacob and put him over your knee and give him twenty whacks with a hairbrush."

"But Daddy, he's a *good* little baby."

He heard real distress in her voice, and that pleased him. "Well, you fucked up, and Jacob's got to suffer for it. Listen to me! Listen to me, now. I don't mean little love taps either. You whack him till he cries. And after two, three days, when he's real sore, you whack him twice as hard, hear me? And every tear that child sheds'll be the same as my tears for you, because of your mistake, and Jesus's tears for me and for all of us on this Earth. You go and do that now."

She was crying. He knew she'd do it, but it would hurt her bad. "Lobo say . . ."

"You tell Lobo to lay off right now. Tell him not to do a goddamn thing till further notice. And call me Thursday at six." He disconnected before she could answer.

For obvious reasons, he had his door closed. There was a knock on it now, as if someone had just been waiting for him to end his conversation. He didn't answer. He needed a moment to get back in character. He was pretty sure you couldn't hear more than a mumble from the other side, but he was glad he'd told Bettina to call him next at a time when he could get away. It wasn't safe to take her calls here.

The knock came again.

He cleared his throat and spoke in the cultured voice he'd so lately learned. "Come in."

The person on the other side burst in carrying a clipboard, puffed up with importance. It was his producer, Tracie Hesler, a sloppy looking girl with long curly hair clipped back carelessly. She always wore pants, and they always looked too short for her. She was too dark for his taste, too bohemian; probably the only woman in Texas who didn't give a damn what she wore.

Without being invited, she sat down. "David, I've got something really great coming up. This woman called who ended up in jail because of bank fees. Ever heard of anything like that?"

He thought about it. "Hell, I don't know. What happened?"

"She's perfect for us: an art student, very young but enterprising.

Even has her own business running errands for people. The trouble is, she still barely makes it. You with me so far?"

He leaned forward, smiling at her. "Totally. Isn't that what people your age say?"

She put her hand up for a high five, a practice he rather liked but thought should be reserved for truly celebratory moments. "You got it. So anyway, she's living on the edge. Fits the profile, right? So she has two bank accounts, and she writes checks on one, deposits them in the other before they've cleared . . ."

"Check kiting."

"Yeah, but she's got no idea it's against the law or has a name or anything. Also, she doesn't know the bank's charging her huge fees every time she bounces a check, and, because she's frantically trying to cover her ass, she never has any money in either account, and the bank has the right to put the checks through twice. So she incurs not one but two fees on each check, neither of which she knows about."

An obvious question came to mind, but Tracie held up a hand to stop it. "So she finds out when she gets her statement, right? She panics, borrows money to straighten it out, goes down to make a deal with them; they take her money, then they turn right around and throw her ass in jail."

He felt the beginnings of a smile playing about his formerly thin (now quite attractive) mouth. "This is sounding good."

"It's better than you think. This same thing happened to me in college."

"You got thrown in jail for check kiting?"

"Oh, no. I most certainly didn't. The bank manager sat me down, explained it was illegal, gave me a chance to make good, and that was that. But it gave me an idea. I started asking around. Just in the office and in—uh—a bar last night, I found six people it happened to. And not one of them ended up in jail."

He stroked the lower part of his face. "Viewer empathy."

"Hell, yeah, viewer empathy—like, half the population's been there. I've backgrounded the girl, and she's totally clean. Also dumb as a rock when it comes to math; no way she would have tried to scam the bank. I mean the only way she could do that would be to step into it, which she did. Now get this; I've also researched the bank, and their fees are twenty-five percent higher, on average, than those of other banks, plus they have more of them. They charge teller fees, for God's sake. There's a five-dollar penalty for not using the ATM!"

"I'm liking this a lot."

"Well, that's the tip of the iceberg. I've got incredible stuff on the banking industry in general. This is big, David. This could be one of our best yet."

He was still thinking. "Everybody goes to banks."

"Yeah, and everybody's intimidated by them."

"Tracie, this is terrific. I really can't thank you enough for this."

"It's my job." But he could see she was eating it up.

"No, you always go the extra mile. I admire your work so much."

"Really? Well, I do try to be thorough."

"No, you're great. Really. I'm deeply, deeply impressed."

He could see she left on a cloud, a cloud he knew exactly how to produce. Women were so insecure. All you had to do was praise them a little bit, and they fell in love with you at the very least; if you worked it right, they were your servant for life.

*I*saac had talked Terri into letting him paint her portrait, something he was desperate to do while she still had the blue hair. Or maybe he wanted to do it because it was a way to feel close to her when they were so obviously moving apart. She had bugged him once or twice about lying to her, and all he'd been able to do was shrug and say he was sorry, he didn't know why he'd done it. Which was another lie that drove another wedge between them. He knew exactly why he'd done it: because normal people have mothers that they go to see on Mother's Day; they don't have grown-up nieces whose fathers are incarcerated. He wasn't ready to open the door to conversations about his family.

And now, since her arrest, she'd been so self-absorbed he hardly knew her anymore. As he worked, he argued with himself, about to go nuts with love and frustration. Maybe it wasn't love. Maybe he'd never loved Terri. If he loved her, he had to trust her, right? And if he trusted her, why wouldn't he open up about his family? Maybe it was guilt and frustration. Maybe she wasn't right for him; maybe he needed to break up with her.

As soon as it occurred to him to break up with her, he had to excuse himself.

When he came back from the bathroom, he found that she'd lit up a cigarette. Before he could stop himself, he gasped.

"What?" she asked, drawing her robe around her. She was posing nude. He couldn't stand painting a woman with clothes on, even if he painted her only above the neck; the energy didn't flow right. In his life, he'd spent a lot of time meditating; energy was a big thing to Isaac.

She was out of the pose, back in the robe, and a blue cloud was rising above her. She stank; the room stank. Everything was different from the way it had been three minutes ago. He felt almost as if he wanted to cry.

"Isaac, what is it?" she said again. "You look like you've seen a ghost."

"I didn't expect you to be smoking," he said.

"What do you mean? I've been smoking ever since I got arrested. That and eating chocolate and fries and every kind of junk food—I bet I've gained ten pounds. Christ, I'm a mess!"

She was. The wonderful blue hair was greasy. He didn't even want to paint her today.

"Terri . . ." He didn't know how to talk about it, didn't know how to tell her who he used to be, how repellent these things were to the former White Monk: the smell of smoke, of fast-food grease in her car.

"What?" she said again, asking a different question now.

He sat down on the stool he used for painting. "I'm worried about you. It seems like . . ." Oh, hell, he might as well say it: "It seems like you're falling apart. A little bit."

"You got that one right, bro'." He hated it when she talked like that. In street cliches. She was an educated woman; she had a brain, and she used to use it to a lot better advantage. "Yeah, I'm falling apart! You would be too if you were me. She stubbed out her cigarette, and, to his chagrin, lit another. It was his house; he didn't even have the nerve to ask her not to smoke in his house. She brushed greasy blue hair out of her eyes. "Isaac, I just can't seem to catch a break. I told you what happened before I met you: I caught my boyfriend cheating on me and he kicked *me* out. Now how does something like that happen?"

Isaac had heard the story. "If I recall, it was his apartment."

"And I'd left a really good, cheap one to move in with him. So I had to scrape up the money for a new one. All I could find was that expensive dump I live in, which I *hate*! But at least it would do; it would get me through. And then my transmission got fucked up."

He winced. He really wished she wouldn't swear.

"And now this. Then I get arrested for something I didn't do."

He corrected her. "Didn't know you did."

"Isaac, goddammit." She got up and paced for a moment, then headed for the bathroom. "I'm going to take a shower."

"No!" he shouted, unaware he'd raised his voice.

She stared at him, astonished. "You don't shout. What's this about? You're not acting like yourself."

"I'm sorry. I didn't mean to yell. I need to get in the bathroom first." Before she could argue with him, he went in, closed the door, did what he had to do, and returned five minutes later.

She was smoking another cigarette, half-concerned, half-angry. "Isaac, what's going on? Are you doing drugs?"

"Drugs? Oh, you mean the bathroom. No, uh-uh. I'm not doing drugs."

"Well, why are you going to the bathroom so often? Are you sick?"

"Sick. Well, no. Not in the usual sense." He was trying to decide whether to tell her. "A little nuts, maybe. That's about it."

She surprised him by smiling. "A little nuts." She ruffled his hair. "You're so cute when you're nuts."

She got up, went in the bathroom, and closed the door. A moment later he heard the shower go on.

He took the opportunity to scurry, emptying her ashtray, wiping off all the surfaces they'd both dirtied, washing the glasses from the Diet Coke they'd shared, and then, before he could stop himself, sweeping the floor, counting the strokes.

He was almost in a trance, never even heard her come up behind him. "Don't you think it's clean enough?" she said.

Damn! She'd made him lose count. That meant he had to start over. He did so without speaking, forgetting that he could. The last time he'd done this, he'd been operating under a vow of silence.

"Isaac."

Again he ignored her, but at least this time he didn't lose count. Or did he? Had he lost count? He couldn't be sure. That meant he had to start over. He stopped long enough to speak to her. "I'll just be a moment, Terri."

When he finished, he saw that she'd washed her hair, but she'd lit up another cigarette. She was going to stink again.

Her face was twisted in surprise and fear. Sorrow too, he thought. "Isaac, what's going on?" Her eyes started to swim.

For a moment he loved her again, just as he had a few days ago, just as if nothing had happened. He sat down in his old rocking chair, feeling better about things and thinking to tell her, just wishing he didn't have to breathe cigarette smoke. In fact, he found he couldn't speak as long as she was smoking. He felt as if he were choking. He decided to write it for her, just like in the old days, when he had to write everything. "Can we talk without smoke?"

She looked at him like she was nuts and shrugged. "Sure," she said, and stubbed out her cigarette. She even emptied the ashtray, which pleased him mightily. Once again, he excused himself and went into the bathroom.

"What do you *do* in there?" She asked, her voice high-pitched and pleading.

"I wash my hands," he said.

"That's all?"

"Oh, no. Then I take a clean towel and wipe off the sink and the doorknob, and everything I've touched. Then I have to wash my hands again and then clean everything off again, and after that, if nothing's strange, like the mirror got splashed or something, I can go."

She closed her eyes and opened them. "You *what?*" she said, and the tone of her voice was unfriendly.

"I guess," he said, "you've never heard of OCD."

"Uh . . ." she seemed to be searching her memory. "No."

"Obsessive-compulsive disorder. People who have it wash their hands a lot and check thirty times to see if they've locked the door. And count. I was counting the broom strokes awhile ago."

Her face wasn't looking quite so blank. "Like that movie with Jack Nicholson?"

"*As Good As It Gets.* Yeah, like that."

"But you don't have OCD."

"I did. I used to. I got it under control with meds."

"And now it's coming back?"

"Seems to be."

"Why?"

Yes. That was the question. Why indeed? He thought it was because he was having a crisis of faith in human nature. He had started life among dangerous humans. That he knew intellectually, and, unfortunately, he could remember a great deal as well.

But he'd paid his dues. He'd gotten away from all that. He had been a monk; he had meditated hours and hours a day . . . oh, the things he'd done! He hadn't spoken for weeks at a time.

Now he'd made a new life, a completely new life as an art student with a girlfriend and a family (in the form of Lovelace). And suddenly this thing had happened to Terri. The arrest and then the falling apart. The cigarettes, the overeating, the whining, the worrying. She was suddenly a different person. He was shocked that this could happen to a person, that it could be done to a person. He wondered if he could say this to her. He decided he had to give it a try.

"Why is my OCD coming back? It's complicated, Terri. And it has a lot to do with you."

"Me?" she interrupted him, furious. "You're accusing *me*?"

"No, of course not. It's just that the stress . . ."

"The stress. You think I should plead out, don't you? To something I didn't do."

He wasn't sure whether he did or not. "This thing is so hard on you, Terri . . ."

"It's unjust. It isn't right. It's something that only happens to poor people. The question just doesn't come up if you never have to worry about covering a check."

The thought in the back of his head surged to the forefront: *Did she mean to defraud the bank? How can I be sure she didn't?*

It was a completely unworthy thought. She was really a good person. But he couldn't help thinking it. She looked at his face, and she read it there; he knew this because of what he saw on hers. The comprehension, the disappointment, the betrayal.

He needed to wash his hands again, but he couldn't move. Couldn't move and couldn't speak, either. He was frozen and might have remained so for a long time if the silence hadn't been ruptured by a ringing telephone.

Terri answered her cell phone as if nothing had happened, and in a moment she squealed with delight. "You're from the *Mr. Right* show? You're kidding! You really want me to? I can't believe it."

Nothing made her happy these days. He couldn't imagine what the call could be.

Chapter NINE

*B*ecause New Orleans is below sea level, its early citizens quickly learned that normal burials were impractical, as their dead relatives tended to float back up. Hence, they learned to build elaborate tombs above ground, miniature buildings in rows like streets, which earned the cemeteries the nickname "Cities of the Dead." At the end of a year, the bones of the latest body could be swept to the back to make room for someone else; thus once a family had its tomb, there was no need to keep buying cemetery plots.

The older tombs tend to be ornate and decorated with gorgeous statues and urns—or at least they used to be. The day the task force took its field trip, it was sad to see the outlines of those that had been removed, and there were lots.

On the whole, the field trip was a great success, like a perfect operation in which the patient dies.

It gave the three officers more than ever a sense of the enormity of territory the thieves had to work from. It was easy to see how they'd been so successful and even how they'd come up with the idea in the first place. New Orleans had acres and acres of unprotected artworks, just there for the taking. There was no way on Earth you could patrol this much property.

But if the trip was daunting, a couple of good things came out of it. It afforded a sense of where the good stuff was (in the older sections, naturally) and how a thief would likely operate in each one. In some, he could simply drive his SUV down the little streets between the rows of tombs, stop whenever he saw something he wanted, pry it up with a crowbar, and load it in full daylight. Because the cemeteries were so vast, it would be easy enough to operate unobserved.

All that could be helpful if they ever got a suspect. They could probably see a crime in progress from the end of a row without being seen, maybe even photograph or tape it. The catch was, they'd have to know about it to be there.

The sting itself wasn't exactly coming together with Germanic precision. However, Hagerty and LeDoux, out on their pavement-pounding missions, were beginning to get a feel for which shopkeepers were honest and which could be tempted with a little illicit action. One or two had actually called to report LeDoux when he came in showing pictures of "family heirlooms" he was selling. These were then questioned as to whether they'd gotten other such offers. So far none had, but they said they'd sure keep their ears open.

Whoopee-do.

Some of them went all righteous on Hagerty, in her decorator role, saying they'd be the last to traffic in that kind of stuff. But several had taken her cell phone number, saying they'd call if they got anything that looked like what she wanted. These—who had to be either bent or out of it—were a lot more interesting. If one of them did call, the task force could get the kind of break that would solve the case.

Skip trudged through the days, wishing she could match the other officers' enthusiasm. She called all the out-of-town antiques dealers on her list, including the ones who'd first been involved—the ones in Los Angeles who claimed they had no idea the merchandise had been stolen. Who they bought it from was a matter of record, but none of the names had rap sheets attached. (Nor true addresses or phone numbers.)

Then she got a brainstorm about a possible information gold mine—real decorators. If ever there was a group that loved to gossip, this was it. And this was her territory, a place she could go as high-profile as she pleased, and it could only help. Raised as an Uptown, private-school girl, she was the daughter of a social-climbing family that had never quite made it to "socially prominent." But she still had plenty of contacts from McGehee's, Valencia, Icebreakers, the Tulane chapter of Kappa Kappa Gamma, and her parents' old neighborhood, most notably her old Kappa sister, Alison Gaillard. If Alison didn't know every decorator in town (or where to find him) no one would. Skip's fingers tingled as she reached for the phone. She was going to rise to this occasion after all.

"Alison? Skip Langdon."

"Why, *Detective* Langdon. We thought you'd forgotten us here at Rumors-R-Us." Her old gossip-buddy sounded a little hurt.

"Never! You'll always be my favorite Deep Throat."

Alison chortled. "Skippy, you watch your language, now."

"It's just that I've had my hands kind of full with lowlife lowlifes. Last I heard your specialty was high-life lowlifes."

Alison's silvery laugh trilled out. Skip had forgotten how beautiful it was—probably the most attractive thing about the woman, who'd never been Skip's type back in college. Not that she wasn't a real knockout in her own way, but she was just a bit too coiffed and manicured and fabulously turned out to resemble a real person. That was how they did things Uptown, which was more or less no-man's-land to someone whose own father refused to speak to her when she became a cop.

A strange thing about Alison, though. She'd come through for Skip every time she'd been asked. She did it as selflessly as if they'd always been best friends, when in fact they'd almost been enemies, owing to a few little things like Skip's "inappropriate attire" (jeans, as a matter of fact) at rush parties.

"Skippy, you are the *craziest* thing," Alison said now. "I'm just an old stay-at-home mom anymore." She paused. "On the other hand, the invention of the cell phone makes gossipmongering easier, faster, and more efficient than ever before, and I was *always* the queen. Why, now I can gossip in the shower if I want to. And I do, Skippy. I do."

This time Skip was the one who laughed. "You aren't kidding, you're the queen. You could probably solve my case on the phone."

"You must mean that cemetery art thing. I'm just so *proud* of you, Miss Head of the Task Force."

"Matter of fact, I do mean that. You wouldn't happen to have seen any art around someone's pool, would you?"

"Oh, no." Alison's voice was shocked. "I know a lot of people who're missing some, though."

"Good. So it's a big Uptown issue. Here's what I was thinking: If I were a thief, I might offer this stuff to decorators and see if I got any takers."

Alison let out a little squeal. "Omigod. Patrick! Patrick Delacroix. I think he did get an offer like that. He told Susu Reynoir about it."

Skip let out her breath in a satisfied little hiss. "Ah. Maybe I should give Patrick a call."

Alison said, "I'm thinking here. I'm thinking. If Patrick got an offer, maybe some of the others did too. Ash Lanasa did our breakfast room. You should see it, Skippy. We have all these great metal chairs. I mean, real sculptures, like Mario Villa does. Only Mario didn't do them; a student of one of his students—"

Skip was sure it was the most fabulous breakfast room in Orleans Parish, but right now she had other things on her mind. "Could you ask Ash if he's heard anything?"

"She."

"Hmm?"

"Ash is a woman. Sure I'll ask her. Get right back to you."

This was the way they'd worked in the past: Alison called to pave the way; Uptown, it made everything smoother.

Without much hope, she called Patrick herself. He hadn't even met the person who made the offer, just received some pictures through the mail with a note saying the sender would phone. He never had.

Which might be good, Skip thought, making a stab at optimism. "Call me if he does, will you?" she said.

Her phone rang as soon as she put it down.

"Skip. It's Dee-Dee."

Jimmy Dee almost never called her at work and he sounded deadly serious. "Skip," he had called her, not "Venus" or "my dainty darling" or even "Margaret." Her heart started to pound.

"Listen, I'm in a bind, and Kenny's at a friend's house. Can you pick him up on his way home?"

"Sure," she squeaked, hoping her voice didn't give her away. Ringing off, she thought that this was no way to live: terrified to hear the voice of her best friend, sure he could only be calling to report disaster, reading danger into haste and distraction.

She thought, *I'm going to find that bastard Jacomine if I have to spend twenty-four hours a day on it.*

She started immediately, scribbling on the nearest yellow pad. She was putting together her game plan when Alison called back. "Bingo. Ash has a friend who has a friend who actually saw a cemetery angel in a shop. This was before anything came out in the media, of course. A client took Ash's friend to see it. Kenny Gilbert is the friend's name. Anyway, Kenny thought it was too Gothic for the look he was going for, so it might still be there. Ash just called him, and he remembers the store." She gave Skip Gilbert's number. "Happy hunting, Kappa girl."

Skip had to laugh; that was a nickname that hadn't even applied in college. Kappa she might be but pretty much in name only.

The store was neither on Magazine nor in the French Quarter. It was a fairly new shop in the Warehouse District, also known, because of its copious galleries, as the Arts District. Skip went herself rather than send Hagerty, and there was the statue, big as life, in a prominent place on the floor. The proprietor, a Middle Eastern man, seemed barely able to speak English. *What the hell,* she thought, and played Hagerty's role. "Hi, I'm Margaret Langdon. From Texas? I'm a decorator, and I was just thinking that angel would be perfect for this job I'm doing in Dallas. The only thing is, I really need about six of 'em. Is there any way you could get more like that one? Or even similar. They don't have to match or anything."

He shook his head vigorously. "No, ma'am. This one of a kind. French—come from château. You not find one like it anywhere."

Ostentatiously, Skip looked at the price tag. "Fifteen thousand dollars," she murmured and stepped back, as if assessing. "Not bad. Not a bad price at all. Are you sure you can't get any more? My client has a *huge* estate—obscene, really—and I want to set six guardian angels at strategic spots around the perimeter. One just isn't going to make it."

The shopkeeper looked unhappy, a man who badly wanted the money but couldn't deliver the goods. "I try. You come back tomorrow. I call dealer." He shrugged. "Maybe. You never know." Like he wanted the sale so much he'd stay up all night making angels himself.

Skip looked at her watch. "I'm sorry. I have to go back to Dallas in an hour. Can't you call him now?"

"Sure, sure, I call now." He got out his Rolodex and picked a card.

Bingo, Skip thought and chose that moment to pull out her badge.

She took him down to the station, calling in Hagerty and LeDoux. The three of them spent an unlovely couple of hours terrifying the poor man, who maintained that he'd bought the angel from a friend of his brother's known only as "Joe." Sure enough, the Rolodex card said simply "Joe." But it did provide a phone number, and that was enough to get an address. A Joseph D'Amico lived there.

Hagerty went out to tackle the brother, while Skip and LeDoux checked out Joe's house. No one was home.

They decided to wait for him, and as they waited, cramped in the car, Skip thought of the people she needed to talk to: Jacomine's sons, the currently incarcerated Daniel and the newly reinvented Isaac, whom she had once known as The White Monk; Daniel's daughter, Lovelace; his wife, Irene (formerly known as Tourmaline), who was a missionary and probably not available; people who'd been close to him in the past. *Particularly,* she thought, *Jacomine's ex-wife, Rosemarie.*

During Skip's last encounter with Jacomine, he'd actually had Rosemarie kidnapped and tried to force her to charter a plane for him. It occurred to Skip she might still be mad about that.

*D*ressing for dinner on a random Thursday night, Karen Wright was hearing things she couldn't believe, things that excited and terrified her, made her go wet between the legs. Her husband's words, the plan he was unfolding, the daring idea he was sharing with her for the first time, actually excited her sexually, made her dizzy, head all muzzy. She'd never in her life felt such a sensation as she felt now, just kind of standing in her walk-in closet, trying to pick out something to wear.

"David." She felt as if she were going to faint. "David, come here." She took his hand and held it to her crotch, so he could feel the impression he was having on her. She wanted him to understand how deeply moved she was, how completely, one hundred percent behind him she was. To her surprise, he snapped at her. "For God's sake, Karen, not now."

He hadn't gotten it. "No, I didn't want to . . . I just wanted you to . . ." She couldn't think of a way to express it. He selected a tie and left the closet. She had an inkling of what was going on here: He thought she was trying to seduce him for some ulterior purpose; he was slightly suspicious of her lately.

They were going to dinner at the home of her Uncle Guy, known to most of his fellow citizens as State Senator Guy McLean. He and David wanted to get to know each other. Just a family thing, Karen had thought, until a few minutes ago, when David unveiled his plan, a plan to change the world in a far, far bigger way than Karen would ever have dared dream. He'd told her her role, what he expected from her tonight and why, and what it could lead to. She was still dizzy from it as she stood there trying to figure out what to wear. For Uncle Guy, and especially for Aunt Carol Ann, nothing too sexy or young or hip. A white linen pantsuit should do it, with a long white scarf. And the diamond earrings David had given her for her birthday.

Hair up or down? She usually wore it down for relatives, thinking it made her look more innocent, less a target of derision. But in view of what she knew now, up. Definitely. Sophisticated. In command. That was who she was from now on.

Guy and Carol Ann lived in Turtle Creek, the fanciest section of Dallas. Before her disgrace, Karen had been there many times, but David never had. It would be her job to be his guide.

Knowing Uncle Guy, she'd told her husband to wear a suit, but knowing David, there was really no need. It was the sort of thing he'd do anyway. Her husband was very formal, very much of the old school, much like her father and uncles.

Carol Ann met them in a black silk flowing pantsuit—a lot fancier than even Karen had counted on. She was wearing her hair up as well. *Power do of the evening,* Karen thought.

"Karen, sweetie, how nice to see you." Her aunt gave her a cursory kiss. "And David. We're *so* pleased to finally get a chance to sit down and really get to know you. We've been so looking forward to it, ever since the wedding."

"I have as well, Carol Ann. I sure have. It's an honor for me." He was handsome in his well-cut suit and well-cut hair. Karen felt a burst of wifely pride.

The men poured themselves some bourbon, while the ladies indulged in a little white wine. Karen had to talk to Carol Ann the whole cocktail hour, which pretty much bored her, but it was good practice. If things turned out as David dared to hope, she'd be spending a lot of time talking to the wives of powerful men.

She asked politely after Carol Ann's children—her own cousins, Dennis, Kevin, and Beth—and Carol Ann asked about Karen's life, which so far in her marriage had consisted mostly of working with contractors and decorators, and one other thing—something close to her heart—the foundation she and David had planned out together. She had an office already and a phone number, but that was about it. She hadn't yet told more than a handful of people about it. "I'm ready to move on," she heard herself saying.

Carol Ann raised an eyebrow. "Move on? Are you thinking of going back to school?"

"Well, some day. Some day, when the kids are old enough, I'd love to go back to school."

Carol Ann sat back, as if suddenly gratified. "Ah. Kids."

Karen smiled at her. "'Course I have to hatch some first. That's what I want to move on to—that and . . ." She took a deep breath. Okay, she was going to tell Carol Ann about *her* plan, one she'd had for a long time. ". . . that and the foundation I'm starting. Right Woman, it's going to be called. The idea is to do some of the things the show does, on a broader scale, for women like me. I mean, women in the kind of trouble I was in when I met David."

"Ah." Carol Ann sounded supremely uninterested.

Karen was suddenly self-conscious. "We'd . . . uh . . . provide loans, services, maybe, uh, child care. For, uh, women. Maybe other stuff; it's still in the planning stages."

"I see."

"You seem skeptical." At the very least.

"I was just wondering, how will you fund it?"

"I'm looking into funding sources now."

Carol Ann cast her eyes down, probably hoping not to be tapped for a donation. But that wasn't at all what Karen had in mind. She wasn't going to family and friends for money; she was going to do this right: learn to write grant proposals, make formal calls on potential donors. She wasn't about to hit up an aunt and uncle at a dinner party. But all that seemed a bit too much to explain at the moment. Perhaps she'd jumped the gun by mentioning it.

She gave Carol Ann a reassuring smile. "Actually, about all I've done so far is rent and furnish a little office. I've only been working on the foundation proper for a couple of weeks."

Carol Ann's eyebrows shot up. "Oh! You're actually working on it."

Lovely family, Karen thought to herself, suddenly realizing that Carol Ann thought her too stupid to run a foundation. But she was determined not to let her aunt dampen her spirits. She shrugged. "I'm pretty serious about it."

Her aunt changed the subject abruptly. "You mentioned having children."

"Oh, yes. That's very much in our plans. The sooner the better."

Carol Ann didn't pause for a second. "Are you pregnant?" she asked avidly, as if pregnancy wasn't quite respectable.

Or so Karen thought at first. Actually, she realized later, it was probably the opposite, probably a lot safer and more interesting and comprehensible to her than any foundation.

"I wish," Karen said. "So far no luck, but I've got my fingers crossed."

Carol Ann gave her an older sister kind of smile. "Well. Dinner's ready."

Despite the formal clothes and the elegant surroundings, dinner was on the simple side, as Karen had predicted earlier when she told David what to expect. These people were old-fashioned Texans, and they didn't hold with foreign cuisines outside of a restaurant.

The first course was a potato soup, followed by perfectly prepared pork chops and fresh vegetables, with strawberry shortcake for dessert.

During dinner, the conversation was mostly about sports and David's show, with a sprinkling of current events, but afterward the talk turned to politics: whether Guy would run again and against whom. It happened so fast Karen wasn't sure who had initiated it, her husband or her uncle. But it was clear to her that this was the subject the two of them had wanted to meet to discuss, each for his own reasons.

As David had predicted, Guy wanted to move up: He wanted to run for governor. Karen gushed as if she were surprised, "Oh, Uncle Guy, that's wonderful. I know we'd . . . I know we'd love to . . ."

Her uncle wasn't even looking at her; he was staring straight at David. Karen was used to that kind of thing. In a family of powerful men, if you didn't have a penis, you hardly ever got to finish a sentence. She didn't now.

Her husband gave her a sharp look—a *shut-up* look—and cut in on her. "Why, Guy, I'm delighted to hear that. I was just telling Karen here I was hoping you were going to come up with that. Fact is, I was going to suggest it if you hadn't thought of it first."

They all laughed at the absurdity of Guy's not thinking of it first. Karen was all puffed up about her husband; he really knew how to make people like him. He kept going, as if the words were tumbling spontaneously out of his heart. "I want you to know I'm with you a thousand percent, Guy. Karen and I will do whatever it takes to help you financially, and . . . well . . . any way you can think of."

Uncle Guy made a stab at modesty—not his natural state. "Well, David, I really appreciate that. It sure means a lot to Carol Ann and me."

"There's so much I'd like to do," David said. "Really. So much."

Karen hid a giggle. *There sure is,* she thought. *Uncle Guy doesn't even have a clue.* She now understood why her husband, the world's staunchest Democrat, read everything he could get his hands on about Ronald Reagan, a man logic would tell you he had every reason to hate. In fact, Reagan was his hero. Reagan had done what David Wright wanted to do and believed he could do and intended to do: He had gained a popular following through the world of entertainment and parlayed it into the presidency.

This was the amazing fact her husband had shared with her in the closet, and in an instant she'd grasped how easy it was going to be for him. People loved him. They were drawn to him. And he had a lot more than show biz going for him: He was on the side of the people; he was already changing the world, showing what could be done with the tiniest bit of effort. He not only had a following, he had a track record, and he'd never even run for anything.

She was going to be First Lady. Oh, and that was going to be delicious! Unbeknownst to her male relatives, Karen had causes that went far beyond her modest foundation idea. They had to do not only with women but with children. And education. And the IRS. She didn't want girls to make the same mistakes she'd made; she wanted tax reform on a scale nobody'd ever even talked about. For openers. In the last two hours, she'd barely listened to Aunt Carol Ann prattle on about her children. She couldn't wait till she had some influence, a voice of her own.

David put a hand on her leg in the car going home. "You did well tonight."

She was thrilled with the praise. "It all worked out, just like you said."

"We're going all the way, baby. We're going all the way!" He was yelling like a football fan, something she'd never expected of her generally reserved husband. "We're going to do it, you know that?"

Karen was staring up at him, beaming, in a state of dreamy adoration, so rapt she didn't hear him unzip his pants till he had guided her hand to him. "Suck me, baby. Come on, suck me. Let's celebrate."

She felt confused. "But I thought you said . . ."

"You thought I said what?" He shouted, flashing furious eyes at her.

She felt like crying. This was no way to have a baby. If she did what he wanted, he wouldn't want to make love for days. "I thought we were going to start working on the baby."

"Karen, for God's sake, you act like tonight was nothing. You know what I accomplished in there? That was big, what happened in there. Don't I deserve a little recreation? Give me what I want, Goddammit." He pushed her head toward his crotch and, despite her plans for motherhood, she felt herself becoming aroused.

Chapter TEN

*T*he day after, sated with good conversation and good sex, David was in his slate-blue home study, door shut, cigar lit, looking out the window at his wife doing laps in the pool—his gorgeous, young, luscious wife with the unfashionable figure of a latter-day Marilyn Monroe.

Not the face, though. Monroe had a fuck-me face; Karen had the face of an angel, of a well-brought-up girl from a good family. It was a WASPy face, a high-school-sweetheart, Peggy Sue kind of face. And a sweetheart she most assuredly was. A beautiful, blonde, sweet-tempered, well-connected sweetheart, whom God had caused to fight with her family just so David could get them all back together again.

It might have seemed amazing luck to anyone else, but, though David would never again be able to work as a minister, there was still enough preacher in him to know how his luck had come about. God had done amazing things for him over the years, and the partnership continued.

What David had realized, watching TV back in that squalid Gulf Coast motel room, was that he really could be another Ronald Reagan. By putting his many talents to use—and he had some Reagan didn't—he could go all the way. All it took was that sudden flash of divine inspiration to show him how.

He was well on the way already. He had the show, which meant access to increasing numbers of followers. He had Karen and her politically influential family. And he had Rosemarie's money. The problem was, he didn't have enough of it.

After his makeover, she'd given him a substantial little grubstake, but most of that was gone. Gone, granted, to good causes, but undeniably gone. Causes like getting a complete new identity in place. If he was going to run for office, things would be checked out. He couldn't get by with the minimum kit: a professionally forged driver's license and passport.

Rosemarie could fabricate—for free—a complete employment record at companies owned by the Owens empire, but there were little things. His story involved lifelong friendship with Rosemarie's late husband, a tale that required manipulated photos showing the two of them together, cash gifts to people who'd swear the two men were inseparable, even an ex-wife and child who couldn't be traced to any organization with which Errol Jacomine had ever been associated.

That kind of thing. There had to be records at universities he'd never even seen, much less graduated from. There were even newspaper stories to explain how his fingerprints were altered—about a burning building from which he'd rescued a four-year-old child, resulting in severe burns on his hands. Coming out of nowhere was both labor- and cash-intensive.

Not only did the past have to be created, so did the present: His current identity as David Wright required current affluence and not just the appearance of it. He really did have to own a house in University Park and a BMW. He couldn't just rent, lease, or lie. These things would all be checked. They all had to be perfect. And it was now abundantly obvious that, without them, he'd never have attracted a woman like Karen. (Odd about Karen: Rosemarie hadn't balked at all, had seemed to find it a grand joke, in fact, his marrying into the McLean family.)

However, having found another man herself, she could hardly complain. But she hadn't exactly remarried. Knowing Rosemarie, you could bet she wouldn't compromise so much as a penny of her considerable and hard-won fortune (and David was in a position to know exactly *how* hard-won it was). But getting the million or so he needed might require a little maneuvering, and he wasn't sure how to go about it.

Because right now, he needed an army. He watched Karen towel off and disappear inside.

All of a sudden he was furious. He realized that watching her was the only thing keeping him calm, and once more he stopped to thank God for her, as he did a dozen times a day. But with his view of her gone, his thoughts turned once more to his immediate needs: 1. To eliminate the Devil-Woman and 2. To raise an army.

Dammit, why couldn't he have a goddamn army? He'd had one before, and, true, Bettina still seemed to have a few people to call on, but he couldn't have any connection with them. Ever. Even Bettina couldn't know about his transformation. No one could.

He got up and paced. The problem was this: How to recruit people to kill the Devil-Spawn? It was hard to recruit when you had a reputation as a multiple murderer. Thus, he couldn't. His ragtag army would have to consist only of those who already knew him (working far behind the scenes) and those money could buy.

He stopped in his tracks, hit between the eyes with a strange idea. Would money buy Langdon?

No. Hell, no. The thing was personal between them. If he didn't kill her first, she'd bring him down no matter what it cost her.

He wished it weren't so damn hard to get good help, what with his son and his trusted lieutenants in prison, nobody was left to run things except Bettina. Bettina was as loyal as a poodle, but she also had the brains of one.

David had to really, really think about Bettina, ask himself a hard question: Could she be trusted to head up a mercenary army?

Joan of Arc she ain't, he thought, and the vision of her in armor, riding a horse to victory was so funny he had to laugh.

Hell, she had organizational skills. She'd run two or three of the programs back in the church—a children's soup kitchen and a sort of labor pool the church had for people down on their luck, folks who needed temporary jobs. She'd even run an event for a campaign once or twice. She just didn't have a lot of imagination. She couldn't think on her feet or, for that matter, at all. She had to be given direct orders.

But here was his problem: Except for a couple of contacts in California, she was all he had. And she was certainly the only soldier he had whose loyalty couldn't be questioned. So she was it—general of the army, chief of staff, and head latrine digger. There wasn't a choice.

He took a big puff of his cigar, inhaling even though he knew you weren't supposed to. Maybe it was the sudden lightheadedness, or maybe he was just inspired. Because his mind hared off in a whole new direction.

Maybe there was another way to get Langdon. If he couldn't kill her, maybe he could disable her. Bring her down big time. There was sure as hell more than one way to skin a cat.

These days, as May got hotter and hotter, Terri's life was all about the show, all about her vindication and the new life she was about to lead as a crusader for the rights of innocent citizens beset by evil banks.

She'd even said those very words ironically to Isaac, who had laughed at her. Okay, it was a fantasy—she was having a lot of those these days—but it was something to live for, something to get her mind off her court case. She'd called up Tiffie and run *Mr. Right* by her.

"You're what?" Tiffie's voice was scathing, as if Terri'd just announced a detailed plan to kill her grandmother. "You're going to be on *television*?" Like a TV studio was an opium den.

Terri tried not to let it bother her. She bubbled on like some merry little fountain. "Yeah, it's this great show about . . . uh . . . righting wrongs. I know it sounds corny, I mean, kind of unbeliev-able, but that's what they actually do. See, they had this woman . . ."

"Terri, I really can't continue to represent you if you do that."

Terri didn't even hesitate. "Oh. Well, okay then. Thanks for everything, Tiffie." And she hung up before Tiffie could say another word. That was the way she fired her lawyer—as if she wasn't doing it at all. She didn't look back, either. She might need another lawyer, but she wasn't going to think about that for a while. She was feeling better, and she didn't want anything bumming her out.

She was still smoking, but that was by choice. She'd quit stuffing her face with junk food, and now she had to take off the five pounds she'd gained—fast, before her TV debut. Cigarettes would help with that.

She wanted to look a certain way; this was show biz, and she was going to treat it as such. Innocent was how she wanted to come across. She had it all planned out.

Justin, her hairstylist, had a hissy fit. "Honey, get a wig," he sniffed. "I don't *do* innocent."

"What if I were an actress? Think Judy Garland as Dorothy."

"*Brown*? You want to go brown?" Like she'd said give her antlers.

"No, I just want to go Kansas."

So he gave her light brown hair with blonde highlights and styled it smooth and straight in a little schoolgirl thing. She couldn't believe it when she looked in the mirror. "Omigod! I just pledged TriDelt."

"Honey, if you tell even one soul who mutilated you, I swear to God I'll slash my wrists."

"It's perfect, Justin. My lips are sealed." She fished out money for a tip.

"Well, just be sure you wear something with sleeves; the tattoo is *so* not Kansas."

She'd already figured that out. She was going to wear a light blue dress. She was going to go some place like Dillard's and walk into the Dowdy Shop, or whatever they called their soccer mom department, and get herself something a Metairie lady would wear, maybe with a little jacket, so the tattoo wouldn't be an issue. And she was going to dig out the little gold cross her parents had given her for her sixteenth birthday, and she was going to wear that around her neck. The lights would shine on it; the camera would pick it up; and it would shimmer. Her own mother wouldn't recognize her.

Even Isaac barely recognized her. But once he did, once he realized it was really Terri sitting in Terri's chair without Terri's blue hair and Terri's tattoo and one of Terri's navel-baring T-shirts, his eyes bugged out, and his voice came out in a hoot. "You look like somebody's Baptist sister!"

She nodded primly. "That's the general idea."

"Uh-oh. We can't have sex then. I couldn't defile you."

She thought he was kidding, but that night he really wasn't interested—an entirely new development in their relationship.

She used it as a jumping-off point to get to some dimly lit corners of her mind, places she'd been trying not to go. She had tapes of *Mr. Right* now, and she watched them over and over. And the more she played them, the more she thought about David Wright.

It wasn't something she wanted to admit, even to herself. But now Isaac had opened the door . . . and it really did occur to her that she was changing and he wasn't changing with her. Maybe he wasn't working out any more. Maybe the relationship had run its course.

Otherwise, why would she be finding David Wright so attractive? At first, she'd found him sleazy and cornball; so what was this about? Maybe she was shallow, a victim of reverse snobbism. Ergo, if he had on a suit, he was cornball. If his hair was sprayed, he was sleazy. The man was in show biz, she reminded herself. Of course he used hair spray. Maybe she was getting through that, getting to who he really was. After all, he had a really lovely accent; that had to count for something.

She thought about having sex with an older man. Maybe it was true what they said, about experience and all that. She wouldn't know and wasn't sure it mattered. David Wright seemed so feeling, so caring. That was what impressed her. Isaac, with his brittle humor about Baptists, turned her off right now. She wondered if she would have erotic dreams about Mr. Right.

But she dreamed only of Isaac and woke in the night to find him ready for her. She rolled on her back for a lovely, sleepy midnighter. "So much," he said, "for the Baptist angle," which made her laugh. She loved his humor, couldn't imagine why she'd felt so mean about it a few hours ago.

She awakened feeling happy and once again hopeful, but cleaning off her desk squelched that. She found records she hadn't mentioned to Isaac—traffic citations she'd been handed in jail, for two hundred dollars plus court costs. When they got you, they really got you; this had nothing to do with the bank problem but everything to do with the negligence that led to it. It made Terri feel ashamed and hopeless. Her depression came back like a blow to the head. She wanted to shake the bars of her cage like an animal and was surprised at the metaphor.

But she had an insight about it. She thought it came less from jail than from the life she had chosen for herself. It wouldn't be like this if she had money. If she didn't have her head in the clouds all the time, thinking of images, trying to translate her life into colors and shapes. Maybe there was an easier way.

Before that moment, the notion of her life as a crusader had extended only until the end of the show. But what if it really were her life? What if she changed everything? Moved to Dallas and became a researcher for *Mr. Right*? She cut class that day and spent the day online, researching bank scams. She drank iced tea and reveled in learning, dreaming of doing good in the world, saving others like herself. Her own cozy head was a good place to be.

Chapter ELEVEN

Skip and LeDoux were still waiting for "Joe" when Hagerty called on the cell phone. Her voice was excited. "I got lucky. I mean, real lucky. When I got to the brother's house—you know, the antique dealer's brother—these three guys were coming out looking like they were dressed for work. Manual labor kind of work. Got in a van registered to a Joseph D'Amico. Is that your Joe?"

"Yeah. Guess he's not home. Could he be on his way?"

"Uh-uh. I'm tailing him now. We're on I-10, headed west."

"Stay with him. We're on our way."

Skip hung up and said to LeDoux, "Hagerty thinks she's got something. Want to take a ride?"

LeDoux shrugged elaborately, barely able to contain his pent-up energy. *Ride, hell*, his body language said. *Fly'd be more like it.* He was oozing so much testosterone Skip could hardly stand to be in the car with him.

She stomped on the accelerator and wove her way to I-10, hoping to hear from Hagerty again soon, trying to keep her own pulse rate down.

If these were their guys, they might be onto something big. Maybe they were going to Lake Lawn Metairie Cemetery. And if so, they'd be there soon. It was just on the outskirts of the parish.

Impatient, LeDoux radioed Hagerty. "Where are they?"

"They're there, kids." Her voice was triumphant. "They're rolling into Lake Lawn Metairie right now. I can't follow any more or they'll make me. I'm going to wait for you at the entrance."

"Damn!" LeDoux said. "Damn!" He was like a dog straining at a leash. *It must have killed him,* Skip thought, *not to be driving.* But a little smile flickered on his lips and what he said surprised her. "I got an idea. Let's stop and get some flowers."

She got it instantly. "Got a better one. Let's, you know, borrow some from that huge mausoleum."

He chortled, "All right!" Truth to tell, the man was enjoying his work so much it was contagious. Skip reached for the radio. "Hagerty, you there?"

"I'm here."

"What are you wearing?"

"Hey, I'm way ahead of you. Perfectly acceptable grave-visiting threads."

"Okay, proceed to the All Saints Mausoleum—remember that huge one?—and liberate a lovely bouquet."

"Woo. Good thinking."

Hagerty sounded as excited as LeDoux.

The mausoleum was in the northeast quadrant of the cemetery, quite a distance from the older section, with its desirable artworks, but, for that reason, it would make an excellent meeting place. Inside, they knew from their previous explorations, were hundreds and hundreds of vases and urns full of silk flowers. (Signs strictly forbidding plastic ones were posted prominently.)

Hagerty could take one blossom from each of ten or fifteen vases and nobody's relative would miss his funeral tribute. Maybe the dead would even approve the small theft in the service of catching grave robbers.

Skip and LeDoux found her holding her bouquet like a bride, practicing looking mournful. "I take it," she said, "I'm the point person?"

"It has to be you," Skip said. "LeDoux'll stand out, and if these guys don't know my face, they haven't been watching the tube." She looked at her notes from the day of the field trip. "Okay, the old part's the south side, east to west the entire width of the cemetery. Hey, here's something: The best stuff's on Avenue A through O."

"That's where they'll be," LeDoux said.

"Okay," Skip said. "Got a camera?"

"No."

"I do." She opened her trunk and took it out. "Fully loaded. You might not be able to get close enough, but here it is. Ready?"

"Ready. I'm just going to walk up the east side till I see them. If I hear them first, I'll know they're working close to that side and retrace my steps and cross over to the west to make sure they don't hear me. I should have an unobstructed view from either side, and there's plenty of stuff to hide behind."

"Including your bouquet."

Hagerty grinned. "Here I go to find Great Aunt Ethel."

Skip and LeDoux waited, discussing strategy. It was nearly ten minutes before Hagerty reached them on the radio. "We have a madonna theft in progress: Three grown men are huffing and puffing to get a four-foot lady off the ground. Would you care to bust 'em?"

"Maybe not yet. Can you get pictures?"

"I think so."

"Okay, get what you can. Danny and I aren't inclined to let them rip up the whole cemetery, but they've already pried the madonna loose—is that what you're saying?"

"They're not there yet, but they've done some damage."

"Our thought is to let them load her up and see what happens. If they try to steal something else, we bust 'em then. If they don't, we follow 'em."

"Ten-four. I'll see if I can get some pictures."

"What row are you on?"

"Avenue K."

"You're on the east, right?"

"Right."

"Okay. We're coming up on the west, one at a time, just so we'll have all three of us as witnesses. If they spot us and spook, we bust 'em. Got it?"

"Got it."

"Let us know if they start moving."

LeDoux did the walking tour first, leaving Skip with the car, in case she needed to move fast.

The plan was a risk. They could have called for backup and made a noisy, high-profile bust that would have guaranteed a burst of publicity on the evening news, but it might have backfired; if these were copycats or small-timers, only one family would get its funeral art back.

The whole object of the exercise was to return the objects that had everyone gnashing their teeth and grabbing crying time in the press. The Great Madonna-and-Cherub Graveyard was what they were looking for.

Skip hopped in her car and got ready. In about five minutes, she saw LeDoux running back. Hagerty called her on the radio: "Skip. They've got the statue in the car. They're rolling. Stand by."

She opened the door for LeDoux.

"Looks to me like they're leaving," Hagerty said.

"Ten-four. LeDoux's back. Take your time getting back to your car. We'll follow and radio our location."

Sure enough, in a moment the truck eased into view, the occupants obviously happy with their haul for the day. Skip gave them a slight head start, but not too much, and then followed. She let out a sigh of relief when the vehicle turned toward New Orleans. That meant no Jefferson Parish deputies had to be involved. It was still their case.

The truck more or less ambled back into town and out St. Claude, plunging deeper and deeper into the Ninth Ward. Here, depending on where they ended up, a strange car might be noticeable and two twice as suspicious.

"Hagerty, how's it going?"

"Fine. Where are you?"

Skip told her.

"Shit. Hope they don't go to St. Bernard Parish."

"Amen," LeDoux said.

Their wishes were granted. The truck came to rest in a quiet, residential Ninth Ward neighborhood and drove into a free-standing garage that looked as if it might be used for some kind of workshop. The two police vehicles could only drive by, and that only once; to do it twice, rubberneck a little, wouldn't be good. Skip wondered if the men were armed and decided not to chance it.

The officers met at an intersection a few blocks away, a busy well-lit one where cops, plainclothes or otherwise, wouldn't be out of place, and had a powwow.

"I'm calling for backup. LeDoux, I'm partnering up with Hagerty; you go and make sure they stay where they are." All three knew LeDoux was the necessary choice; it was a mostly black neighborhood. "Let's synchronize our watches. I want to make the bust in half an hour, assuming they don't move."

She got in the car with Hagerty and called Abasolo to fill him in and get his higher-level assistance: "I want three district cars here. No sirens." She gave her location. "We'll do a five-minute run-through and then make the bust. Sound good?"

Abasolo couldn't keep the jubilance out of his voice. "Sounds great."

The district cars straggled in, and it was half an hour before everyone was assembled. Quickly, they made a plan. Skip radioed LeDoux. "What's happening?"

"They're in there."

They started toward the garage in a caravan. LeDoux came back on the air. "There's a television van here. Who called them?"

"Oh, shit. They probably just monitored the radio." Unless Abasolo had tipped them. "Can you get them out of there?"

"I've already tried. They're throwing First Amendment stuff at me."

"All right. Hell. Tell them we're sealing the area. You take the far end of the block; one of the district cars will take this one. Just make sure we don't have to argue when we get there; read them their rights if they won't move."

When they got there, the van was well outside the area to be sealed, the crew already unloading their gear. Making a solemn vow to murder Abasolo if he'd tipped them, Skip thought about praying, settled instead for crossing her fingers. If things went bad, they went bad in front of the whole city.

Quickly (and very quietly), with no lights, the cars took their places, all officers out. The garage door was steel, the sort that required a remote to open. No way in hell to kick it in. But there were paths to the back on either side. Two officers started up each one, Skip and one of the uniforms—Chuck Cramer—on the left, where they found a high, wooden gate. Skip's scalp crawled. This hadn't been a good idea. Who knew what was behind there?

The silence was nearly intolerable until she heard someone laughing. Evidently, the laugher was inside the garage. She and Cramer returned to the front, as did the two other officers. They also reported a gate.

They modified the plan slightly and put it into action. Skip approached the front and listened for a moment. Again, she heard laughing, loud talking. She banged on the door. "Excuse me. Excuse me, is anybody here?"

Inside, everything went quiet.

"Listen, I've got an emergency. Mrs. D'Amico's been in a wreck. She's gonna be okay, but she's unconscious, and I really need . . ." She was going to say ". . . someone to give blood," but the garage door began to go up. Quickly, she and two uniforms rolled under it, while LeDoux shouted: "You are under arrest. Put your hands on your heads. You are under arrest."

Skip came out of the roll kneeling, her hand on her gun. What she saw almost made her laugh: three horror-stricken thieves, slowly, very slowly raising their hands. One was in the splashy process of wetting his pants. "That's it. Come on; take it easy now. Just cooperate, and nobody'll get hurt."

She heard Cramer behind her, making a similar croon. She got to her feet. The garage door was completely open now, and the other officers had poured in. Quickly, they patted down the three men and handcuffed them, while Skip assessed the situation.

Evidently, the men were simply sitting around having a couple of beers and a cigarette. The statue from the cemetery was still here, still wrapped in quilts, and there were quite a few others as well. But not as many as Skip had hoped.

She opened a door at the back of the structure, felt for a light, and stepped into the backyard. The sight she beheld was more beautiful than moonlight on the ocean—the biggest trove of stolen angels ever assembled, she was willing to bet. Angels and madonnas and saints, iron crosses and gates, even a deer. She recognized quite a few pieces from pictures people had brought in, photos of their angels in happier times.

"Hey, LeDoux," she said. "Hagerty. Check this out."

Hagerty said, "Holy shit!"

LeDoux settled for "Jesus God Almighty."

Skip called Abasolo again, and this time her own voice tingled with jubilation. "Mission accomplished. We've got enough angels here for our own little heaven on Earth. It's going to take days to move all this stuff."

"Yes! All *right*, Langdon! Like they say in the movies, 'You de man.'"

"Gee, thanks." She braced herself for a night of crime scene photographers. After that, she planned to seal the scene and post guards. Morning would be early enough to find a place to put the art and start the transfer process.

It was nearly one A.M. when she used her key to Steve's house and climbed into bed with him. He woke up, startled, but not so startled he couldn't pull her tight against him. It was the first time they'd been together since Napoleon's death. "I wasn't expecting you."

"Well, you got me."

He looked at the time. "You have an earlier date or something?"

"Bust," she said. "Got the Angel Gang."

He sat up. "The cemetery thieves? You got 'em?"

She smiled with her lips closed, trying for modesty. "It's the kind of thing makes me horny."

"You got 'em?" Steve took childish pleasure in her small triumphs. "Way to go! We've got to celebrate." He had huge brown eyes that looked as innocent as Kenny's sometimes. She hugged him and snuggled down for something a little more serious, thinking maybe their rift was over.

"I love you, Skip. I'm sorry I was so . . . um . . ."

"Mean?"

"I was going to say judgmental. I was just upset."

"I know."

"I really am sorry about Napoleon."

"No, you aren't."

"Oh, sure I am. Kiss me, okay?"

"Okay."

She was grateful to have a self-employed boyfriend. He could afford to be frolicsome, since he could sleep all morning if he wanted to, which was more than she could say for herself. For her, there was still a world of details and logistics to attend to, not to mention the hordes of reporters Abasolo was going to make her talk to.

*M*r. Right was furious. He'd come all the way to Texas to get away from the woman, and here she was on page one of the Dallas paper. It seemed she'd caught a gang of crooks.

Well, big deal. Wasn't that her job? The way the paper described it, it didn't even sound very difficult, what she'd done. It was just a crowd-pleaser, one big, fat, giant crowd-pleaser, just like her. She was ugly as sin, mean as the devil, and dumb as dirt, but she was made of nonstick Teflon, and she always landed on her feet. He didn't understand how it had come about that she was being lionized yet again. If ever anyone didn't deserve it, it was this bitch. If he didn't believe in the devil—and he did—this would be enough to convince him. The woman was on the wrong side. She was a woman who stood between him and what God wanted from him—a truly evil woman. And yet no one could see that. Everywhere she turned, she met with success.

This deeply, deeply rankled David Wright. In his heart, he felt that every bit of the acclaim that came to Skip Langdon should have come to him. She had beaten him repeatedly, and he hated her for it, felt shame for it, and knew that only Satan himself—or his nearest representative—could have caused such a feeling.

"Karen! Get me some water, will you?" He was still in bed, but he was having trouble breathing. This was probably giving him a heart attack.

He got no answer from his wife. What the hell was wrong?

He yelled again.

And then he was aware not of sound but the absence of sound, as she turned off the shower. She stepped into their bedroom, hair dripping, wrapping a soft white robe around her. "Did you call me?"

"Sorry. I didn't know you were in the shower."

"Are you all right? What's wrong with you?" Her voice was urgent.

Fear flashed through his body. "Nothing, why? What's the matter?"

"You're red. Your face is all flushed, like you've been running or something."

He wondered if he was having a stroke. Not wanting to show weakness, he said nothing.

"David? You sure you're all right?" He hated it when she looked at him like that, like he might be old, weaker than she was. "Here, let me get you some water."

She brought it and sat down beside him and stroked his hair while he drank it. "That's better," she said.

"What is?"

"Your color's back to normal."

Okay, so he didn't stroke out that time. He got up and got dressed, trying to think of a way to bring down the Devil-Woman. He read the article again. It was accompanied by a picture of a warehouse into which the police were moving an entire yardful of stolen cemetery art. In a week or so, they were going to open it up like some great department store where you could shop for your own stuff—or for your late Aunt Bessie's. Langdon was overseeing the whole damn operation, which was bound to be as popular as a tax cut.

He took the paper into his home office, cut out the article, and put it up on his bulletin board, the picture of Langdon thumbtacked right through the nose.

A plan was shaping in his head, the notion that maybe this thing was an opportunity. But he needed money to bring it off. He dialed Rosemarie, but he didn't get her. Damn caller I.D.! She was probably ducking him, but she couldn't do it forever. Not when she owed him the way she did.

Karen came back in, dressed in a pair of shorts and smiling, her hair still wet. "Breakfast?"

"Well, now. Aren't you as pretty as a picture."

She took a step toward him, and he braced for a lapful of pulchritude, but instead she peered over his head at the board behind him, staring right at Langdon's picture. "Who is that woman?"

"What woman?" He swiveled his chair.

"That one. With the tack in her nose."

"Hell, honey, I don't know. What the hell you talkin' about?" He was aware he wasn't supposed to speak like that—to drop his *g*'s, to say "hail" for "hell"; today he did it anyway.

"She's attractive."

David didn't even bother turning around. "She's ugly as a mud fence."

"You're not even looking at her."

"Honey, I saw the newspaper article. I know what she looks like."

"Why did you put it up on the board?"

He was about at the end of his patience. "Karen, for God's sake! I got bigger fish to fry than some woman's petty jealousies."

She made a little sound like a whimper and stared for a moment, pupils dilating. Then, apparently getting it, she whirled and fled, sandals flapping lightly on the slate floor.

For a moment he felt badly at having snapped at her, wondered briefly if he shouldn't have been a bit more politic under the circumstances. "Bullshit," he decided. "She's just gonna have to learn."

He decided to forget about breakfast. He went to a pay phone, dialed Bettina's cell number, and let it ring once. Then he phoned back and let it ring twice—their emergency signal. Not very imaginative, but it worked. Hell, any more complicated and Bettina probably couldn't handle it. As it was, half the time she picked up.

He went on to the office and awaited her call, which ought to be coming in approximately forty minutes from the time of the signal. An hour at the most. He was lenient about this because he didn't want her panicking and getting careless.

This time the call came in twenty-eight minutes exactly. "Hey, baby," he drawled. "Been missin' ya. How's little Jacob?"

"Our baby fine, Daddy. He a beautiful little man."

Again, she had said "our baby," something he'd forbidden her to do, but he decided to let it go this time. He had much, much bigger fish to fry. She seemed to sense it. "What you need, Daddy? What you need from little Bettina?"

"Bettina, I'm over these dog-killing incompetents of yours. I've been doing a lot of thinking lately, and I need to deal with our man directly."

"You mean Lo—"

"For Christ sake, Bettina. No names. How many fucking times do I have to tell you? Give me his number."

"All he got's a pager, Daddy. You know you never mess with that kind of shit. It's disrespectful to ya."

"You don't have the number, do you, Bettina?"

"Daddy, I—" her voice was panicky. "Daddy, I didn't know you wanted it, or I woulda . . ."

"Bettina. Listen, honey, it's all right. Your Daddy's proud of you. Everything's just fine. You just get me the number by noon." He rang off.

That would give him time to get a new cell phone under a name he'd never used before. He'd have to use a different one every time with Lobo.

When Bettina called with the man's number, he dialled it immediately, not wanting to keep Lobo waiting. If Lobo had caller I.D., the name he'd used to get the cell phone would ring a real bell with him; it was somebody he'd executed.

Lobo answered the page in about fifteen minutes, keeping him waiting, David thought, to show disrespect, gain a little power. Well, hell. Money was power. He threw some at Lobo immediately.

"Lobo, my bro'. You know who this is?"

"I got an idea."

"Ya want another chance at that ten grand? Same money you would have made for the job you fucked up?"

"It ain't over yet. I'm gon' get the bitch."

"Yeah, sure. Meanwhile you got five thousand dollars of my money, and I got nothin' but promises."

"Look, just forget about it, okay? I'll send you ya money back. I never did want to hit no cop; it was a favor to Bettina, tha's all."

"Hold on, Lobo. We worked together before, and it turned out fine, right?"

"Yeah, I guess.

"This isn't a hit. It's a little more complicated than that."

"Well, what is it, then?"

"Let's just call it Plan B."

Chapter TWELVE

*O*vernight Skip had the highest profile in town. Once again, she was everybody's favorite Good Girl, an extremely ironic development, in her opinion, for a chronic Bad Girl. She would have gone out to smoke some weed with Jimmy Dee, just for balance, if they hadn't both given it up when his sister died and the kids came to live with him.

Sheila huffed around, mightily unimpressed, but Kenny asked Skip to come speak to his class about police work. It was the kind of thing that made her grit her teeth. But it had to be done, and not just because the chief and Abasolo wanted it but because Kenny had taken Napoleon's death hard. He loved the monster. What a sweet-tempered boy like Kenny—or like Steve, for that matter—saw in that vicious animal. . . .

Unable to solve the problem of who had poisoned the beast, she did penance by going to Kenny's school when she should have been working.

The FBI hadn't solved the case, either. All they really had was evidence that somebody had lobbed some poison over the fence. Steve's neighbors were out of town, making it an easy operation. Their flower beds were disturbed, and the kind of poison wasn't even slightly in doubt. The autopsy showed metaldehyde, a common ingredient in snail and slug bait, handily bought at a garden center and often found on garage shelves. The perp could as easily be a dog-hating crazy as a Skip-hating fanatic.

Skip found it was altogether better for her love life just not to bring it up. She and Steve seemed to have gotten over the rough spot, he attributing his bad temper to grief, she admitting to a streak of paranoia. After that, what with the termites and increasing May mugginess, she found it best to pretend it never happened. Steve had announced a sudden trip, and that ought to help too, she thought.

She still intended to work the Jacomine case but not till after the spotlight from the angel caper dimmed. The FBI was keeping good tabs on Bettina, who was all they had at the moment. What Skip really wanted to do was get to Dallas and check out Rosemarie, Jacomine's child bride. There was something intriguing there; she could feel it. And there was sure as hell no way to do that with the little decorating project her superiors had so kindly given her. She had an angel warehouse to set up. For that, she needed an assistant, and she happened to know an expert who worked free. She nipped across the courtyard to her landlord's house and slipped into the kitchen, where she found only a pot of fabulous-smelling beans and Sheila, making a salad.

For once, the kid was in a half-decent mood. "Hey, Auntie."

"Hiya, Martha Stewart."

"Puh-lease. This is cassoulet." She favored Skip with a rare smile. "You can call me Julia, though."

"Oh. Roberts or Child?"

Sheila just sniffed. "The uncles are teaching me to cook. Want to know something? I think I've got a talent for it."

"I think you might," Skip said, though she really had no idea. She was just glad to see Sheila interested in something that didn't involve shopping or makeup. Not that the kid was shallow; she was a kid. This could be a sign of impending adulthood. "Uncle Jimmy around?"

"Upstairs. You better holler."

"Dee-Dee!" Skip trilled. "Dee-Dee *darling!*"

"My ears!" Sheila winced.

"Margaret?" Jimmy Dee's voice was unmistakably welcoming. He was the only person in the world allowed to call her by her given name. "Is that you, my dainty darling?"

"Ewwwwww," said Sheila, but Skip could see her mouth twitching. For a few years after the kids came, Uncle Jimmy had tried to squelch his exuberantly campy side. ("Mustn't upset the Martians, you know"—Mars being his nickname for Minnesota, where they came from.) Lately, they'd all relaxed—Uncle Jimmy, Skip, Steve, and Uncle Layne. Nowadays the kids called every hooker and queen in the neighborhood by name. Minnesota was a distant memory.

Dee-Dee clattered down the stairs and into the kitchen. "Lovely as always, I see. Adore the torn T-shirt."

"Dee-Dee, have I got a job for you. Want to organize the most exclusive antiques boutique in town?"

"Omigod, deco fun! You mean the Madonna Barn?"

Skip smiled smugly. "It's yours if you want it."

"How much does it pay?"

Sheila stopped stripping ribs from Romaine lettuce and gave him a grin. "Oh, cut it out. It's a maiden uncle's wet dream."

"True, pearl of a girl. True. A Krispy Kreme of a scene, simply made for a queen."

The pearl of a girl snorted. "Sorry I butted in."

"I shall hang the walls with gold lamé, drape all the statues with old piano shawls and festoon them with Mardi Gras beads. For background music, Bach, I think."

Jimmy Dee was a lawyer who passed for straight in most circles. Skip thanked Bacchus his clients couldn't hear him now. "You got the idea," she said. "But you might have to downscale it." In her heart, though, she thought the beads might be a pretty good touch.

"When do we start?"

"It's going to take them a week or two to haul the statues to this old warehouse we're using. I thought maybe you could come in at night and arrange them artfully."

"Arrange them? Me and what army? Some of those things weigh half a ton."

"Don't worry, we've got the army—police volunteers. Great, hulking, gorgeous ones."

That got Sheila's attention. "Count me in," she said without looking up.

Skip had no idea whether the girl was serious or not, but she sure was growing up.

"How about the bear?" Jimmy Dee said.

"We'll have to do without him; he's going to L.A. for a few days to raise some money. He wants to do a documentary on the whole cemetery art phenomenon."

"Brilliant idea."

Maybe, Skip thought. *And maybe Steve just wanted to get away for a while.*

Meanwhile, she had a job to do, and it was getting good. The three grave robbers, Joe D'Amico, Lance Fortenberry, and Jerome Bowen, hadn't made bond. At first, the task force had concentrated on the brother and the dealer, Adnan and Bilal Rashid, preferring to let the others cool their heels in Parish Prison. Neither proved particularly proficient in English, and, even with a translator, they didn't have a whole lot to say.

The brother, Bilal, also a dealer, said he'd met the gang about a month ago and bought one statue and two urns from them. They'd come to his house for payment the day Hagerty picked them up there. Bilal claimed he had no idea the merchandise was stolen; the gang said it came from a relative's plantation. Since all that turned up was indeed the statue and a receipt for the urns (which had since been recovered), the officers sensed they weren't going to get any more. They turned their attention to the gang.

Skip and Hagerty took D'Amico, who by now had had two days to think things over. Hagerty did the questioning. She had a persuasive way about her. D'Amico, a big, shy guy with a thick head of hair and moustache to match seemed to take a shine to her. *What the hell,* Skip thought. *Whatever worked.*

"Joe, you got a couple of priors here. Ever think about yourself? You like women, don't you? Not many of those in Angola."

He shifted toward her. "Look, I got a family."

"You probably like to see them once in awhile too. Want to see your kids grow up, or you want to spend the next ten years pumping iron so you don't end up some thug's bitch?"

"I ain't gon' be nobody's *bitch*."

Skip said, "They grab you and hold you down, Joe. Three of them at a time jump you."

"You shut up!"

She stood. At six feet in her uniform (worn specially for the occasion), she looked like nobody to mess with. "*You* shut up, punk! We got pictures of you robbing people's graves. You know how unpopular that is? There aren't twelve people in this town *wouldn't* convict you. We got a whole yardful of people's precious little angels and urns where they plant mums and pansies for dear departed papa from the old country. You gonna plead innocent? Innocent of what? Leaving the bones?"

Hagerty said, "Was this thing your idea, Joe? Or did somebody put you up to it? If anybody did, all you have to do is tell us who it was, and the D.A.'ll be nice to you. See, he knows he can't solve this case without you, and he really needs to solve this case. You could get off with a couple of years, max; be home in time for little Stacy's sweet sixteen party."

Joe rubbed his eyebrows. "I had me a job in construction, real good job, but man, I'm getting too old for that shit. My joints are giving out, you know? And Maureen needs clothes, and the kids got to have school uniforms . . ."

Hagerty practically had tears in her eyes. "Mmmph, mmph."

"You're disgusting," Skip said. "Are you trying to say . . ."

"Look, here's what I'm trying to say. Just let me spit it out, okay? This guy had termite damage—had to take out some walls in his shop . . ."

"What shop?"

"Little antique shop in the Quarter."

"The French Quarter?"

The man nodded. "Chartres Street. Guy had this real pretty marble saint in his window. I said I liked it, and he said, 'Wish I had a hundred just like her. I could sell two, three every day.' After a while, he said, 'You wouldn't know where to get more, would you'? I went, 'Me? How the hell would I know? I ain't no antique dealer.' And he said, 'Well, I just thought, you bein' Italian and all, maybe you had some in the family. People put 'em in cemeteries and stuff.' And I got to thinkin' that, yep, they sure did. So I told him maybe I could get him one. And I just went out to Lake Lawn in broad daylight and got him one. Easiest thing I ever did. I picked this old, deserted-looking tomb, you know, nobody was gonna miss it."

Right, Skip thought. *That's just how it happened, all right. Forget the lady in the window; you're the saint in this story.* She might have said it aloud, except that Joe was on a roll.

"I brought it in, and he just about went crazy. Said could I get him some urns too, and maybe some crosses. Said people love those things. He couldn't get enough of 'em."

"Did you tell him where the statue came from?"

"Hell, no, I didn't tell him. I didn't know him yet. He'd have to be crazy not to know, though. Right?"

"You tell me."

Hagerty offered him a cigarette. He pounced on it like it was a hamburger. "Once, when I brought him this real nice statue, a little girl holding a bouquet, he said he'd seen one like it once. Axed me, wasn't there a pair of 'em. And there was. I said, sure, I could get him the other one. After that, he'd describe stuff: tell me exactly what he wanted and where to get it."

"Where to get it?" Hagerty repeated mildly.

"Oh, yeah. He told me where to get it. That was when I brought in Lance and Jerome. We'd go get what he wanted, and while we was at it, we'd pick up other stuff too. Figured he wasn't the only game in town. Pretty soon we had a list of regulars."

"The Rashid brothers."

"Naah, they only bought from us once."

"Come on. We tailed you from Bilal's house."

"Would you listen to me? They're nothin', small-time nothin'." Like it was disgusting. "We was just there to kind of talk them into payin' up, you know?"

Hagerty sighed. "It's a cash-and-carry business, Joe. You telling us you just gave them the stuff?"

"That idiot Jerome took half on delivery; felt sorry for 'em. Ain't important. Would you *listen*? We had three regulars givin' us art lessons: tellin' us to go for the marble, not the concrete; how to tell the good stuff, like if the fingers was separate, ya know?"

"You tell us."

"If the hand's just carved out of one block, that's one thing, see? But if they got each finger separate, like you can see through, then that's real fine work. Desirable to collectors."

He had Skip's interest. "Go on."

"Well, we worked for 'em reg'lar. Got 'em anything they axed for. They propably sold it out of town, a lot of it, but I know they got stuff right now. I *know*. Hadn't had time to move it." His face took on a sly look. "I can tell you where it is."

"Okay, Joe. You tell us. Names and addresses."

"Listen, y'all, I got a family. You gon' make me a deal?"

"That's up to the D.A., but if I had to guess, I'd give it about ninety-nine percent. You cooperate with us; we cooperate with you."

"Promise me."

"Who was that first guy—the one on Chartres Steet?"

"Neil. Neil Gibson, like Mel. Real easy name to remember. He bought fifty thousand dollars' worth of stuff from us."

Skip felt slightly sick.

Joe said, "I gave you something; now you give me something. I want to make a deal."

"Give us the other names, and we're through here. We can take a break."

"Can I have another cigarette?"

"Two names, Joe, and then we're through."

The man hunched over, thinking, and came up with a face full of fury. "Fuck you cunts! Just fuck you! I try to cooperate, and you just take advantage."

Hagerty burst in, her voice soothing. "Now take it easy, Joe. You just take it easy."

"Fuck you! I want a lawyer."

Sometimes it went like that. Out of the blue, they got scared and balked. Skip and Hagerty tried to cajole him, but in the end they had to give up and let him call his lawyer. But they'd gotten a lot—more than they had a right to count on. Hagerty was excited. "Skip, this is gonna be big. A *whole* lot bigger than we thought."

"I gotta go talk to A.A."

"What's wrong? Hey, we did great in there."

She went to find Abasolo. "Okay, here's what we got. Three Mr. Bigs, and we know the name of one of them."

"What about the other two?"

"He clammed up. Asked for a lawyer."

"Shit. Let's see how LeDoux's doing with Jerome."

"A.A., wait a minute. I know the guy."

"What, you know Mr. Big? Who is he?"

"Antique dealer named Neil Gibson. He's a friend of Jimmy Dee and Layne's; I've had dinner with him."

"Christ!"

"I've been to his Mardi Gras party. I can't work this case."

"That's all? Dinner and a party? That's the whole thing? That's no conflict."

"A.A., I just can't do it. I couldn't look Jimmy Dee in the eye."

"Langdon, look at me. This is your old buddy, AA. They love you out in TV-land. Christ, the *mayor* loves you. You can do it, and you're gonna do it. You're gonna get a search warrant, and if you find anything, you're gonna slap the cuffs on him and bring him in. This city needs that, you understand? We need a victory. We need a bigger budget for more recruits. We gotta get better equipment. How do you think we're going to get it? Here's how: You're going to be our little Cemetery Angel."

"You don't get it: People love Neil Gibson too. It's going to be divisive."

"Who loves him? Rich, white, Quarter rats? Everybody else is gonna hate him."

"Oh, hell. It doesn't matter." It didn't if he was guilty; he was just like anybody else, no matter whose friend he was. "All right, A.A. Whatever you say."

She got the warrant, served it, found stolen art, and marched her pal Neil down Chartres Street in handcuffs. It was one of the worst moments of her career.

She got the two others too—William Marks and Michael Layburn, also prominent antique dealers. Layburn was the biggest catch of all: A well-known preservationist, he was particularly active in Save Our Cemeteries.

Whether A.A. gave them the nickname or they made it up, the media did dub her the Cemetery Angel.

She could have died.

Almost the worst part was losing her decorator. Jimmy Dee just didn't have the stomach for it anymore; she had to make do with the burly straight guys. One of them picked up Dee-Dee's idea for Mardi Gras beads and music, though he chose marching tunes instead of Bach. Despite Skip's own conflicts, the Madonna Market opened on such a festive note that she was able to muster up the requisite smile wreaths.

She dressed carefully for the occasion, in a plum-colored pantsuit that brought out her green eyes. Her job, she figured, was to be a hostess. It wasn't all bad. People cried when they found their lost possessions; some of them hugged her.

It was nearly noon when a young woman approached her with a picture of a lost statue, a little boy who looked too sweet to be real, dressed in some kind of elaborate, maybe Victorian, outfit. She was nearly frantic. "I can't find Billy. Billy just ain't here."

This was the down side. A lot of the stolen stuff would never be recovered. But there was something unusual about this young woman: She was the only black person in the place. Skip noted this only in passing—no time to worry about it now—and grabbed another officer, one of her burly decorators. "Hey, have you seen this statue?"

He screwed up his face. "I think so. It sure looks familiar."

"Got any idea where it might be?"

"Let me look in the back." Seeing the avid look on the woman's face, he made his escape.

Skip was trying to think of something comforting to say to her when she felt someone's presence, someone listening just over her shoulder. It was Kevin O'Malley, a new kid from the *Times-Picayune*, whom Skip had just met. He was trying to horn in on the conversation. Seeing his notebook, the young woman took the opportunity to glom on. "Hey, you a reporter? Could you help me—just listen a minute. I can't find my mama's Billy. Please, talk to me. Maybe you could publish this—" She held up the picture. "Maybe somebody know where he is."

The kid lit up. He'd found exactly what he wanted, or thought he had. Skip felt slightly uneasy about the woman, but Kevin was a big boy. If the woman's story rang false, it was up to him to figure it out. Skip left the two of them alone and moved on. It was only a tiny vignette in a very long day, forgotten in an instant, remembered only when she saw the next day's paper.

Once again, the *Times-Picayune* made a hero out of her. The paper ran plenty of pictures of crying people, so overcome by finding their wandering statues you'd have thought they were all Michelangelos. As a sidebar, it also ran a piece about people who'd been disappointed, including the young woman looking for "Billy." The reporter had granted the supplicant's wish and published Billy in all his glory. If Skip hadn't been so cynical, it would have brought a tear to her eye.

But cynic that she was, she didn't give it a thought until that afternoon, when she got a call from Kevin O'Malley. "Hey, guess what? I found Billy."

She pricked up her ears. There could be something in this for her. "Congratulations. That's great."

"And I've got something else for you—a whole new cache of cemetery art."

"No kidding." She picked up a pencil; this could be good.

"Yeah, we ran the picture, and we got a tip about where he was. I went over there to take a look, and no one was home, so I, you know, kind of peeked over the fence. And there it was, all this stuff, just sitting there in some guy's backyard."

"Oh. Well, thanks for calling. I'll go over and take a look. Where is it?"

"Five eighty-nine Spain Street." Skip could hear papers rattling somewhere in the station. An ordinary sound, but at the moment it seemed to come from a great, great, distance. Her whole life had just split apart. "Some guy named Steve Steinman owns the building."

Chapter THIRTEEN

*S*kip had only a moment of pure fatalistic understanding—the sort you might have if you looked up and saw a meterorite headed for Earth—before the news hit her bloodstream like a jolt of caffeine. Her heart accelerated and her stomach flipped over. She went into hyperspeed.

First, she fished the morning paper out of the trash and checked for the woman's name and address: Mary Jones, 4805 St. Charles. A black curtain seemed to fall around her; she knew there was no Mary Jones at that address, but she had to go through the motions. First she tried the phone book, then she took a ride. The house was a mansion, as were all the dwellings on this part of the showiest street in New Orleans. Ringing the bell with little hope, Skip was greeted by an African-American woman in a maid's uniform. She didn't even bother to smile and make her manners. Just blurted, "I'm looking for Mary Jones."

"I'm sorry," the woman said. "This the Gerson residence."

Skip produced her badge. "Police," she said. "May I speak to Mr. or Mrs. Gerson?"

There followed an uncomfortable twenty minutes in which Skip tried to pry coherent answers from a half-potted Mrs. Gerson, with help from the maid, a Hazel Brown, both of them, in the end, agreeing that no Mary Jones nor in fact any Jones at all had ever worked there, nor was Hazel herself related to a Mary Jones.

It was about what Skip had expected. Hazel could have an acquaintance, even a daughter, who knew the address through her. Or "Mary Jones" could have made it up out of whole cloth.

On the way back to the Third District, she cursed Kevin O'Malley for not suspecting something, but on the other hand, what did it matter to him what the woman's address was? She had a great story to tell; who cared whether it was true? No one could get hurt by it.

Skip pounded into Abasolo's office and closed the door. "A.A. I've been set up." She knew what was going to happen, but she was too mad to be afraid, even for Steve. "You know that stupid story this morning about the missing statue named Billy? The reporter just found it. Acting on an anonymous tip, he went to a certain address, climbed a fence, and found a cache of what he suspects to be stolen cemetery art, including the statue of Billy. Guess whose address?"

"Skip, for Christ's sake, quit pacing. Sit down and try to calm down."

"Steve Steinman's, Adam. My boyfriend's."

Abasolo whistled and sunk down in his chair. "Have you checked it out?"

"Are you kidding? I checked out the woman, but no way am I going over to Steve's alone; for all I know, the *T-P*'s got photographers lying in wait. Steve's in L.A, by the way. The last time I saw him was three days ago, and there was no statuary of any kind in his backyard. And, no, I haven't phoned him."

"Do it now, with me as a witness. We've got to get permission to search. Don't tell him what it's about."

"Shit!"

"Skip, calm down, for God's sake. We've got to do it by the book."

For all his talk of calm, she noticed a muscle twitching in his jaw.

She made the call, and they were out of there, on the way calling for a district car to meet them there. (A.A. thought of everything: "What if the *T-P* team is there? You want to look like a couple of dirty cops sneaking around?")

But the street was its usual quiet self. Skip let them in with her key, and when they opened the back door, the sight that greeted them caused the same words to issue from both pairs of lips: "Oh, shit."

The backyard was littered with urns and statues, crosses and gates, even a couple of the prized metal chairs. "Billy" was there, of course, but he was way beside the point. The point was, they'd been had or Kevin O'Malley had, and it was going to rebound nastily on Skip and Abasolo—and poor Steve.

"All right," A.A. said, "here's what we do. As of now, the task force is disbanded; neither you nor Hagerty nor LeDoux is to speak to any of the prisoners again. We'll impound this stuff tonight and hope no media show up to whip our asses. No matter what happens, from now on, you refer all press inquiries to me. Oh, and one more thing: Tell Steinman to get his ass on the next plane back to town."

"Why?"

"You know why."

She thought it through. A warrant could be issued for his arrest, that was why.

They left the district officers to guard the trove, and, on the ride back, Abasolo called the chief to break the news that his great PR coup had become a disaster.

When he was off the phone, Skip said, "Adam, thanks for sticking by me."

Abasolo said nothing. Again, his jaw worked.

She couldn't let it go. "You, uh, think maybe I helped myself while I was setting up the warehouse? You know Steve was out of town. So it would have been just me. Acting alone."

"Okay, for the record: How did that stuff get there?"

"Somebody climbed over the gate, opened it, and unloaded a truck."

"Why not you? You're even friends with one of the suspects."

"He's an acquaintance, not a friend." She couldn't believe Abasolo hadn't gotten it. Absolutely couldn't conceive of it. The scam was so obvious to her, she hadn't even bothered to spell it out. She pulled his own trick on him: "Think about it."

He didn't speak until they got back to the station, and when he did, it was with resignation. "Jacomine."

She was cut to the bone. "You actually suspected me, A.A.?"

He laughed. "Hell, no, Skip. You acted properly on this; you had no reason to come to me unless it really went down the way you say it did."

"Well, why'd you take so long thinking it over?"

"I was just trying to think if it could have been anybody else. I guess it could have been—Neil Gibson, for instance. He knows who your boyfriend is, right?"

"Right. And he might have had another cache of stuff he could have moved to Steve's backyard, but, as a practical matter, who'd move it? All his crime buddies are in jail."

"He could find somebody. And it would be a hell of a lot better for us if it played out that way."

"You're not kidding."

"But we have to prepare for the possibility that it's a blind alley. You can see exactly how the shit's going to fly."

The expression seemed woefully inadequate when she looked ahead; the thing coming at her was more like an avalanche than a sewage shower. It began the next morning, with the publication of a picture of Steve's backyard, probably obtained by climbing the same fence the dog poisoner used. The picture identified the home owner and included the information that he wasn't available for comment.

By the time Skip got to work, Kevin O'Malley had left her half a dozen messages. Foolishly, she picked up when the phone rang again. It was O'Malley: "Why didn't you tell me Steve Steinman was your boyfriend?"

That just killed her. Talk about your stupid questions. "Good morning to you too, Kevin." *Ever consider that I'm having a worse one than you are?* "I'm referring all press inquiries to Sergeant Adam Abasolo. Let me transfer you."

She did so with an odd feeling of numbness in her fingers. Two days ago she was the department's golden girl. Now she was officially dirty.

Hagerty and LeDoux were like a couple of Rottweilers penned up in the middle of a sheep herd. They kept throwing themselves against their cage, stomping all over the station growling and barking. Skip had hardly put down the phone when they rampaged into her office. "Skip, we were set up!" Hagerty yelled, her voice shrill. "None of us ever saw that stupid Billy statue. We never had the damn thing! We all worked on the warehouse. We were there all the time; nobody could have walked off with anything. And we've got a really good inventory. We can *prove* nothing happened." She took a breath through flared nostrils. "Goddamn Gibson!" That's who it was, wasn't it? Viper in your goddamn midst." She was pacing and waving her hands.

LeDoux sat instead, still and deadly. "Somebody's going down over this one," he rumbled.

"Guys, I appreciate the 'we' part, but I'm the one who's been set up."

"We should have *known*; none of our other victims are black. Hell, black people didn't have that kind of money in those days. Some of those things date back to slave days. After that, they didn't go in for damn *cemetery* statues, what little money they did have." Ledoux gave the word a kind of derisive emphasis, as if he was suddenly over angels and madonnas. "We should have known when we saw that woman."

In a way, Skip had known, at least that something was out of whack—perhaps they all had—but no one could say it; no one had even thought it through. She said, "What were we going to do? Treat her different because she was black?"

"We just should have suspected something," LeDoux grumped.

Hagerty said, "Damn, I hate this. Yeah, you were the one set up, but it reflects on all of us, goddammit. Like we couldn't even protect the stuff. Like we're as goddamn corrupt as everybody thinks."

It was true. Especially the part about what everybody thought. All the average reader would think was "corrupt police." Which could work to Skip's advantage; the department would pull out all the stops on this one, and not just for her.

Skip thought for a minute. "We're disbanded, but that doesn't mean we can't do a few things. Adam's got people interrogating the prisoners now. We could try to find Mary Jones."

LeDoux snorted. "She probably comes from some neighborhood where people would rather take a bullet than talk to the po-lice."

"We could try to connect her to Hazel Brown; there might be a reason she gave the address she did, like maybe she didn't think she'd be asked. Maybe it was the only one she knew that wasn't her own."

Hagerty said, "There's something about that Brown-Jones thing. Damn similar names. I'm willing to work on it."

Skip raised an eyebrow at LeDoux. "Danny?"

"Hell. I'm just gon' go find me somebody to kill."

Skip would have liked to work on Mary Jones herself, but Abasolo had strictly forbidden her to have anything at all to do with the case, and she had to agree with him. One false move and the already-dirty cop was covered in the aforementioned sewage.

She tried to get back to her other cases, the things that had seemed so important a month ago, but all she could think about was Jacomine. Gibson really could have set her up; he was out on bail and easily had the means. But what good it would do him, she wasn't sure.

Jacomine, on the other hand, would do anything to take her out. Till now, she'd never considered anything like this; she'd thought only of violence from Jacomine.

But it had his signature on it—a petty deviousness that would embarrass a child, coupled with a thoroughness that would do the marines proud. It would take several people to do it, and he'd always been good at getting volunteer armies together.

Well, hell. She'd done what A.A. wanted. If there was ever a good time for a leave of absence, this was it. She went to find him.

"Hey, Skip. Good news. None of the prisoners ever saw the Billy statue—they all drew a blank—and the rest of the stuff's generic. And Mary hasn't come in to claim her little treasure—no surprises there. We're trying to get some reward money, see if we can find her through the tip line. When's Steve coming in?"

She looked at her watch. "One o'clock. I'm leaving for the airport in a few minutes. Listen, A.A., I've got an idea."

"You do? Shoot." He looked like he expected something good.

"No matter what happens, we're dirty and we're gonna get dirtier. The evening news tonight's gonna say something like 'This just in: The head of the cemetery theft task force has been linked to a new cache of stolen art. Police deny wrongdoing.' See what I'm saying? There's no way to get out of this semigracefully. Hell, they're probably going to call it Angelgate."

The sergeant winced.

"What if you could throw them a bone?"

"I'm listening."

"Tell them I've taken a voluntary leave of absence."

"Are you crazy? That practically convicts you."

"Yeah, but it takes some of the heat off the department. Look, I'll even go on TV if you like. Steve and I both will. She crossed her fingers, hoping she was right. "We can do a great big press conference. The chief'll say we can't find Mary; the department's doing a thorough investigation and also an internal investigation. Steve and I will say we couldn't be more surprised, and I'll say I think it's only right to remove myself from the scene till my name's cleared." She could see he was considering it. "Come on, A.A. I'll look *real* sincere."

"I'll think about it."

Steve was a basket case when he got off the plane. "Skip, what's happening?"

At heart, he was a cowboy who'd always kind of wished he was the one chasing bad guys, never content to be a mere observer. But he wasn't half as street smart as he thought he was.

She said, "Someone broke into your backyard and brought you a band of angels. Simple as that. You check any bags?"

"No, I'm good to go." They started walking. "My neighbors must have seen something."

"They did. Some guys unloading a truck. Needless to say, they didn't think to get a plate number."

"But they'd know I wasn't home."

"Maybe."

They reached the car and loaded the baggage. They were nearly out of the parking garage before Steve spoke again. "Who would *do* something like that?"

She decided to confront the issue directly. "Probably the same person who poisoned your dog."

He went white. "*That's* why they killed Napoleon?"

"I can't tell you the specifics. I think they did it because Jimmy Dee's house is practically a fortress. If anyone wanted to get me, your house is better, except for that one little thing."

He was sweating, and his color showed no sign of returning. "You really think it was Jacomine, don't you?"

"Either him or Neil Gibson."

"Neil? Are you kidding? He's got those two cute little pugs. And Evangeline the cat. Remember her?"

"You don't forget a cat like Vangy." She was a twenty-pound long-haired Siamese, with azure eyes that looked like the marbles named after kitty orbs.

"Neil loves animals. He'd never hurt an animal."

Skip stifled a small feeling of triumph. Maybe this meant he'd be more open to her Jacomine fears. Playing the devil's advocate, she said, "You've got to consider the idea that it might have been him, Steve. Even before this statue thing, half the French Quarter hated me for arresting him; they just can't believe he'd do something like this."

"He had angels in his shop, right?"

"Lots of 'em. And the thieves were the ones that tipped us."

"Well, I guess I can go with the phrase 'caught red-handed.' But Neil would never, ever harm an animal—of that I'm sure. It could have been one of the other Mr. Bigs, but it wasn't Neil." That was the way the whole city was: sure, one way or another, of Gibson's guilt or innocence. She wondered if people felt the same about her.

Skip left Steve to give his statement to Abasolo, and when it was over, Steve joined her again. "How'd it go?" she asked.

"He watched me like a hawk. Made me nervous."

"Could have been 'cause you've got a yardful of stolen goods. Ever think of that?"

"You mean . . . I'm a suspect?"

Skip was speechless, realizing the seriousness of the find hadn't sunk in yet.

At the end of the day, Abasolo approached her desk. "Interesting development. *Extremely* interesting. We're due in half an hour for a meeting with McGuire, Hingle, and Fuzzy Begue—at headquarters. I think maybe somebody got their ear bent by Shellmire." He left her to chew on it. "Let me go get McGuire. Hingle's meeting us there."

She was so astounded she couldn't even sputter. Kelly McGuire was their lieutenant—Abasolo's immediate superior—and Rondell Hingle was captain of the Third District. A conference with those two would have been a little unusual in itself, but Fuzzy was the big surprise here. And the big gun—he was Deputy Chief of Operations.

Abasolo came back to get her, McGuire in tow. "You ready?"

"Sure."

Herbert "Fuzzy" Begue greeted them in his office. He was a big, old-fashioned beer-gut kind of cop, with a shaved head left over from the days when the style was military rather than fashionable. Shellmire and Hingle, a tall, taciturn African-American, were already there.

Begue seemed excited. "Y'all come in. Detective Langdon, we got some trouble for ya."

Skip picked up his mood. "Thanks, Chief. I've been thinking I needed some."

Everybody laughed but Hingle. He was a by-the-book kind of cop without a lot of sense of humor. Whatever was going down, she sensed he didn't really approve. Or maybe he was just angry. The cemetery fiasco made him look almost as bad as Skip. She resolved to do a little politicking.

When they were all seated, Begue said, "Agent Shellmire has been talking to me and Captain Hingle about something. Wanted to run it by you three and see what you think."

She and Abasolo and McGuire nodded, like kids in a classroom.

He kept talking. "We've been talking about this Mary Jones thing. We think somebody's out to get ya, Langdon, and we think we know who. Captain Hingle's been having talks with Sergeant LeDoux and Officer Hagerty, who're kind of thinking along the same lines. Now, we've turned this thing over to PID." He meant the Public Integrity Division, New Orleans' version of internal affairs. "Got to cross our *t*'s and dot our *i*'s. You aren't off the hook yet, and of course we've got to reassign you. But Agent Shellmire's got a real interestin' idea about that.

"Look, we don't think Gibson did this thing. First off, we don't think he'd have screwed up by sending an African-American gal. Second, the rest of the gang couldn't wait to rat him out on everything else, but they say they never saw the stuff in Steinman's yard. Bottom line, we think Errol Jacomine's back—we've always known he wasn't done with ya. And the fact that somebody took a shot at you a while back kind of bolsters that theory."

"Yessir," Skip said. "That was my thought."

"Here's the long and short of it, then. Agent Shellmire wants to go after him big-time, wants you to help him. Truth is, that might be the best thing for the department right now; it gets you out of our hair, and I don't have to tell you, if you get him, we'll all rest easier."

Plus, Skip thought, *it'll be a big feather in the department's cap.* But she couldn't feel too cynical about it; the plan could hardly be more to her liking.

"There's something big we have to talk about, though. There's a real big 'if' here. You've got to agree to some things."

Uh-oh, she thought.

"First off, this is top secret multiplied by ten. You can't even tell ya mother."

Skip nodded. *Not likely*, she thought.

Begue paused and sat up straighter, getting down to business at last. "Here's what we're gon' do. We're gon' announce that an internal investigation's in progress and you've been reassigned. Just like we would if we thought you were guilty." He paused. "Ya' just gon' have to be in disgrace for a while as far as the rest of the world's concerned. Won't make anybody else look good either—not Sergeant Abasolo, not Lieutenant McGuire, and, most especially, not Captain Hingle. But he's agreed anyway." Skip glanced at Hingle. He looked pretty grim.

"What about the rest of y'all?" Begue asked.

Abasolo said, "Sounds good to me."

McGuire nodded. "What have we got to lose?"

Skip wanted this. She wanted it badly. But there was a problem. "What about Steve Steinman? He's going to be tarnished."

Begue nodded. He'd been expecting that. "Look, whatever happens, there's no way out of that right now. Main thing is, you can't tell him what's really going on."

He'd called it: There was no way out. She didn't have to like it, but she had no choice about accepting it. "All right. I agree."

"It's a done deal then. Just so you know, we've got to hold a press conference first thing tomorrow morning."

"Oh." She tried smiling. "Gonna be a tough day tomorrow."

"You bet it is. Prepare for a shitstorm."

After the meeting, she and Shellmire got together and plotted strategy. First thing on the agenda, they decided, was a trip to the Louisiana State Penitentiary at Angola. This was where the best sources were: Jacomine's son, Daniel, who'd been one of his father's top lieutenants for a while; a man named Potter Menard, a "campaign aide" during Jacomine's catastrophic run for mayor; and a couple of lesser followers. If anybody could help them, these guys topped the list. "Who knows?" Shellmire said. "Maybe one of them found Jesus."

"They all did," Skip retorted. "Problem is, they think his first name's Errol."

It would take a day to set up, so it was decided that the next day, Skip would go to the office as usual to retrieve her Jacomine files and tie up any loose ends she had.

She regretted that decision by mid-morning; even she hadn't expected the strength and pain of the predicted avalanche. By noon, she was buried in sympathy calls and press inquiries (which she fielded back to Abasolo). By six P.M., the word *Angelgate* had entered the language.

That night, after the news, she discovered the part she hated worst was watching Sheila and Kenny's attempts to digest the concept of Auntie in disgrace. Steve wasn't much better, and, what was worse, he was angry, not at her, especially, just at having been caught in a trap.

She'd gotten her fondest wish, and she'd rarely been so miserable.

Chapter FOURTEEN

$\mathcal{M}$r. *Right*, the television show, paid Terri's plane fare to Dallas but didn't send a limousine. Tracie, the producer, picked her up and drove her to her motel, an older one near the studio, in an iffy section of town. All of which served to remind her that this was only a cable station she was going to be on, not exactly Oprah.

But the minute she was in David Wright's presence, her misgivings melted. Tracie took her to his office so they could get acquainted before the show. When he stood to shake her hand, she felt an electricity radiating from him, a force field around him. She wanted to step into it and did, when she took his hand. It was dizzying. It was warmth and sexuality and . . . genuine love. She could feel it. Not love just for her—she wasn't stupid enough to think that; it was love for his fellow human beings.

She thought it possible she was in the presence of greatness. She looked at Tracie to see if she felt it too and saw that the other woman seemed transformed; she was softer and gentler, somehow, the way men are when their sweethearts enter a room.

He said, "You're a brave lady, Terri Whittaker. I'd give you a hug, but I don't know you well enough."

She wished he would hug her. She was attracted to him. At the same time, she felt safe with him. It wasn't something she could explain. She just felt he wouldn't let any harm come to her. He wasn't extraordinary looking; in fact, he was quite a bit shorter than she thought he'd be. And his eyes were small. But he had thick, curly gray hair worn combed back to show off a widow's peak. It was sprayed down—she knew you had to do that for television—but it was still his best feature. It sure wasn't his looks that attracted her. But whatever it was, she was suddenly overcome with shyness.

"Thank you, sir," she said, uncharacteristically respectful.

"Oh, forget that 'sir' stuff, even if we are in Texas. Call me David." He leaned over to her. "I can call you Terri, can't I?"

"Sure."

"Sit down and we'll have a nice little chat before the show. Coffee or Coke or anything? Tracie can bring you anything you want."

A cigarette, Terri thought, but she asked only for water.

"I always like to meet my guests before the show. This isn't like other shows, you know. Everyone who goes on my show has been through something bad, real bad. I feel I owe them the respect of getting to know them before I put them in front of those harsh lights." He paused to give her a little smile. "But those lights'll be kind to you, Miss Terri. Yes, ma'am, you're going to look just beautiful on television."

With my Tri-Delt haircut and my soccer mom dress, she thought, and knew her choices were perfect.

David might have been flirting or not—Terri really couldn't tell—but one way or another he was certainly seducing her. She felt safe and warm, wrapped in a soft fluff of something pink and cottony.

"Now, all our guests have gone through something that could

happen to anybody, but wouldn't happen to anyone with enough money to dig out of their hole. You follow?"

Terri nodded. "That's sure true in my case."

"Tracie tells me you're an artist and a student. That's kind of a double whammy, isn't it?"

She smiled, happy to be understood. "They didn't invent the phrase 'starving artist' for nothing. Art isn't a calling that's even recognized as a real job by most people; they think it's some sort of self-indulgent hobby, usually. And since it's not particularly valued by our society, there aren't many grants for art students; hence, the concept of the day job."

"You have your own business, I hear. 'Aunt Terri's Rent-a-Wife.'"

"Umm-hmm. I run errands for the people whose jobs are actually respected by society. They work twelve hours a day and can't do their own grocery shopping. But I don't have twelve hours a day for my chosen profession, or even six or four, because I'm so busy trying to make ends meet with my day job." She glanced at him nervously, hoping she wasn't losing him.

He clicked his tongue and shook his head in utter sympathy. "Mmm. Mmm. A real vicious cycle you've got there." He smiled, as if to take her mind off her troubles. "Well, I sure hope someone nice takes you out to dinner now and then."

"Oh, my boyfriend's an artist too. We don't actually go out much, but Isaac's a great vegetarian cook. You'd be amazed, the things he can do with rice and beans."

"Well, I'm so glad you've got a boyfriend." For the first time, Terri detected a false note; the temperature in the room seemed to have dropped. Had Mr. Right been hitting on her, she wondered? Maybe the mention of a boyfriend had turned him. "What kind of art does your boyfriend do?"

She laughed. "He's kind of having an identity crisis. He used to be quite well-known as an outsider artist. Do you know what that is?"

"I believe I do; my wife Karen's kind of got a weakness for 'em. They're those people who paint angels and aliens, aren't they?"

Terri had to laugh. "A lot of them do. Isaac never was into close encounters, but he painted nothing but angels for a while."

"Was he good? Karen's kind of a collector."

"I don't know. He never shows me anything from that period. See, the term *outsider* is usually used to describe artists with no formal training. When he decided to go to art school, he even changed his name."

"I guess I should have known. Isaac's kind of an unusual name."

"Oh, he was always Isaac. But he used to be—are you ready for this?—the White Monk."

She had expected Mr. Right to share a big old laugh with her, but he didn't even bother to smile. Simply glanced at his watch and said, "Well, we're running out of time here. Excuse me while I do a few last-minute things." He called Tracie to take her to the Green Room.

The producer came in looking disconcerted. "Is—uh—is everything all right?"

Mr. Right flashed a splashy television smile; he had beautiful teeth, Terri noticed. "Everything's wonderful. Miss Whittaker's going to be just spectacular. You mind running down the format for her?"

On the way to the Green Room, Tracie kept glancing over her shoulder, as if looking for something. She was sneaking peeks at her watch too. She seemed distinctly ill at ease.

Finally, when they'd arrived at their destination, Tracie said, "Usually he . . . um—he didn't tell you how the show's going to go?"

"No. We just gabbed. He's very easy to talk to, isn't he?"

"It's funny he . . . well, listen, I've got to be quick. I guess he really must be pressed for time, or he'd have gone over it with you. Because this is one of our biggest shows ever. Usually we have two guests, one who's had their wrong righted and the new one—the one with a problem. You follow?"

Terri nodded, though she was slightly confused. She understood the format, but there was some kind of strange vibe in the air.

"This time we cancelled the other, because your problem is too important; it affects too many people."

"Really?" Terri was starting to get stage fright.

"You'll be on for the full hour." She paused and held up a reassuring hand. "But don't worry; you won't have to do anything but describe what happened to you. We're also going to have an expert on, talking about how banks cheat their depositors—the very people they're supposed to be serving."

"Hey, you sound like you could go on yourself."

"Listen, Terri, the same thing that happened to you happened to me. Only I didn't go to jail for it. You got a real raw deal." She gave Terri an impulsive hug. "I'll be back in a few minutes."

When she'd gone, Terri looked around for the first time. More drab. The room wasn't green, despite what they called it. It was a whitish gray—actually more like white with a layer of dirt on it—and the furniture had obviously come from a thrift shop. She remembered that this was a struggling cable station, but it would have been hard to imagine surroundings more drab.

She had a sense of failure, and she hadn't even been on yet. Worse, she had no means of distraction. She hadn't realized she was going to have half an hour to cool her heels, or she'd have brought a book.

There was a phone. She could call Isaac. But that seemed ridiculous; she'd call him on her cell phone after the show, when they could rehash it. She tried to remember if she knew anyone in Dallas. Actually, now that she thought of it, she had a friend here, Jessie Newman, a girl she went to high school with, who'd married some guy from Dallas. What was his name? Kincaid, that was it, like some Son of the Confederacy. Donaldson Kincaid. Two last names.

She looked it up in the phone book that lay on the rickety, scarred table next to the phone.

Curiously, he wasn't listed, but a Jessie Kincaid was. Terri thought, *Uh-oh. Divorce.* She wasn't sure she should call at all.

But in the end, it beat the hell out of sitting there wanting a cigarette. When a message answered, she was disappointed but reassured actually to hear Jessie's voice. They'd been good friends; she wondered why they lost touch. At the beep, she said, "Jessie? Here's a voice from your past. It's Terri Whittaker. Remember me? I'm just in Dallas for a day, and I thought I'd give you a call."

There was a click on the line, and Jessie said, "Terri Whittaker! How come you never wrote me?"

"I thought you were the one who never wrote me."

"Oh, forget it. It's a treat to hear from you. Boy is this town *not* New Orleans. How the hell are you?"

"Today, fine. But something pretty bad happened to me. I'm here to be on this television show, *Mr. Right*. Do you know it?"

"Same old Terri." Jessie laughed long and loud at that one, which put the fear of God in Terri. She wondered if she'd done something really stupid.

"Jessie, that's not reassuring. What in hell's so funny?"

"You can always be trusted, that's all, to be in on the hot new thing. You're the first person I know who had acupuncture. You were always first at every new club and restaurant, and you were onto a fashion trend six months before it hit *Vogue*."

"Hey, I'm kind of flattered by that." Terri wondered if she'd just learned something about herself. "But *Mr. Right*'s this low-rent cable show where poor sad people go to cry. It's not like, uh, crayon-colored hair or something."

"Terri, you are *amazing*. You do it without even knowing you're doing it, don't you? *Mr. Right*'s the hottest thing in Texas. It's a *phe-nomenon*. They just went to an evening format, and everyone in town's talking about it. Hey, have you met David Wright? He's kind of sexy, don't you think? He met his wife on the show. She was one of his first guests—girl from a prominent family that disowned her when she married a boy they didn't like. She hit the skids and embar-rassed them in front of the whole town by going on the show. It might seem like a grandstanding thing to do, but, Terri, she was des-perate, just a sweet innocent kid who didn't know what else to do. It really put the show on the map."

"I can imagine."

"So the family had no choice but to welcome her back into the fold—again in front of the whole town—and then she married Mr. Right. Talk about creating a sensation!"

Tracie appeared and mouthed: "Five minutes."

"Oh, gosh. The producer's calling me."

"Okay, I'm tuning you in right now. My husband's out of town, by the way. You here alone?"

"Oh, good. That's a relief."

"What?"

"I couldn't find his name in the phone book. I thought you might be divorced."

She laughed again. "Oh, hell, no. He's completely wireless these days—only uses his cell phone. Listen, where are you staying? Can you have dinner with me?"

"The Bluebonnet Motor Lodge."

"Ughhh. Terri, you can't stay there. I'm shocked that's where they put you. You'll *have* to stay with me. Will you? I'll get a babysitter, and we'll go someplace nice for dinner."

Terri had actually given some thought to where she was going to find a restaurant. The thought of the depressing motel, of a night alone in a slightly scary neighborhood, had been weighing on her. "Jessie, you know what? You're cheering me right up. I'd love to stay with you."

"Get them to take you back to the Bluebonnet to get your stuff. I'll pick you up there."

The next few minutes were a blur. Someone slapped some powder on Terri's nose, someone else led her to the set (which was much nicer than the rest of the studio), and she had time, looking out at the expectant audience, to get nervous while someone else clipped a microphone on her. She'd forgotten about the audience.

There was no sign at all of David Wright.

And then he was introduced, and he came out of the wings and made his bow. The audience went crazy. Jessie wasn't kidding; this thing really was a phenomenon. She was scared to death.

Her nervousness wasn't even slightly helped by the fact that the onscreen David seemed very different from the offscreen one. He seemed distant now, no doubt focused on doing his job rather than on her. Oddly, he wasn't nearly so attractive under the lights. His eyes suddenly seemed small and calculating, way too intense for comfort.

It's charisma, she said to herself. *That's what makes him a star.*

The first thing he said was, "Terri, where you from, gal?"

She was a little taken aback by the sudden change of accent—from semi-English to full-out Texas—but the warmth appeared to be back in his eyes. She went with it.

He asked her a bit about school and her art, and then he said, "Well, they sure didn't invent the phrase 'starving artist' for nothing. It's not a calling that's even recognized as a real job by most people, is it?"

"No, it isn't. Most people think—"

"They just think it's some kind of a self-indulgent hobby, don't they? And since it's not particularly valued by society, there aren't many grants for art students."

I should have seen this coming, she thought. *That intimate little talk was all about stealing my material. I'm going to come off looking like an idiot if I just let him rip me off.*

"Hence," she said quickly. "the concept of the day job."

"You're a real hard-working girl, Terri. I hear your day job is running errands for people who have bigger fish to fry, people whose jobs—unlike that of fine artist—are actually respected by society."

Once again, she dove in before he could spew her whole life out of his own mouth. "Yes, they work really hard too. But I don't have twelve hours a day for my chosen profession . . ."

As she finished her speech, she made the mistake of glancing briefly at her host's eyes. They were not merely focused; she could have sworn they were downright malevolent.

Like Corinne Kay Walker, the woman whose landlord had tangled with *Mr. Right*, she got to tell her story—Terri against the bank—and then Mr. Right asked, "Can we right this wrong?"

I must have done well, she thought. The whole audience was on its feet. The theme music seemed even more urgent and frenetic than it had when she watched the show at home. The collection baskets were passed and people dug deep into their pockets. That part made her feel a little cheesy, but later, Jessie just shrugged. "It's show biz."

After the screaming, yelling, stomping, and pocket-emptying, an older woman came on, a consumer advocate who'd written a book called *Banking on Big*, and she ended up getting almost more applause than Terri. "Know what they do?" she'd say. "They know you're on vacation in July and August, and might not see your statements. So that's when they introduce the new fees." The audience booed loudly.

"How do they get away with it? They're banking on big: No one's going to challenge a corporation named Bank of the Western Hemisphere. Did you ever notice their names? Calculated to intimidate."

Or, "Do you realize many banks now penalize you for not using the ATM? Fees for teller transactions aren't uncommon. And have you noticed how large the fees are these days compared to what they used to be?"

By the time she had finished, she'd whipped the audience into a meringue. But Mr. Right wasn't yet done. "Ladies and gentlemen, we have a surprise guest today—a gentleman who phoned us when he found out about Ms. Whittaker's plight and asked if she needed a lawyer. Would you welcome, please, Mr. George Pastorek."

Terri's jaw dropped. George Pastorek was going to be her lawyer? She knew only two names in the world of consumer advocacy, and the other one was Ralph Nader.

"What happened to Ms. Whittaker is an outrage," Pastorek began, but he couldn't get another word out before the audience was on its feet, cheering. "It's the kind of thing that can only happen to someone who's too poor to get out of the hole these so-called guardians of your money can put you in."

They loved that one too. But Mr. Right wasn't one not to have the last word. He signed off with a final rabble-rousing speech: "Ladies and gentlemen, we are *not* going to let some corporate leviathan get away with this! With outlandish and outrageous fees! With backing a young woman—a poor student, a struggling artist— into a corner like a dog! With never even giving her a chance to make it right! But *we* will make it right! The day when a solid citizen, a young woman who has done nothing wrong except to fall into the jaws of a greedy monster, can be wrongfully imprisoned and harassed is a black day indeed for America! But a new and brighter one dawns for Terri Whittaker tomorrow."

Again, the audience stood and cheered. Some threw coins at the set; others threw hats into the air. Still others fisted their hands and chanted: "Terri! Terri!"

Terri left the studio feeling dazed and strangely upbeat. *I should be,* she thought. *I've got a suitcase full of money.*

She'd barely gotten back to the hotel when Jessie called from the lobby. "Get your Louisiana butt down here."

That made her laugh. She nearly ran from the dismal little room, riding an adrenaline high.

*I*saac tried calling Terri before she went on the air, just to say, "break a leg," but he wasn't all that surprised when she didn't answer; she was forever letting the battery run down. But he really wished he knew where she was staying; he wanted to make sure he had a message waiting for her when she got back from the studio. Well, no problem, he called the station and talked to the producer, who said Terri was at that moment being interviewed by the host, but she was staying at the Bluebonnet Motor Lodge.

He made himself a big bowl of popcorn, got himself an unaccustomed beer, and sat down to watch his girlfriend wow 'em. At first, he had eyes only for her. To him, she was beautiful, even with the brown hair. At first, he'd disapproved of her wearing the gold cross, thinking it too calculated, but it sure looked good glinting in the lights.

The host gave him the creeps from the get-go. Everything about him looked and sounded phony, from his carefully styled hair to his weirdly familiar voice, with the ersatz English accent. The way he moved gave Isaac the creeps.

When Terri started to talk, the camera came to rest on Mr. Right, showing the compassion in his face. Isaac had a weird, creepy sense of déjà vu. Something wasn't right with this guy, and he'd seen it before.

But where?

He lost all interest in the content of the show. He put his entire focus on observing Mr. Right, listening to him, watching his eyes.

Chapter FIFTEEN

*M*r. Right's first thought was that everything was fine, it was just a coincidence. *No one*, absolutely no one could penetrate his disguise. He was going all the way, and he'd thought of everything. He was Mr. Right; he was no longer Errol Jacomine. Even his own son wouldn't know him.

His second thought was that it was a setup. He felt sweat popping out under his fine mane of white hair. It had happened before. Even at his finest moments in his other lives, he had felt the clammy grip of fear, had felt himself zigzagging wildly between his trademark sublime confidence and a crazy, paralyzing terror. This was just one of the zigzags, the first of many he'd suffer before he achieved his final goal. It was nothing, just one of those moments of panic the great have to live with, the kind of thing a president must feel before pushing the button.

He tried to calm himself, to let in the suggestion that he'd been wrong about this, that somehow he'd overlooked something. This was his own son's girlfriend, or somebody who claimed to be, and she was about to be on his show.

Oh, hell, no! No, it wasn't that. The truth hit like him like an anvil. This was someone sent by the Devil-Spawn to make him blow his own cover.

Oh, yeah. Oh, yeah. He could see it. Nobody knew who he was, except Rosemarie, and she had everything to gain by keeping him where he was. But somebody who knew him might have seen the show, picked up some little thing—hell, maybe the way he moved or something—and dropped a dime to Devil-Cop. His confidence came back for a moment: Was that conceivable?

He had to be calm here. After all, he had a contingency plan; he never did anything without a contingency plan. But was it good enough? He had to think. His instinct was to do nothing. *Act normal,* he told himself. *No one can touch you. No one can do a thing unless you give them a reason.*

But his panic told him to get away from the woman as fast as he could. Hell, she could be a cop herself. He didn't have spies anymore. Without his following, he was like a quadriplegic. He had no idea whether his son Isaac was alive or dead, much less whether he was in art school and had a girlfriend named Terri Whittaker.

Okay, even if Whittaker was a cop, she couldn't observe him if he didn't let her.

He called Tracie to get Terri put on ice. When the girl finally came in a good five minutes later, she looked as if the sky was falling. "David? What's wrong? You said you wanted another full half hour to talk to her. This is our biggest show ever . . ."

"*Who is that woman?*" he shouted, not bothering to keep his voice normal, to try to seem unruffled, as if nothing had happened. Not even caring.

Tracie, pink and fast getting red, cringed, taking baby steps away from him. "Who is she? She's Terri Whittaker, the woman the bank sent to jail. Who did she say she is? Is she . . . I mean, did she say something crazy or something? Is she a nut case? Listen, I checked everything out: called the school where she goes; called the bank, of course; saw the police records."

"You saw the police records? What police records?"

"She sent us copies of them."

"*She* sent the copies."

"Well, yes. She did. David, what's going on? What's happening?"

"I don't want her on the show." He had seated himself sometime during the interchange. Tracie's quaking was calming him. He now sat in his executive swivel chair, steepling his fingers, regaining his calm, and he spoke icily.

"Don't want her . . . ?" Tracie was turning pale, going through a different kind of panic. "But this is our biggest show ever. We don't even have a backup. We've flown in an expert and a lawyer for her. We've got a full house out there, not to mention that this is only our second show in the nighttime format, and, quite frankly, Mr. Right, the eyes of Texas are upon us."

It was that phrase that got him. He'd been about to demand they send Terri home and simply go with the bank expert, when the producer's words brought him up short. He'd already talked to the damn girl; if she really was his son's girlfriend and had somehow blundered onto the show, canceling was the worst thing he could do. It would draw the wrong kind of attention to him, make Tracie suspicious, if nothing else.

He dropped his head into his cupped hands. "Oh, hell, girl. I'm sorry. I've got an absolutely splitting headache. I guess . . . the . . . pain . . . got to me." He drew out the words like he could barely speak.

"Omigod, I'll get you some Vicodin." Tracie flashed out of his office and came back with a plastic vial. "I keep a supply for occasions like this." She poured one out in his hand and gave it to him. "Here. Take this. You've just got nerves, that's all, because it's such an important show. I've seen it a million times."

She seemed back in control now, no longer red, no longer white. Somehow or other—he really had no idea how it happened—Mr. Right actually had in his employ a person he couldn't control, a person who hadn't gotten the message that nothing he said was to be questioned. Ever.

Somehow, he didn't think there was any getting through to her. He'd just have to fire her and start over.

"I've got things to do," she said. "The expert's plane was late. You lie down, okay? And let that stuff kick in." She left without asking permission.

He threw out the Vicodin—above all, he needed a clear head—and tried to think. Okay, okay, okay. His first instinct was right. The best thing he could do was act normal. Pretend nothing had happened. After all, if David Wright was who he said he was, he'd never have heard of an outsider artist named The White Monk; the name "Isaac" would mean nothing at all to him. Therefore, he would have to behave as if that were the case. He'd do it, and he'd do a spectacular job. No one would ever be the wiser.

One thing he knew he was good at was *dissembling*. That was a word he'd learned in England. The thing he was good at was lying. He'd made a career of it. He was an accomplished actor long before he ever became a TV star; it was his stock-in-trade. There was no doubt in his mind he could pull this thing off.

He breathed deeply till showtime, and then he went out and knocked their socks off. He could tell by the audience reaction, by the applause. And it fed him.

He loved that applause. The more of it he heard, the better at his job he got. He damn near convinced himself that little Miss Prissy Whittaker was a saint who'd been wronged.

Karen was in the front row tonight. Strange. She hadn't told him she was coming. Tracie'd probably invited her, because it was such a big fucking show, the biggest since Karen's own. Damn, what they could do with the IRS now! They were just getting started when Karen walked in with her precious gift, and even as it was—kind of half-assed, compared to tonight's extravaganza—it had caused a statewide sensation. Of course, he realized in retrospect, a lot of it had to do with who Karen was.

He had to do twice as good a job with Karen there. He focused deeply on getting the thing done, and he knew he did it well. Better than well. Better than any talk-show host in America could have. If he had a network show today, he'd be halfway to the presidency. Just look at the way people stood up to applaud; look at the way they parted with their money—dollars, too, not just coins; look at the way the women practically swooned. That was one of the best by-products of this whole thing. Tonight he could probably have any woman in the whole studio, and his stupid wife had picked this night of all nights to show up!

Easy there. Settle down, he told himself. He knew that was crazy. Karen was the only woman in his life now. He was thinking like he used to.

After the show, he headed for the men's room to wash his face. He had to have a moment alone to piece things together. On the way there, he began to feel nauseated, and in fact he just barely made it, throwing up before he even got the toilet seat up. He sat on the floor, recovering, and it was only a moment before the nausea came back. *Shit!* He was going to puke again. How the hell could that happen to him?

The second time was almost worse; there was very little left, so it was mostly heaving. God, it was painful. His throat hurt, his stomach hurt, his breath was something out of a rhino. Jesus, who had done this to him?

He was sitting there on the cold tile, when it came to him what had just happened. He had focused on the wrong fucking thing. He should have staged a fainting fit or something. A heart attack. Christ, why couldn't he have thrown up like this in his damn office?

What he should have done was stay off the air no matter what it cost him. Because if the girl was who she said she was, Isaac would watch the show.

He tried to tell himself it was no big deal. He and Isaac had had practically no contact in recent years. Once, he'd wanted his whole family together so badly he'd actually sent his son Dan to take his granddaughter forcibly from her college campus. But he hadn't even tried to get Isaac.

Isaac was barely a Jacomine at all—at any rate, not like the others. He and Rosemarie had made Dan, and Dan and Jacqueline had made Lovelace. Isaac was Irene's boy—plain, tired, stupid Irene whom he had rechristened Tourmaline, just to give her a little style. Hell, he had no fucking idea why he'd ever married her, and he wished to hell he hadn't. She was about as far from Rosemarie and Karen as Mamie Eisenhower was from Nancy Reagan. No style, no savvy, no nothing. She'd birthed a son who might as well be from another planet, he was so peculiar.

Errol had tried like hell to love him, even turned him into a preacher for a while. In those days the kid was a pleaser, a sad little thing always looking for attention, a child who'd do anything if he thought it was going to get him some brownie points. That was what gave Errol the idea; he thought if the kid tried that hard with his own parents, he'd probably be great with an audience. He was also a cute little bugger who, after a little coaching, would probably be pretty good at making the folks turn loose of their dollars. So Errol invested his good time and energy into teaching the little bastard to preach. Wouldn't you know, he picked that one thing to say no to? He was shy, the little coward. Hated getting up in front of the crowds. His father had had to beat some sense into him.

It took a long damn time, but dear little Isaac finally came around. Turned into a right fine seven-year-old evangelist if Errol said so himself. Didn't quit wetting the bed till he was nearly ten, but he could preach pretty good.

But when he was twelve or thirteen, something like that, he got . . . how the hell did you describe it? He didn't get religion; he got the opposite of religion. Refused to preach any more and started stuffing his face with everything he could find: hamburgers, milkshakes, french fries. Turned into a regular little butterball. Hell, that wouldn't have been so bad, but his face broke out in zits the size of eyeballs. God, the kid was ugly. Hell, good thing he wouldn't preach; nobody could stand to look at him. And ornery! Errol had to go back to the strap again.

Little bastard. Years later, he'd betrayed his whole family in the perfidious manner of an enemy. He had lain with his brother's wife and brought shame to the house of Jacomine.

After that, not a one of them had any use for him. Errol wasn't sure he'd recognize him if he passed him on the street. Why the hell should a dumb fuck like Isaac recognize *him*? Especially now that he'd changed his appearance, his accent, even his height. He probably had nothing to fear from his lesser son. But he admitted to himself that there was a chance. This crazy thing had brought that home to him. There was a chance, and he'd overlooked it. He couldn't believe he hadn't had the little bastard killed.

Karen was in his office, on her feet, beaming, squealing, waving her arms. She was wearing a short paisley skirt and a black T-shirt kind of thing with long sleeves. Her hair was up.

"Ohhhhh, it's Mr. Riiiiiight!" She leapt up and grabbed his face between her two hands and forcibly kissed him. He was in no mood to kiss back. God, she was irritating. "Sugar, that is gon' put you over the top! That was the best, best, *best* thing I have ever seen in my entire life!"

"Well, that hasn't been very long, has it?"

The joy drained out of her face. He liked that. He liked being able to put it there and take it away. It didn't belong there now.

She looked as if she'd gotten a war telegram—"regret-to-inform-you" kind of thing—and then compassion replaced the shock. She grabbbed the back of his head, pulling his face close to hers. "Oh, sweetheart, don't feel insecure. People loved it. They loved that poor girl, Terri, and they just hated the big bad bank. And they think Mr. Right is their knight in shining armor, just like I do." She actually rubbed her nose against his. He was revolted. Before he thought, he shoved a hand in her stomach and pushed her.

"Get the hell away from me, whore!"

She landed in a chair, breathing hard, some of her hair coming out of its tight twist. This time she registered only amazement. "What did you call me?" She pushed at the errant strand.

Pushing her had felt good. He grabbed her by the wrist and pulled her up, drew her close. "Whore," he whispered. "You look like a whore in that outfit."

He brought his mouth down on hers like a weapon. She shook him off. "What's wrong with you?"

He answered her in a loud whisper, more or less a hiss, partly designed to keep anyone outside from hearing. But it unnerved people even more than yelling. "You're my wife, bitch. Act like it!" He pulled her back toward him.

She twisted sideways and tried to pull away, but he still had a firm hold on her wrist. He reeled her back in, and now she shoved him with her free hand. That infuriated him. He backhanded her across the face, and before she could recover, he slung her by the arm he held and let go. She sailed across the room like a scarecrow, coming to rest only when she smacked the opposite wall, losing her balance and sliding down it.

Suddenly alarmed, he knelt beside her, "Darling. Karen, are you all right?"

There was a tiny, almost inaudible knock, and the door opened. Tracie said, "Oh, God. What happened? Is there anything I can do?"

He held Karen so tightly around the wrist that she had to take his meaning. "Mrs. Jacomine . . . tripped. She's fine, aren't you, darling?"

Dutifully, as he had known she would, Karen smiled up at the producer. "New shoes," she said. "David calls them Jezebel pumps."

"Ever the gentleman. That's not what most people call them." Tracie left and closed the door behind her.

As soon as it clicked, he went into full-tilt apology. "Omigod, Karen, I don't know what happened there. I saw you, and I was so excited . . . then when you wouldn't . . . I don't know . . . the adrenaline . . . we had so much riding on that show . . . I've really been under a lot of pressure."

He tried to help her up, but once again she writhed out of his grasp, and this time he let her go. "Don't you touch me, you bastard." She strode out of the room on her fuck-me pumps.

Well, hell, she'd be all right. Mr. Right was philosophical about it. Why shouldn't she be? No one was more of an expert on women than he was. They got upset; they got over it. In the end, it just made them more passionate. But this thing was going to cost him: He was going to have to give up sex with his wife tonight, and he was going to have to buy her some kind of fancy present to make up, and it was going to be tedious going through all the crap he was going to have to go through.

Fuck! Fuck! Fuck! He wished he'd never seen that goddamn Terri Whittaker. Well, one thing—he sure wasn't going to be betrayed by his own son.

He went into the hollowed-out book where he'd kept the cell phone he'd bought to deal with Lobo and punched in the gang-banger's pager number.

When the phone rang, Lobo said nothing, just breathed.

"It's me."

"I know ya. Bettina frien'."

He told Lobo what he wanted him to do, and as he did so, a Bible verse came into his head. He thought that he had named his sons well: Daniel had certainly ended up in the lion's den, and the Lord had his own plans for Isaac.

Chapter SIXTEEN

*A*fter the show, Isaac spent half an hour shaking, trying to recover. Several times, he picked up his phone, but he couldn't get his fingers to work. And when his coordination finally returned, he couldn't reach Terri; either she had her phone off, or she'd forgotten to charge it, as usual.

He dialed the station and asked for her.

"I believe Miss Whittaker's left, sir."

"But you don't know for sure?"

"I didn't see her walk out, but I'm fairly sure she's gone."

"This is her boyfriend," he told the receptionist. "Can you tell me where she's staying? She left me a message, but it was garbled. The, uh . . ." He held his breath, hoping she wasn't the suspicious type.

"We put our guests up at the Bluebonnet Motor Lodge."

He exhaled. "Did she leave alone?"

"The producer probably took her back."

"But you don't know for sure?"

"No sir."

He pushed it. "Does Mr. Right produce his own show?"

"Sorry, sir. I have another call." She rang off, having apparently gotten suspicious.

She could be with his father. Errol could have asked her out to dinner or something, and she, in all innocence, would have been flattered, would have accepted. If his father understood the connection between her and Isaac, he'd kill her the second he thought he could get away with it.

Hands shaking, he called the Bluebonnet Motor Lodge. "Whittaker?" a female clerk said. "Just a moment, please."

Isaac breathed a sigh of relief. At least he could leave a message here.

The operator came back on the line. "Ms. Whittaker has checked out."

"What? When?"

"I'm sorry, sir. I do not have that information."

"Give me the front desk, please." Maybe someone would remember her.

"This is the front desk, sir."

"Oh. Do you remember Ms. Whittaker?"

"No sir, I don't."

"Is anyone else there?"

"Mr. Ramos is helping a customer, sir."

Isaac gave up, thinking, *Okay, that was that.* She was supposed to stay overnight; if she wasn't there, something was wrong. Seriously wrong.

He felt like he was going to pass out.

His hands slick with his sweat, he picked up the phone to call the Dallas police, then realized how futile that would be. *Well-known television personality's about to kill my girlfriend?* Uh-uh, it wouldn't fly.

Langdon! he thought. Langdon could get to them—they'd believe another cop. Where the hell had he put her number? He fumbled for it, his fingers dull and uncooperative. Eventually, he thought of calling the Third District.

"Officer Langdon has been reassigned," he was told. "Can someone else help you?"

"No. No one."

Absolutely no one, he thought.

*K*aren left the studio with dignity, heels clicking, even mustering a smile for anyone who passed. Once in her car, she sat there in shock, trying to convince herself that what had happened was real, to give it some kind of a name.

What about if I were trying to tell it? she thought. *What would I say? Would I say my own husband tried to rape me? Would it be true?*

She couldn't explain that part at all. She wondered if, in some crazy, sick fashion, he was sexually excited by the thrill of his performance, turned on in some kind of twisted, violent way. But there were two kinds of violence at issue: sexual and physical. He may or may not have tried to rape her, but he'd most certainly knocked her around. You really couldn't call it anything else, and you couldn't forgive or excuse it. She wanted to; she really, really wanted to pretend it hadn't happened. But her back hurt too badly.

Falling against the wall, she'd hurt herself. Her back was killing her; she had to get some ice on it. And she couldn't go home. David would be home soon; if he wasn't, so much the worse. She'd be there alone, contemplating the ruins of her marriage.

She wanted her mama.

Without thinking much about it, she drove to her parents' house. If she'd analyzed it, she'd have remembered that they had fought and then made up, would still have gone there, as countless women did when their husbands hit them. But she didn't think; she just drove. After her first marriage exploded, she'd had to live at first simply and then in poverty. Now, with David, she was slowly, painfully trying to re-create the warmth and luxury of her parents' home, but she wasn't succeeding, and she felt it, felt the lack of warmth she didn't know how to find. She hadn't her mother's knack or, for that matter, her mother's money. She really didn't know where to start, and she was too proud to ask anyone except a decorator. Her wonderful new home looked like someone else's; it had an iciness, an aloofness. It didn't look loved.

She thought of her parents' den, with its two wide-screen TVs and its books; its worn, cozy furniture and her mother's needlework; its framed photos of family vacations; its seldom-used fireplace; her dad's golf trophies. Now that was home. She wanted nothing more than to be in that room, with her mother's arms around her as if she were a little girl again. She realized with surprise that her own home had hardly a book in it, hadn't any of the earmarks of two people's mutual interests, their shared life.

She knocked shave-and-a-haircut (the family signal) and entered through the door that was never locked till bedtime. Her parents were having dinner on trays in front of one of the televisions. Even though she'd grown up in this house, in this room, she felt like an intruder. "Oh. I'm sorry to interrupt your dinner."

Her father didn't speak. He returned to his lamb chop with an aggrieved air.

Her mother was gracious as always. She crossed the room to kiss her daughter lightly. "Karen. Congratulations. We saw the show and it was wonderful." She sounded underwhelmed.

"Mother . . . Mother . . ." Karen felt her face breaking; no need to hold it in anymore. "Mother, he hit me." She let it all out as she collapsed in her mother's arms—the tears, the sobs, the body shakes, everything that conveyed her desperation. She wasn't just hurt; she was heartbroken. And she'd had to walk out of that studio and drive over here as if nothing had happened. Now she was screaming.

Her mother said, "Calm down now. Calm down." That was the last thing she wanted to do; she'd been calm for the last forty-five minutes. She wanted to be her mother's child. "Boyd, get her some water."

In a moment, she looked up to see her father holding a glass of water. The expression on his face terrified her almost more than the thought of her husband.

Her mother took the glass and held it out to her. "Drink this now. Drink this." Karen hated the way people repeated themselves when someone lost it. She took the glass, and she sipped, momentarily quiet. And then she began hicupping.

Her dad sat down on one of the big, shabby sofas, looking like something that belonged on Mt. Rushmore. He didn't speak at all, didn't even look at her, just stared at the wall. He had turned off the television.

"You're all right now. Tell us what happened."

"Oh, Mother, I was so happy tonight! I wanted to surprise him. So I went to the studio and sat in the front row." Her mother nodded. Karen hiccupped.

Her father said, "For God's sake, drink that water."

Karen obeyed. "He wasn't happy to see me. I don't . . . know why. I tried to kiss him, and he called me a whore."

At this, her father's face whipped toward her, stonier than ever, as if he agreed with David. "Then he started to get . . . sexual . . ." She glanced furtively at her father, oddly embarrassed. ". . . and I pushed him away."

Her father spoke angrily. "Now why the hell would you do a thing like that? You just said you tried to kiss him."

She was taken aback. "Because . . . uh . . . he called me a whore."

Her mother reached to stroke her forearm. Her father said, "Hmmph," to acknowledge her answer. "And because . . . uh . . ." She was finding it hard to tell. "He got rough. He scared me. So I pushed him away. And then he tried to pull me back . . ."

Her father's stare was like an icepick. "Y'all into little games?"

She couldn't believe what she'd just heard. She felt herself blushing, not out of embarrassment but out of shame. "No! No, we're not into little games. Daddy, this was no game. What do I have to do to make you understand? He threw me against a wall." Her hiccups were gone.

Her mother pulled her close again. "Oh, honey."

Her father got up and paced. The phone rang. All three of them ignored it.

Finally, Karen said, "Mama, my back really hurts. Do you think I could have some ice for it?"

"Oh, *honey*," her mother said again and got up to get the ice.

When she was gone, her dad turned to her, furious. "Now you listen to me, Missy. You're supposed to be grown up, but you don't ever grow up. You just make one bad decision after another and expect this family to clean up your messes. You're going to have to figure this one out on your time, you understand? You leave your mother and me out of your filth."

Karen felt sick. "Excuse me, Daddy," she said, and ran to throw up. After washing her face and rubbing it with some of the ice meant for her back, she started to feel a little better.

Damn the McLeans, she thought later, lying on the bed in her old room. *Why couldn't I have the kind of Southern father who'd kill any bastard who messed with his little girl?* It was all her mother could do to persuade Boyd to let Karen stay the night.

She was dozing, trying to cope with the pain, when she heard the doorbell ring. She knew who it was even before she heard her father's heavy footsteps on the stairs. "Come on down. Your husband's here." He didn't wait for an answer.

David was waiting in the den, her parents having tactfully melted away. "Karen. My poor little lamb." He crossed the room and tried to put his arms around her. She grabbed them and shoved him away. "All right, I deserved that. I came to apologize."

"I'm not going home with you, David." She would have to tomorrow, but at least she could have one night of peace.

"Karen, darlin', you mean the world to me."

"David, you *hit* me!"

"I most certainly did not. I've never hit a woman in my life."

She shrugged. "Shoved then. What's the difference?"

A strange look came over him, something she'd never seen

before. It was pain, she thought. Trouble—the kind the guests on his show had, nothing she'd ever associate with Mr. Right. "Honey, something bad happened tonight." He held up a hand to stave her off. "I mean besides my hurting you. I am truly sorry about that, Karen. You may not believe it, but I am. When I said I was under pressure, I didn't mean from some stupid television show. I was afraid for my life, honey. And yours."

She couldn't believe what she was hearing.

"Baby, I've got some things to tell you. I've got some enemies. I saw someone tonight, someone from my past . . . and I couldn't help it, I just went nuts. I was so crazy with worry—and so *damn* upset to see you at the studio—I just lashed out at you. Honey, I swear to God nothing like that'll ever happen again."

"What do you mean 'enemies,' David?" She heard the edge in her voice and hoped he did.

"It was a long time ago. Back when I was running this little company in Phoenix, somebody was getting picked on and I took his side. Fired a couple people."

Karen didn't get it. "So? That's enough to hit your wife over?"

"Fired was just the beginning. Once these two guys were gone, we discovered they'd been stealing from the business—"

"Ah." It was starting to come clear. "And they were going to pin it on the picked-on guy."

"That's my girl! You got it. Long story short, we prosecuted, and I didn't know they were out of jail till I saw one of them in our studio tonight. Now, this man's from Phoenix, and he turns up in Texas. *Last* thing I wanted was my wife in the same building with him so I saw you and I just . . . lost it. Can you find it in your heart to forgive me?"

She wasn't sure. On the one hand, it sure wasn't a reason to call her a whore. On the other hand, this was Mr. Right, the man she'd loved unequivocally before tonight. She'd be a fool to kiss her marriage good-bye without even hearing him out. "I think," she said carefully, "I need the details."

He looked so relieved she almost wanted to hug him. He even chuckled. "Well. At least you aren't throwing me out." He reached out to her; still guarded, she put her hand in his. "Come on. Let's go home. Details at eleven."

She let him take her home and tuck her into bed with more ice and plenty of aspirin, and a thousand more apologies. She was glad to have been talked into this, glad not to have to wake up contemplating a second divorce before her twenty-seventh birthday.

Sometime in the night, the aspirin wore off. She woke up moaning, disoriented. She was still in pain, but a different sort, like menstrual cramps. And something else was wrong. "David!" She shook him. "David, turn on the light."

He reached his lamp and blinked in the glare. "Why? What's wrong?"

"I feel . . . wet." She threw off the covers.

The bed was soaked with her blood.

Chapter SEVENTEEN

Skip and Shellmire spent the day on a wild goose chase, driving to the state penitentiary at Angola. Daniel Jacomine (the big prize) refused to talk to them, but two former followers agreed, including Potter Menard. Skip held high hopes for Menard, and, indeed, seeing him was gratifying in its way. He'd turned on Jacomine, done a complete one-eighty. That was the gratifying part. But he couldn't tell them a single thing about where his former leader was now. The other guy was still loyal to Jacomine and, it appeared, had only agreed to see Skip so he could threaten to kill her when he got out. It wasn't a surprise, but it was a loss.

Skip was so disheartened Shellmire took her to dinner when they got back to New Orleans, a dinner that included several glasses of wine and a lot more obsessing. "Bettina next?" Shellmire suggested.

"Nah, I think we've already milked that one, unless we could get a search warrant. But we sure don't have probable cause. I think Rosemarie's our best bet. She's got money, and I'm betting he's not going to leave her alone as long as he thinks he can get some. Maybe he had to pay for that botched hit on me. Could be he's run out of thugs who'll work for free. Why don't we go to Dallas?"

Shellmire set down his glass. "Yeah. Let's try for tomorrow afternoon; spend the morning going over past cases, see if we can dredge up anybody else, figure out if we overlooked anything."

"Or anybody," Skip said. But she couldn't help feeling discouraged. "I brought a lot of stuff home. I'll work on that, and you can work at your office. We can meet at the airport."

He signaled for the bill. "I'll see if we can get a flight around three. Give us plenty of time to get to the airport."

"Sounds good."

She got home shortly after ten and felt a little shiver when she heard LeDoux's message on her voicemail. "You had a call from an Isaac James. Said to tell you he used to be the White Monk. A weirdo, am I right?"

Skip had to laugh. One of her favorite weirdos. You couldn't forget the White Monk even if he weren't the son of your worst enemy. She wondered briefly if his father had been in contact with him. *Not likely,* she thought, but hope sprang eternal. More likely, he was calling to commiserate about Angelgate.

She got ready to write down his phone number, but it wasn't on the message. Oh, well, she probably had it somewhere.

She looked it up and gave him a quick call but got only his voicemail. She found that, even though chances were about ninety percent that Jacomine wouldn't contact his son, couldn't possibly access his voicemail, she was a little queasy about leaving her home number. She put Isaac's number by the phone, to remind herself to call him first thing in the morning.

But she was tired from the trip to Angola and slept later than she'd intended. He'd evidently already left the house by the time she called.

Despite his mnemonic device with LeDoux, it hadn't been that long since she'd seen him. She knew he was in school at UNO, which could mean any kind of schedule in the world. Well, hell. She shrugged and decided to call back later, maybe drive by his house.

She called Steve, thinking it was odd that she hadn't heard from him. "Hi. It's me."

"Oh. Hi." Very distant.

"You don't sound so good."

"I just feel so helpless." No wonder, with the whole town thinking he was a thief. It was her fault, and she wasn't even free to tell him it was going to come right.

"Baby, you don't know the meaning of helpless. But it'll be okay, really. You've just got to have faith."

"Yeah. Yeah, I know. We just have to get through this. Somehow." It broke her heart to hear him sound so dejected.

"Listen," she said. "I've got to get out of here; I'm going out of town for a couple of days."

"Oh? Where?" Even more distant. She hadn't asked him to come with her; that had to hurt.

"Just . . . uh . . . I think I'm going to drive to the Gulf Coast. Try to cool out a little."

"Oh. Well, I've got the bug men coming today." The termite people.

"Steve, listen. We'll get through this. I just need a couple of days . . ."

"Sure. No matter what, Skip—"

"What?"

"I love you. I'm just a little down right now."

God, that must have cost him! "Me too, Steve. Let's just hold on to that."

She rang off, feeling disoriented and sad. She sat down to read the paper with her coffee, see if she could wake up a little before tackling her files. She didn't really want to face the fact that the Angola trip had been profoundly disappointing. She hadn't actually dared hope that any of Jacomine's followers had had a change of heart, and come to find out, the toughest hombre in the bunch had cracked. Or claimed he had. But still he couldn't tell her a damn thing.

Or claimed he couldn't.

When she really thought about it, what Menard had actually told her was to back off and flee for her life. Maybe he was a rattlesnake in a bunny suit, like Bettina. He looked sincere, sounded sincere. The best con men always did.

He had said unequivocally, *Daddy set you up.* Maybe he knew it for a fact.

Damn! She couldn't seem to catch a break. But maybe she had, and didn't know it. There was still the call from Isaac. She hadn't left a message the first time, thinking to try him every thirty minutes. But an hour had gone by. She phoned him again, and again got no answer. She said, "Isaac, it's Skip Langdon. Got your message; I'm around if you want to try me again." She left her home number and went over to see if there was anything new at the Big House.

Only Layne and Angel were home, Layne working in his study, and Angel curled up beside his desk. Being a puzzle maker by trade (which went over great with the kids), Layne did all his work at home.

"The news," he said "is large. Kenny actually succeeded in teaching Angel that trick. You know, jumping up to his shoulder."

"Hey, show me!"

"Nope. Only Kenny can do it. Right, girl?" The little dog wagged her tail and stared up at him, totally devoted. "We've come a long way, haven't we?"

Time was when he was so allergic to her, it almost ended his relationship with Jimmy Dee. But Kenny saved the day in a thoroughly unexpected way. Now Layne and Angel were inseparable, he being the human who was home the most.

"Enough about us and our domestic triumphs. How about you?" Layne asked. The uncles were understandably worried about her.

"Well, I'm . . . uh . . . 'working at home' until they figure out what to do with me." She hated lying to Layne.

"Skip, I'm just so sorry about all this." He'd said it before, the first night of Angelgate, but it was the kind of thing you couldn't get off your mind.

"Yeah. Me too. I know it's tough on the kids."

"Listen, you tried eating anything?"

"Maybe I should make myself some oatmeal."

"Ha! I can do better than that. I was about to whip up some *pain perdu*." The New Orleans version of French toast. "Sheila doesn't know it, but I'm barely managing to keep a recipe ahead of her in this cooking project we're doing. I practice when the kids are at school."

"Thanks, but I don't think I'm up to company right now. I'm just—" She was about to say she was going over some old files but thought even that might be saying too much.

He interpreted her hesitation as depression. "I understand."

She went back and picked up her phone to try Isaac again. There was a a message from Shellmire. "Skip, call me right away. It's urgent."

Damn! She'd only been gone a few minutes. She should have taken her cell phone. She punched in Shellmire's number, fingers fumbling. "Turner, it's Skip."

"Bad news, kid. Somebody's shot Isaac Jacomine."

She drew in her breath. *Hell! I should have known.*

"They took him to Charity."

She breathed again; he was alive. "How bad is it?"

"It doesn't look good. It's . . ." He didn't want to tell her, she could tell. "It's a head shot."

"Shit!"

"You said it. Look, I've got to go; I've got to wrestle your guys to let me assist."

"Wait a minute. Where are you?"

"On my way to his house—he was shot in the front yard."

"He must have been coming home. Did it just happen?"

"Few minutes ago. Why do you say that?"

"We've been playing phone tag. He was 'it.' I'm coming over,

Turner." She didn't give him a chance to answer and regretted having to do that; it meant she couldn't ask any of the questions on the tip of her tongue.

But she had to; she had no official place in this investigation, and Turner needed to manufacture a way to get her in. She'd given him a few minutes to think.

As she drove up, so did a young woman in a beat-up old car—a pretty woman but a little straight for Isaac, maybe not his girlfriend. She figured he'd go for a more Bohemian-looking babe. Ah, but on closer inspection she did have a tattoo on her arm. That was more like it.

"Hi," she said, as if she knew the girl. "You a friend of Isaac's?"

The girl looked terrified. "What's wrong? Why are these police cars here?"

Behind her, she heard someone call, "Terri? Terri, stay right there. He's all right. I'm coming right over to talk to you. Everything's all right, now. Just stay right there."

Skip turned to see who it was. "Pamela!" she cried, genuinely delighted to see the large woman who'd befriended Isaac so long and so often.

And at that, Pamela's face fell apart. She collapsed on Skip's shoulder. "Oh, Skip. Omigod, Skip! Those bastards." She was sobbing so hard she couldn't say any more.

The young woman—Terri, evidently—walked around Skip and the sobbing Pamela, so that she faced Skip. She'd apparently figured out that everything wasn't all right, despite Pamela's protestations. Her face was chalk-white, and she had a wild look in her eye. Skip said, "Terri? Sit down. Right there, right now. Put your head down."

That brought Pamela out of it. "Terri, I'm so sorry." she knelt and put her arm around the girl, who had—apparently gratefully—obeyed Skip's instructions. "Isaac's in the hospital. Someone, uh . . . it looks like someone . . . uh . . . someone shot him."

A huge wail escaped from Terri, clueing Skip in that she probably was Isaac's girlfriend. Seeing her on the sidewalk, so young and vulnerable, made her think of Isaac's niece. She said to Pamela, "Has anyone called Lovelace?" at which point Terri said, "How do you know Lovelace? Who are you?"

"I'm an old friend of Isaac's."

"Detective Skip Langdon," Pamela said. "She's the cop that almost got blown up by Isaac's father a few years ago. You remember that."

"Isaac's father?" the girl said. "Isaac's never mentioned his father."

Pamela and Skip looked at each other. "Oh, Jesus," the fat woman murmured. "Let's all three of us all go in for a cup of . . . Oh, shit! I was making tea for Isaac when he was . . . Oh, fuck!"

While she collected herself, Skip turned to Terri. "You okay now?"

The girl nodded, looking anything but.

"Let me help you up."

"You're a . . . cop?"

Skip gave her a smile she didn't feel—anything to put her at ease. "Yeah, but I've posed for Isaac; you might even have seen the picture."

Terri looked at her critically. "Yeah. I know you . . . sure, I've seen it many times."

Skip gave her another weak smile. She had to get to Shellmire. "Listen, go with Pamela and let her tell you what she knows. I'm going to see if I can get some more details."

Obediently, they went into Pamela's house, the thin young woman and the fat middle-aged one, united in their affection for Isaac. Skip had wondered often how Pamela and Isaac managed to strike up a friendship when one of them didn't even talk, but the truth was, Isaac's sweetness was obvious from the next parish. He got to everybody.

There were several district cars at the scene and one unmarked one, along with a couple of white crime lab vans. Some of the uniforms stared at her curiously, maybe recognizing her, maybe not; she didn't see anyone she knew. She didn't see Shellmire, thought he must be inside. She walked over and paused at the yellow tape already stretching around the scene.

One of the uniforms swaggered over. "Ma'am, this area's restricted."

She produced her badge. "I'm Detective Skip Langdon. Turner Shellmire inside?"

The man looked confused. "Aren't you . . . uh . . . ?"

He knew exactly who she was, but she didn't help him out. What was she supposed to say? *Yeah, but I'm innocent?* "Tell Shellmire I'm next door, will you?"

When she arrived in Pamela's cheerful kitchen, Terri was sitting at a wooden table Pamela had painted yellow, sipping hot tea, a rare commodity in New Orleans this time of year. Pamela was hovering, her brow creased. "Skip, Terri wants to know if Isaac has enemies."

Skip sat down at the table and put a hand over Terri's. "How long have y'all been going out?"

"A couple of months. Why?"

"And he never mentioned his father to you?"

Terri shook her head, clearly dreading what was about to come. "What's wrong? Is his dad in the mob or something?"

"No, it's not that. Have you ever heard of a man named Errol Jacomine?"

"Errol Jacomine! The guy who ran for mayor and then tried to blow up that little girl and everything? *That's Isaac's father?*"

Pamela muttered, "The good news is, they're not close."

Terri let out a short bark of mirthless laughter.

"You know about Lovelace?" Skip said. "That's why she and Isaac are so close. Her father got involved with her grandfather's crimes, which left Isaac and Lovelace pretty much the only family either of them has. They changed their names legally to 'James'."

"I thought Isaac's mother was a missionary."

"She is; she stays as far away from her ex-husband as she can."

Terri was clenching and unclenching her hands, trying to let out some of the tension. "Jacomine's killed a lot of people, right?"

Skip nodded.

"So, do you think he had some enemy or other who went after Isaac? Just because they're related?"

"Could be." It wasn't what she thought at all. "But here's what you should know: By tomorrow, the media are going to have the story about Jacomine's son being shot, and the cops are going to treat this like a very big deal; in other words, they probably won't think it's a random shooting . . ."

Terri interrupted. "Why are you saying 'they'? I thought you were a cop."

"It's not my investigation."

Terri stared at her. Stared long enough to figure out this was a face she'd seen before and not just in a painting. "Oh! You're the one, uh . . . you're the Cemetery Angel."

Yes, but I was set up! The words crowded to her lips, primed to shoot out like arrows. Skip pushed them back. She parted her lips in a tight, fake smile. "I'm afraid I'm persona non grata right now. But I still have contacts; I'll do whatever I can to help."

"Isaac told me about you."

"He did?"

"He didn't tell me you were a cop. He just talked about the woman in the picture as his friend. You know what he said about you? He said you were the bravest person he'd ever met."

Pamela nodded. "He adores Skip."

Terri bit her lip. "Damn, I wished I'd called him last night!"

Skip raised an eyebrow.

"I was out of town. I went out with a girlfriend, and I forgot to call him. I only remembered in the airport, and my cell phone was dead." She gulped, getting it all together. "I still could have called, but you know why I didn't? Did you know a long-distance call from a pay phone costs five dollars now? At least that one did. I wanted to save five dollars! I didn't call my boyfriend because of five crummy dollars." She was fighting tears. "What if he dies? I mean, what if I missed my one last chance to talk to him?"

Pamela came up behind Terri and put her hands on her shoulders. "He's not dying, you hear me? Monkie's tough."

Skip wasn't in the mood for melodrama. She stood up. "I'm going to go try to find Shellmire again. I'll be back."

She met him coming up Pamela's nicely edged walk, and he wasn't alone. With him was Sergeant Frank O'Rourke, NOPD, Skip's least-favorite colleague. In fact, it seemed a travesty even to call him a colleague; he was really more like an enemy. She'd been detailed to work with him on her first important case, long before she'd become a detective, and he'd hated her on sight. Some of the reasons eventually came to light. They had to do with his wife, also a police officer. But part of it was unexplainable, at least so far as Skip was concerned.

"He's just jealous, my dainty darling," Jimmy Dee used to say, but jealous of what she could never quite figure out.

O'Rourke spoke first: "Langdon, for Christ's sake! What the fuck you doin' here?"

She gave him one of the fake smiles she was specializing in today. "Nice to see you too, Frank. Hi, Turner. How're you doing?"

Shellmire grinned and saluted. O'Rourke said, "I axed you a question, goddammit."

"I'm visiting a friend."

"Ms. . . . uh . . . Fontenot? How the hell do you know her?"

"I met her through the victim, Isaac James." She was almost enjoying this. "I'll tell her you're here." She retraced her steps, calling Pamela to the door. "Pamela? Pamela, there's a detective and a real nice fed here to see you." Shellmire and O'Rourke followed Skip up the steps. "This is my good friend, Turner Shellmire of the FBI, and this is Frank O'Rourke." She let her voice drop on O'Rourke's name, so that the point she was making wouldn't be lost.

O'Rourke said, "The officers posted outside said you've got another guest, looked like someone who's a friend of James. Young lady who almost fainted?"

Terri came up behind Pamela, peering around her considerable shoulder. "Yes. I'm Terri Whittaker."

"Like to come in and talk to you both if you don't mind."

Pamela opened the door wide, as if she were having a party and they were the honored guests. "Of course. Have you talked to the hospital lately?"

"No, ma'am. It's too early; they'll still be working on him."

Terri was frantic. "I need to go soon. I have to be there for him."

"Oh," said Shellmire. "You were close?"

"We were dating."

O'Rourke muscled into the conversation. "Ms. Fontenot, you got any place where we can talk privately?"

"That won't be necessary. I have nothing to hide from my friends."

Skip caught Turner's eye, and she could have sworn he winked, ever so subtly; as for herself, she smirked openly.

Pamela said, "Why don't we all sit down?" She offered tea, but there were no takers. And then she brought a couple of folding chairs to accommodate everyone.

When they were seated in her tiny living room, Skip included, O'Rourke turned to Pamela. "Understand you saw the shooting."

"Yes. It was a drive-by. Isaac was on his way over to talk. I think he was worried about Terri. I went out on the porch to meet him, and just as he stepped off his porch and turned right toward my house, I heard the shot and saw him fall. I looked to see where the shot came from, but all I really saw was a dark car. It's kind of a blur."

"Oh, God." Terri looked guilt stricken. "I was supposed to call him from Dallas, and I forgot to. I did call this morning, but I didn't get him."

"Dallas? When were you in Dallas?"

"Last night. Just overnight. I went yesterday and I flew back this morning . . ." She stopped and covered her mouth. "Oh. Maybe that was why he was worried. My flight was cancelled. I was supposed to get back early, but I didn't make it until just now. I came straight from the airport."

"Was he expecting you?"

"No. But I felt guilty about not calling. And I was excited. I wanted to tell him about my trip."

"Your trip?" Shellmire asked. "What about your trip?"

"I went there to be on a TV show." Her shoulders heaved gently in a modest shrug. "And it was a big success."

"You an actress?"

"Oh, no, it's not that. It's kind of like a talk show: They take a person with a problem, and they help them. I had a problem with a bank, and not just some dispute, a really *bad* problem. And they got me a lawyer and everything. I was dying to tell Isaac about it."

O'Rourke spoke harshly. "Miss Whittaker, did you have plans to go to Dallas with Mr. James?"

"With Isaac? No. This wasn't a pleasure trip."

"Would he have surprised you by flying up and meeting you?"

"What are you talking about? He didn't even know the name of my hotel."

"Just wondering," O'Rourke said.

"Tell me," she said. "What the hell are you talking about?"

But of course he wasn't about to. It was the police way: to grab all the information they could and never give anything away. The interview went on for quite a while after that: Did Pamela get a plate number? (She hadn't.) Did either of the two women know of anyone who might want to kill Isaac? Anyone with a grudge? Any enemies? Did Isaac use drugs? Did he deal drugs? Had he seemed worried lately? Did he have any special problems?

Skip sat through it knowing she wasn't going to find out what she wanted to know till she could get Shellmire alone. When Shellmire and O'Rourke were done, she walked outside with them. "Somebody's got to call his mother and his niece. I know them both, Frank. Would you like me to do it?"

"Langdon, you aren't even supposed to be here." He turned away.

"Just trying to help. I'll just say good-bye to Pamela and Terri."

She went back in. "Either of you have Lovelace's number?"

"Sure," they said in unison.

"I'll get it," Pamela said. "I was going to call her as soon as y'all left."

"I'll be happy to do it for you."

Pamela looked relieved. "Thanks, Skip. You're a good friend."

Skip took the number and said good-bye. As soon as she was in her car, she called Shellmire on his cell phone. "Turner. What's this Dallas stuff?"

"Damnedest thing. Looks like Isaac was there last night. We found a used airline ticket in a wastebasket."

"Oh my God! Looks like our instincts were right." She looked at her watch. "Did you get us a flight?"

"Yeah, but we better follow up on this, maybe try to go later."

"Yeah. I'm going to call Lovelace and then talk to Terri again. There's got to be more on that Dallas thing. Maybe something'll come to her."

"Okay, I'll work it from this end. We're about to canvass the neighbors."

"Okay. One more thing. Can you make sure O'Rourke puts a guard on Isaac?"

"Will do."

Chapter EIGHTEEN

*T*he deal with Lobo was simple: half up front, half when the job was done. All Mr. Right had to do was transfer five thousand from a special account he kept under the name Thomas Washington into one Lobo mentioned (which he did by pay phone first thing in the morning), then sit back and chew his nails.

He wanted to pace. He needed to work off some energy. But Tracie appeared almost the minute he arrived at the studio: "Great response on the bank show. E-mail and phone calls pouring in."

He tried to smile. "Great. That's great news." His face wouldn't work.

Tracie's sunny countenance turned dark. "Still feeling under the weather? Hang on, I'll get you another Vicodin."

"No thanks. No. It's the after-show letdown, I guess. I'll be fine."
Once again, he tried out the smile.

"You sure? You really don't seem . . ."

"Just leave me alone, goddammit!" Then, seeing her hurt look, he
said, "I just haven't had coffee yet."

And then, of course, she had to get him some. He felt like throwing it in her ugly face. But he took a minute to compose himself.
When she came back in, he said, "Tracie, I'm sorry I snapped at you.
I'm going to be honest with you. I hate it when people bring their
problems to the office, but I just couldn't help it this morning. My
wife's in the hospital."

The girl looked alarmed. "Oh. That fall she took—"

"No, no, it wasn't that at all. She woke up hemorrhaging in the
middle of the night."

"Omigod, a miscarriage! I'm just so, so sorry." She was quiet a
minute, as if mourning the Wrights' unborn child, and then she
brightened. "But Karen's young and healthy. Y'all can always try
again."

His paranoia kicked in instantly. "How the hell do you know
what it was?"

"I just thought . . . isn't that usually what that means—'hem-
morhaging'?"

"I don't know." This time he executed a successful grin; he could
feel it looking right. "Men are clueless. Listen, thank you for your
concern."

"You're welcome."

The damn woman finally left. She wanted him, just like they all
did—hero-worshipped him. She'd be as easy to manage as Bettina if
he'd just quit losing it.

She blew him away when she said "miscarriage," though. He
wasn't lying when he said he was clueless. He'd thought cancer; he'd
thought everything you could think when they found the bed soaked
with blood, even internal injuries caused by his knocking her around.

The idea of a miscarriage hadn't occurred to him until the doctor told him.

Well, hell. That was a *good* thing. Last thing he wanted right now was another damn kid. But it struck him as ironic that he was about to lose two in one day.

And to his amazement, putting out a contract on his own kid was a lot more nerve-wracking than the expectant-father thing. He was going out of his skull. He paced. He drummed his fingers. He tried to work on his next show.

He thought the top of his head was coming off.

Finally, he took a long lunch break that consisted mostly of a long, long drive. Once safely on the road, he dug out his newest cell phone and called Lobo. "You get the money?"

"Send me the second half."

"What do you mean? Our deal was half up front."

"It's done."

The phone went dead.

Just like that. *It's done.* That was how the scumbag announced that David's son was dead.

Mr. Right was actually saddened by it, a fact that surprised him. He'd never really had a relationship with Isaac, and now he never would. He'd had a chance at another kid too, one he never even knew about. For some reason, he even felt regret about that one.

He hurried back to the office and turned on the television in his office. It was on CNN, on the little super: "Son of Errol Jacomine gunned down in front of his house."

"Errol Jacomine" with no I.D. at all. That was how famous he was. There ought to be satisfaction in that, but there wasn't. He wasn't yet famous for the right things—and he never would be, under his own name. Not till after he died. He thought about that for a moment, wandered off on a tangent, and then he saw a reporter talking to a New Orleans cop. He turned up the volume. "Can you tell us the extent of his injuries, Sergeant O'Rourke?"

"All I can say at this time is that he remains in a coma."

Coma! the bastard said. *A fucking coma!*

His mother-fucking worthless son wasn't even dead, and he'd paid that asshole Lobo five thousand dollars.

Oh shit oh shit oh shit, he definitely wasn't paying the rest. He got up and kicked his desk. Kicked a chair and knocked it over. Kicked another.

Then he heard running footsteps, and there was that damn Tracie again, peeking in like she thought she was his guardian angel or something.

He beat her to the punch. "It's okay, Tracie, I know I'm acting like a child. I'm just worried about Karen, that's all."

She nodded, looking frightened, and ducked out again, closing the door fast. He wondered if he looked like a wild man. He phoned her extension and left a message. "I'm really sorry for acting like a jackass. I think I better take the rest of the day off before I do something to embarrass myself."

He was out of there like a shot. He hadn't even gotten the car out of the garage before he'd called Lobo and left his number pager. It took an hour for the man to call back. "Yeah? You transfer the money?"

Mr. Right shouted, *"Kill him, you asshole! Goddammit, kill him!"* He threw the cell phone out the window onto the freeway. The car behind him screeched trying not to hit it.

S kip waited till she got home to call Lovelace, hoping O'Rourke would get to her first, but evidently she hadn't waited long enough. As soon as the girl heard her name, she said, "Isaac. Omigod, What's happened?"

Skip wondered if her somber tone of voice had said it all, or if Lovelace had reason to fear for her uncle. She said, "It's bad, Lovelace. He's alive, but it's bad. Some bastard shot him in front of his house."

"Oh, shit." She paused to catch her breath. Skip heard a couple of gulps as she fought tears. "How bad?" she finally managed.

"It's a head injury. He's in a coma."

"Oh, shit. Omigod. Did they get the guy? He just called me this morning. She said he might have seen his father. Could my grandfather have done this?"

Seen his father? Skip stood up and paced, her blood racing. This was big. This was the key to it all. She tried to calm down, to make her voice soothing. "We don't know anything yet. He's going to need you, though. Can you come?"

"Oh, yeah. Sure." Lovelace sounded dazed, as if traveling hadn't occurred to her yet. "I'll get on a plane as soon as I can."

"I'll pick you up at the airport. Listen, did he say where he saw his father?"

"Well." She drew out the word and hesitated afterward. "You know Isaac, Skip. He wasn't even sure he saw him. He was heavy into OCD mode."

"I thought he was medicated these days."

"I don't know . . . maybe he got off the meds. But if the OCD ever went away, it came back—with a vengeance. He kept saying he couldn't be sure."

"Well, maybe he really wasn't sure."

"He even said it was the OCD. Listen, I've got to call the airlines." Panic was starting to rise in her voice.

"Lovelace, wait. Did he call you, or did you call?"

"He did. He told me to be extra careful for a few days."

"Did he give you any idea why the time limit?"

"To figure out if the guy was actually Errol, I guess. I don't really know." The line went quiet; she was apparently trying to remember the conversation. "Oh, I know! I asked if his father was in New Orleans, and Isaac said *he* wasn't in New Orleans. But he kind of slid off my question."

"So he didn't say where the guy was?"

"No."

"Okay. Is this a cell phone?"

"Yes. Do you have one?"

Skip gave Lovelace her number and made her promise to call

when she had an arrival time. When she hung up, she debated whether or not to call O'Rourke. No need, she decided. He was perfectly capable of asking the same questions she had—so long as he had the sense to think of them.

She called Terri instead. "Listen, I need to come over right now."

"I'm not home. I'm at the hospital."

"Charity?" Charity Hospital was where gunshot victims were almost always sent.

"Yes."

"Good. I'll come there. Any word?"

"He's still in the accident room."

She found Terri twisting a tissue in the waiting room. She'd changed into torn jeans and a tank top with a skull on the front—an outfit strangely at odds with her neat haircut, as was the tattoo it showed. "How is he?"

Terri shrugged. "No news. I'm just . . . waiting."

"Look, Terri, I spoke to Lovelace. She's flying in, by the way."

"Oh! Does she need a ride from the airport?"

"Maybe. I'll let you know. She told me something really interesting. She said Isaac called her this morning and said he might have seen his father."

"You mean Errol Jacomine?" Skip realized she still hadn't taken it in that Jacomine was really his father.

She only nodded. "And that isn't all. I think he flew to Dallas last night."

"But—"

Skip nodded again, to indicate she'd already gone where Terri was headed. "There was enough time. He could have flown there and back this morning. What time was the show?"

"Seven o'clock. But why? Why the hell would he go to Dallas?"

"Let's think it through. I see you went home and changed. Had he left any voice mails for you?"

Terri barked a laugh. "About ten of them: 'Terri, it's Isaac. Guess you're not there yet.' Pretty much like that."

"Nothing else?"

"No." Terri quit playing with the tissue and folded her hands, sitting quietly for a moment. "He sounded scared, though. I might not have thought that if I didn't know what I do now. But I think it's right; he might have been scared."

"When were the calls made?"

"Oh." She jerked her head, startled. "I didn't pay attention, but I'm sure it says on the voice mail." She looked at her hands. "I saved them. I wanted them. In case . . ."

In case he dies, Skip thought. She understood. She'd have done the same thing in Terri's place.

"You can't think of any reason he'd have gone to Dallas?"

"Not unless it had something to do with me. But that's crazy; I was coming right back home. And, anyway, he didn't know where to find me; I'd left my hotel room, and I hadn't called him."

"Listen, I'm going to ask you to focus on something."

"Sure." Terri closed her eyes.

Skip's cell phone rang. It was Lovelace, giving her flight number and arrival time, late that evening. Skip said, "Good. I might have to work overtime. If I can't make it, okay if Terri picks you up?"

"Sure. Is she okay?"

"She's here. We're in the hospital, waiting."

"Can I talk to her?"

It was another few minutes before Skip had Terri back. "Okay, here's my question. I want you to think carefully. What, exactly, did you say on that show?"

"You think it had something to do with that?"

"If he'd seen his father, and he thought you were in danger, it might have been something you said. Did you say anything about Jacomine?"

She shrugged, as if the idea were preposterous. "No. Why would I?"

"Anything about Isaac?"

Terri closed her eyes again and thought. Finally she opened them and shook her head. "I don't know. It's hard to remember what I said on and off the air."

"You talked about Isaac off the air?"

"Just to the host. He interviewed me before the show."

"The host."

Terri nodded.

"Was anyone else in the room?"

"No. Why?"

The back of Skip's neck was beginning to prickle. It felt as if the temperature in the room had gone down twenty degrees. "What does the host look like?"

"Oh! Handsome. Really attractive in an older-man kind of way. I mean, he grows on you. At first I thought he was kind of smarmy, but that's just because he's so nice. He's one of the few people I've ever met that really has charisma, you know?"

Skip was feeling chilled to the bone. "Terri. Could he be the man Isaac saw?"

Terri did a literal double take. "David Wright? Are you kidding? No way. Jacomine's a dried-up ratty-looking little turd who talks like a redneck—I saw him on TV a million times when he ran for mayor. David Wright's educated; he has this really cultured voice, almost British. You can't change the way you speak."

Skip was acutely disappointed. "I guess not."

"And believe me, there's no physical resemblance whatsoever. I mean none. I told you, this guy's really kind of cool. He has this very worldly gray hair and . . . I don't know, nice clothes and a sort of TV *presence*. Jacomine had a weak chin, remember that?"

"All too vividly." She sighed. "Okay. Let's start over. I want you to tell me every word of the conversation you had, both on- and off-camera."

Again, Terri closed her eyes. "Well, I told him about my troubles and my work, and how I have my own business." She filled in the details, digressing briefly to complain that the host had stolen her lines. "He asked me if I had a boyfriend and . . . no, it wasn't exactly that. He said, 'I hope someone nice takes you out to dinner sometime.' And I said my boyfriend was also a starving artist, so he cooked instead."

Skip couldn't sit still any more. She stood up and pretended to stretch. "Did you say Isaac's name?"

"Let me think. Yeah. Yeah, I did. First name only, though. Isaac."

That would be enough, Skip thought. An artist named Isaac.

"And then he started asking me about Isaac." She stopped talking. "Oh."

"What?"

"Oh, shit. He made me tell him about Isaac's art and define 'outsider art' . . . oh, *shit*! I said The White Monk. I actually used that name. That would identify him, right?"

"You're sure you didn't do that on the air?"

"Positive because . . . oh, *shit*!"

"What?"

"The minute I said that phrase, he blew me off. Called Tracie, the producer, to come take me back to the green room." She sat up straight and took handfuls of her hair in her hands. "Yes! And she was very taken aback. Asked him if everything was all right."

Skip's mind was racing. This was it, had to be it. And yet . . .

"All that's suspicious as hell, right? The only thing is, he wasn't Errol Jacomine. Absolutely wasn't. That's all there was to it. I mean, you'd have to see him to know what I mean." She stopped dead. "Hey! Hey, you can see him. You absolutely can. I've got a tape of the show."

Skip was practically salivating. "Terri. I have to see that tape. I can't overstress the importance. I need to see it now. I know you think you can't leave Isaac . . ." She stopped, trying to find a delicate way to insist that Terri play the tape for her immediately.

But Terri was shaking her head and rummaging in her backpack. "Oh, no problem. Why don't I just give you the key, and you go to my place and watch it?"

"You sure?" Skip said, holding out her hand for the key. But the question was a Southernism; if Terri'd changed her mind, she'd have grabbed the key out of her hand. "What's your address?"

Skip broke every traffic law on the books getting to Terri's and nearly broke the door getting in, she was so impatient. *Poor kid,* she thought, rifling Terri's unpacked duffel, as instructed. Terri had practically no furniture, and what she had appeared to have been picked up at garage sales. Her protestations of poverty were no joke. However, she did have a VCR, a gift, she'd explained, from her parents. Skip found the tape under a pouf of soiled clothing, popped it into the machine, and settled on the double mattress that evidently served both as bed and daybed. It had a faded purple cover on it, along with a collection of mismatched throw pillows.

The show's theme music came up, David Wright was introduced. Skip braced herself—and let out her breath with disappointment. No way that nice-looking man could be Errol Jacomine, who looked like a weasel at best. She felt cheated. She had to be missing something. Maybe it was something Terri said in the interview. She turned up the volume.

"Hello, I'm David Wright," said the star, "and tonight we have an extremely relevant show, relevant to each of us who has a bank account, that is. And that's all of us, isn't it?" The audience applauded. "I mean, if we're lucky enough." He spoke the last part with modesty and sympathy, not ridicule.

Terri was right: His accent was slightly British, nothing at all like Errol Jacomine's redneck twang. The man was actually somewhat likable. She wouldn't go so far as "charismatic," but she wasn't repelled by him, and that alone indicated he wasn't Jacomine.

She took a good look at the man's neck—Jacomine's neck was stringy and sinewy, old before its time. Could you change a person's neck?

She knew the answer to that: Sure you could. This guy's neck didn't look anything like Jacomine's. Did anything else? Yes! The widow's peak. Jacomine had worn his hair combed to the side, evidently to tame it; had hidden the birthmark, though anyone who looked closely could see it.

Mr. Right wore his hair combed back, so that it looked luxuriant. And it was gray. Jacomine's hadn't been; could he have dyed his hair? *Certainly*, she thought, or, more likely, he could have let it go natural. But that didn't prove anything.

She watched the way the man moved his jaw—kind of clipped and impatient. She saw the *shut-up* look that popped into his eyes when the attention went to Terri. But, hell, he was a TV personality; that was what they were like.

She paused the machine, got up to get herself a drink of water, and when she looked again, she saw something. What, she wasn't exactly sure, just something that made her go alert again. A gesture? *Maybe*, she thought.

She closed her eyes and listened, and the more she listened, the more she was sure she'd heard the voice before. A person could change his accent, but he couldn't really change his voice.

She started to get excited. There were plenty of Jacomine recordings; she could get voiceprint analysis. *Stop, fool*, she said to herself. *Voiceprint, hell! If that's Jacomine, he just put out a contract on his son. You've got to move faster than that.*

Mr. Right was saying, "Now you probably think your bank is there to serve you. But, after hearing about Ms. Whittaker's problem, we looked into it a little bit. And ladies and gentlemen, serving you is about as far as you can get from the whole story. Yes, indeed, these pillars of the financial community have bigger fish to fry by far. Oh, yes, much much bigger fish to fry."

Skip froze. She'd heard that before, that voice, saying those words. "Bigger fish to fry" was one of Jacomine's favorite expressions. She stopped the tape, rewound, and listened again with her eyes closed.

Her scalp prickled. It was Jacomine.

She called Shellmire. "Turner, Where are you?"

"I'm back at my office."

"Anything new?"

"Nothing."

"Well, I've got something. I'm bringing you a tape."

She sped to FBI headquarters, once again managing not to get a ticket. She played the tape for Shellmire, watching him watch Mr. Right. She saw him go through what she'd experienced, moving from utter disbelief to wary alertness to excitement. It wasn't the fish phrase that did it to him, it was a growing familiarity. "See the way he shrugs? Kind of bucking his head up first? I always thought he did that when he was lying—a 'tell,' you know what I mean?"

Skip nodded, suprised she'd never noticed.

"I'm going to go get some more tapes."

He brought an armload of tapes of Jacomine, being interviewed, giving campaign speeches, even giving a sermon. The more he and Skip compared, the more excited they got.

Skip thought she was going to go nuts; it was like having an itchy trigger finger. "Look, let's go to the airport, get the first flight out to Dallas."

"My thought exactly. Just let me set some stuff up with the Dallas guys, have some agents there discreetly check out the employment record he gave the station, maybe his references . . ."

Skip stopped him in mid-sentence. "Okay, okay, fine. Meanwhile, I'm going to the airport. I'll rent a car and find a hotel, meet you when you get there."

"Skip, you've got to calm down. You're going to do some damage if you don't watch out."

"Right." She was standing now. "See you there."

Maybe she could calm down on the plane. Meditate or something.

Chapter *NINETEEN*

$\mathcal{D}$avid Wright had shaken off his absurd panic, had understood that was probably all it was. It was a mistake not to have whacked Isaac months ago, but now the problem was under control. The glitch, he should say; that was all it was.

There was another now. Karen had taken her miscarriage unreasonably hard. She was practically a vegetable. Two days after her miscarriage, David got up early and made coffee, toast, and scrambled eggs for his wife. They were the first scrambled eggs he'd ever made in his whole life, but he figured any fool could scramble eggs. And he was right. As far as he could tell, they were no different from anybody else's scrambled eggs.

He made a plate for Karen and put it on a tray, on which he'd already placed a rose from their garden. He took it into their bedroom and shook her gently.

"Come on, sleeping beauty. Breakfast time."

All day yesterday, so far as he knew, she'd done nothing but sleep. She opened her eyes. "What is it?"

"Look. I made you some breakfast."

She made a kind of grimace, though she may have meant it as a smile. "Thanks."

But she didn't budge.

"Karen, now, come on. You can't stay in bed the rest of your life. Come on and eat now." He could barely believe the words coming out of his mouth. No more than he could believe what he'd just been doing for half an hour. Earl Errol David Jackson Jacomine Wright had never made so much as a sandwich for himself, much less for a woman. And here he was, begging.

Karen didn't answer. It was like she was in a coma or something. "Come on, baby, just a little bit." He held the toast to her mouth. Her eyes had closed again, and she didn't even notice.

"Karen!" He spoke sharply. "You can't do this."

She didn't answer.

He left the room to keep from hitting her. That was one thing he absolutely could not do. It was bad enough what she'd told her parents, though her father, thank God, had the sense to believe him instead of his bimbo daughter, but it could not, under any circumstances, happen again.

What had to happen was, he had to win her back. He came back and sat on the edge of the bed, took her hand.

To his surprise, she opened her eyes, stretched, and sat up. "David, this is sweet of you."

"I need my girl back." He looked into her WASP-blue eyes, and almost believed what he was about to say. "Karen, I'm nothing without you."

She picked up the coffee. "I'll be okay." She patted his hand. "Thanks to Dr. Wright."

"You promise you'll get dressed and do something fun today?"

She nodded. "Cross my heart and hope to die." Unlike most women, who slept in T-shirts these days (if you believed what you saw in the movies), Karen still wore lacy nightgowns. She had on a white one, and the lace against her white shoulders was unbearably lovely. He absolutely couldn't believe he'd ended up with a woman like this. The thing was to keep her.

He left fifteen minutes late, but with a terrific feeling of accomplishment. He was pulling it off. He felt elated. His life was coming together again: Karen was coming out of her coma, Isaac was still in his, and *Mr. Right* had had great response to the banking show.

Walking through to his office, he noticed that Tracie actually had on a dress. Was it his imagination or was she dressing better these days? He mimed tipping his hat. "Looking lovely this morning."

She gave him a wave that was actually a little finger-wiggle. Definitely seductive. "Got a great idea," she said. "How about overmedication of elders? I've got this woman whose mother's on fifteen different prescription drugs. Poor thing's so out of it her speech is slurred."

"Can we get the mother on the show?"

"Whoo! That might be too much, don't you think?"

"How about a tape? We could go to her house and talk to her in the comfort of her own bed."

"You are so *smart*, David Wright. Sure. Let's do it. I left a memo for you."

Tracie was falling for him; it was ever more obvious. She'd have to be kept at bay. He absolutely could not mess up this thing with Karen. Did Ronald Reagan mess around with bimbos? Hell, no. That was for losers like Clinton. He, Mr. Right, must be above reproach.

He wasn't in his office twenty minutes when Tracie busted in, not even bothering to knock. He glared at her over the rims of his reading glasses, a trick he'd seen in movies, and spoke in his most supercilious pseudo-British. "Ms. Hesler. Do we need to talk about privacy?"

She ignored him. "David, listen." He noticed for the first time how pale she was, how her hands were flying aimlessly through the air, working off nervous energy. "I need to talk to you." She closed the door behind her. "Something bad's going down. Two feds just walked into the station manager's office."

"What the hell are you talking about?"

"It's all right, it's all right." She patted the air in front of his chest, not touching him. "It can't affect us directly—unless we get fired. The bank must have leaned on somebody. I've seen it before. Every time you have a really controversial story, this kind of thing happens."

Mr. Right was no longer listening. His attention had gone ten minutes into the future. His panic flashed back for a second and then disappeared. One thing about it, panic was an illusion at worst, a warning at best. When the worst had happened, the very worst that could possibly happen, it was replaced almost instantly by an icy calm.

He knew at once that there was no way this could be coincidental. Isaac had awakened and ratted him out. No doubt in his mind. Well, there was his contingency plan. He cracked the door and looked around the corner. Nobody was there.

He said to Tracie, "Well, they're damn well not going to get away with it. I'm going in there and bust this little party up."

"You can't do that!"

"I damn well can, and I will. Stay here, and I'll let you know what's going on. Here." He held out a folder. "Been working on a strategy for next season. Look it over, will you? Be back in a few." He strode out purposefully, and after a few steps, reversed his direction, slipped out the back door, and drove away. He figured he had about twenty minutes till anyone noticed he was missing. It was still a long way from that to connecting David Wright to Errol Jacomine. His television career might or might not be over; there was still half a chance Tracie was right and the feds were there for some relatively benign shakedown, but he didn't think so.

He drove to Highland Park Mall, near one of his banks, the one with the Thomas Washington account. He parked his car in the lot, leaving his sports jacket on the seat. He opened the trunk, extracted a baseball cap, shades, and tan windbreaker, all of which he put on, making sure the cap covered his now-famous gray hair. And then he pulled out a canvas briefcase, the kind meant to carry a laptop. This one contained his life—lives, actually. He'd taken the precaution of having a number of documents forged at once. You never knew when one persona was going to have to die and another was going to be needed. There was one other thing in the case—a gun.

He went into the bank, looking warily around. A woman employee caught his eye, and he saw the flash of recognition. She started toward him happily, smiling and waving, and he knew she wanted to tell him what a fan she was, to be the person who helped Mr. Right that fine day. He absolutely could not have that encounter; Mr. Right could not be connected to Thomas Washington. He turned and fled, pretending he hadn't noticed her.

He walked briskly to the nearest men's room, which was by no means near, and called a cab. He waited in a stall for fifteen minutes, then slowly, warily, ventured out.

He gave the cab an address a block from Rosemarie Owens' house and walked blithely up to her door. But on the way he phoned her. "Morning, ma'am. UPS. I'm at the service entrance."

She had a back door, but not a service entrance. The message was a prearranged signal, in code in case her phone was tapped. It was only to be used in cases of direst emergency.

*R*osemarie was trying to keep it together, just keep her heart inside her chest. She'd spent a lot of time thinking about what to do if this moment came, and she was somewhat prepared: She had a gun. She made her voice casual. "Mr. Right. As I live and breathe."

"Rosemarie, you're a sight for sore eyes." She was wearing a pair of flowered capris and a white sleeveless sweater-thing. She was his age, but in her own opinion, she could be thirty years younger.

"How's your wife?" she said.

"Guess that means you're not in the mood for a little slap-and-tickle."

She put her finger to her lips, walked outside and closed the door, took his arm, and begin to circle the garden.

"Hubby's home, I guess? Or hubby-facsimile."

"Earl, Earl, how the hell am I going to explain you?"

"You had the phones swept lately?"

"Once a week, just like we agreed. Yesterday was the day. On the lam, are you?" She smiled when she said it, letting her surgically enhanced eyes crinkle prettily. The whole thing was to appear cool as a creek bed, as if the entire Dallas police department could descend on her and she'd ask them in for tea.

"Afraid so, old girl." The "old girl" thing was something he'd learned from his English voice coach. "Possible situation unfolding."

"Oh?"

"Feds at the office. I went out the back door."

"Damn! I was so hoping that rotten cable station was finally going to turn a profit." She sighed. "I guess all good things must come to an end. I've got to hand it to you, babycakes. *Mr. Right* was a great idea, and you were the perfect Mr. Right."

"Rosemarie, if you don't mind, we're a little exposed out here."

Good. He'd blinked first.

"I'm just waiting for the maid to go home. Sistine takes a few minutes to pack up. How do you like that name? Sistine. Too much, isn't it?"

"Quit trying to distract me, and let's think."

The front door thwacked shut. "Ah. She's left. But Todd's in there watching TV in his den and getting stoned. With any luck he won't even come out, but if he does . . ."

"Ah, yes. The boy toy. Well if he does, I'm the best friend of your late husband. Bit of bad luck—unfortunate investment, wife bankrupting me, little wager that went awry."

She burst out laughing, ignoring his obvious urgency to get in the house. "Why, Eliza Dolittle, you *are* a quick study." When her eyes uncrinkled, she made them hard as marbles. "Is that your little way of asking me for money?"

"Rosemarie, for Christ's sake, I have plenty of money. Can we go inside, please?"

She shrugged. "Come in." But she spoke coldly, stripping all the amusement, all the welcoming banter from her manner.

He stepped into her restaurant-sized kitchen, and she saw him taking in its polished wood floors and gleaming granite counters, its little lights under the cabinets, its lavish bowl of fruit. Earl said, "In case Todd comes out, let me shave first. My head, I mean. He figures out who I am—I mean, even the Mr. Right part—we're both going down."

She sat down on a barstool. "Have it your way, darling. Use the downstairs guest room."

"Well? Aren't you going to show me?" She'd forgotten he didn't know where it was.

"I suppose." She got up languidly, as if her fate wasn't inextricably tied to his, and walked him leisurely through the house. She'd taken care to make it look like the manor to which she certainly hadn't been born. Instead of being lavish, her house was comfortable. It had hardwood floors and good, well-kept furniture with plenty of personal touches, like a piano covered with photographs, and there were books (though she never read) and flowers.

She led Earl into a room with a four-poster bed covered with a red toile print. The wallpaper matched the bed cover. Light streamed in the windows; French doors opened to the backyard they'd just strolled. The pool was steps away. A very soothing room.

"Nice," he said.

"Last I heard," Rosemarie remarked, "you were doing pretty well yourself." She rummaged in the bathroom and handed him an electric razor. "Go to it, kid."

She thought she was finally freaking him. He was starting to sweat.

He made his voice seductive, clearly trying to match her *sangfroid*. "Why don't you do it for me?"

"A bit intimate for a married woman, don't you think?"

"You're not legally married to that twinky, are you? Even you aren't that crazy."

She laughed genuinely again, the way she had when she called him Eliza Dolittle. She was still in the bathroom, where she'd gone to look for the razor. "Of course not, darling. It makes it easier for him socially." She paused. "Not that he hasn't asked."

He stepped close to her, deliberately invading her space. She knew he could feel her breasts, and her breathing. He grabbed the hand that held the razor and lifted it above her head, against the wall, pinning her. "We wouldn't want to endanger that lovely money, would we?"

"Let me go, Earl." She made her voice low and threatening.

"That lovely money you wouldn't have if it weren't for me. You haven't forgotten that, have you?"

"What the hell do you want?" She couldn't keep the bite out of her voice.

He shoved her into the wall, stepping back, but retaining a threatening distance. His voice was smooth and uncaring. "How about a shave and a haircut?"

"Sit down," she said, indicating a little vanity bench.

He sat, staring into the mirror. She stood behind him, also staring at their tableau. They would have made a lovely couple if not for the fury on their faces.

She cooled her face down and saw him see her do it. Not good. She rummaged in a drawer and came up with scissors. "Let's cut it first." How about stabbing? she wondered. Could she do it? It might be her best bet. She'd hidden the gun on her way to answer the door, but she needed time to retrieve it.

"Whatever the lady wishes." The proximity of their bodies, the heat from the mirror lights, maybe even the anger did something that might work well for her. He was starting to get turned on. She could feel his breathing change.

"Take off your shirt," she said.

Daily workouts had been part of his transformation. She knew how proud he was of his torso. For full dramatic effect, he pulled the shirt over his head instead of unbuttoning it.

Rosemarie pretended not to notice. She took it and stomped it under her feet. "To catch the hair," she explained. And she began cutting his hair with an energetic focus that might also, it occurred to her, be described as violent.

She hadn't gotten where she was by being a shrinking violet, and nobody knew that better than Earl. She saw a light sweat break out on his upper lip.

She wasn't quite sure when she'd have a better moment. She had the scissors. All she had to do was . . . what? Bury the blade in his back? Or maybe his ribs.

"Too warm?" she said. "Let me turn up the AC."

"Ever the perfect hostess."

How much pressure would it take to kill him?

"Ow! Do you have to pull it so hard?"

She didn't answer. Maybe she was hurting him on purpose. She didn't think she could stab him. Shoot, yes. But thinking of that blade and how it would feel, cutting through him . . . no. Uh-uh. She couldn't do it.

His head was now covered with a steel-gray cap of quarter-inch hair. *Not a bad look,* she thought. *But way too Mr. Right for today.* She picked up the razor.

He grabbed for it. "Never mind. I'll do this part."

Letting it go, she leaned languidly against a wall. "Oh, really? I thought you were kind of enjoying the attention."

He threw the razor down and pinned her once again, giving her a whiff of his sweat. Before she could move, he kissed her, and she let herself melt against him, thinking maybe the tiny submission would reassure him. For the moment, it seemed to work. He let her go. "Mmm. Yeah."

She smiled, lifting an eyebrow in a bemused, slightly superior way. "Later, maybe?"

He fired up the razor and buzzed it over his skull. "What about the semi-hubby?"

"He's probably passed out in front of the TV."

"What do you see in him, anyway?'

"I never have had good taste in men."

"Except for that last husband of yours." The one who had left her the lovely money. "And of course your first."

"Not everybody marries Mr. Right the first time around."

"Including you, baby. We've come a long way since then."

He put the razor down and turned to her. "What do you think?"

"I think you're about to go a lot farther." She wasn't sure what she meant by it, just hoped it would give him the idea to get the hell out of her life.

He said, "I meant the look."

"Very hip. Come on out where I can see you." She led him into the guest room proper, lounged on the bed, and gave him the onceover. "Too bad there's no time to grow a goatee or something."

He shrugged. "I'll be okay with shades and a cap. I need clothes."

She nodded, licking her lips. Good. Maybe an excuse to get the gun. Todd's clothes wouldn't fit him, but she didn't have to mention that.

"And money," he said.

"Oh?"

There it was. Finally on the table. "Look, I've got plenty under another name. But I can't go in the bank. I mean I did, and someone recognized me; so I split and came here."

"I don't believe you."

"For Christ's sake, Rosemarie, give me the phone and the number of your bank account. I'll have it transferred right now. I need cash; Mr. Right's dead. I've got to get the hell out of here or I am too."

"What about Karen?"

"Karen." He stood stock-still, as if he hadn't even thought of her. Finally, he said, "Don't you get it, Rosemarie? I'm Number Two on the FBI'S Most Wanted list. I've got to get out of the country. Today."

"That's all Karen means to you? What about if it were us?" She stretched back on the pillows. He sat down on the bed and caressed her cheek. She curled her body close to him.

"Come with me," he said.

"Where?"

"Wherever you like. I have passports to burn—that's one little one precaution I took. What I don't have is cash."

"Neither do I." She snuggled closer.

He swung a leg over, straddling her, and pinned her shoulders. "Goddammmit, find some," he shouted.

Almost instantly, Rosemarie heard running. Todd. He must have heard the shout. Damn. He didn't know where the gun was and wouldn't think to bring it if he did. He was bigger than most men in Texas; he didn't think in terms of guns.

Earl rolled off Rosemarie, grabbed for his briefcase, unsnapped the outer pocket, and extracted his own gun. She tried to stand, but he grabbed her arm. When Todd came into the room, at a dead trot, Earl was holding Rosemarie's elbow with one hand and the gun with the other, pointing at the door. "Whoa, boy. Slow down," he said.

That was the last thing Todd was about to do. Poor Earl didn't know him at all. One reason she'd picked him was that he was part bodyguard. He was about six-five, had shoulders like a table, and the long hair of a blue-collar worker. Earl rolled off the bed; Todd crashed onto it.

Earl rocked back, training the gun on the big man. "Take it easy, now. Let's all just catch our breath here."

Todd said, "What the hell is going on here?" He pronounced it "hay-ull." "You okay, darlin'?"

Rosemarie stood up and smoothed down her flowered capris. "He didn't rape me, if that's what you mean."

She realized Todd didn't recognize him. Maybe the shaved head worked better than she thought.

Earl was swiveling his head, looking at Rosemarie, then Todd, then back again. She could tell he was getting furious, the way he always had when he didn't get his way. "*Rosemarie, you whore!*" he shouted.

Okay, it was now or never. She looked at Todd, caught his eye, and inclined her chin very, very slightly, giving the go-ahead sign. Todd turned to Earl, but he wasn't quick enough. As if in a dream, she saw her ex-husband steadying his weapon. Todd leapt on him. Earl fired.

Todd fell backward, blood spurting. Rosemarie screamed.

Earl fired again and then he seized her and pounded her face with the butt of the gun.

She screamed again, knowing it was over, the game she was playing, unable to feel a thing for Todd, even to worry about her face; just terrified, knowing Earl was going to kill her. But he pulled back before he hurt her too badly. Why, she didn't know. Maybe he needed her for something. With Earl, it was always that. She had to convince him she was his devoted slave in about a millisecond. But she knew he'd seen her signal Todd.

"You killed him," she said, putting all the shock she could muster into her voice.

"Oh, come on, Dragon Lady. One of us was going to die; you set it up like that, didn't you? Only the plan was, it was going to be me."

"Earl, look at me." He obeyed, as she knew he would. "Earl, I love you, baby. You were my first love. And my only love . . ." She was pleading for her life.

"And your best love, kid. Because I got rid of that surplus husband of yours that time, enabling us both to be rich for the rest of our lives." In spite of herself, she felt something like hatred cross her face. "Yeah, baby." he said. "We've been over this territory. What's yours is mine."

She looked at Todd's body lying on her bed, blood seeping into the mattress, the carpet, the pretty, red-figured cover. Jail looked kind of attractive at the moment; she could easily end up like he had.

She said, "Of course, sweetheart. Let's get out of the country."

Perhaps he'd try to use her as a hostage. That might be good; if she got out alive, she'd be a victim. The whole thing was to buy time.

Chapter TWENTY

*A*fter her husband had left for work (quite a long while after) Karen got up and dressed for the first time in two days—in black pants and white T-shirt—and moved out to the garden to think.

She sat in an Adirondack chair, staring at the annuals she'd so laboriously and lovingly planted that spring. The jasmine was just starting to bloom. The smell of it was slightly nauseating.

She'd thought maybe she was pregnant the night she had the talk with Carol Ann; sitting there talking about how she wanted a baby, she'd been thinking, *and maybe I'm carrying one.* And so, the day of the show, she went and got a home pregnancy kit. She tested positive, only about ten hours before she lost the baby. She thought she was over her crying, but when she thought of that now, silent tears ran down her face. It hurt to remember how excited she was, how she had first fallen into a reverie and decorated the baby's room in her head, then thought how much fun it would be to go to the show and surprise her husband with the news. That was the whole point of the visit. That was what she had come for, and he'd hit her and killed their baby. Ever since then, those two facts had been her whole world. Now she was working on moving out the other side.

The question was this: Could she forgive him? The promised "details at eleven" had never been provided.

But anyone deserved a second chance, right?

Fool me once, shame on you. Fool me twice, shame on me. The old saying echoed in her brain. The complicated thing about it was that David hadn't fooled her twice. Charlie Bennett had fooled her the first time.

Then there's my father, she thought. He'd fooled her more than once. What she wondered was, was there any man she could trust? Other women trusted men. Why not Karen? David really had been under a lot of pressure, and he really had acted in anger. And she loved him, and she wanted to be with him.

Or at any rate, there was so much about being with him that she wanted. She was Mrs. Right. Wife of an up-and-coming local celeb. There was pride in that. Even if future First Lady was only a pipe dream.

And she had this nice house, and security, and love, and the possibility of a baby. . . . She teared up. *But not the baby I was carrying two days ago.*

Everywhere she turned, it was like that. Good, then bad; bad, then good.

I need to work it through, she thought.

She looked at her watch. Two hours had passed. Without even making the decision to do so, she went back into the house, found a yoga tape, slipped it into the VCR, and changed into workout clothes.

The tape began with breathing. And after the breathing, what the teacher called "The Potted Palm" series, sitting stretches: bending, grabbing for her toes . . .

And after that, standing stretches. She had her butt high in the air, deep in Downward Facing Dog, Mr. Right and her problem forgotten, nothing in the world on her mind but pushing up with her thigh muscles, shifting the weight to the outsides of her feet, trying, as always, to get her heels a little closer to the ground, when the phone rang. She ignored it.

In a moment, someone knocked on the door. She ignored that too. And then the knock became louder, more insistent, like the police knock you hear on television.

She righted herself, frowning, trying to figure out who on earth it could be. The phone rang again. Automatically, she answered it. "Just a minute, there's someone at the door . . ."

The voice on the phone said, "FBI. Come out with your hands up."

She heard a noise like an explosion and then running footsteps. And there in her bedroom were a phalanx of men in riot gear, pointing guns at her.

"Don't forget to breathe," the yoga master said. The tape was still running.

She dropped the phone, screaming. *This wasn't her life.*

"Don't move or I'll blow your fucking head off." She couldn't really be hearing that.

Someone grabbed her, stuck a gun in her back, pulled her hands behind her. She felt cold metal on her wrists.

Some of the men were pointing their guns inanely at the television. Others swarmed the house, opening doors, stomping . . .

Her captor marched her into the street, where her neighbors had started to gather. They shoved her into a car. "All right, where is he?"

She was light-headed. Her heart thumped. She was crying. "Where is who?" she screamed.

One of the soldiers—feds, she knew, but they looked like soldiers—walked up to the car, and said, "It's clear."

"Where's your husband?" her captor asked.

"My husband? He's at work," she said stupidly. "Why? What's this about?"

The man who'd cuffed her read her her rights.

They drove her to the federal building, took her inside, took off the handcuffs, and left her in a room, alone. She was too numb even to cry.

After a long while, two men came into the room, with a woman, a tall woman with wild, curly hair. They didn't bother to introduce themselves. The woman looked familiar.

One of the men said, "Mrs. David Wright?"

She knew she didn't have to answer, but maybe things would go easier if she did. Still, she was furious. "That's a matter of record," she snapped.

"Very well. We'd like to ask you some questions, Mrs. Wright. Before we start, I'm going to read you your rights."

"Somebody already did."

"We're going to do it again."

Oh, God, she didn't want to listen again. She could ask for a lawyer right away and end the session, but she was out of her mind with anxiety—absolutely couldn't sit there till a lawyer arrived. When the second man had finished, she snapped again, "Would you mind telling me what this is all about?"

"Sure. It's about harboring a fugitive."

"What fugitive? What are you talking about? We've never even had a houseguest."

One of the men spoke kindly. He was a rumpled man, a little soft-looking, not what she imagined an FBI agent would look like. "Are you aware that your husband uses an alias?

"You mean Mr. Right? The name he uses on television?"

The other man sneered.

"No, David Wright. Are you aware of his other name?"

"What other name?"

"Errol," the nice one said.

"Errol? Errol Wright?"

"Errol Jacomine."

"Errol Jacomine?" She came suddenly alert. "I know who that is. That's the guy from New Orleans who . . . uh . . ." She couldn't think what he'd done, exactly. "Wait a minute! Isn't he a serial killer or something?" She looked at the woman, and saw on her face a look of such misery, such tragedy, that she had to look away. She knew that it was for her. It was not the woman's misery; it was hers. The woman was suffering on her account. And at that moment she began to grasp what had happened to her.

She needed to say it: "You think that my husband is Errol Jacomine?" She was aware that Jacomine had never been caught.

The woman looked as if she were about to cry.

"How long have you known him?"

She shrugged self-consciously, suddenly feeling stupid and gullible. "Almost a year. We were married two months ago. We met on his show." The words seemed to march out of her mouth on their own, like some strange little parade. Two months with a perfect stranger? She looked at the woman's face and she thought about the night he hit her, the way his eyes had narrowed, become mean little slits. Animal eyes. At the time, she'd thought, *This is a stranger.* Thought it, and at the same time not allowed herself to think it.

She looked at the woman's face, and she knew that the face didn't lie. "Omigod," she said. "Omigod."

Remember to breathe, she told herself.

"I don't know his people. He said he was the last of his family." And then a ray of hope shot through her. "No, wait. He has pictures. Of him and Rosemarie Owens's husband . . . I forget his first name. He can't be Errol Jacomine; he was in Dallas all that time . . . when . . . uh . . . He can't be Errol Jacomine. He knows people."

"What people?"

She searched her memory. "Rosemarie! She's a very well-known woman in town. My family knows her. He was in her crowd."

"Shit!" someone said, one of the men, maybe both of them.

Karen was remembering that she and David had been to Owens's house, the two of them, and that David knew everyone there. He was no stranger; he had friends, he had bona fides. It was all a big mistake. She was about to say more, but no one was interested anymore. The other three were exchanging glances. The bad cop—the unrumpled one—got up and left the room.

"What's happening?" she said.

For the first time, the woman spoke. "I'm so sorry for what happened to you."

That confused her. "What happened to me? You know about the baby?"

The two of them looked straight at her, pointedly didn't look at each other. The man said, "What about the baby, Mrs. Wright?"

Karen spoke to the woman. "How do you know about that?"

"Talk to me, Mrs. Wright," the man said, and she had a sudden, terrible fear that he was going to send the woman away.

Karen said, "Who are you? Who are you both?"

The man said, "Special Agent Turner Shellmire. And this is Detective Skip Langdon, New Orleans Police Department. She's here in an unofficial capacity only."

Langdon. This was why the woman's face was familiar. Her picture was on Karen's husband's bulletin board, with a thumbtack through the nose. He hated her. Maybe she was framing him for all this. Maybe that explained it. But she was sympathetic, Karen could sense it. No cop was *that* good an actor.

"I can't talk to you?" she said.

"You need to talk to Agent Shellmire."

Karen had been distracted by those few moments away from the issue, taken a few moments to collect herself. She breathed deeply. These people had broken into her house, handcuffed her, falsely imprisoned her, and bullied her. And her father was one of the most influential men in Dallas.

Not that she could trust him.

But she'd have to. Surely he'd come down and get her out of this.

Suddenly she had a better idea. "What if I want to talk to you?" she said to the woman.

"You need to talk to Agent Shellmire," Langdon repeated.

That was unacceptable. These people couldn't do this to her unless they arrested her. She blurted, "Am I under arrest or am I free to go?"

They both shifted uncomfortably. No one answered. Finally, Shellmire spoke. "Excuse us for a moment." They left her alone again.

They haven't decided, she realized. *They've gone to talk about whether they believe me.*

They were back in ten minutes. She stood up without giving them a chance to speak. "I'm going to leave now unless you arrest me."

Shellmire said, "Sit down, please."

"You're not letting me go?" She couldn't believe it.

"We're arresting you." Just like that. No explanation, no nothing.

"For what? I haven't done anything."

"For harboring a fugitive."

Tears of fury flowed into her eyes. She kept her voice even. "I'd like to talk to my attorney."

"Very well," Shellmire said.

She phoned her uncle, State Senator Guy McLean.

Chapter TWENTY-ONE

$\mathcal{I}$saac couldn't move. He was in a strange bed. Nothing felt right. In fact, something hurt; he just wasn't sure what. And in his dream, there was something awful happening. Something very scary that only he could stop. It was a really unpleasant dream, one of those disconcerting early-morning dreams. He stirred and tried to go back under. Instead, his mind drifted, and came to focus: Terri. This was no dream. He had to save Terri.

His eyes flipped open.

"Isaac! Omigod, you're back!" It was Lovelace who was squealing, not Terri. She wore denim shorts and a halter T-shirt that covered only half her midriff.

"You had your navel pierced." He was riveted.

"Omigod, you're fine!" She bent over his bed to hug him, jarring something that really hurt. "I've got to get a nurse in here." She fiddled with some mechanism on his bed.

He realized for the first time that he was in a hospital room. It was his head that hurt. He tried wiggling his toes and fingers; things seemed to work okay.

"What happened?" he said, like someone in an old movie, but Lovelace had no time to answer before the room was overrun with doctors and nurses welcoming him back to the world with their own little agendas.

First a nurse came in and then a doctor, a female neurosurgery resident. They told him where he was—Charity Hospital in New Orleans—and what had happened—that he had a gunshot wound to the head, a grazing wound, he was very lucky, but there was a slight skull fracture and he was probably going to have something called "postconcussion syndrome."

He couldn't follow very well after the word *gunshot*. "Someone shot me?"

"You don't remember? Well, that's very normal; there's nearly always memory loss with a concussion. You may also feel groggy or confused, have headaches; you could even hallucinate."

"I think I'm hallucinating now."

Lovelace laughed, but the doctor said "No, you're not." All business.

Who the hell had shot him?

The doctor asked him a series of questions about the year and the season, the date, the state, the city, and other things. She asked him to remember three words for three minutes, and, absurdly, to count backward in serial sevens from one hundred.

That one he failed immediately. "Ninety-two," he said.

"Ninety-three," Lovelace chimed in, eliciting a glare from the doctor.

There were other questions, including a strange little task that involved folding paper, and a reflex check and a neurological exam.

Except for the sevens, he felt he did pretty well. "So I'm not brain-damaged?" He finally got up the nerve to touch his head and felt bandages.

"The initial tests show no substantial structural damage, but your postconcussion symptoms could be quite variable."

God, she was a stick. He looked at Lovelace. "Well, the hell with that. Am I bald?"

Uptight as she was, the doctor chortled. Lovelace howled, literally laughed till she cried. Brain-damaged or not, Isaac knew the joke was nowhere near that funny, knew his niece was just relieved that he was coherent. He wished the two of them would shut up because he had a much more important question to ask. "Is Terri okay?" he said. They kept right on laughing, didn't even hear him.

He tried it louder, raising his voice a little. "Hello out there. Is Terri okay?"

They wound down. Lovelace said, "Sure. She sat up all night with you. She's just gone home to rest for a while. Let's call her."

"Ummm. Just a second. How did I get here?"

Both of the women looked dismayed. "Someone shot you," the doctor began.

"In New Orleans?"

She nodded patiently. "Remember? We're at Charity Hospital in New Orleans."

"I remember something about Dallas." He couldn't remember anything much, except driving aimlessly, looking for Terri. "I dreamed Terri was in terrible trouble. You sure she's okay?"

Lovelace said, "Yeah, she's fine. But I think you were in Dallas. The cops found a used plane ticket at your house. Do you remember why you went there?"

*W*hen he couldn't get Langdon, he'd driven to the airport and caught the first plane to Dallas.

Not until he was airborne did he start planning what to do. He couldn't go to the Dallas cops. He'd already considered that. They'd think he was crazy, and precious time would be lost.

He rented a car and drove to the Bluebonnet Motor Lodge and thought, *No wonder she left; anybody would.* Which made him think she might be all right. But why hadn't she called?

The desk clerk who'd been busy when he called, a Hispanic-looking man in his forties, also couldn't remember a Terri Whittaker, which nearly drove Isaac crazy; Terri had only been there three hours ago, and she wasn't exactly forgettable. Finally, he pulled out his wallet and set it on the counter, feeling slightly cheesy. He had no clue how to offer a bribe without being offensive. He finally settled on "Hey, I know what might help. She was here for the *Mr. Right* show; they would have booked her."

The clerk beamed as if he'd had a revelation. "Oh, that lady. Sure, I remember her. Miss Hesler booked her. She lef' in a hurry."

Isaac felt a vein twitch in his neck. "A hurry?" He tried to speak nonchalantly.

"A lady come for her. She call from the lobby, and all of a sudden your frien', Miss . . ."

"Whittaker."

"Miss Whittaker come, lookin' around her, kind of, like she just packed and she think she's forgotten something."

"Was the lady Miss Hesler?"

"No. I never seen her before."

"What can you remember about her?"

"Nice car."

"Nice *car*?" Isaac was close to losing it. Who remembered people by their cars?

"Brand-new Lexus."

"Okay, brand-new Lexus. What color Lexus?"

The man thought about it. "I didn' notice."

He figured the damn Lexus was white—they all seemed to be. But he sure as hell didn't know anybody who drove one, and didn't see how Terri could. So the question was this: Was the Lexus woman dangerous? He had to assume so; so far as he knew, Terri had no friends or acquaintances in Dallas.

He needed Langdon. But how to get her? He didn't have either her home or pager number with him. He left a message at the Third District.

He ended up driving the streets with his cell phone on, hoping Terri would phone, hoping to catch a glimpse of her somewhere, somehow. "Go to Deep Ellum," the desk clerk said. "That's where the action is." He went; saw nothing. Drove more; saw more nothing. Eventually, he found himself a hotel only slightly better than the Bluebonnet.

He slept for a few hours, waking up early and thinking what a foolish thing he'd done, flying to Dallas to try to find Terri. He should have waited till morning, and now it *was* morning and he wasn't even in New Orleans where he damn well ought to be. He tried her again, and again didn't get her. He got up and headed to the airport; he'd made a return reservation for nine A.M.

On the way, he called Langdon at her office again, leaving another message, begging them to track her down and have her call him. Having no idea if they would or not.

Mentally, he ticked off avenues he'd followed, trying to decide if he'd left out anything. *Lovelace!* he thought. He hadn't called his niece. The thought filled him with panic. Anxiously, he dialed her number.

"Hi, Uncle Isaac." She must have caller I.D.

He could hardly get his breath. "Lovelace. I saw a man who looked like my father. It can't be him, but I can't be sure it's not." There was a tiny trickle of calculation in what he was saying, the way he was saying it.

She picked up on his peculiar phrasing. "Isaac, your OCD is back, isn't it? Oh, Isaac, I'm so sorry."

"Lovelace, I can't be sure. It might be him and it might not." This was one of the manifestations of his OCD: When it was in full force, he couldn't be sure of certain things. "Can you be extra careful for a few days? I'll call back when I can be sure."

"Are you all right? Is the man in New Orleans?"

"Of course, I'm all right. I'm not even in New Orleans. Listen, you shouldn't have to suffer for this problem; it's my problem. I'm really sorry I frightened you, but I just . . . can't be sure."

He hung up sweating, thinking, *I really blew that one.* The last thing he wanted to do was terrify her, but he'd had to talk to her, to make sure she was where she was supposed to be, if nothing else.

Before he was even off the plane, Isaac accessed his messages. Terri's cheerful voice chirped out at him: "Hi, Isaac, I'm really sorry I forgot to call. I had dinner with an old friend from New Orleans . . ." Here she laughed. ". . . dinner and a whole lot of drinks. Somehow, it just slipped my mind. Everything went great with the show. See you later this morning."

He'd heard Terri's voice; he knew she was fine. But he couldn't be *sure.* Okay, he was obsessing; he knew it. But he also knew it when he washed his hands twenty times a day and checked ten times to make sure he'd locked the door. It wasn't something he could help. He hardly even bothered apologizing to himself—just took a taxi home, jumped on his scooter, and sped to her house.

But she wasn't home. He was deeply disappointed. Her mail had come and hadn't been collected. That argued that she hadn't gotten back yet. He could wait for her. Should he? On the other hand, she could have gone to the store or something, maybe out to lunch.

He obsessed so long about it, it actually constituted waiting. His cell phone battery was dangerously low, but he didn't dare leave his phone off. And finally, inevitably, he ran out of juice.

That made his decision: Nothing to do but go home. He half-hoped she'd be there, and he was disappointed when he didn't see her car. The minute he walked in, he began cleaning. He cleaned the already spotless kitchen; he swept the floor, carefully counting each stroke; he stripped the bed and put the linens in the washing machine. Then and only then did he permit himself a shower. He ran it till the hot water gave out, and still he stayed in. His fingers and toes were like raisins—ice-cold raisins—by the time he stepped out.

He wished he had something white to dress in. The White

Monk, his former persona, had dressed only in white, and it was what he needed now, but he'd thrown out all his white to begin his new life.

He picked up his broom and started sweeping again. When he'd swept the requisite number of strokes, he called Terri again and then his next-door neighbor, Pamela, his best friend in the world. "You haven't seen Terri, have you?"

"No, why?

"Pamela, I think I'm going crazy."

"Oh, really?" she sighed. "So who'd notice, here in the Bywater?" She paused, and Isaac knew he was supposed to laugh, but he couldn't force even a chuckle.

"Okay, okay. I'll dig out my grandmother's secret recipe for sanity-inducing tea—she was a witch, you know. I'm putting on the kettle now. Meet you at the door in thirty."

Good old Pamela! He knew she meant seconds, not minutes, and that was so typical of her: always there for him in situations a neighbor should never have to go through. And those situations had occurred at a time he'd never even spoken to her! It was during the period of his famous vow of silence, which hadn't fazed her even slightly. She wasn't kidding about sanity standards in the neighborhood.

Sighing, he put his newly charged cell phone in his pocket (in case Terri called) and picked up a tissue to open the door. When his OCD was in full flower, he couldn't touch doorknobs.

Stepping onto his porch, he glanced toward Pamela's, saw that she was on her porch, waved briefly, and started down his steps.

*T*he young doctor slipped out of the room, probably to find some equipment to torture him with.

He said to Lovelace, "I went to Dallas because Terri disappeared on me. I thought my father might . . . oh! You don't know."

His niece looked sad for some reason, as if he'd said something that reminded her of a tragedy.

"What's wrong? You told me Terri was okay."

Lovelace sat down on the bed. "Isaac. Terri's fine. It's you that got shot in the head."

He didn't see what she was getting at. By the time he'd put it together, the resident was back with another doctor. "I *am* brain-damaged," he said, just as they walked in.

They didn't have all the answers he needed, but they did have one: He'd only been out about a day. Not too bad, considering. He made a stab at more info: "Hey, do you guys know who my father is?"

The resident, the young woman, pursed her lips. "Look, you're going to get the best care we can give you whether your daddy's the governor or the garbageman."

Isaac was mortified. But it must mean his father hadn't been arrested.

When he was alone with Lovelace again, he said, "My father tried to kill me, right?"

She looked at something out the window, then turned back to him before she spoke. "If he didn't, it's a hell of a coincidence. Here's all I know: Skip Langdon was supposed to pick me up at the airport last night, but she ended up sending Terri because she had to take a sudden trip."

"To Dallas?" Isaac whispered.

Lovelace shrugged in frustration. "Terri thinks so. Skip asked her if Mr. Right could be your father . . ."

"Terri knows about my father?"

"Isaac, for Christ's sake! That's the least of your worries now. Terri gave Skip a tape of the show, and then Skip suddenly had to go somewhere. Terri and I watched the tape last night."

"It's him, isn't it?"

Lovelace hesitated. "I don't know; I just don't know. I don't know him well enough to say."

"It's him, Lovelace."

"Okay, let's say it is. So here's what we think happened. He catches on that Terri's your girlfriend because of what she told him, and he knows you'll be watching the show. And if you see the show, you'll know it's him."

"Which I did. So then what?"

"Then he gets someone to try to kill you."

"Who?"

She shrugged, as if she answered the question every day.

"Terri and I think it has to be someone from the past. From the church."

"If there's anyone left. Maybe he hired someone." He adjusted the bed so he could sit up.

Lovelace put a hand on his. "You know what? It doesn't matter. You've got to face something, Uncle dear."

"You mean that my own father tried to kill me? It could have been a lot worse. It could have been *your* father."

His brother Daniel.

Chapter TWENTY-TWO

By the time Shellmire caught up with Skip in Dallas, their prey was gone. Getting there ahead of him had only meant waiting for him in a hotel room, but in a way, that was good. She used the time to calm down, and, given the personality of Paul Hargett, the special agent in charge, she needed all the serenity she could muster.

Hargett was a distinguished-looking guy, graying, in his early fifties, with a tight set around the mouth. He had been in Dallas less than a year, having recently been transferred from Philadelphia. He looked like a man who didn't care either for heat or for Texans, a man driven by nightmares about the grassy knoll and Waco, terrified that something equally nasty would happen on his watch.

Shellmire had faced a major fight to get Skip in on the anti-Jacomine effort. As a general rule, the feds didn't like letting anyone in, much less some "disgraced" cop from another city, and Hargett was guarding his fiefdom like it was the Vatican. The easiest thing for Shellmire would have been to cave.

But he and Skip had worked this case too long together. He knew for a fact that she knew more about Jacomine than any living person in law enforcement. He probably knew, as well, that this was a situation in which fine points weren't really going to be important. But he had a well-developed sense of fair play. He talked her in as a consultant. The thing that tipped it was the debacle at the television station.

Hargett was in a fury, mad at himself, probably. Until then, he claimed he'd proceeded cautiously, knowing he couldn't just go and arrest a popular television personality on her say-so and Shellmire's. He had to be absolutely sure; he had to set a trap that Jacomine couldn't wiggle out of, but he'd disappeared before the trap was set. In reality, Skip figured, he probably hadn't taken the Jacomine sighting all that seriously.

But, boy, he was making up for lost time now, sending those goons out to Jacomine's house. He had that "poor little wife," as he called her, at the office already.

"Good," Skip said. "Don't let her go for any reason." She spoke way too strongly for diplomacy's sake, especially under the circumstances. She had reasons for saying it—two, at least—but Hargett didn't ask what they were. He just set his mouth a little tighter and added a frown.

Seeing her mistake, she tried to get him back. "Look, you can't overestimate this man. Whatever you think is the worst-case scenario, he'll up the ante. And he loves kidnapping; he has a history of kidnapping whoever he wants to spend time with—along with whoever he wants to kill." She hesitated. There was something she needed to get on the table, but she didn't want to insult the man. "Like Rosemarie Owens," she said. He only grunted.

He might be blowing her off, but then again, he might not have read the file. "You know he kidnapped her once before," she added, thinking it said everything he needed to hear without bludgeoning him. And then she thought, *Hell, bludgeon him.* "I'm sure you've already sent someone to her house, but if you haven't, my advice is to do it immediately." The man's balls were not her problem; Jacomine was.

He didn't go with them into the interview room, only introduced them quickly to Agent Stirling Pennell and admonished her, "Officer Langdon, you're sitting in on the interview as an observer only. Please refrain from participating."

Pennell said to Shellmire, "We might be barking up the wrong tree here. I don't think the wife had a clue."

Shellmire sighed. "Gotta start somewhere," and Pennell led them into the room where she waited.

She wasn't at all what Skip imagined: someone on whom Jacomine could prey; someone beaten down, poor, vulnerable; someone looking for a hero—even Owens (who was nothing like that now) had been only thirteen when they met. This woman was young, but she looked way too bright to fall for Jacomine's routine, too privileged to need him. She was pretty, in a Texas kind of way— the blonde hair, nicely styled, the blue eyes, the manicured nails—but she wore no makeup, and that was unusual for a suburban Southern woman, even one who planned to spend the day at home. That could indicate something was wrong, that she was depressed.

That could be good. Maybe her marriage wasn't going well.

Ideally, the way Skip would have conducted the interview would have been to start there, to find out what their connection was, what hooks he had in her.

And then it came out they'd met on the show; there it was. Karen wouldn't have been on the show if everything had been going well in her life. She did fit the profile, at least in one way. Usually they were blind-loyal as well. If this one was, they had to deprogram her, bombard her with tapes and newspaper articles, evidence of his crimes. Or maybe it didn't matter; maybe Jacomine had already left the country.

And then Karen had said the magic words, "Rosemarie Owens." Skip could see by Pennell's face that they surprised him, made him realize his boss was new in town, might not know who she was, Jacomine's history with her. He left the room.

The next few minutes were as excruciating as any Skip had ever spent—imprisoned in a room with a witness she was forbidden to speak to, a potentially excellent witness, and almost worse, not knowing if Hargett had thought to cover Owens's house. The impotence was unbearable.

Things went rapidly downhill from there. The witness got tough. And then it turned out that not only had Hargett failed to pick up on the Owens connection, he apparently hadn't realized that pretty little Mrs. Wright came from a family with juice, a family that was going to be outraged at her treatment.

Her lawyer—whose name was Scott Frentz—came barreling in like Wyatt Earp, having apparently first called a judge. He wanted her released now, this minute. Skip bit her lip: *No!* She figured Karen for a dupe, but she desperately wanted her in jail to protect her from Jacomine.

She must have made an involuntary sound. Pennell glared. He wanted her out of there; it was obvious. He said to Frentz, "I don't care if the whole McLean dynasty comes down here and *pickets*; do you realize who this man is? The most dangerous criminal in the country is who! Number Two on the FBI's Most Wanted List!"

"Her family wants her home with them."

It wasn't a negotiation; it was just a way of wasting time. Karen was going to jail all right, that was decided, but only for minutes. Juice had already been applied. Frentz had her bonded out almost before the cell door slammed. Evidently, her uncle the state senator had something going on a federal level. The only thing left to do was keep her under surveillance.

Skip could have spat. And then Hargett called her into his office. "Agent Pennell feels you were a disruption during the interview."

"With all due respect, Agent Hargett, I followed my instructions to the letter. The witness did ask to speak to me, and, honestly, I think we'd all have been better served if she'd been permitted to."

It wasn't tactful, but he was throwing her out anyhow; she was sick of tactful. "As we would have if you'd sent someone immediately to Owens's house."

A dangerous flush spread over his face; Skip hoped she'd never have to work with him again. She'd burned her bridges. "We won't be needing your services any longer, Officer Langdon."

She said, "Yes, you will," rose from her chair, and left.

He'd need her services, and he was going to get them, whether he wanted to or not. She wasn't going to be in on any FBI action, but now she could damn well talk to Karen.

Shellmire was waiting for her outside Hargett's office. "He threw me off the case."

"Shit!"

There wasn't time for more before Hargett opened his door and shouted, "Shellmire, get in here!"

Feeling slightly dazed by the speed at which things were going, Skip left the building—to make Hargett happy—and pulled out her phone on the sidewalk.

Her only shot was Karen. She figured if Senator McLean had come riding so handsomely to her rescue, he'd probably know where she was going. She phoned his office and asked for him.

"Who may I say is calling, Ma'am?"

"My name's Skip Langdon. I'm a police officer who met his niece this morning."

"Just a moment."

To her surprise, she was connected almost immediately with the senator. "Officer Langdon. I've heard about you. Karen likes you; that ass Hargett hates you."

She laughed. "Well, that was quick. Actually I didn't get a chance to talk to Karen before Hargett threw me out, which he did, five minutes ago. Listen, Senator, she's been through hell, and there's a good chance it's about to get worse. I'm unofficial here, but I think I can honestly say I know the man she married better than anybody else in America; I need to talk to her, and she needs to talk to me. Any chance you can put us in touch?"

"Up to her," he said. "You got a cell phone? This is a hell of a thing. *Hell* of a thing." She pictured a handsome, white-haired man shaking his head; for all she knew he was as ugly as Jacomine before the doctors.

She gave him her number, rang off, and waited—but not for long. Karen called back almost immediately.

"Officer Langdon! I . . ."

"Call me Skip."

"Skip. I'm dying to talk to you. I think you know things—about me."

"You mean about what you've been through?"

"What I'm going through."

"Look, can I see you?"

"Please. Yes. Please. I'm at my uncle's house. Just get me a pack of cigarettes on the way. Ultralights."

"What brand?"

"Any brand." She gave Skip the address. "I feel so . . . I don't know. Like I'm running on empty."

Skip was about to reholster her phone when it rang. It was Shellmire: "Bad news, Skip. They found a body at Owens's house. No sign of either Jacomine or Owens. We're trying to figure out if any of her cars are missing."

"Whose body, for Christ's sake?"

"Young white male, shot in the chest. No I.D. yet."

"He'll go after Karen next."

"Yeah, I know. I'll lean on Hargett."

"Fat lot of good that'll do."

"Skip, for what it's worth, he made a big mistake dumping you. You're getting a rotten deal all around."

"Yeah, well, it's not my day, but at least I'm doing better than that poor bastard at Owens's house."

But not a hell of a lot better, she thought.

*K*aren hated that throw-your-weight-around thing the McLeans always did. Until today, that is. Until today.

When they tell you your husband's America's Most Wanted and

threaten to lock you up, you'll do what you have to. Even form an alliance with a fat, pink-faced, perspiring fool like Scottie Frentz. *He must be happy now,* she thought. He'd been trying to date her for years. Now he'd had the chance to be her rescuing knight.

Still, she had to give him his due. He'd made short work of the overbearing, asshole feds who wouldn't even let her talk to a cop in the same room with them! What the hell was up with that? Was it some kind of sexism? It seemed to her like the worst form of petty bureaucratism.

Of course, even that couldn't keep her out of jail. Being processed was the most humiliating thing she'd ever experienced—and she'd gotten the short form. Scottie said they could have drawn it out for hours.

She was unexpectedly angry. It felt good. Actually, it felt great. And she had David Wright to thank for it. She was getting her second wind now, thinking things through, and there was a hell of a lot to think about. She wouldn't have felt like this before she went on his show and got a new life and married him and learned by his fine example—learned to be strong, to care about people who needed caring for. She would have just been some scared little tangle of raw ganglia, afraid to open her mouth, afraid of the feds, afraid of the McLeans, afraid of her ex-husband, just plain scared of everything. And hopeless.

Right now she had hope—hope that her life as she knew it wasn't over, that David Wright wasn't Public Enemy Number One, that there was all some big mistake, and that she could untangle the whole thing—with the use of McLean clout if she needed it. So far it was standing her in good stead.

Her uncle must have made some high-level phone call—maybe to the governor or something—because she really didn't think that fat fool Scottie Frentz was capable of getting her out of that place by himself. He'd also made her agree to stay with him and Carol Ann, to keep an eye on her, maybe. She'd insisted on going home to get clothes, however, and for more than one reason.

Scottie sat happily on her sofa, reading magazines and drinking coffee, while she packed a suitcase. That left her all the leeway in the world to include the emergency cell phone her husband had given her when they were first married. *"If anything ever happens, turn it on."*

"Anything like what?"

"If we get separated."

"You mean like a terrorist attack or something?"

"Baby, don't even think about that! But take the phone, will you? I'll feel better."

So what did that mean? That he was Errol Jacomine and he foresaw this? In that case, what did he expect from her? That she was going to go running into the arms of a serial killer? Or whatever he was. Not exactly a serial killer, she was pretty sure, if that was the sort of person who tortured women before filleting them. But he'd killed people. Jacomine had killed people.

She kept shoes in boxes on a shelf in her closet, piled three deep, and in one of the boxes, in one of the shoes, was the cell phone. She hadn't thought about it since she put it there.

When she got to the guest room of her uncle's house, she turned it on and plugged the charger in. And then, unhappily, she called her parents, fortunately getting only the machine.

She was all alone in her uncle and aunt's house and feeling odd. Not sad, not angry, but strangely excited. And kind of coolly distant, like she couldn't really *feel* what was going on in her life, like she was watching a movie or something. If she had to put a name to the way she felt, "curious" might be as close as she could get. Curious and on edge, waiting for the other shoe to drop. She was dying for a cigarette, though she hadn't had one since she first started to work for the station. She'd started smoking when the thing happened with Charlie and hadn't stopped until it was over.

She was about to go get a pack when the call from the cop came. Skip Langdon was one woman she wanted to talk to. She asked her to bring the damn cigarettes. She showered and changed clothes, to give herself something to do, taking the cell phone into the bathroom with her. She didn't know if David would even remember it.

Having dressed in jeans and a tank top and little slide sandals, she tidied the pillows in the living room and in so doing, noticed something odd: a car on the street that shouldn't be there.

Her heart jumped into her throat. *Okay,* she thought, *if they want me, why don't they just come get me? And who was "they"? It sure wasn't her husband out there.*

She phoned her uncle (who was being exceptionally nice to her), but he couldn't help because she didn't have the plate number. And he said whatever she did, don't go outside to get it; he'd call the Dallas cops to come check it out.

Skip Langdon got there while she was making iced tea, carrying a plastic Walgreen's bag. Karen was all hopped up. "Check out that car. Somebody's watching me."

Karen watched the cop make a show of studying the car, finally saying, "I wouldn't worry about it," and that was how she found out the feds had her under surveillance. Why the hell else would the cop tell her not to worry?

"Are you alone here?" the cop said.

Karen nodded. "Want some iced tea?"

Skip said, "Thanks. Are you scared?"

Karen considered. *Probably not,* she thought, *if that car was only feds.* "No, she said finally. "I'm just . . . discombobulated. Did you bring the cigarettes?"

"Sure." The cop handed over the pack. She followed her into the kitchen and took a glass of tea, saving Karen the trouble of fixing a tray. They went back and sat on the newly tidied sofa in the living room, Karen bringing an ashtray she'd found in the pantry.

She lit up, feeling guilty.

"It must be an awful thing," the cop said, "having your world come apart like this."

Karen shrugged. "I guess I'm in denial. I don't feel like my world's come apart. I guess I won't really understand anything until I talk to my husband."

"You sure are in denial, girlfriend." The cop spoke harshly and then she settled down. "Look. Tell me about your life together. And I'll tell you what I know about him."

Karen didn't want to talk at all, just wanted all the information this woman could give her. She felt light-headed from the cigarette and wanted to blame what happened next on that. But maybe she needed to talk more than she thought she did. In the end she told the cop all about the show, and David's slow courtship of her, and their happy life together, and her new work, her fledgling foundation, Right Women.

When the cop said, "You said something about a baby. Are you pregnant?" Karen was shocked. She'd forgotten for a minute. Forgotten in the rush of love she felt for her husband now that he wasn't there. Her eyes filled. "I had a miscarriage."

"Oh?" The cop let the silence fill the room.

"It was two days ago," Karen said. And then, "I don't want to talk about it."

"All right, then. Are you okay with talking about Rosemarie Owens?"

"Sure. Why not?"

Skip frowned then, but whatever that was about, she put it aside. "Does she live with a man? Maybe a houseboy or . . ."

In spite of herself, Karen laughed. "You mean her very much younger 'husband,' Billy Bob Bubba? Oh, excuse me, I think his name is Todd. He's an ex–Dallas Cowboy."

Skip looked very serious all of a sudden. "Todd who?"

Karen thought, *What the hell does it matter?* but something in the woman's manner was intimidating. She searched her memory. "Todd Lyman, I think. Layton, maybe. Something like that."

Skip said, "Excuse me a minute," pulled out her cell phone and made a call: "Hey, Turner! Any I.D. yet on that guy they found at the Owens house? She lived with a man named Todd Lyman or Layton. Oh, you did? Okay." She rang off.

Karen picked up the past tense like a dog grabbing a scent. "What's happened?"

"Todd's dead. Somebody shot him at Rosemarie's house."

Karen's hands fluttered. "David . . ."

"No sign of either him or Rosemarie. May I ask you something, Karen?"

"Sure." *How can it get worse?* she thought.

"Did you know your husband was once married to Rosemarie Owens?"

That almost made her laugh. "No, uh-uh. He was her husband's best friend. Not Todd, the real husband. That's the connection. David wasn't married to her."

"Oh, really? He was if he's Errol Jacomine. They got married in their teens, ran away to Alabama, had one son, Dan, now serving time for crimes he committed with his father. Anyway, he and Rosemarie split up, and years later he married Irene, whom he renamed Tourmaline. He likes to control everything, Karen. Haven't you noticed that? They had one son, Isaac."

"Where's Isaac now?" It was kind of an automatic question, just making conversation. This had nothing to do with her.

"He's an art student in New Orleans. Where he lives with his girlfriend, Terri Whittaker."

There was something familiar about the name. A shiver ran up Karen's spine.

"Terri was a guest on *Mr. Right* earlier this week. Haven't you wondered about the timing on all this?"

Karen lifted her iced-tea glass but somehow missed her lips. She busied herself wiping spilled tea while she thought about timing. That was the night David hit her. The night he changed.

"Isaac was shot yesterday morning in New Orleans."

Karen didn't get it. "What does that . . . mean?"

"It means he put out a contract on his own son." Skip's voice was gentle. "He found out before the show that Terri's boyfriend was Isaac, and he knew Isaac would watch. He was the one person in the world who might both watch the show and recognize him." She smiled. "I would have recognized him. I'd know him anywhere. But I had no reason to see the show."

"You're telling me that you actually know Errol Jacomine and that he's my husband?"

The cop pulled a videotape out of the Walgreen's bag. "You can see for yourself. We've got lots of tapes of him. He ran for mayor of New Orleans, you know. He's always got something grandiose going."

Karen felt as if a ghost had laid a cold hand on her neck.

Like running for president? she thought. *Would that be grandiose enough?* God, what a fool she'd been!

Skip was staring at her, assessing. She was holding up the tape. "You up for this?"

Karen nodded, not speaking. She wasn't sure she could speak.

She led Skip into a little den on the first floor where her uncle and aunt liked to watch the news and sat down while Skip popped the tape into the machine.

At first, she didn't get it at all. "*That's* Errol Jacomine?" The weak-chinned little rodent with the redneck accent was no more her husband than Harrison Ford was.

But as the tape ran, she began to hear the voice and not the accent, began to see familiarity in the way the rodent moved and, without warning, felt nausea rising so fast she had to run to the bathroom.

After a discreet minute or two, Skip followed. Karen had left the door open. She was rinsing her mouth. "You okay?" the cop said.

Karen felt oddly violated. "Just give me a minute." The cop left. This time she did close the door and she started over, washing her whole face, wanting to rip off her clothes and stand under a hot shower, but there was no shower, this was just a powder room, and so, for the moment, there was no escape.

She more or less staggered back into the little den, where, she was glad to note, it was blessedly silent. Skip had taken the tape out and was waiting quietly.

"Let's go back in the living room. It's too claustrophobic in here." She needed as much air as she could get.

When they were once again seated in her aunt and uncle's tranquil living room, sunlight streaming in, Skip spoke again. "You're sure you're all right?"

Karen said, "This is so weird," and thought she sounded like some Valley girl on a television show. She sat up straight and made an effort to restart her mind. "I'm sorry. I'm a little disoriented."

"You've had a bad shock."

Several of them, Karen thought. *Several of them.*

"You've been living with an entirely different man from the person you thought was your husband. Do you believe that now?"

Karen nodded. She'd sort of more or less thought she had the hang of it, but viewing that tape was like watching science fiction, some awful end-of-the-world story in which aliens took over the minds and bodies of your loved ones. Except in this case it was the other way around: They wore people suits; they made you think they were human, and handsome, and loving . . .

But there was only one, and it was her own husband. She really had to get that through her head. "But . . . how can you *do* that?" she said, not meaning how could anyone be so sick and vicious and conniving but how was it possible to accomplish such a thing.

To her relief, the cop understood. "It would take a hell of a lot of money. Surgery; hair implants, maybe; speech lessons. He has sort of a British accent now—it could have been done in another country."

"But the pictures . . ."

"Ah, yes. The ones you mentioned, of David with Rosemarie's former husband. Photographs can be altered. But he'd have to get the photos first."

She was speaking very carefully, and Karen was beginning to get her drift. She was beginning to have a small epiphany. "Rosemarie!"

Skip nodded.

Karen said, "She has the money, and she'd be the only one in the world—or almost—who had the pictures. And she must have hired him; the cable station belongs to her." She stopped to work it out. "But why didn't they just get remarried?"

"Educated guess? Way, way too close for comfort. It's known that they know each other, also that he had recent contact with her—either he had her kidnapped and tried to make her help him once before, or they set it up to look like he did. No way could they be seen together. Let me ask you a question. You say he was in Rosemarie's social set. How do you know that?"

"We've been to parties at her house, parties for the cable station, that sort of thing; he knew the same people she knew."

"How many people?"

Karen thought about it. "Not very many. Two or three, maybe."

"Uh-huh. She probably introduced him around at large gatherings, like the ones you went to, and by the time you met him, it seemed as if he was a close friend of her close friends."

"We never socialized with those people."

"There was probably a very good reason for that. Karen, listen. This man will do anything. If he tries to contact you, you've got to promise you won't see him."

She tilted her head at the car across the street. "How could I see him with my babysitter out there?"

"Don't hedge. Your life could depend on it."

"You honestly think I have anything at all to say to the man I just saw on that videotape?"

"I hope not."

"But what if he calls?"

"Keep him talking. See if you can get him to agree to meet you. Then call the FBI and tell them when and where."

"Fuck the FBI!"

"Okay. Call me then." She wrote something on a card. "Call me if you hear from him. And whatever you do, don't keep the appointment. Do I need to mention that?"

Karen stubbed out her butt in the ashtray. "You think I'm crazy? The only place I'm going is out for cigarettes."

Skip pulled out another pack. "Brought you two. Just in case."

Chapter TWENTY-THREE

*M*r. Right was at his best in a crisis; as soon as the worst happened, it was like having a weight lifted from his shoulders. Right now, his mind was in high gear, juices flowing, thoughts coming so fast he could hardly process them. He felt alive. He should have seen it coming, the way the bitch had set him up. He toyed with the idea of killing her now, trying to make it look as if she and her mini-Tarzan had killed each other in a lover's quarrel. But with Rosemarie dead, there was no chance in hell of getting his hands on any of his money—the blood money he'd earned by freeing her from husband number whatever-it-was.

His course of action was obvious. There was only one way out of this, and it was Karen. But he had to keep Rosemarie with him as a last resort. You always had to have a backup plan.

He said, "We don't have time for anything fancy. Let's just get out of here before the cops come and find Todd's body. You game?"

Rosemarie said, "Where to, big fella?"

The way she talked made him nervous, way too cool for school. He didn't know what else she had up her sleeve, but it was something. Now that she'd showed her ass, there was no question of that.

He said, "Got a nice plane we could gas up?"

She shook her head. "Fresh out of those."

"Mexico, then. We'll drive to Brownsville and find us a border to cross." He was trying to match her cool.

She said lazily, "José Cuervo, you are a friend of mine." She let it lie there a minute. "Only one problem. Do we steal a car or what?"

"Nope. We take one of yours."

"No good. Plates." Once again, she let it lie there, appeared to be thinking. He was ahead of her though.

He patted his briefcase. "Got an extra set. Right in here."

She shrugged, as if they were going to the movies. "I'll get my toothbrush."

He put the gun back in the case, put the strap over his shoulder. "Uh-uh. No time. We'll get one in Margaritaville."

She got up lazily and started toward the door.

"Got your keys?" he said.

"I'll get my purse." *Not alone you won't*, he thought, and dogged her footsteps.

They were already in the garage, he following with a show of meekness, when he slipped the gun out and cracked it over her skull. She gave a little sigh as she sank to the floor.

Okay, he thought, *duct tape.* There had to be some; they were in a garage. There was a sort of workshop Todd or someone had set up in there. Of course there was tape. He found it quickly and bound her wrists and ankles, cutting the tape with his Swiss Army knife, and threw the rest of the roll into his briefcase. Then he made sure he had working keys and opened the trunk of her least noticeable car—a fairly late-model dark-colored sedan. There was nothing much in it but jumper cables and a can of gasoline. He left them both. Never knew when you might need a Molotov cocktail. And the cables were a big set with little teeth on them; they'd hurt like hell with an arm, say, pressed between them. Excellent for persuading purposes.

Working at top speed, he changed the plates and shoved Rosemarie in the trunk, first taping her lying mouth in case she regained consciousness.

Then he barreled out of there, reaching after a few blocks for his last unused cell phone, the one in which he'd programmed his emergency numbers, Rosemarie's and the one for the phone he'd given Karen. Dialing, he had no doubt in the world that his wife would answer.

On the fourth ring, she said, "David! Dear God, David, what's going on? I've spent the morning at the federal building. They arrested me, David. My uncle had to bail me out."

They'd moved fast. Much faster than he would have thought.

"It's okay, baby. Look, it's okay. Everything's going to be fine."

"They stormed in with guns and everything. Jesus, David, it's about you; that's all I know. They said you're dangerous and I shouldn't even talk to you, but . . ."

"But what? You love me, don't you?"

"Oh, hell, David, I'm so scared!"

"Honey, you've got to hang on. You've got to be really brave and really, really cool. It's okay; it's really okay. I'll get us out of this. I had no idea they'd go this far. It's all a setup. You know that, don't you? You know I love you. I was getting too powerful, that's all. They had to do something to stop me. But it's too late, you understand? Look, I've got some very important people working with me. We'll get out of this, you know that, don't you? Sweetheart?"

"What?"

"You love me?"

"David, they say you're somebody else."

Oh, Christ. "Baby, am I your Mr. Right? How could I be somebody else?"

The line was quiet.

"Karen?"

"What?"

"Listen, I'm on my way home. Everything's going to be fine. We'll work it all out." This was a test. Her reaction might tell him something.

"No! Oh, God, don't! I'm at my uncle's. They've probably got our house set up like a command post. You can't go there." That was a good sign.

"Karen, you've really got to be reasonable. I didn't want to tell you this, but some very high-up people are backing me. It's okay. I'll just go home and . . ."

"They'll shoot you."

"Don't be ridiculous. It's our house. They can't shoot a man in his own house."

"David, you can't go there."

"Okay, okay. Why don't we meet someplace else? We'll just call the police from wherever it is, and, by then, everything will be all set up for the stupid feds to call off their dogs, and we can just put our feet up till our friends give us the word. And then we can go home. Together."

"Look, David. You really have no idea of the scope of this thing."

"And you really have no idea of the scope of my operation—*our* operation—sweetie pie. Remember what we talked about?" He made his voice turn to velvet. "It's already in motion—has been for a long time. Just trust me, okay? How about your office? Why don't you just go to the Right Women office, and I'll be there, and we'll just ride this thing out together."

"My office?" She sounded like a zombie.

"The storm troopers aren't there, are they?"

"No. At least I don't think so. But they're here. I can't get away."

"Oh, yes you can. I've got an idea."

She didn't speak, was probably too numb to answer him.

"I know a place they won't go." He outlined his plan. "What do you think?"

"Omigod," she said. "You're a genius. I'd never in a million years have thought of something like that."

"Just trust me, baby. Trust me, and do what I say, and we'll be together real soon."

Skip had left the McLeans' house with a bad feeling. Exactly what was causing it she wasn't sure, except the near-mythic way Jacomine loomed in her consciousness. He had no notion of his own limitations. He'd try to contact Karen, there was no question in her mind. But the question was this: Was Karen enough of a fool to believe the line of garbage he was bound to try to feed her?

She didn't seem a fool. Skip liked her. But she did seem a victim. Skip wished to hell she knew more about that baby thing.

She went out and got in her rented car and sat there. The two feds watching Karen probably saw her, but she was betting they'd leave her alone.

Karen didn't even bother to check the street when she came out some twenty minutes later, probably trying to put on a casual show for the feds. She was still in her jeans and tank top, carrying a huge straw tote, clearly meant for the beach.

She got in her car and started driving. The feds followed. Skip followed the feds. The caravan they made would have been comical seen from a satellite. On the ground, it probably wasn't even noticeable. If the feds knew she was there, they evidently didn't care.

Bigger fish to fry, Skip thought.

Karen drove down Preston Road, past a huge, high-fenced area that looked like some oil man's private estate. She took a right on Mockingbird Lane and in half a block, another right, driving through a gate in the high fence she'd been following. A plaque on the wall said DALLAS COUNTRY CLUB. The feds followed her in, past tennis courts on the left, a golf court on the right. On the other side of the tennis courts was a large parking lot for the clubhouse. Karen parked, unloaded her straw tote, which, Skip now saw, was piled high with towels. She sauntered up to the clubhouse and sidestepped to the left, where she looked down, called something to someone, and then entered the clubhouse. One of the feds got out of the car, ran to the place where she'd yelled to someone, and then followed Karen into the building. The other moved the car to a side entrance. If she came out there, the driver had her, but he could also see the front of the building.

Skip parked, got out, and approached the building. She saw that to the left was a stairway down to a pool. Evidently Karen had yelled to someone there, perhaps along the lines of "see you in a minute."

Skip had three choices that she could see: watch Karen's car, follow the fed following Karen, or try something else. Well, hell, if she waited here, she could see Karen's car, the FBI car, and the pool area. If Karen came out for a swim, she could watch without being noticed.

Karen hadn't even had time to change to her swimsuit before the pedestrian fed scooted out, looking around wildly for his buddy. Evidently, Karen had escaped—or had made him think she had.

To wait for her here or follow the feds? Maybe they knew something she didn't. She opted for following.

But within five minutes, she saw it was hopeless; the FBI guys were returning to the McLean house where, Skip was certain, Karen wasn't going.

*K*aren had no idea it was possible to have so much fury in her, boiling, coursing, like a toxin blasting through her veins. How dare David treat her like a child? How was it possible for an adult human being to think his wife was as dumb as she'd have to be to buy that crap on the phone?

Her uncle had a gun; every Texan had a gun. All she had to do was to find it.

And how in the name of the baby she'd lost had she for one minute entered into his puerile little fantasy about being president? President, for God's sake. Talk about folie à deux! How the hell had he done it to her?

The gun would be in the bedroom, she thought. People always thought a burglar was going to surprise them in bed, and they'd just surprise the burglar first. Her own father kept a gun in the drawer of his bedside table.

And the damn escape plan! It was ingenious, something he'd taken a long time to think out, something he'd worked out long before today. *"I've got an idea,"* hell! He probably had a trunkful of ideas.

First, she did exactly as her husband had told her: called a town car to pick her up at a particular time, at exactly the place he told her. A car with tinted windows.

Then she tackled the bedroom. Her uncle's nightstand, she figured, would be the one without the hand lotion on top. Gingerly, she opened the drawer, hoping she didn't find sex toys.

There were two pairs of spectacles in there and a box of tissues. No gun.

Where else then? She checked under the pillow, feeling like a burglar herself, and then under the mattress. Her fingers closed on something hard and cold. *Please, God, don't let it be a dildo.*

She lifted up the mattress to take a look. There it was, the obligatory Texas firearm. She wondered if it was loaded and if she could fire it.

It felt way too light. She checked under the mattress again and found what must be a clip for it, meaning it must be an automatic. Good. Those were said to be easier. She loaded both items into a tote she'd brought from home.

Now to lose the damned FBI and get to her office.

She drove to the club, called the car service on her cell phone, verified that the car was in place, and went in, walking slowly, exactly as David had told her. Once she was in, she moved fast.

She moved swiftly through the lobby, into the ballroom (which was currently bare), and turned right at the rear, vaguely aware of motion behind her. The damned feds were probably following. She tried to keep calm. The key from here on out was to move fast. She belonged here; no one cared about her speed. But two men chasing her would be noticed.

She turned right at the far side of the ballroom, proceeded down the hall, and then downstairs to the restaurant. Here, there were two choices: You could turn right and go out the side entrance, or you could go through a door at the rear of the restaurant. Karen chose the rear entrance, which opened onto a short breezeway.

Quickly, she loped through the breezeway, opened a door at the far side, and stepped into a small dining room, the sort where private lunches are held. At the rear of that, she opened another unmarked door and entered the ladies locker room. It was ladies' golf day, and the place was full. She hurried through, and just as she was turning right again, to enter the golf shop, she heard the screams.

Ha! Home free. The feds—or at least one of them—*had* followed her. They'd have no choice except to apologize, leave the locker room, and retrace their steps. So now they were on the opposite side of the club; absolutely no way in hell they could catch her. She strode casually through the golf shop, saying her "hellos" as she went, exited, and slid into the waiting town car, already pointed toward the entrance opposite the main one at Mockingbird Lane.

She had to hand it to David; that was one carefully thought-out plan. She asked the driver to take her to an intersection near the Quadrangle and told him to hurry.

She kept watch out the back, but there was no sign of the FBI car.

She got out at the intersection, paid the driver, watched the town car disappear, and strolled to the building that housed her office. The first thing she noticed was that the security guard wasn't in his usual place. Gone on rounds, maybe. A half-smoked cigarette had gone out in the ashtray on his desk. She frowned and thought, *Who leaves a cigarette burning in the ashtray?* The answer was obvious. Someone who had to leave in a hurry. She wondered if he'd gotten to her husband first. *No need to worry,* she thought. He wasn't armed. He was just an old guy paid to take people's names when they came in. She hoped her husband wasn't holding him hostage or something. That would complicate things.

The building was a small stand-alone box across from a park, not more than four stories, with a parking lot in back and nice landscaping. The offices in the street—including hers, had wonderful glass fronts that opened onto little balconies. The building didn't get a whole lot of foot traffic, but there were people working in the offices. They'd be bound to hear the shot. She thought about that, and let a closed smile play at her lips. Who cared? By then he'd be dead.

*S*kip could have cried with frustration. She couldn't believe that it was this simple, that Karen had actually managed to shake two feds and one cop. And yet logic told her she was defeated. Karen Wright could be headed toward her death at this moment, and there wasn't a damn thing Skip could do about it.

Okay, she told herself. *Accept it. You can't do anything except what you can do.* Was there anything left? Where to start?

Start. That was it. Start. Okay, where would Karen go? Where would Mr. Wright tell his wife to meet him? Maybe a favorite restaurant, a street corner, but Skip couldn't know that, she couldn't find a place she didn't know about. That left what she did know: Karen's home, her parents' house, the McLeans' house, the television station, her office, maybe a church. It would be unlike Errol Jacomine not to belong to one, if only to compare himself to the preacher. But Karen hadn't mentioned a church. She called Karen's parents' house; got no answer. Rang Senator McLean again.

She tried to sound calm. "Hi. Had a nice talk with your niece."

"How is she?"

"Can I be honest with you? I'm a little worried she might try to meet her husband."

"Oh, no, Karen's much too smart for that. Besides, isn't the FBI out front? They're supposed to be."

"She left the house, Senator."

"Well? Didn't they follow?"

"Oh, yes, they followed. And they lost her."

He laughed. "She probably went to a mall or something. They wouldn't be the first people she's left behind in a mall."

"Senator, with all due respect, she could be in danger."

His voice turned hard. "What do you want me to do?"

"Tell me any place she and her husband went together. Some place private she might try to meet him."

"To be honest, I barely know the man."

Skip didn't give him time to elaborate. "How about a church. Do they go to church?"

"I don't know. They don't go to ours."

"Her office then. How about that?"

"Her office? She doesn't work, that I know of."

"She runs a foundation."

"I'm sorry, detective. I don't know a thing about that."

Now there was a stopper. "Okay, thanks for your help."

The feds didn't know about the office; neither did Karen's own uncle. What the hell was the name of that foundation?

Chapter *TWENTY-FOUR*

*R*osemarie woke up while the car was in motion. She could tell she was in a car, but she couldn't figure out why it was pitch black in there. Her head hurt and she couldn't move. She could hardly breathe. And her mouth—something was keeping her from opening her mouth.

She sucked air through her nose and smelled fumes—and the newness of the car. Her hands were bound behind her, her ankles stuck tightly together. She was on her side, curled up in a fetal position. She was sweating.

Gradually, she took in the sensations, fighting rising panic. And then she remembered. Remembered going into the garage ahead of Earl, worrying that he'd do something like this, wondering how to prevent it, trying to be cool. He must have knocked her out and stolen her car. He must have loaded her in the trunk.

Okay, if he'd do that, he'd kill her. If she didn't smother first. She tried to remember if you could smother in the trunk of a car. *Maybe,* she thought, *if it was hot enough.* And it was. It was a hot May day, boiling hot. She'd certainly smother if he tried to drive to Mexico.

The only thing to do was breathe, breathe and try to survive as long as she could. She'd taken yoga on and off for years; she knew how to breathe, knew it would calm her. And that it was the only thing she could do. So she breathed, focusing on each breath, trying not to think, just to stay alive.

And, finally, the car stopped. She heard Earl get out, slam the door, and walk away. Fleetingly, it occurred to her to make throat noises to attract his attention, but she knew it was a bad idea. Better he should think she was still unconscious—or dead.

Coming out of the breathing-trance was like waking up a second time; only this time she wasn't panicked. She was furious.

I've got to kill the bastard, she realized, and wondered why she hadn't already done it, done it when it would have been easy. In those months when she was supporting him instead, with that stupid job at her little cable station. But, hell, that was hindsight.

Now she was going to do it. All she had to do was get out of here. She started kicking and felt a large metal object. It dawned on her that it was Todd's gas can. She was in Todd's car! It was the gas he kept for his stupid boat. This was good; the car had an escape button, in case you got locked in the trunk. Earl must have realized that; he was a maniac for details. He must have thought she couldn't get to the button with her wrists bound. And she probably couldn't. She didn't even know where it was, needed her fingers to poke around for it. So she'd have to get the tape off. It was tape, wasn't it? It seemed to her that it was; wire or rope wouldn't be so wide or so tight against her skin. She'd have more wiggle room.

It was a nice big trunk she was in. They'd gotten the car so Todd could haul stuff. She could maneuver in it, find the jack or something, get to a taillight maybe, break it . . .

Wait a minute. She was wearing her watch. Perhaps she could break the crystal, use it to saw through the tape. She slammed her hands against the floor of the trunk.

No. The angle was wrong. She couldn't even feel the watch, couldn't know if she'd cracked the glass.

She started moving, slowly, her limbs hurting from the confinement. Her feet hit something. Could you die of gas fumes? Or, maybe, with all that heat, could you burn up from spontaneous combustion? Maybe she'd be barbecued in her own little oven. The panic started rising again.

Again, she breathed, moving her head, trying to straighten out. And she felt something else. But what? She'd have to use the top of her head like fingers, depend on it to tell her what she was feeling.

She rocked her head back and forth on the object, like a kid playing some stupid game with a pillow, finally easing her neck on top of the object. That was better. Her neck could differentiate textures.

It felt like some kind of rope, something coiled up. But harder than rope, something with less give. She kept moving until she felt metal—a long finger of metal—finger-long but fist-wide.

She understood what the object was. It was a set of jumper cables. She tried to remember how they worked. You held them in your hand and opened them and locked them onto screws or something on the battery. And they held. She tried picturing them. Yes! They had teeth.

Her heartbeat sped up. This could be it. But how to get them in position? Kick them there, maybe. Could she turn her whole body around? She starting working on it.

Gradually, painfully, she flipped herself, like an embryo in a womb, using her feet for leverage, then for kicking, kicking the cables back behind her, sitting up a little, raising her head till it hit the roof and set off new waves of pain.

She took a few moments for a few more breaths, but the air was poisonous with gas fumes. She abandoned the effort and just kicked, kicked, kicked some more. She couldn't gauge how well she was doing; her feet were nearly numb. But she could feel the cables with her feet, feel the length of them inching up her back, feel the grip digging into her.

She kept at it till she could feel the grip with her elbow; she pushed down on it, and to her surprise, felt it open. She needed to get her wrist into the metal jaws, but she couldn't do it from this angle. She kept working.

Finally she had the grip in her fingers. She opened it, tried to work her wrist in, but she couldn't hold it. She tried again. And again. And a third time.

Sweat poured off her. Fumes engulfed her. And finally, on the sixth try, she felt the excruciating bite of the grip. She worked it between her wrists, whimpering from the effort. And when she had it in position, she pulled her wrists apart. The fabric gave, a little. But she could do it. She knew now that she could do it.

She kept working, wondering where they were, what Earl was doing in there, how long he'd be, whether she was going to make it. And finally, with a mighty tug, she did. Her elbows hit the padded sides of the trunk, and she brought her hands around to her front, rubbing them together to restore circulation. And then she sent those fingers out to work, not even bothering to tear the tape off her mouth.

The button would be near the front, she thought, *near the lock.* In a moment she found it. The trunk flew up, and she breathed real air, not even moving for a moment, except to free her mouth. Then she tore at the tape on her ankles, using a combination of the cable grips and her own fingers, nails torn and ragged, to rip it off. Still, she couldn't walk. Her feet had no feeling at all.

She sat on the edge of the trunk and rubbed them till she could stand, then stomped like a child whose foot has fallen asleep. Slowly, the feeling returned, and, as it did, she surveyed her surroundings. She was behind a small building, in a parking lot. There were other cars there. She realized how fortunate it was that no one had come to rescue her. Because how the hell was she going to kill her husband in front of witnesses? How was she going to do it, anyway, without a weapon?

Maybe she could improvise one. She set the gas can on the pavement.

He must be in the building. She walked to the front and opened the door. No guard, she noticed, though there was a desk for one, with an ashtray and a pack of cigarettes beside it, a lighter neatly laid on top. *A gift from God,* she thought, palming the lighter.

Thinking Earl might be back any second, she took stock quickly, wondering what the hell he was doing here. She grabbed the guard's sign-in book and started leafing through it. She had to go back two weeks before she found what she was looking for: an entry for Karen Wright, Room 214.

That was where he'd be. She went back for the gas can.

S kip parked her car in front of the building, illegally. She walked into the building, noted that the guard was missing, and wondered briefly if that meant anything. She checked the directory and took the elevator to the second floor.

The door to 214 was closed, but she could hear voices, a woman's voice, at any rate. She thought briefly of calling for backup but decided it was too soon. Two little old ladies could be in there, phoning around in aid of making the world right for women.

She leaned close and listened. And there it was, a voice she knew, silky and smooth as ever, saying, "Now, Karen, no need to get excited; just put the gun away, now. This is not the bogeyman; nobody's here but your loving husband."

Okay, she told herself. Be calm. Take a minute. She walked back down the hall and called Shellmire. "Turner. I've got him. I think he's armed." Well, somebody was armed, anyway. She gave the address, walked back down the hall, drew her gun, listened a moment more. "You asshole!" Karen screamed, and Skip heard the desperation in her voice. So, apparently, did Jacomine. "Karen, no!" he yelled.

Skip kicked the door open.

The two people in the room turned toward her, shocked. Karen was holding a gun, hands shaking, and Jacomine was completely bald. For a second, Skip was unnerved, not so much by the gun, which she'd expected, as by seeing Jacomine looking so much like his old self; somehow, hairless, he was no longer Mr. Right, just her old enemy with a better jawline.

He recovered first, making some sort of motion that could have started out to be a step. Karen fired, but the shot went wild. Jacomine jumped her, knocked the gun out of her hand.

Skip shouted, "Hands up, or I'll blow your fucking head off."

The two kept struggling. He was on top of Karen, had her nearly on the ground. Skip had no shot.

She took a step forward and kicked him, but he grabbed upward for her gun. He caught her by surprise, nearly twisting it out of her hand, and held on. She kicked again. Karen grunted, at the bottom of the pile.

Jacomine still had the gun in his grip; Skip felt her own grip loosening. He was getting it. She held tighter, kept kicking. He twisted, hard, and she dropped it, heard it skitter across the room.

They both dived for it, giving Karen a chance to struggle out of the pile. Skip could sense people in the hall, having come out of their offices. She shouted, "Karen! Get out of here." And wriggled toward her gun.

She heard movement, maybe Karen running, and then a sudden exclamation, "Rosemarie!"

A throaty voice, female, spoke behind her: "Well, hi, Earl, honey."

Not even slightly fazed, Jacomine continued to inch toward the gun. Skip held onto his leg, but he was stronger. She couldn't hold on much longer. Someone walked around her. And then liquid splashed into the room, onto Jacomine mostly. The ominous odor of fumes filled the room.

Skip shouted, "Everybody, get out of here! Call 911! Hurry!"

She heard scurrying, then a faint sound, as of a match struck, maybe a lighter flicked. She held onto the leg. The throaty voice said, "Know what that is, Earl? You drop that gun, or I'm gonna burn you alive."

Jacomine's foot went dead in Skip's hands. He twisted his neck toward the voice. "Rosemarie, you know you don't mean that."

The voice said, "Get up, Earl."

He sat up, giving Skip time to grab him and haul him to his feet. She threw him across the room, against a desk, and bent to pick up her gun.

The woman she saw as she pivoted back was no more who she expected than Karen had been. She'd seen plenty of pictures of Rosemarie Owens, a cool blonde—the sort who married money, repeatedly. This woman was a wreck: hair disheveled, bruised, soaked in sweat, holding a lighter.

Skip thought, *Shit, the fumes. The whole room could go up.*

She said evenly, "Put that out, Rosemarie."

Smiling, as if her life were complete, Rosemarie doused the lighter.

Then Skip heard a scraping sound, definitely a match this time, and Karen said, "No. Let's burn him."

The room exploded in flame.

The women screamed. Skip heard them run into the hall. Jacomine erupted before her eyes into a fireball. Karen had thrown the matchbook at him.

Skip swiveled her head, scanning for a fire extinguisher, blanket, anything. But the fire went out almost immediately. Jacomine leapt up and ran toward the full-length window that led to the balcony. Skip fired, but she'd been distracted a moment too long; her aim was off. If she hit him, it didn't stop him. He ran straight through the glass.

Skip caught her breath and ran after him. By the time she caught up, he had pitched over the balcony and landed in a stand of shrubbery. She stared for a moment, wondering where the hell her backup was and whether she should jump on top of him.

She couldn't bring herself to do it; damned if she was going to risk breaking a leg when she was this close to catching him. Instead, she turned and ran down the stairs, fighting her way through the crowd, yelling, "Police! Let me through! Police!"

He was gone when she got there.

Gun still drawn, she ran behind the building into the parking lot. A car was barreling down on her. Jacomine? She leapt to the side, raced back to get her own car.

He had to be badly burned, and he might be shot; he could be dying. But you didn't feel burns immediately; she'd read plenty about it. He could do a lot of damage before he passed out. And he was probably doing seventy already. She ought to call Shellmire, give him an update, but her hands were shaking too badly. All she could do was drive.

He turned onto Cedar Springs, headed downtown, then onto Harry Hines Boulevard. To the right loomed the new arena, the American Airlines Center. She tried to think, to give 911 a location. She didn't know Dallas, but Jacomine did. In his shoes, she'd try to find the nearest freeway entrance, an idea she truly hated.

She picked up her phone, then realized she'd have to look at it to call 911. There wasn't time. She tried to speed up, but it wasn't safe; there was too much traffic.

She saw what she dreaded ahead of her, an entrance to the Stemmons Freeway. But it was a very narrow entrance, with barriers on either side. If she could just get close enough to force him . . .

He skimmed through the barriers before she could reach him. She was gaining, though. She wondered how in God's name he could be doing all this. She had to force him to the right, get him off the freeway, before he passed out.

He'd gone only about a quarter of a mile when his car began to weave. He was losing it, but he wasn't slowing down.

She managed to pull up on his left and rode him.

His car veered dangerously close to hers, then back the other way. She kept crowding him. A sign ahead said VICTORY AVENUE and HI LINE DR. Maybe she could force him off at the exit. He corrected too much to avoid hitting a car, then had to swing wide back to the right—and that was where he lost control. His car hit the barrier, just in view of the back side of the new arena, on a little overpass.

It flipped over and landed with a thud like a tank crashing.

Chapter TWENTY-FIVE

Skip stared at herself in the hospital bathroom, and thought, for the first time in two days, of Steve Steinman. She needed to call him right away, along with Adam Abasolo, then Jimmy Dee and the kids, to let them know that it was over.

She splashed water on her face.

Jacomine was alive, with one gunshot wound, and third-degree burns on his torso and face. She'd actually seen him in the hospital, lying on a gurney, unconscious, helpless, and it was important to see. If she hadn't, she'd never believe he hadn't somehow slipped away again. She felt like crying, perhaps with relief, perhaps simply to relieve tension. The hospital gave him about a fifty-fifty chance of survival. But there was a piece of her that couldn't believe he wouldn't somehow get up and walk out of there when no one was lookng.

She combed her singed hair and returned to the emergency room to find Shellmire. "Some scene over there. They cut me loose to come get you. How you feeling?"

She thought about it. "Kind of shaky."

"You're lucky that whole room didn't go up."

"You're not kidding. It could have, easily. I just kept thinking about how many times I've seen people smoking in gas stations. So far I've never seen it cause a fire."

"Could, though." Shellmire shivered, thinking about it.

"What was weird, when she threw the matches, it was kind of like an explosion. Just a little pouf of flame, then it went out."

He nodded. "Yeah. Sometimes it'll flash and go right out."

"Oh, that's what the doctor meant. He said Jacomine had flash burns."

"Lots of 'em, it looked like." He stood up. "I've got to get some coffee. You need some?"

"Make mine a Valium."

And he left, giving her a few minutes to make her phone calls. When he returned, she made a show of drinking the coffee, which was probably the last thing her body needed after its enormous expenditure of adrenaline, but they both knew she still had to maintain alertness.

"I just called Abasolo. Good news: Isaac came out of the coma. Looks like he got away clean. No brain damage at all."

"All right!" For a moment, a grin cracked the agent's face, but it disappeared almost immediately. There was still a long way to go to close the case.

"I've got a question," Skip said. "Where the hell was the security guard?"

"I'm glad you asked. Taped up and locked in a closet."

"Might have known."

Shellmire drove her to the federal building and, along with Hargett, another agent, and a Dallas cop, listened to her story.

They exchanged glances when she got to the part about the matchbook. Hargett said, "You're sure Karen was the one who threw it?"

"Absolutely. Why?"

"Tell us again what she said."

"She said, 'No. Let's burn him.' Right after I told Rosemarie to put out the lighter."

"Did Rosemarie put out the lighter?"

"I told you. She did. The situation was defused. Karen was very deliberate about it."

Hargett persisted. "Did you actually see her throw the matchbook?"

"I couldn't. She was behind me. But I heard her strike the match, and I heard what she said."

The other four looked miserable. Her stomach flip-flopped. They knew something she didn't.

"What's going on?"

The cop was the one who told her. "We didn't find the matchbook. She and Rosemarie both say Rosemarie threw the lighter to save your ass, because he refused to drop the gun."

"Wait a minute! I already had the gun."

"That's not what they say."

"They." She was beginning to see what had happened. "Hold it. They were alone together before any officers got to the scene. They cooked this thing up. Rosemarie's boyfriend's dead, right? Plus, she's the one who *made* Mr. Right; she not only harbored a fugitive, she mentored him! She's going to have a million charges against her . . ."

"And Karen comes from one of the most powerful families in Dallas." Shellmire spoke grimly.

Skip felt lightheaded. "But . . . there were witnesses."

Shellmire shook his head. "We'll keep trying. But so far, nothing.

When Rosemarie threw the gasoline, you gave the order to get out of there, right?"

Skip nodded.

"Good police work. And know what those law-abiding citizens did? Ran for their pitiful little lives."

"Oh, hell."

"Yeah."

The adrenaline high was over, and even Shellmire's coffee had worn off. "You guys gonna charge me with anything?"

The special agent in charge spoke up. "I'd sure like to," Hargett said. "But looks like you've got friends . . ."

"Also, she did a damn good job," the Dallas cop said. Skip hadn't caught her name, but evidently she didn't care much for Hargett.

"Yeah. You did," Shellmire said. So maybe she had.

"I appreciate the vote of confidence. Could I get out of here now? I need to go and sleep for about a day and a half."

Shellmire took her to her hotel, where she tossed and turned, and intermittently cried, and talked on the phone to Steve and Jimmy Dee, and Adam Abasolo, and occasionally did sleep until the next morning, when she caught a plane home.

The crying still puzzled her. She should have been dancing in the streets. But she put it down to the fact that it's a horrible sight to see a flaming man jump from a second-story window—and even more horrible that both Karen and Rosemarie were probably going to wiggle out from under their crimes.

Then, too, there was the question of what she was going back to. There was still a big hurdle to get over. She might have just captured America's Most Wanted, but she was still in semidisgrace in her hometown—at least till she could prove Jacomine had set her up.

There was one note of hope, though. When she phoned him, Abasolo had offered to meet her at the airport. She'd kind of had in mind a reunion with Steve, but it could wait. She sensed that whatever Adam had to say couldn't.

The first thing he said was, "You look like hell."

Skip winced.

"Hey, I'm sorry," he said. "I didn't think you were that sensitive."

"It isn't that. I was all set to say, 'You should have seen the other guy,' and then I remembered how he actually looked." She shuddered. "You shouldn't see him. Nobody should."

"I hear they don't think he'll live out the week."

"He lost a whole lot of skin. Blood too, from the gunshot wound. It was something to see, Adam, those two women hell bent on killing him. You hear what really happened? One threw the gasoline, the other threw a book of matches at him."

"Cold."

They were talking as they walked to his car. They paused to get in, and Skip said, "Why'd you want to see me, Adam?"

"It's not me," he said. "It's Isaac."

"Isaac? I need an escort to go see Isaac?"

"I think he's got something, Skip."

It took Skip a moment to recognize the young woman with the worried expression in Isaac's hospital room, but close inspection revealed that it was only another version of Terri. "Hi, Terri. Nice hair." It was short, spiky, and orange.

"Thanks, I'm trying to cheer Isaac up."

Skip turned her attention to the patient, afraid of what she might see. But Isaac looked surprisingly like himself; his head was bandaged, but he wasn't bruised and swollen. He had a bit of tension around the eyes, and Skip remembered what she knew about head injuries. Probably he wouldn't be out of pain for quite awhile.

"Hey, hardhead."

"Hey, Skip." He gave her such a sweet smile that she couldn't resist trying to hug him. A hug is always awkward when one party has an IV, and this was no exception. But she needed it.

"You look pretty good," she said.

"So do you."

"Not according to my partner here. You guys know Sergeant Abasolo?"

Terri rolled her eyes. "He's been hanging out with us."

"He says you've got something for me." She was expecting to hear that Isaac had seen the shooter—hoping for it anyhow—but what he said was, "Daniel called."

"Daniel? Daniel Jacomine called you?" There was a serious rift between the brothers.

Isaac's sweet, pale face scrunched a little, as if he were trying not to cry. "It was so sad to talk to him, Skip. He wanted to believe in something, and he bought into the wrong thing."

In spades, Skip thought.

"He told me about something really bad our dad did to him . . ."

"When he was a kid?"

"No, uh-uh. The last night he saw him. He thought it was his fault. Errol told him he deserved it, and Daniel believed him. But . . ." Isaac actively fought tears. ". . . here's what's sad. He says he knows I didn't deserve to get shot, that anyone who could do that to me . . ."

"But, wait. How did he know who did it?"

"He knew. Even before the story started to come out on the news—about Errol, I mean. When I talked to him first, the only thing he'd heard was that somebody tried to whack me. There was no doubt in his mind who it was."

"Any doubt in yours?"

"No." Isaac answered as matter-of-factly as if he were telling her the time. He'd never had illusions about his father. "But I knew why he did it. Daniel didn't even know about Terri and the show. He didn't know about Mr. Right or anything. He just knew, that's all."

Skip understood it. If she'd heard out of the clear blue that Isaac had been gunned down, she'd have known too. But for Daniel it was undoubtedly a breakthrough; she cordially hoped it was going to lead to something productive. "What did he say that you thought I'd be interested in?"

"He asked for you. He said to tell you to come see him."

"You really think he has something to say?"

"He sounded . . ."

He paused so long Skip had to prompt him. "What?"

". . . like a completely different person."

When Skip and Abasolo had said their good-byes and walked down the hall to the elevator, Skip said, "You want to go with me, is that the idea?"

"I heard somewhere you were a quick study."

They stepped into the elevator and, in keeping with elevator etiquette, remained quiet until they were alone again.

"There's the car over there. Isn't there a song called 'Angola Bound'?"

"If there isn't, there ought to be." She headed toward the unmarked vehicle.

Chapter TWENTY-SIX

Seeing Abasolo, Daniel was visibly disappointed. Wouldn't even look at him. "Who's this?"

"My good friend, Sergeant Adam Abasolo."

Daniel turned his gaze on the other man. "I know you. You testified in some of the cases." Meaning the Jacomine cases.

"That's right."

"I asked for Langdon."

Abasolo raised an eyebrow, telling Skip it was her call. She needed him there in the worst kind of way. "Daniel, listen. If you have something important to tell me, I need a witness."

"Come on! You don't need a witness—what the hell for?"

"I have to tread lightly these days."

Unexpectedly Daniel laughed, if you could call a derisive honk a laugh. "Oh, yeah, I forgot. You're dirty now."

Skip winced before she could stop herself.

"Or did you get set up?"

"Yeah, I got set up." She was aware that she was barking at him but not able to soften it. "You know anything about it?"

He shook his head. "No. But I might know who does." He sent a sneer Abasolo's way. "The Testosterone Kid can stay. As long as he keeps his mouth shut."

She and Abasolo sat in the chairs the guards had provided for them. Daniel had somehow put up a mental curtain in the corner of the room occupied by Abasolo. Maybe it was something you learned to do in prison. He focused entirely on Skip, not holding back, and what she saw was an entirely new Daniel. She hadn't seen him since his trial and had never really talked to him, only interrogated him. She remembered him as a fierce, angry fanatic, someone who wore a perpetual scowl, was probably paranoid. Some kind of crazy, at the very least.

His hair was very short now; his face seemed rounder as a result. Calmer. If Skip had seen him on the street or in a bus station, she might have said he looked more confused than otherwise. In a sad sort of way. Like a child who'd had the kind of shock that makes him question everything he thought he understood. She suspected Daniel had been questioning things for quite some time.

He said, "I'm sorry I wouldn't see you when you came up last week. Maybe I could have stopped some of this shit."

"Did you know your father had become David Wright?"

He shook his head. "Hell, no. Sure as hell didn't." He sounded outraged, though Skip couldn't tell whether his fury was directed at what his father had done or the fact that he hadn't told Daniel about it.

"Then probably you couldn't have helped," she said. "Don't worry about it."

Daniel fumbled in a pocket, found a cigarette, lit it, and stared past

Skip and Abasolo into the depths of the prison. "I do know some things."

Skip felt her stomach jump.

"How's my father?"

Skip shrugged. "He's still alive."

"You know, yesterday I talked to my daughter for the first time in a year. Lovelace answered when I phoned Isaac. Started me thinking about her." He leveled his eyes at Skip. "About why she's alive."

Skip nodded. She knew what he was getting at: In one sense, Lovelace was alive because of Skip. *Nice of you to notice*, she wanted to say. But it was no time for sarcasm.

"You know, she writes me? Wrote while I was in Parish Prison, waiting for trial, on trial, all that time. Sends me Christmas cards, everything—Christ, a fucking Father's Day card! But the cards were always mailed from New Orleans, by Isaac I presume. She never says where she's living, or going to school, or what she's doing; never even told me about her name change. I had to find out from the newspapers."

In spite of Skip's efforts, sarcasm won the day. "Maybe she doesn't trust you. For some reason."

Abasolo gave her what were known in the Third District as his reproachful guinea eyes, but Daniel ignored her. "Look, I know how good Isaac's been to her; that she does talk about. And another thing. He's my baby brother, goddammit!" He banged the table. His face had suddenly turned red, veins popping out like tunnels. The old Daniel was back, but the anger was redirected. "He can't fucking kill my baby brother!"

"Hey. Daniel." She spoke almost in a whisper, low and soothing. "He's not going to be hurting anyone anymore. And Isaac's going to be fine. It's over now."

"Isaac told me to ask for you, but, fuck, any cop would have done fine. I asked for you for one reason and one reason only. I've seen the news. I want to know what really happened in that room. You were there; you tell me."

"You have something for me?"

"Hell, that ain't how it works. I've made up my mind. I've got something for you whether you talk to me or not. But my mother and my father were both in that room. Sounds like they tried to kill each other. If you're halfway decent, you're gonna tell me."

Skip told him, glad she could honestly say that Rosemarie had put out the lighter, finishing up with the fact that neither she nor Karen, in all likelihood, would ever be charged with any of their crimes.

"Mmm. Mmm," Daniel said. "Serves him right. Serves him just goddamn right."

"What do you know, Daniel?" She spoke in her give-it-up cop voice.

He put out his cigarette, lit another one. "Daddy did a little favor for my mother once. Took care of that superfluous husband for her."

"Ah."

"He didn't think I knew, but I did. I put it together, anyhow. See, Bettina has a very talented friend. You know Bettina?"

"Oh, yeah. Teflon Bettina. Everybody goes to jail; not Bettina. Know her well."

"Bettina used to brag about this guy, offer him to Daddy in case he needed somebody whacked." He let out his derisive honk again. "'Course Daddy had his own trained assassins." He stared at his cigarette to avoid looking at Skip. "I ought to know." He flicked his gaze back to her face. "But some things you just can't ask your firstborn son to do. Even if his mama needs a favor. Lobo came up in a gang outside L.A. Learned lots of stuff there, some of it kind of subtle, I'm gathering."

"Lobo who?"

"Lobo's all I know. Anyway, what it's worth, I always thought Daddy got him to off Rosemarie's husband."

"Now what made you think that?"

He shrugged. "Besides common sense? One thing, a cash withdrawal Daddy had me make. I know he gave the cash to Bettina. And the time was right. Look." Daniel squared his shoulders, tapped the cigarette impatiently. "Y'all pretty much broke Daddy's whole well-oiled machine. That's why it took him so long to come back. Soon's I heard that Mr. Right shit, heard he was in Dallas, I knew exactly what happened. He had to play the Rosemarie card 'cause it was the second to last one he had left. But Rosemarie couldn't fix him up with an assassin for his second and most poorly loved son—he never gave a tinker's damn about Isaac! If she knew one, she'd have offed her *own* fuckin' husband. You see where I'm goin' with this?"

"Yeah. You think he played the Bettina card."

Daniel wiped all expression off his face; his work was done. "Shouldn't be that hard to find; name's Bettina Starnes. Got a kid."

"I think we can find her."

"Take care of the kid, okay? He's my little brother."

Skip was elated. On the ride home, she was practically burbling. "I've always thought Bettina was our only chance."

"But we never had probable cause," Abasolo finished for her.

"And we still don't." Skip sighed. "Well, we can go talk to her. See if we can get her to give up Lobo."

"Yeah, if we can't find him some other way."

"Gonna be pretty hard without more of a name." She shrugged in frustration. "She's our only chance. She's stubborn as hell, but she's got to know we got Jacomine. We can drag her in; say he ratted her out."

"For what?"

"You name it, Bettina probably did it. She's got a kid; he's got to mean more to her than Lobo."

"So you're thinking maybe she'll get chatty. Hope sure springs eternal."

"We've got to cut Shellmire in."

The sergeant winced. "Yeah, I guess so. But this is our operation, not the FBI's."

"Let's roll first thing in the morning," Abasolo said. "One car only, I think."

"I'm going to be at Steve's tonight. Shellmire knows how to get there. Why don't I get him to meet me at Steve's, and we'll pick you up at your place? We can go in my car."

She called Shellmire from Steve's and then began concocting a vegetable pasta sauce.

Steve overheard the conversation. "Man, I hope you get something, Skip. I'm sorry for thinking you were paranoid. I mean, I knew Jacomine, but I didn't really think . . ." He stopped talking, trying to figure out how to finish the sentence, but she knew perfectly well what he meant.

You could know Jacomine, think you knew what he was capable of, and yet not really know. You could underestimate him because he'd go so much farther than anyone else, was so much crazier on a grander scale. And, it seemed, had a secret source of money and power. Maybe if they got Lobo, they could get Rosemarie.

Terri had been doing a lot of thinking the last couple of days. Her mother was always saying "You need to reevaluate your values and go to church." She hadn't felt the need of the latter, but she'd done a pretty thorough job of the former.

She couldn't believe what an idiot she'd been. She flinched when she remembered she'd actually had fantasies about a murderer and con man, had stupid, adolescent doubts about whether Isaac was right for her. Especially after all the doctors and nurses and Lovelace had left them alone and he told her how much he loved her, how he realized it when he saw his father on the show, how much he regretted the doubts he'd had about her.

That part absolutely embarrassed her to tears. "Oh, Isaac, I was such a whiny little asshole then. I'm so, so sorry," she'd wailed.

He'd sketched out his trip to Dallas for her—what he could remember of it—and she was so deeply moved, she wanted to be with him forever.

She felt like a different person now; that period was behind her. One good thing was left: her desire to do something besides paint. She was still an artist; that was a given. It wasn't about to go away. But she was going to paint differently now, maybe with more of an edge. It was a metamorphosis Isaac had gone through, after he'd given up being The White Monk, and she could feel it happening to her. But she was going to do some other work as well; she'd been given an opportunity, and she was going to grab it. She bustled into the hospital full of news.

"Isaac, guess what? The bank dropped the charges. I just had a call from my lawyer. George Pastorek's still my lawyer! Can you believe it? After all this, he still went right ahead and worked on my problem. He said I have to pay him, though—I have to do some more TV appearances with him, tell what happened to me—and he gave me a chance to work for his consumer group this summer, to help pay my way through school. I have to go to New York, but that's okay, it's only for a few months."

She was a little worried about that part, how Isaac was going to take it. She scrutinized his face; he looked like he'd lost his last friend.

"Oh, Isaac, I won't go! I'm sorry, I didn't realize."

"It's not that. You go. I'm happy for you."

"What is it then?"

"My father died. It was just on CNN."

The news hit her like a bullet. "Your father? I'm sorry. But . . ." She was about to say "You didn't love him at all," but she stopped herself.

"I didn't think I'd be sad, but I am; you only get one father. Terri, he never had a chance."

She was flabbergasted. The truth was, he'd never given anyone a chance, including his two sons. "I don't follow."

"He could have been a good person—a normal, regular, happy person. Something happened, and he just never was; I don't know what."

"You mean, like something in his childhood?"

"Maybe. Or maybe not. Maybe he was born the way he was. Which makes you wonder—" He left the thought unfinished, apparently unwilling to venture into philosophical territory. "Terri, imagine having to live that way! Always suspicious, always afraid, always scheming, seeing enemies everywhere. Never having someone to love. God, it's just so sad."

Terri thought his father was the personification of evil. Isaac might be crazy, he might be in denial, but you couldn't say he wasn't generous. She'd never loved him more.

Chapter *TWENTY-SEVEN*

S kip awakened to a fine May morning, with a kiss of breeze off the river and hardly a drop of humidity. She and Shellmire stopped at PJ's for a *grande* to go and one for Abasolo.

Afterward, Shellmire took off his seersucker jacket and tucked it into Skip's backseat.

"Hot day," she said.

"But lovely, isn't it? Too bad old Errol isn't here to enjoy it with us. Swear to God, I miss him already."

"Spare me the black humor, Turner." Skip spoke more sourly than she intended.

He raised an eyebrow as she got in and started the car. "I thought you'd be in a great mood this morning."

"Couldn't sleep," she said, and barely said a word on the drive to

Mid-City. She was still trying to process the news: that her old enemy was really dead, the years of threat and fear truly over.

By the time they got Abasolo, the coffee had started to kick in. It was almost farther to the sergeant's house than to the East itself. On the Interstate, it's no more than seven minutes away, far, far closer than the hour's drive to the North Shore, though the psychological distance is the length of California.

As she took the high-rise to the East, across the Industrial Canal, she listened to the men banter and noticed that, though it didn't grate on her particularly, she still wasn't ready to contribute. She was in the mood that had caused her mother to inquire, when she was a kid, whether she had ants in her pants. *Termites*, she thought. She'd dreamed about them again.

Still joking when they turned onto Bettina's street, the men missed seeing the young woman approaching her building. Skip snapped, "Hey! Something's going down. Let's see if that woman goes to Bettina's apartment. I'm going to cruise by and then stop. Y'all watch her."

But Skip could see too, out of the corner of her eye. The woman went to Bettina's door, rang the doorbell, and waited, not even slightly nervous, as if she belonged there and wasn't expecting cops for breakfast.

Skip cut her motor and parked, still attracting no attention.

Abasolo said, "Let's go."

"No, wait. Let's see if she gets in."

The woman rang the bell again and knocked. For good measure, she hollered something they couldn't hear, and even held her ear to the door. When she turned around and for the first time, Skip saw her face, she yelled, "Oh, shit. Let's get her!"

She got out of the car and started walking. The woman, realizing someone was on the street, looked in her direction and registered nothing.

Skip heard the men get out behind her, and suddenly the woman took off running. Must have looked scary as hell, Skip realized.

She hollered, "Halt! Police!" but the woman wasn't about to halt. It was a fairly neat little block, mostly single-family homes with front yards unencumbered by fences. Provided there were no cars in driveways (at the moment there weren't), you could race across them at will, and the woman did.

"Fuck!" Skip muttered to herself and pounded after her. She didn't hear the men behind her. The woman was younger, smaller, and faster. She rounded the corner, slowing down only a second, but that, and the fact that the girl was not a sprinter, not in shape at all, began to give Skip an advantage. She yelled again, "Halt! Police!" and wondered why she bothered.

But another half block and . . . yes! A running tackle. She had the girl on the ground, and she was just realizing she was too exhausted to cuff her.

Abasolo loped up. "Turner's waiting. He's getting too old for this shit. And by the way, what shit would that be?"

Skip's breath was ragged. "Cuff her, would you? I can't move."

The girl came to life. "You cain't arrest me. I ain' done nothin'."

"Oh, yeah? Then why'd you run?" Abasolo didn't even know why Skip had run, but he was right there, bless his heart.

"Meet Mary Jones," Skip finally managed to gasp.

"Ah. As in, 'Mary had a little statue.' Well, that just do explain things."

"That ain' my name," the girl said.

Abasolo cuffed her while Skip dusted herself off. "Now, Mary . . ."

"I said that ain' my name."

"All right, what is your name?"

"Trenice."

"Okay, Trenice, what were you doing at the Starnes apartment this morning?"

"I take care of Jacob."

"You're the babysitter?"

"Yes, ma'am. Nobody answer this mornin', though. I don't know why. Bettina ain' call me or nothin'; car's there and everything. And I *know* I heard Jacob cryin'."

Skip and Abasolo let their eyes meet. He said, "You and Shellmire go. I'll take care of her."

Once again, Skip broke into a dead run; realizing how far she had to go, though, she slowed to a jog, and it irritated her, watching Shellmire watch her toil. He hadn't put his jacket back on. *Maybe getting older isn't so bad*, she thought.

"That was the babysitter. Says she got no answer, but she heard the baby crying and the car's still there."

"You beat that out of her or what?"

"I'll explain later. You do the honors." Her speech was ragged; she was still out of breath and sweating heavily.

Shellmire banged loudly, and they waited. And in the silence, a loud wail came back at them, obviously a baby's cry.

"Jacob?" Skip yelled. "Jacob, it's okay." Her dream of termites came back to her, the termites that, in her mind, meant Jacomine; meant disaster.

"Do you smell something?" Shellmire asked.

She sniffed the hot air. "Very faintly. I've got a bad feeling, Turner."

On impulse she tried the door; to her amazement, it opened.

The smell was stronger, not overpowering but unmistakable. Something was dead in there. Except for the baby's cries, all was quiet.

"Bettina? Jacob?"

They split up, guns drawn, Skip down the hall to the bedrooms, Shellmire to the living room and kitchen.

She found the baby first, standing up in his crib, now evidently so frightened—or fascinated—he'd stopped crying.

"Hi, Jacob," she whispered. "You okay, Buddy? Hang tight one more minute, okay?"

Bettina was in the next room, very obviously dead in her bed, an empty medicine vial and a Jim Beam bottle on the table beside her.

The room was hot; green flies were already crawling on her. "Turner! In here!"

About that time, the baby started howling again. Shellmire stopped on his way to pick Jacob up. Skip met him in the hall and took the kid. "She's dead; go look. I don't want the baby in there."

She took Jacob into the living room, where she rocked and petted him, not even stopping to open windows. Shellmire came back in, glancing nervously at Jacob. He said, "Ambulance and Child Abuse guys on the way." He pressed his lips together a moment. "Skip, there's a note. It's just lying on the bureau—no envelope, nothing."

"Take the baby, would you?" Jacob howled anew when she left.

"Without Him, I am nothing," the note said. And then, without further ado, it got down to business: "I do hereby bequeathe my only son, Jacob Starnes, to the custidy of my sister, Rose Maintree. All my worldly goods I leave to my sister Rose. I am sorry to leave this way."

It was signed "Bettina Starnes."

So probably, despite the speed of decomposition, she'd killed herself only the night before. The late spring heat was merciless.

In the past, Skip might have suspected that somehow this had been engineered by Jacomine himself.

Maybe, in a way, it had. Maybe he'd told Bettina to kill herself if he died. Or maybe it was her own idea. If you believed what she wrote, it amounted to the same thing. She must have left the door unlocked, figuring the babysitter would try the door when she got no answer.

It was another hour before the baby had been called for, the body removed, and the crime lab satisfied. In the course of it, Mary Jones had been sent back to the Third in a district car, to await questioning—something Skip was going to enjoy—and Turner, who didn't have to hang around for the formalities, had left to get an address on Rose Maintree.

When they were all free, Abasolo said, "You can do the talking at Rose's."

"Thanks a lot," Skip said.

"Not at Rose's house, though," Shellmire said. "The woman's a math teacher at Warren Easton High School."

That might bode well for Jacob, Skip thought. It had to be better than being raised by Bettina, who might be a child who needed a father, a religious fanatic, or just a crazy person, depending on how you looked at it.

Skip went in alone and broke the news to a dry-eyed, distant Rose Maintree, who, to her surprise, thanked her politely but didn't ask a word about Jacob. Skip revised her opinion: The little boy, born with physical problems and now orphaned before age two, simply couldn't catch a break.

Shellmire eyed her when she got back. "How'd it go?"

"Might as well have been talking to a robot. That's some family; she didn't even ask about Jacob."

The agent made a sound like "ooof."

Chapter TWENTY-EIGHT

The termites swarmed that night, driving the whole party— Skip, Steve, and the Scoggin-Ritter family—out of the courtyard and into the Big House.

Sheila had made the entire dinner—a light summer supper, really—to practice her new skills and to celebrate the family's delivery from what Uncle Jimmy had taken to calling "The Fear Years." Skip had just told the story of her day.

"It's almost like Jacomine wasn't human," Sheila said.

Skip nodded. "No sociopath has human feelings; that wasn't what was so scary. Jacomine had no sense of his own limits. Karen told me he actually thought he could be president!"

Steve stopped his fork in midair, like somebody'd ordered him to halt. "Come on!"

"Swear to God. He was going to use the Mr. Right gig to become the most popular man in America—follow right in Ronald Reagan's footsteps."

"Oh, my God. Bat shit doesn't begin to describe . . ."

"Well, it never stopped him before; all in all, being nuts was his biggest asset. That and knowing how to tap into emotional veins. No question that *Mr. Right* show was becoming a phenomenon in Dallas."

"I'm just curious," Layne said. "How far do you think he'd have gotten if Terri hadn't been on his show?"

"Actually, not much farther. The producer told the FBI she thought he'd knocked his wife around after the show, and Karen kept talking about losing a baby. I just wonder if he caused her to miscarry."

"Meaning he was starting to decompensate?"

"Yeah. He was used to giving all the orders. In the real world—without his precious 'following'—he couldn't be his usual megalomaniac self."

Kenny looked puzzled.

"What's the matter, sport? Don't you know that word—*megalomaniac?*"

"Oh, please. You can't live in this house and not know *megalomaniac.* "Power crazy, right? I was thinking of Mary Jones. How'd she pull that scam off, just her and Bettina?"

"Oh, Trenice. I forgot. That's the best part. She completely caved, told the whole story. She's just a neighbor of Bettina's, not a Jacomine follower or anything like that. Bettina offered her money to do that little impersonation she did. Looks like that's the whole gang, just Bettina and the babysitter. Plus a couple of guys Bettina hired to steal the stuff they put in Steve's backyard."

"Either of them named Lobo, by any chance?"

"That's the bad news. Darnell and William."

Steve grumped, "Lobo's probably the asshole that poisoned Napoleon."

"And shot at me."

"So what's gonna happen?" Kenny asked.

Skip shrugged.

"Lobo's Frank O'Rourke's headache; O'Rourke's the point man on Isaac's case, and good luck to him. But Trenice'll probably go down. And maybe somebody at the *Times-Picayune*'ll get a good yarn out of it all."

"Like Jane Storey." Jimmy Dee said, naming a reporter friend of Skip's. "Should we go call her?"

Skip tried to look innocent. "Adam and I sort of talked to her this afternoon. Adam felt pretty bad about what happened to me. And I felt bad about Rooster Blanchard. Jane's even doing a special little feature on him."

"Who the hell is Rooster Blanchard?"

"Guy who saved my life when this whole thing started. Remember that? We gave him a real bad day back then, poor bastard. But now he's probably going to get some sort of commendation. Whatever that's worth."

"Ah. And you're vindicated. Things are shaping up."

"I'll drink to that." Skip smiled and raised her glass.

Things were good tonight. At the moment, she could hardly remember Dallas.